WITHERED
by
SHADOWS

ADA MARLOWE

ISBN: 979-8-9939765-0-1

Cover design: Ada Marlowe
Printed in the United States of America

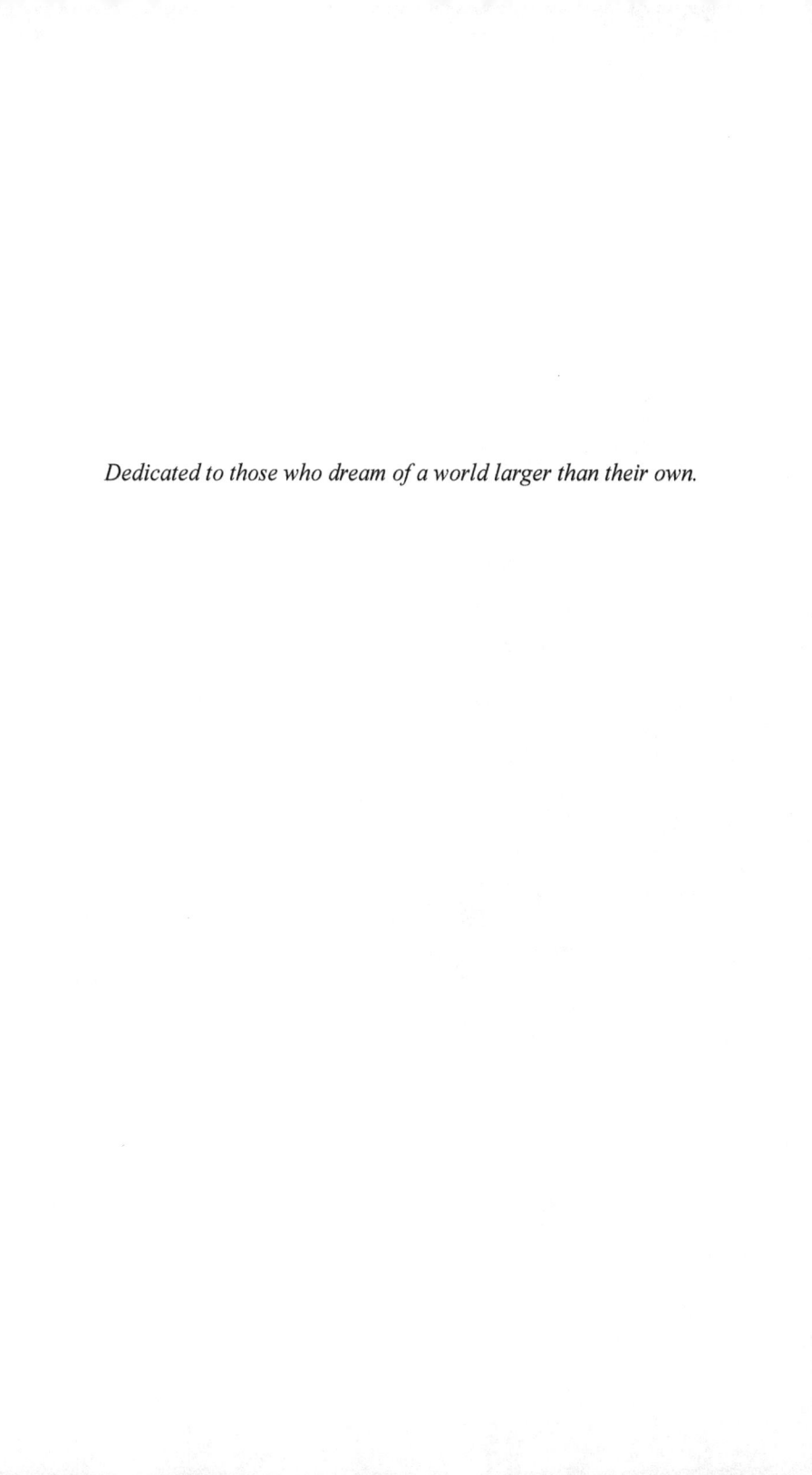

Dedicated to those who dream of a world larger than their own.

PROLOGUE

<u>Withered by Shadows</u>

In shadowed realms where light dares not tread,
A soul lay withered, nearly dead.
Petals of hope, once blooming bright,
Crumble to dust in eternal night.

Whispers of wind through barren trees,
Echo the loss of what used to be.
Faded dreams in the gloom entwine,
Weaving new threads in grand design.

Thorns of despair may pierce the heart,
Ravaged by time, torn apart.
Hollowed eyes now glimpse the void,
Where joy was stolen, peace destroyed.

Yet in the dark, a spark may gleam,
A withered seed in a forgotten dream.
Shadows may claim, but deep within,
Resilience stirs, to rise again.

CHAPTER ONE

Fish. Barter. Survive.

That's the mantra of Eldwick that pulses through every cracked cobblestone, every weathered dock, every roughened hand hauling nets from the gray, churning sea. As the southernmost town in Aelthar's mortal lands, we're a forgotten speck, cut off from the world by jagged cliffs and treacherous, wind-lashed waters that deter trade routes and visitors alike. Everything we have, kelp-woven baskets, iron hooks, smoked fish, is all we'll ever get. And in a place this small, everyone knows your name, your secrets, and the weight of your family's past. Step out of line, and trouble finds you fast, turning a hard life even harder.

My family keeps to ourselves, a small unit carved from this harsh existence. It's just me, my younger brother Rory, and Ma. Rory, wiry and sea-roughened, labors as a boat hand, hauling ropes and gutting fish for men who would sooner spit than speak to him. Ma tends her tea and herb stall in the market, her fingers stained green from bundling thyme and sea lavender, her smile tight as she navigates the townsfolk's wary glances.

And me, I'm the fixer. I mend what's broken: tangled fishing lines, torn sails, cracked oars, rusted pots. If it's snapped, frayed, or shattered, I can put it back together with a steady hand. It's not much, but it keeps us fed and keeps my mind from wandering to places it shouldn't—like dreams of faerie kingdoms with glass spires or oceans so blue they steal your breath. Those fantasies faded long ago, ground down by Eldwick's relentless tides. My life is here, in this salt-soaked village where nothing ever changes.

The market square hums with its usual chaos as I weave through the crowd, a heavy sail slung over my shoulder, its coarse canvas chafing my skin. The air is thick with the briny tang of smoked fish, the musk of damp kelp, and the faint sweetness of Ma's herbs drifting from her stall.

Voices clash, merchants haggling over crabs, fishermen cursing a bad trade, and hushed whispers about "cursed tides" and shadow figures gliding atop the waves, their void-like eyes fixed on Eldwick. Most dismiss it as sea-madness, the ravings of men worn down by the ocean's whims, but I know better.

Two months ago, I felt it. A tremor in the air, like the world was holding its breath, vibrating with an electric hum that set my nerves alight. It wasn't just the wind or the waves; it was as if reality itself quivered, poised to crack open. I mentioned it to Rory, hoping he'd felt it too, but his eyes darkened, and he hushed me sharply.

"Don't talk about it, Kiera, not to anyone," he whispered, his voice low as if the cliffs might overhear, so I didn't push. Our family's reputation already carries enough weight.

When I was thirteen, Father lost his mind, or so the town claims, raving about fae and a mystical creature called a vyrskal. He swore he saw them darting through the northern forest and claimed he fought alongside the fierce, scaled vyrskal to shield the place from evil faeries coming for Eldwick. But no one believed him. Faeries in Eldwick? The mortal lands haven't seen such beings in generations. So when he vanished at sea months later, no one searched. Some whispered relief at the "madman's" departure, but I was just a girl at the time, and the sting of their words lingers, a wound that never fully heals.

"Kiera!" a gruff voice cuts through the market's din. Thom, a burly fisherman with a gap-toothed grin and a beard flecked with fish scales, leans against his stall, his weathered tunic stretched over thick arms. "That my sail?"

"Try to keep it in one piece this time," I say, heaving the folded canvas toward him. He catches it with ease, inspecting my work with a nod. Thom's a reliable client, always breaking something at sea, always needing me to patch it up. And more work means more bartered goods for Ma and Rory.

"Tell Rory I need him for a trip in three days. Make sure he's available," he says, lighting a pipe that releases a pungent mix of burnt kelp and tar. "Unless you want to try your luck as a boat hand. I'll pay you double what I pay the boy." His eyes glint, half-joking, half-testing my resolve.

"I'll let Rory know," I reply, turning away before he can press further.

I catch sight of Ma at the end of an aisle, her graying braid swaying as she chats with a cluster of women, her hands gesturing with practiced ease. But I keep moving. Interrupting her mid-transaction is a mistake, especially when those women shoot me sidelong glares, their disapproval of my trousers, my knife at my hip, and my unladylike ways palpable.

They especially disapprove of me turning down all the men that offer trinkets or fish to prove their worth. They say I should be grateful anyone is interested at all. But no one in Eldwick sparks anything in me. I've seen every face, heard every story, there's no one here I want.

I pause at Widow Maud's booth, where trinkets gleam under the dim light: coils of wire, spools of sturdy thread, needles sharp enough to pierce leather, and hooks delicate enough for intricate repairs. With those, I could turn my odd jobs into a real trade. But Maud, her eyes cold as the sea, always rebuffs me.

"You don't have anything I need, girl. Go make yourself useful elsewhere." So I scavenge, dismantling broken tools to salvage parts, making do with what Eldwick grudgingly offers.

"I'd get going if I were you," a familiar voice says softly from behind. I glance over my shoulder to see Lira, her auburn hair catching the faint sunlight like polished copper, a vision in her pale blue dress, her hands folded delicately.

We were inseparable as kids, scaling cliffs and daring the tides, laughing until our sides ached. But time carved different paths, she blossomed into a maiden men fawn over, while I stayed rough-edged, practical, unbothered by the town's expectations.

"Calen's looking for you," she says, a playful glint in her eyes.

"He's persistent, isn't he?" I mutter, shaking my head. Her grin widens, a flicker of our old mischief resurfacing.

"Looked like he was holding something important to show you," she teases, tilting her head.

"So, I should run then?" I quip, and she laughs, a sound like

4

bells over the market's clamor.

"As fast as you can," she replies, her voice light but warm, a bridge to our shared past. She stands out here, a wildflower amid the mud and salt. I want to say more, to close the gap that's grown between us, but the words feel clumsy.

"You look great, Lira. I hope Hale's treating you well," I say, the formality stiff on my tongue.

"He is," she replies softly, a wistful note in her voice. "And I hope your mother and Rory are doing well." Her politeness stings, a reminder of how far we've drifted.

"Shit," I hiss, spotting Calen's lanky figure weaving through the crowd, his eyes, no doubt, scanning for me.

"I'll hold him off," Lira offers, her eyes sparking with that old, reckless excitement. "Go!" I flash her a grin, then duck through the flaps of a nearby tent.

Lira's voice fades as she intercepts Calen, her words bright and distracting. I slip out the back, emerging onto the rocky path that snakes toward the sea. The market's noise dulls, replaced by the rhythmic crash of waves and the mournful whistle of wind through jagged rocks.

Alone now, I slow my pace, glancing over my shoulder to ensure no one follows. The path to the dock is a gentle slope, strewn with pebbles that crunch under my boots, and the dock itself is Eldwick's oldest relic. A sagging skeleton of weathered planks, warped and splintered by decades of relentless tides. Each board creaks under my weight as I reach the end and sit, my legs dangling above the churning water.

A shadow shifts nearby, and I glance up to see a black bird land on a warped spindle. It's no ordinary creature, larger than the gulls, its feathers sleek and iridescent, shimmering like stardust when a rare ray of sunlight pierces the clouds. Its eyes, deep and unblinking, fix on me with an uncanny intelligence. I've seen it before, this solitary watcher, always alone, always observing. I've kept it secret, even from Rory. Eldwick turns anything unusual into whispers of madness, and our family's borne enough of that burden.

"I don't have any fish for you today," I say, pulling my knife from its sheath at my hip. The blade, nicked but sharp, glints as I wipe it clean on my sleeve.

I pry a splintered chunk of wood from the dock and begin carving, my fingers tracing the bird's angular beak and sleek wings. I've tried this before, whittling its likeness, but it always flies off before I finish, as if it refuses to be captured. But today, I notice a jagged slash across its chest, feathers matted with dried blood, and a red, raised scar circling its bony leg.

"Are you injured?" I ask, lowering the knife and wood to my lap. The bird tilts its head, as if considering my words, then turns its gaze to the ocean. I follow its stare, expecting Rory's boat, though he's not due back for another day, but the sea is empty, save for the endless roll of waves.

"Is something wrong?" I press, my voice barely audible over the wind's howl. The bird's eyes snap back to me, piercing and almost commanding. Then a chill prickles my skin, and the hairs on my arms rise. It's trying to tell me something.

I lean to the side and scan the horizon. My heart quickens as the clouds shift swiftly, their edges tinged with an unnatural dark violet. The air hums again, that same electric tremor from months ago, but stronger now, as if the world is teetering on the brink of splitting apart.

The bird lets out a sharp, guttural caw, and I shoot to my feet, gripping my knife steadily. The dock trembles beneath me, a low rumble rising from the ground. Then black smoke curls on the horizon, and three shadowy figures hover above the water, their forms indistinct but unmistakably alive, staring as if waiting for something.

The cursed tides. The shadow figures. This must be what the fishermen have been whispering about. My pulse hammers in my throat as I stare, the knife firm in my hand.

"What are those things?" I whisper, glancing at the bird, half-expecting an answer. Then the ground shakes harder, and I lower myself to the deck, bracing as Eldwick sways behind me.

Pulses of light, jagged and blinding, arc across the sky, and the air crackles with electric energy. Then, a deafening CRACK splits the heavens, like glass shattering. I clap my hands over my ears, squinting upward through narrowed eyes as shards of light cascade down, as if an invisible dome encasing Eldwick has fractured, its pieces dissolving into the wind.

"Ma," I whisper, my voice lost in the gale, my thoughts racing to her, defenseless against whatever's coming.

I turn and sprint down the dock, sheathing my knife at my hip, the bird soaring ahead as if leading the way. But as I reach the rocky shore, I slam into something solid and invisible. I press my hands forward, meeting resistance. A barrier, smooth and impenetrable, humming with faint energy. I'm trapped, cut off from Eldwick.

"Hey!" I yell, pounding my fists against the unseen barrier, but the sound muffles as if I'm underwater. I strike again, and a jolt of electric current buzzes through me, sharp enough to make my teeth clench.

"Kiera of Eldwick, you are summoned," a voice intones, cool, melodic, sending a shiver down my spine as I spin around.

Three figures stand before me—faeries, their slender forms clad in green tunics and pants embroidered with gold vines. Two males and one female, their pointed ears peeking through cascades of light-brown hair, their shimmering eyes piercing. The female steps forward, her movements fluid.

"Who are you, and what do you want from me?" I demand, my voice trembling, but defiant as I adjust my knife in my hand.

"You must come with us," she replies, her voice like wind over a frozen lake.

"I'm not going anywhere with you," I sputter, her calm certainty grating against my nerves. Her lips curl into a grin, as if my defiance is a jest.

I draw my arm back, ready to throw my knife, but she raises her arms and green vines shoot from the dock's cracks, coiling around my ankles with unnatural speed.

I crash backward and my head strikes the wood with a dull thud as my knife clatters just out of reach. I lunge for it, but the vines reel me in like a fish on a hook, my left arm trapped against my body as they tighten.

"Let me go!" I cry, desperation clawing at my throat. Ma is back there, I can't leave her to face this alone.

The vines creep to my neck, and with another gesture, she lifts me, my body hovering inches above the dock, suspended in the air.

Another CRACK splits the sky, and even the faeries flinch, their eyes darting towards the end of the pier. I twist my head, catching sight of a lone figure at the dock's end, cloaked in black, his back to us. Beyond him, the shadow figures draw closer, their forms grotesque, faeries, but warped, their skin gray and peeling, their mouths moving in silent, sinister chants.

The man in black raises his arms, and black flames roar from his hands, a wall of writhing smoke that slams against the barrier around us, curling harmlessly away.

"We have to go. NOW!" one of the male faeries cries, his voice sharp with panic.

As the man in black turns, our eyes lock, his silver gaze slicing through the chaos, a beacon of intensity that stirs a strange, unshakable familiarity deep within me—like a half-remembered dream tugging at my soul. For a fleeting moment, the world narrows to that connection, a pull I can't explain or resist. But before I can grasp its meaning, the ground beneath me seems to dissolve.

Darkness swallows me whole, and I'm falling. Not through water or air, but through a boundless void, weightless and untethered, as Eldwick, my family, and everything I've ever known fade into an abyss of the unknown.

CHAPTER
TWO

My body slams into the ground with a jarring thud, my knees cracking against the floor, sending a shockwave of pain up my legs. The green vines that bind my wrists and ankles dissolve in a hiss, searing my skin raw with their retreat. I stagger to my feet, my heart hammering a frantic rhythm, and take in the surreal scene unfolding around me.

This is no longer Eldwick's salt-crusted pier; its familiar decay replaced by a foreign grandeur. The air hangs heavy, thick with a damp scent of moss, the delicate crush of petals, and a cloying sweetness that chokes my lungs and makes my head spin. Beneath my scuffed boots, the floor is green marble, veined with gold that shimmers faintly, as if the stone itself breathes with a life I can't comprehend.

I'm in a throne room, there's no mistaking it. The chamber

stretches vast and cavernous, its walls a living tapestry of writhing vines and roots that coil into graceful arches, where flowers bloom mid-air, their petals glowing with an eerie, otherworldly light. Stained-glass windows tower overhead, dwarfing Eldwick's tallest cottages, casting emerald and gold patterns that dance across the floor like liquid sunlight. The air hums with a palpable energy, and my skin prickles under the weight of countless eyes.

Dozens of fae encircle me, their green tunics and cloaks shimmering with embroidery that mimics leaves and thorns. Their beauty is sharp, almost painful, like blades sheathed in silk, ethereal yet threatening. Some regard me with curiosity, their luminous eyes tracing my every move, while others fix on me with open contempt, their murmurs slithering through the air.

At the far end of the room, a throne of twisted roots draped with cascading ivy commands attention. Upon it sits a male faerie, young yet striking, his chestnut hair falling in loose waves around a sharp jaw softened by a crooked smirk that hints at both charm and cynicism. His eyes are every shade of green and pierce through me, cold and calculating, as if he's weighing my worth and finding it lacking. His robe is a cascade of green and gold that clings to his frame, and a crown of thin branches studded with emeralds rests lightly on his head.

His gaze locks onto mine as he rises and descends the throne's steps with the fluid grace of a predator stalking its prey, the room holding its breath in his wake.

"Kiera of Eldwick," he intones, his voice smooth yet edged with a bitter undertone. "A mortal girl, dragged from a nowhere village. Tell me, what makes you worth the trouble?"

"I'm nobody," I snap, straightening my shoulders despite the tremble in my hands. "Where am I? And why am I here?"

He stops mere inches from me, too close for comfort, his scent, pine mingled with crushed mint, invades my senses and makes my head spin.

"You're bold for a mortal reeking of fish and desperation," he says, his voice low and faintly amused, a smirk tugging at the corners of his lips. "I am Tormen, Lord of the Verdant Dominion. This is my court, my home, and you, " he leans closer, his breath warm against my cheek, "are staying until I decide otherwise."

"You have no claim over me," I growl, stepping into his space. The fae around us erupt into murmurs, a wave of hisses and whispers that ripple through the chamber, but I keep my eyes locked on Tormen. He's the real threat, the one pulling the strings. "Take me home. *Now.*"

"Home," Tormen echoes, the word dripping with scorn as he circles me slowly, his gaze never wavering. "Eldwick, was it? A rotting village clinging to a dying sea. What's there for you, Kiera? A family, perhaps? Someone you'd bleed to protect?" His tone is casual, almost mocking, but his eyes are daggers, probing for vulnerabilities.

"None of your business," I snarl, my fists clench at my sides as the whispers turn hostile, a storm brewing among the fae.

A sharp-faced female fae in a fern-green tunic steps forward, her lips curled into a sneer. "Insolent mortal," she hisses. "She reeks of defiance and filth, unworthy of the Dominion's grace." Others nod, their eyes glinting with malice. My muscles coil, every instinct screaming to fight, though I know it's a battle I can't win.

"*Enough,*" Tormen's voice cracks like a whip. The fae freezes, her face paling under his gaze, and the room falls silent, the air thick with his authority. "We've been waiting for you longer than you know," he continues, his voice softening to a near-reverent murmur. "Marked by the stars to reshape our fate." He pauses, letting the weight of his words settle, but offers no further clarity, leaving me to grapple with their meaning.

"Sounds like you grabbed the wrong girl," I retort. "I'm not your chosen one. I know nothing about your world."

"Not all here believe in the prophecy's promise," he says, his eyes shifting to the fae around us, then returning to me, a shrewd gleam in his eyes. "I, however, see... potential." There's a hunger in his voice, a predatory gleam that sets my nerves on edge. He wants something—power, control, a way to tip the scales in his favor. I'm a piece in a game I don't understand, and the realization ignites a fire in my blood.

"She's a mistake," another fae spits, his voice cutting through the tension. "End her now, before she taints us all."

Tormen raises a hand, and the room stills. "She stays," he declares, his voice a quiet thunder that silences the court. His eyes hold mine, amusement and challenge mingling with something darker, as if he's daring me to shatter his world. "You'll learn your place, Kiera, or you'll break. Either way, you're mine to shape."

"I'll tear you down before I let you use me," I snarl, stepping closer, my fists trembling with barely contained rage. "Whatever you're scheming, I'm not part of it."

"Oh, Kiera," he says, his voice low and intimate, a velvet blade sliding under my skin. "You're already part of it. You just don't see the board yet." With a fluid motion, he turns, his robe swirling, and stalks back to his throne, settling into it with the effortless confidence of a Lord who's never known doubt.

"Escort her to her chambers," he orders, then gestures to the rest of the room. "The court is dismissed."

The fae disperse, their green tunics blending into the vines as they slip through arches and shadowed doorways, their whispers trailing like ghosts. Two guards in moss-green armor step forward, their breastplates etched with thorn patterns, and their faces are blank.

"Touch me, and you'll lose a hand," I growl, though it's a bluff, and their steady gazes suggest they see through it.

"You walk, or we drag you. Choose now," one guard says, his voice flat, but commanding.

My instincts scream to fight, to kick and claw until I'm free, but reality crashes in—I'm trapped, surrounded by magic I can't counter, in a world that's not mine. Even if I escaped this room, I have no map, no path back to Eldwick, to Ma and Rory, to the life I know.

I glance at Tormen, lounging on his throne, watching me like a storm he's unleashed for his own amusement. He sees me as a key to some grand plan, a tool to shift the Dominion's balance, but he's wrong. I won't be molded so easily.

"Move," the guard says, his staff nudging my shoulder. I walk, flanked by the guards, their vines hovering close, a constant threat.

The throne room's light fades as we pass through a vine-covered archway, the air growing cooler, heavier with the scent of damp moss and blooming flowers. The hall stretches endlessly and my boots resound with a hollow rhythm, each sound a stark reminder of how far I am from home. But then something catches my eye, and I pause, ignoring the guard's impatient grunt.

Through an ivy-framed window, I spot a familiar silhouette. The black bird from Eldwick, perched on an arch outside. Its feathers shimmer, black with hints of deep violet, lending it an otherworldly grace. Its eyes meet mine, too knowing, too familiar.

Perhaps it's Tormen's spy who's been watching me all along.

But the way it looked at me on the pier, guiding me with its caw, makes me doubt it serves him. This bird doesn't belong to the Verdant Dominion, it answers to someone else.

for the way it looked at me on the pier, mocking me with its soft glow, the shell it seems almost like a liar, sweet betrayal it could never hope to possess someday.

CHAPTER THREE

Three days blur into four, perhaps more; time slips away in this relentless glow. My stomach gnaws at itself, a hollow void, my throat raw from the meager water dripping into a shallow stone basin, just enough to sustain life but not to quench the burning ache. They've tossed in stale bread, a cruel mockery of sustenance, but I force it down, clinging to whatever strength it provides.

I huddle with my knees drawn up, back pressed against the cool crystal wall. Guilt slices deeper than the hunger, sharper than the cold: Ma, alone in our crumbling cottage, her herb stall untended; Rory, hauling nets without me to mend them. Do they think I'm dead? Lost at sea like Father? I can't let that happen. I won't.

"I'm not dying here," I rasp to the empty air, my voice hoarse but defiant. I've tried everything, clawing at the vines until my nails bleed, probing for hidden cracks in the crystal, pounding the walls until my fists ache. But nothing gives. This prison was built for beings far stronger than a mortal girl from Eldwick, and that realization twists dread tight in my chest.

The crystal door suddenly grinds open with a low rumble, and two guards walk in, their moss-green armor clinking softly, hands ready with those familiar cursed vines. Their eyes fix on me, cold and impassive, like I'm nothing more than prey already ensnared.

"Up," one grunts, gesturing sharply with his glowing hand. But I remain still, glaring back with a clenched jaw.

The other acts swiftly, gripping my arm and pulling me upright. My legs buckle under the weakness of starvation, but I swallow a curse and lock my knees, forcing stability. No weakness. Not for them. Not ever.

They propel me out into a long, winding hallway, its walls embedded with glittering emeralds and twisting roots. I scan desperately for any escape route—shadowed alcoves, half-hidden doorways, a loose panel, but the guards' hold is firm, their vines hovering just inches from my skin.

As we pass a high, arched window framed in ivy, my breath catches. There it is again. The black bird, perched on the sill, its feathers shimmering with that subtle violet sheen. It lets out a sharp caw, identical to the one on Eldwick's pier before the fae descended, then launches into the air, wings slicing the light as it vanishes. A chill sinks into my bones, deeper than the cell's cold. What are you? A spy? A warning? If you're not Tormen's, then whose?

The guards shove me through an ornate arched doorway into an intimate dining hall. A long table of dark, polished wood dominates the center, laden with platters of ripe fruits, steaming loaves of bread, succulent roasted meats, and pitchers of what smells like honeyed wine spiced with unfamiliar herbs. The aromas assault me, making my mouth water traitorously, but I clench my fists, refusing to let the hunger show.

Tormen sits at the head of the table, solitary and composed, his gold-and-green robe catching the light. His eyes gleam with a mix of amusement and that ever-present predatory hunger. He gestures to the chair across from him, the motion slow and deliberate.

"Sit, Kiera," he says, his voice smooth, carrying an undercurrent of command. "You're half-starved. A proper meal might keep you on your feet long enough to be useful."

I pause at the threshold, pride clashing with the hollow ache in my stomach. The scent of fresh bread is pure torment, but I cross the room and sink into the chair, spine rigid, hands folded tightly in my lap, well away from the tempting spread.

"I'm fine," I lie, my tone even as my stomach betrays me with a faint growl. "I didn't come here to play dinner guest. What do you want from me, Tormen?"

His smirk deepens, sharpening the angles of his face as he plucks a plump grape from a silver bowl, rolling it idly between his fingers. "Still so stubborn," he murmurs, almost approvingly. "But starvation won't buy you freedom, it'll only weaken you further. Eat." He pops the grape into his mouth, chewing deliberately, his gaze locked on mine, unblinking. "Or do you think I'd waste a feast on a cheap trick?"

"I think you're wasting my time," I retort, my voice slicing through the air. "You locked me in a glowing cage, surviving on scraps, and now you're playing the gracious host? Say what you really want, or let me go."

He laughs, a low, jagged sound that echoes off the ivy-clad walls. "You wound me, Kiera. I'm offering hospitality, and you

18

throw it back in my face." He leans forward, elbows resting on the table, his gaze probing for cracks. "Very well, let's dispense with pretenses. Tell me about Eldwick—your life there, the rhythms of your days. Have you ever felt... something unusual stirring within you? A spark, perhaps, or an inexplicable pull? Something that felt out of place in your mundane world?"

I stiffen, my mind racing. He's hunting for magic, some hidden power he believes the prophecy planted in me. "I'm nobody," I growl, my voice low and edged with warning. "I mend nets, barter for scraps, and watch over my family so we don't starve. That's it. You've got the wrong girl."

"The prophecy marked you for a reason, one I intend to uncover. Deny it all you like; you're only postponing what must be." He takes a slow sip from an ornate goblet, the contents gleaming like liquid amber, then leans closer. "What tales of magic linger in Eldwick? Even a forsaken village like yours must whisper of power, of realms beyond the mortal veil. Faeries or ancient forces."

"In Eldwick, we talk about tides, storms, and the next catch," I snort, crossing my arms tightly over my chest. "Not your faerie nonsense or prophecies. If you're searching for a mage, go kidnap someone else. I just want to go home."

"And what makes that miserable little village so precious?" he presses, his words making me flinch despite myself. "You're a fighter, Kiera. I see it in every defiant glare. That's why the stars chose you. But there's more beneath that surface, isn't there? A depth you hide even from yourself."

"Stop pretending you know me," I snarl, leaning forward, fury trembling through my words. "You don't. None of you do."

Tormen's smile fades, his fingers tightening around the goblet until his knuckles pale. He rises fluidly, his movements laced with a dangerous grace, and I tense, every muscle coiled for whatever comes next.

"Walk with me," he commands, his voice clipped, irritation simmering just below the surface. The double doors at the far end swing open with a wave of his hand, revealing a sun-dappled path beyond, and he stands there, eyes challenging me to refuse. "Don't make me ask again."

My instincts scream trap, but with the guards looming nearby, choice is an illusion. I stand, legs still unsteady, and step into the hall, feeling his presence like a shadow at my back, ready to strike.

We emerge into a lush garden courtyard, sunlight filtering through a canopy of towering trees whose leaves glow with an inner luminescence, casting dappled patterns on moss-covered paths. Flowers bloom in impossible colors, and the air is thick with the sweet, decaying scent of overripe blossoms and rich soil.

"There are forces at work in Aelthar you couldn't begin to comprehend," Tormen says, his voice low and measured, as if the very trees might eavesdrop. "Every lord, every creature here harbors motives. Some overt, others buried deep. Truth is a scarce commodity in these realms, Kiera."

"I don't trust you," I snap, keeping my voice sharp and low, matching his pace along the winding path. "Not your words, not your motives, not this entire twisted world."

He chuckles, but it's a cold, brittle sound that doesn't reach his eyes. "That's perhaps the wisest thing you've said since arriving."

I bristle, heat rising in my cheeks. He thinks I'm ignorant, a backwater mortal stumbling through his grand game. And maybe I am, but that doesn't make him right. I know nothing of Aelthar's maps, its politics, or its players; Eldwick's cliffs might as well be worlds away. He's a lord, born to power, he'll always hold the advantage.

"I may seem like your enemy now," he continues, his tone shifting to something almost persuasive, "but if you remain here, under my protection, you'll come to see this as your best path to survival."

I scoff, unable to hold back. "Protection? Seems to me you've struck some deal that's turned you into a coward."

His eyes flash with a stern intensity, hands balling into fists at his sides, as if restraining the urge to lash out. Hit a nerve, did I? Good. There's truth there, buried under his polish. Who did he bargain with? And what did it cost?

"The realms are unraveling at the edges," he says, his voice steadying, though tension lingers. "This isn't about victory or defeat anymore. It's survival, pure and simple." He turns his head sharply as the clink of armor echoes from a side path, a guard stumbling into view, breathless and wide-eyed.

"My lord," the guard pants, bowing quickly, "Lord Soren of the Umbral Expanse has arrived. Uninvited and demanding an audience."

Tormen's expression hardens to stone, but I catch a flicker of unease in the way his fingers tap the air. "Let him in," he replies, his voice calm but taut. His eyes dart to me, calculating, reassessing. I keep my face neutral, but my pulse quickens as the air thickens, charged with the promise of a storm.

Soren enters the garden moments later, shadows clinging to him like tendrils of mist, dulling the vivid shimmer of the leaves. He's breathtaking in a lethal way. Sharp cheekbones accentuating warm bronze skin that absorbs the sunlight, wavy jet-black hair falling just past his ears to frame a face that's equal parts allure and threat.

His silver eyes, cold as distant stars, burn with arrogance and hidden depths, and his attire, tailored black leather and silk embroidered with subtle silver threads, seems to devour the light, making the garden feel confined.

I recognize him in an instant, a jolt slamming through my chest: the man—fae—from Eldwick's pier, watching impassively as the vines dragged me away. His presence tugs at me, magnetic and perilous, stirring something I can't name, or afford. I force my gaze away, heart hammering. What does he want? Is he here for me, or to settle some faerie grudge?

"Tormen," Soren says, his voice silk-smooth but laced with venom, each syllable a precise strike. "Sulking in your garden while Aelthar crumbles? How utterly predictable."

The air crackles with tension, the two lords circling each other like rival predators, and I'm trapped in the crossfire, the garden's humming life suddenly stifled.

"And you're barging into my court without invitation," Tormen retorts, his tone light but undercut with a tremor, a fissure in his composure. He steps closer. "Your audacity is as tiresome as ever. What drags you from your shadows this time?"

Soren's eyes flick to me, a spark of curiosity igniting in their silver depths. Too knowing, too probing. How much does he know about the prophecy? About me? Is he an ally, or just another chain?

"And who might this be?" he asks, his voice softening to something almost intimate, though edged with sharpness, as if stripping away my defenses layer by layer. His gaze lingers, stirring an unwelcome heat. "A mortal in your court, Tormen? You're slipping."

"She's no concern of yours," Tormen retorts, stepping slightly between us, his voice lowering with a protective, or possessive, edge. "State your purpose, Soren. I have no time for your games today."

Soren's laugh cuts through the garden like a blade, sharp and unyielding. "Games? Rifts tear through Aelthar, yet your precious Dominion remains pristine. What bargain have you made to shield it from the chaos?"

Tormen's hand twitches, a telltale crack in his facade. "You're chasing phantoms, Soren. My lands thrive because I'm no fool, unlike you, letting shadows overrun your domain."

"Fool?" Soren advances, his presence swelling like an incoming storm. "The rifts devour Aelthar's essence, and you know it. Your silence endangers us all. Including her." His gaze snaps to me, pinning me in place, and my heart stutters.

"You're desperate, weaving fairy tales to cover your own failings," Tormen counters, his voice steady but strained. "If your Expanse falters, blame your weaknesses, not me. Let my forests flourish in peace."

Soren's tone drops to a lethal whisper, eyes narrowing. "Your Dominion's immunity won't last. The rifts hunger without prejudice. They'll consume your forests, my shadows, and Eldwick alike. Confess what you're concealing, or I'll extract it myself."

My stomach twists. Eldwick, obliterated? Ma, Rory... I can't let that be true. I want to dismiss it as a ploy, but Soren's conviction shakes me. Tormen's jaw clenches, but he meets the glare head-on. "You dare threaten me in my own Dominion?" His hand hovers, as if summoning the surrounding vines, the garden's hum intensifying. "Crawl back to your darkness, Soren. You'll find no answers here."

"Keep them buried," Soren hisses, his voice dripping with contempt, "but when the rifts consume everything, don't come begging." He pivots to me, eyes locking onto mine, that magnetic pull tightening. My breath hitches under the intensity. It's as if he's silently asking whose side I've chosen, or warning me to choose wisely. "And you, mortal. What role do you play in his tangled web?"

"I'm not playing anyone's role," I reply, forcing my voice steady, holding his gaze despite the storm inside. "I don't know your rifts or your realms, and I don't want to. Leave me out of it."

Soren's smirk unfurls slowly, almost appreciative, hinting at unspoken alliances. "Defiant to the core," he murmurs, as if sharing a private jest, then turns back to Tormen. "Hide your truths if you must, but they'll surface. And I'll be there to witness the fallout." He strides away, his black form trailing faint shadows that linger like echoes, leaving the garden chilled and unsettled.

Tormen's gaze whips to me, his calm shattered, suspicion etching deep lines on his face. "What was that?" he demands, voice low and accusatory, stepping closer. "Soren doesn't deign to notice mortals. What connection do you have to him?"

"How should I know?" I snap, exhaustion fueling my ire. "I've never met him. Deal with your rivals and keep me out of your faerie wars."

His jaw tightens further, fingers curling as if itching to summon vines. "Guards," he calls sharply, his tone deceptively even but laced with menace. "Return her to her cell."

The guards seize my arms once more, their vines growing ominously, and I'm too weary to resist as they drag me away.

Tormen's stare burns into my back. Intense, recalculating, as if rewriting his schemes around this new variable. But Soren's eyes haunt my thoughts, a dangerous ember igniting questions I'm not prepared to face.

CHAPTER
FOUR

After Tormen's guards dragged me back from the garden encounter, a tray of food materialized at the door—remnants from his lavish feast: crusty bread still warm, ripe fruits glistening with dew, and slices of roasted meat. I stared at it for what felt like an hour, suspicion gnawing at me. Is it poisoned? A trick to make me compliant? But hunger was a fiercer enemy, a gnawing void that weakened my resolve. I devoured it all, the flavors bursting on my tongue like a betrayal. Sweet and savory, a stark contrast to the stale scraps I'd survived on before. Now, my body hums with renewed strength, muscles no longer trembling from starvation, but my mind is churning through Tormen's cryptic words, Soren's dire warnings, and the impossible weight of this faerie world that has upended everything I knew.

Tormen's probing questions in the dining hall echo in my mind:

prophecy, chosen one, a mortal girl destined to shift Aelthar's fate. It claws at me, this idea that I'm some key in their grand game. If that's true, why do I feel nothing? No spark of power, no surge of magic coursing through my veins. I close my eyes, leaning against the cold crystal wall, searching inward with desperate focus.

Come on, if there's something in me, show yourself. A flicker, a whisper. Anything to prove I'm not just a mistake they snatched from the docks. My fingers graze the veined surface, its icy bite tingling under my skin, sending a faint vibration up my arm. But there's no rush of energy, no glow igniting from my touch. Just the vines' taunting hum, vibrating like laughter.

"*Come on,*" I whisper, my voice sounding thin and fragile in the confined space. "Show me something." I press harder, picturing the radiant glow that emanates from the vines and the walls, imagining it bending to my will.

"Open. Break. Do something. Anything!" The crystal remains unchanged. Frustration burns hot in my chest, a blade twisting deeper. I slam my fist against the wall, pain exploding through my knuckles like fire, but it grounds me, reminds me I'm still alive, still fighting.

"Useless," I hiss, cradling my throbbing hand, the sting a sharp counterpoint to my powerlessness. What am I even doing? I'm no faerie ruler, no wielder of prophecies. I'm Kiera from Eldwick, fixer of broken things. Not worlds.

I slump to the floor, head in my hands, the cool crystal pressing against my back. Tormen's words loop like a curse in my mind: a mortal to reshape Aelthar. If this realm is fracturing, what does that mean for home? Could the rifts Soren spoke of swallow Eldwick whole, dragging Ma and Rory into some shadowy abyss? Or, if I somehow escape, could I return to my old life? Mending nets under the gray sky, bartering for potatoes in the market, pretending this nightmare never happened? Eldwick feels like a lifeline, but it's fraying, tangled in the undeniable truth of Aelthar's magic. Even if I make it back, I'll never unsee this place. The living vines that pulse with life, the palace's halls that seem to breathe, Soren's silver eyes, sharp and magnetic, pulling at something deep inside me.

I curse myself under my breath, shoving the thought of Soren away. He's a faerie lord, a schemer just like Tormen. Dangerous and untrustworthy. Yet, why does his gaze linger in my mind like that, a spark I can't extinguish? *Focus, Kiera.* You're not here to moon over silver-eyed strangers.

Then, my eyes snap to the door as a sudden commotion shatters the oppressive silence. Muffled thuds, piercing screams that cut through the crystal, and the sharp clatter of metal clashing against stone. My heart slams against my ribs, adrenaline surging as I press myself against the wall, the vines searing my shoulders with an electric jolt that makes me grit my teeth. I swallow the pain, eyes locked on the door, every muscle tensed. What's happening out there? Guards fighting? Another rift tearing open?

Black smoke seeps beneath the door, oily and alive, curling upward like grasping fingers. It slithers through invisible cracks in the crystal, spreading like ink in water, and the door groans under some immense pressure. With a deafening crack that reverberates through my bones, it shatters inward, shards exploding like broken emeralds, glittering in the green light. I stifle a scream, ducking low and shielding my face as the fragments rain down, the smoke stinging my eyes and filling my lungs with choking coughs. Peering through my fingers, I brace for whatever horror is coming, my body tense, survival instincts screaming to run, fight, anything

27

but cower.

A massive beast fills the doorway, a nightmare forged from shadow and malice that makes my blood run cold. Its form is hulking, spikes jutting from its head and shoulders like obsidian daggers, bloody claws gouging deep furrows into the crystal floor with each step. Leathery wings, frayed at the edges into wisps of smoke, fold against its back, and a whip-like tail lashes behind it, its barbed tip gleaming wickedly. Its crimson eyes cut through the haze like glowing embers, and black steam curls from its snarling maw, carrying the reek of brimstone. But my heart lurches with a jolt of recognition.

It's a vyrskal. Exactly like the fierce, scaled being my father swore he fought alongside in the northern woods, its image etched into the sketches he drew obsessively, sketches I've studied hundreds of times by the hearth's dim light. It's identical, a living echo of his tales, pulling me back to those nights when his voice wove magic into our small world.

Its red eyes lock on me, and I freeze, my heart pounding so hard it drowns out everything else. Fear roots me in place. No escape, no way past this monstrosity in the narrow cell. This is it. It's going to tear me apart like those guards. My mind screams to fight, to grab a shard of crystal as a makeshift weapon, but my hands are empty, trembling. I'm no match for this creature, but I'm not dying curled up like prey in a corner.

I straighten slowly, legs trembling but voice steady as I can make it. "If you're here to kill me, get it over with," I say, staring into its burning eyes. If this is my end, at least I'll face it standing, not begging.

Slowly, it extends a clawed hand toward me, the gesture surprisingly careful, like an invitation rather than a threat. I stare at

28

it, my mind racing through the chaos. Stay here and rot in Tormen's cell, forgotten and broken, or follow this monster that just slaughtered its way to me? Neither choice is safe, but staying means a slow death. This thing—it has to be tied to Soren. The shadows, the smoke, it fits his dark aura. The beast's eyes hold no malice, only a strange purpose, as if it sees potential in me that I don't. What if it's my only way out?

"I'll come with you," I say, my voice firm despite the fear choking my throat. I don't take its hand, keeping a wary distance, my body tensed for any sudden move. "But don't think I'm yours to command."

The beast huffs, a puff of steam curling from its nostrils like a reluctant acknowledgment, and turns, stepping over the guards' bodies with indifferent grace. I swallow hard, my boots crunching on crystal shards as I follow, my throat tight with a mix of dread and grim determination. This could be a mistake, but it's movement. Better than rotting here.

The beast moves swiftly through the palace's labyrinthine halls, its claws clicking rhythmically on the crystalline floors, wings brushing against the narrow walls and leaving faint trails of smoke that linger in the air. I keep pace as best I can, my boots slipping occasionally on blood-slicked stone, my senses heightened for any sign of traps or pursuing guards. The corridors are dimly lit by bioluminescent orbs embedded in the walls, their light flickering erratically, casting long, dancing shadows that make every corner feel like an ambush waiting to happen. The air grows heavier with the metallic tang of blood and the acrid bite of smoke, a grim testament to the beast's path.

The halls are a gruesome graveyard. Dead faeries sprawled across the floor in twisted poses, guards and courtiers alike torn by claws or choked by tendrils of black smoke that still linger like ghosts. Their once-striking features are frozen in shock, eyes staring blankly at the ceiling, blood pooling in iridescent puddles that reflect the green glow. I avert my eyes, stomach roiling at the sight, but the images burn into my mind. So many dead, just to get to me. This beast is a force of destruction, tied to Soren's darkness, and now I'm bound to it, for better or worse.

We emerge into a vast main hallway, its emerald-veined walls soaring high, bioluminescent torches dimmed as if the palace's magic is faltering under the assault. Shattered chandeliers lie in heaps on the floor, their orbs flickering like dying stars, and uprooted vines dangle from the ceilings like broken limbs, dripping sap that sizzles on the stone. The destruction is terrifying, a chaotic scar on Tormen's pristine domain, but there's a strange thrill in it. A crack in his unassailable world, a sliver of opportunity to slip through and escape.

We press on into an even grander chamber, the heart of the palace, its stained-glass dome arching overhead, fractured light filtering through in hues of green and gold. The air hums with residual magic, tugging at my chest like an invisible thread. It makes my skin crawl, but I shove the sensation down, focusing on the beast's steady pace ahead. Its wings twitch, scanning the chamber with predatory vigilance, and I wonder what it's searching for, what threats it anticipates in this ruined space.

A voice cuts through the silence, venomous and cold, freezing me in place. "Soren, you treacherous snake. Sent your pet to fetch her, did you?" The beast halts abruptly, its red eyes narrowing to slits, and I stop behind it, my heart slamming against my ribs.

Tormen steps from a shadowed alcove at the top of the stairs, his gold-and-green robe pristine amid the wreckage, but his green eyes burn with a cruel, unhinged edge, his usual smirk twisted into a snarl of pure fury. He descends a few steps from a grand staircase that spirals up to the dome, the air around him crackles with green energy, vines twitching at his feet as if eager to obey.

"I knew you two were scheming," Tormen says, his voice low, eyes flicking between me and the beast. "You've picked a dangerous ally, Kiera. The Umbral Expanse is a pit of shadows and lies. Hardly the place for a spark like you."

He pauses, his gaze locking on me with a possessive intensity that makes my skin crawl. He's not just angry; he's unhinged, like I've betrayed some twisted bond he imagined between us.

My fear ignites into defiance, a fire that pushes back the terror. I step forward from behind the beast, hands shaking but eyes locked on Tormen's.

"A cell's no place for me either," I snap, my voice echoing in the vast chamber. "You starved me, caged me like an animal. If Soren's a snake, what does that make you? A coward hiding behind vines?" The words are reckless, fueled by days of pent-up hunger, fear, and betrayal. I don't know the beast's motives or Soren's true intentions, but they're my path out of this glowing abyss, and I'll seize it with both hands.

Tormen's grin sharpens, a blade unsheathed in the dim light, and he laughs. A cold, guttural sound that echoes off the stained-glass dome, sending a shiver down my spine.

"You know nothing of Aelthar, or Soren's games," he says, his voice a growl, eyes glinting with malice as he descends the last steps. "You think you can run? Think this beast will protect you? I'll bury you both before I let you leave this palace alive."

He raises his hands, green light crackling around his fingers like lightning, vines coiling from the floor like whips, their hum vibrating in my bones.

The beast spreads its wings wide, steam curling from its maw, a low growl shaking the floor beneath us.

"Let's see if Soren's pet can bleed," Tormen growls, his body radiating power as he lunges forward.

CHAPTER
FIVE

The chamber erupts into chaos, Tormen's magic surging in a wave of thorny vines that lash toward the beast. The beast charges, its spiked tail slicing the air, claws flashing as it meets the attack head-on. I back away, heart pounding, scanning the chamber for anything—weapon, an exit, a way to tip the scales. Crystal fragments from the shattered chandeliers glint on the floor, sharp enough to cut, but too far to reach without exposing myself. The vines on the walls twitch violently, their hum louder, feeding on the tension like parasites.

I edge toward the side of the chamber, body coiled to run if an opening appears, my survival instincts screaming to stay sharp, to wait for the moment.

The beast roars, a sound that rattles the dome, and swipes at Tormen, its claws tearing through a wall of vines that Tormen summons in defense. Sap sprays like blood, sizzling on the floor. Tormen dodges with unnatural speed, his robe swirling as he counters with a whip of thorns that wraps around the beast's foreleg, sinking deep into scales.

"Soren's desperate, sending his beast to do his bidding," Tormen taunts, his voice sharp over the roar of battle.

The beast snarls, ripping free with a spray of ichor, its tail sweeping in a wide arc that grazes Tormen's shoulder, drawing blood. Tormen laughs again, the sound manic. "You'll never take her from me," he snarls, thrusting his hands forward. Gnarled roots erupt from the floor, wrapping the beast's legs like chains, thorns piercing deep.

I bolt for the side door while they're locked in combat, boots skidding on the slick crystal, the promise of freedom pulling me. Just get out, find a way through the halls, anything but stay here. But Tormen spots me, his cruel grin twisting as he flicks a hand in my direction.

The chamber's vines surge to life, thorny tendrils lashing out and snaring my wrists and ankles with a jolt that steals my breath. They hoist me off the ground and slam me against the wall, electric sting searing my skin as thorns bite into my arms, warm blood trickling down. The vines coil tighter, crushing my ribs until every breath is a ragged gasp.

My vision blurs, panic clawing at my chest. I twist against the grip, but they only squeeze harder, and I'm slipping, fading fast. Not like this. Not crushed against a wall like an insect.

The beast, entangled in roots, roars and breaks free, charging Tormen anew. Its strikes are precise, grazing limbs and missing vital spots. It's not fighting to kill outright, but to disable, to create an opening. It's holding back. But why? Through the haze of pain,

I watch the brutal dance: the beast's claws tearing through vines, Tormen's magic scorching its scales with smoking welts. Tormen's robe is torn now, blood soaking his sleeve from a claw's graze, his grin wild and feral, a hunter reveling in the chase.

"You're outmatched," Tormen sneers, summoning a spear of twisted roots, its tip glowing with venomous light, then hurls it at the beast's chest. The beast twists, the spear carving a deep gash along its side, spilling more ichor that steams on the floor.

Tormen weaves a net of thorns, casting it over the beast to pin its wings. The beast tears it apart, but Tormen counters with another spear targeted at its throat. The beast ducks, charging low to slash at Tormen's legs. Tormen leaps back, forming a shield of vines, but the beast's tail crashes through, knocking him off balance. Blood drips from Tormen's wounds, his breath ragged, but his eyes burn with hunger.

"You think you've won?" he spits, hands glowing brighter.

The vines pull me further into the wall, the crystal softening like quicksand as it envelops my arms and shoulders in a relentless grip. Thorns pierce my skin, drawing a raw, desperate scream from my throat as my vision begins to fade under the crushing pressure.

"Beast!" I cry out, my voice breaking with desperation, my strength waning.

Its head snaps toward me, red eyes widening in sudden recognition, but Tormen seizes the moment. With a flick of his wrist, he hurls a massive orb of green magic that slams into the beast's chest, erupting in a dazzling explosion of sparks and dark ichor. The beast staggers backward, a deep gash splitting its scales as it struggles to maintain its footing.

"Help me!" I plead again, my voice a fragile thread in the chaos.

This time, the beast responds. Its claws lash out, forcing Tormen to retreat, and its powerful tail whips forward, coiling around his waist with precision. With a heave, it hurls him upward, his body arcing through the air before crashing onto the staircase landing with a thunderous echo. Tormen crumples into a heap, blood streaming from his wounds as the impact reverberates through the chamber. The vines around me collapse instantly, their magic severed by his fall, and I tumble to the floor, gasping for air, my limbs trembling and welts burning where the thorns had torn my flesh.

A heavy silence settles over the chamber, broken only by my ragged breaths and the slow drip of ichor pooling on the crystal floor. Tormen lies motionless atop the stairs, the dome's glow dimming like a fading heartbeat, casting long shadows across the wreckage.

The beast turns to face me, its red eyes steady and unreadable, holding a depth I can't decipher. I struggle to my feet, every muscle protesting, and meet its gaze with a mixture of gratitude and wariness. It saved me. But why? What am I to it?

I offer a small, silent nod, a tentative acknowledgment of this fragile alliance that has formed between us. The beast leads the way toward the palace's front doors, its claws clicking rhythmically against the shards littering the floor while my boots crunch through the debris. The hallway stretches out before us, a dismal scene of carnage.

As we approach, the massive doors carved with intricate ivy patterns swing open silently, revealing a lush forest beyond. The air fills with the soft chirping of unseen creatures and the warm glow of sunlight filtering through emerald leaves, igniting a burning desire for freedom in my chest. I sprint past the beast, my legs aching with the effort, my mind racing toward the familiar fog and salt of Eldwick. But before I can gain much ground, its bloodied claws wrap gently around my waist, lifting me skyward with a lurch that steals my breath.

I fight against its hold, pounding my fists against its armored chest in a futile attempt to break free. "Put me down!" I shout, my voice raw with frustration. "I'm not your prisoner!"

I kick wildly, twisting in its grasp, but the ground falls away beneath me, the forest shrinking into a distant blur as the palace recedes into a faint gleam. My stomach plummets with the height, treetops rushing past in a dizzying swirl. If it drops me now, I'm dead.

Forcing myself to still, I take deep, steadying breaths to quell the rising panic. Below, Aelthar unfolds in a breathtaking tapestry of foreign beauty. The Verdant Dominion stretches out with its emerald forests, rivers of liquid light winding through groves where faerie lights dance like fireflies.

To the east, towering mountains pierce the clouds, their slopes cradling floating islands adorned with shimmering castles, their spires glinting like cut glass in the mist. To the west, a coastal city rises from a turquoise sea, its shell-like towers catching the sunlight as waves crash against cliffs of pearlescent stone.

The air turns warm, fragrant with the scent of blooming flora, but as we soar onward, the landscape shifts dramatically. The forest darkens, trees twisting into gnarled shapes with black bark. A volcanic mountain looms to the north, its red glow pulsing ominously as ash drifts like gray snow across the wasteland.

The beast veers northward, bypassing an obsidian fortress amid the volcanic wastes. Then, dark, jagged mountains emerge through the fog, stretching like a scar across the land, their peaks shrouded in mystery. The air cools, carrying the heavy scent of stone and shadow as the beast weaves gracefully through the peaks. The fog parts to reveal a shadowed forest of black and silver trees, their leaves shimmering like moonlight on water.

At the edge of a cliff overlooking an ocean of churning black and silver waves stands a palace crafted from black stone veined with violet light, its thorn-like spires elegant yet menacing, as if carved from the heart of a storm.

The beast descends with a gentle thud, its wings flaring to slow our momentum as we land in the palace's courtyard. It releases me and I stumble back, my legs shaky, the welts on my skin stinging with every movement. The terrain out there—mountains, floating islands, volcanic wastes—is a death sentence if I run. I'd never find Eldwick, not through that.

I turn to face the beast, its wounds stark in the dim light. Deep claw marks from Tormen's vines, a torn wing bleeding dark ichor, gashes across its spiked shoulders. Despite the damage, its scales shimmer with an eerie beauty, a testament to its resilience.

"You're hurt," I say softly, my voice tinged with unexpected concern. It fought for me, spared me from Tormen's grasp. Why does that matter to me now? The beast doesn't react, its red eyes fixed on me with an unfazed gaze, revealing nothing of its intentions.

With a sudden lunge, it ascends skyward, wings flaring with a gust that ruffles my jacket as it perches atop the palace's highest spire. Its silhouette stands stark against the foggy sky, red eyes glinting with what feels like a command or perhaps an invitation.

I turn to face the double doors ahead, their surfaces carved with swirling shadows that seem to writhe in the low light. Fear knots my stomach, a tight coil of uncertainty, but a flicker of resolve burns within me. I've escaped one cage only to step into another, but maybe answers lie beyond these doors. Answers about Soren, the prophecy, my place in this madness. A strange pull stirs in my blood, a whisper I can't yet name, urging me forward.

CHAPTER
SIX

I push open the shadowed doors and enter a cool, cavernous hall where the air holds an ancient, musty scent of stone mixed with a faint metallic edge. The ceiling soars high above, a dark crystal vault speckled with tiny lights that echo a celestial canopy, crafting an illusion of boundless depth. The hall is stark yet elegant, every stone whispering secrets of a realm far older than I can fathom, and I feel the weight of Soren's domain settling over me.

A figure approaches, his boots clicking softly against the tiles, breaking my reverie. He's tall and slender, with tousled black hair draping just above his shoulders, outlining a face illuminated by silver eyes twinkling with mischief. His dark gray tunic, tailored but slightly creased as if charm outranks perfection, contrasts with a silver crescent moon pendant resting at his chest. His smile is easy, disarming, and I brace myself, sensing he's more than he seems. Another faerie lord? No, too casual. Maybe an ally, or a distraction.

"Kiera of Eldwick, I presume?" he says, his voice smooth with a lilt of amusement that dances in the air. "I'm Rennor, Lord Soren's advisor and, on my better days, his conscience. Welcome to the Umbral Expanse."

He offers a slight bow, then rises with a grin. "Are you hungry? We've arranged a meal." He motions toward a side corridor, his look welcoming yet laced with a playful hint that stirs my caution.

My stomach twists at the thought of food, the memory of Tormen's thorny vines and the beast's ichor-smeared claws lingering too vivid and fresh.

"No, thank you," I reply, my voice quieter than I intend, betraying the exhaustion that clings to me. "I'd rather be shown to my room, if that's okay." I need rest, not another trap disguised as hospitality.

Rennor lifts an eyebrow, his grin easing into a nearly understanding expression. "Follow me, and try not to get lost in the shadows." He turns with a flourish, and I fall into step beside him, my boots echoing in the vast hall, a stark contrast to his lighter tread. His easy stride and quick wit stand out against the brooding intensity I associate with Soren, and I steal glances at him, intrigued. Not what I expected here.

"So," I begin, hesitating as we navigate the maze of black stone corridors, "why did Soren send that beast to get me?" My cheeks warm, and I curse myself inwardly for sounding so curious, so invested in this enigmatic lord.

Rennor glances sidelong at me, his expression guarded yet playful. "Let's just say he has his reasons, and they're rarely straightforward." His tone is light, but a cagey edge hints at secrets he's not ready to unveil.

I frown, pressing further despite the risk. "He doesn't strike me as the rescuing type. More like someone who would leave you to the vines." My voice carries a dry edge, but my heart races, fishing for insight into the fae whose silver eyes haunt my thoughts.

Rennor laughs, a bright sound that bounces off the walls, easing the tension momentarily. "You're not wrong. Soren's no hero, but he has a knack for choosing his battles wisely. His reasons are his own, though. Not mine to spill," he says, deftly sidestepping my probe with the grace of a practiced diplomat.

"You're worse than he is, dancing around answers like that," I retort, rolling my eyes as I let out a long breath. He's trained at this, keeping truths buried. "What good are you if you don't give me something to work with?"

Rennor clutches his chest in mock wounded pride, grinning widely. "Ouch! I advise mostly on navigating Soren's moods, which is a full-time job. But I'm betting you'll handle him just fine." His infectious grin tugs at the corners of my mouth, and I shake my head, fighting a laugh despite myself.

"You're not what I expected from this place," I admit. "I thought you'd all be broodier, more like Soren."

"Someone has to keep this palace from drowning in gloom," he quips, pausing before a set of double doors carved with intricate patterns of swirling mist. "Here we are. Your quarters, as requested." His tone changes, growing serious for the first time. "Get some rest, Kiera. Tomorrow morning, we're star-drifting to the Aether Dominion. The Lords and Lady are eager to meet you and discuss… well, everything. Prophecy, rifts, the whole tangled mess." His eyes soften, a rare glimpse of sincerity.

I nod, my stomach tightening at the prospect of facing these powerful figures. "Thanks," I say, meeting his gaze with a hint of gratitude. "For the escort, not the cryptic nonsense."

He laughs again, bowing slightly. "My pleasure. Sleep well, Kiera." With that, he turns, his boots clicking down the corridor, leaving me to push open the doors.

The room that greets me stops me cold, a stark contrast to Tormen's crystal cage. Its walls are polished obsidian veined with silver, catching the soft glow of floating orbs that radiate a warm, steady light like captured moonlight. A massive bed dominates the center, its dark wooden frame carved with subtle elegance, draped in silken sheets of deep indigo that shimmer like liquid night. Above, a black crystal chandelier hangs, its delicate chains dripping with gems that scatter prisms across the space.

A broad window stretches across one wall, showcasing the shadowed forest below, its silver leaves fluttering against the turbulent black and silver waves of a distant sea, a vista both stunning and disquieting. A silver basin filled with steaming water sits beside a carved wardrobe, its doors etched with crescent moons. The air is cool, scented with faint lavender, every detail luxurious yet restrained, as if the room itself guards secrets I've yet to uncover. This is too much. Too grand for a fisherman's daughter.

I collapse onto the bed, my body aching from the thorns and bruises, the silken sheets soothing against my welts as exhaustion pulls me under, and I drift into a restless sleep.

I wake to morning light filtering through the window, arriving far too soon after the exhaustion of yesterday's ordeal. A tray of food awaits on a small table nearby. Warm fresh bread, slices of vibrant fruit, and a pitcher of water sparkling like crystal. I eat quickly, my stomach still twisting uneasily from the chaos, savoring the simple nourishment despite the lingering nausea.

A soft knock at the door interrupts my thoughts; it's the maid, offering an elixir for my bath that she promises will heal and soothe my wounds, while she gathers my tattered clothes for washing. Sinking into the warm water infused with the potion, I scrub away the blood and grime, feeling the sting of scrapes fade under its gentle magic.

Once clean, I find my old clothes, now washed and mended, folded neatly in the wardrobe, alongside a new set in deep black and midnight blue, but I choose the familiar fabrics, seeking their comforting weight against my skin.

Stepping into the corridor, my boots fall silent on the smooth obsidian tiles as I wander the palace halls, absorbing the strange beauty around me. The intricate carvings that seem to shift in the light, the faint hum of unseen magic, and the quiet grandeur that whispers of secrets yet to unfold.

The palace unfolds as a labyrinth of shadow and light, its corridors twisting and turning past arched windows that reveal glimpses of jagged mountains and silver forests, their untamed splendor both haunting and mesmerizing. Tapestries drape at intervals, embroidered with scenes of starry heavens and shadowy beings, their metallic threads shimmering like ensnared starlight. The air hums with quiet power, each step feeling like a journey through a dream I don't fully grasp. My nerves churn, the upcoming meeting with the dominion rulers looming. What do they want from me? A mortal with no magic, no answers. Am I just a pawn in their game?

Eventually, I find myself back in the main hall, its dark crystal ceiling glittering above, and spot Rennor leaning against a pillar, his hazel eyes bright with that familiar mischievous spark. "Lost already?" he teases, pushing off with a grin. "Or just admiring the decor?"

I cross my arms, matching his tone. "Just wondering how you survive all this gloom without tripping over your own ego."

He laughs, clapping a hand to his chest. "You're vicious this morning, Kiera. I like it. Ready for the Aether Dominion? It's a bit brighter than this place." He offers his arm, and I take it, my nerves tingling as the air around us begins to shimmer with light.

"Ready as I'll ever be," I say, my voice steadier than I feel, masking the uncertainty roiling within. The air shimmers brighter, black swirling around us, and the hall fades as the star-drift pulls us toward the Aether Dominion and the waiting council.

CHAPTER
SEVEN

The black light of the star-drift fades, leaving me in a vast hall with Rennor's firm arm supporting me as the magic's hum reverberates in my bones. He releases me, and I take in the grand meeting chamber, its pristine elegance washing over me. Soaring alabaster columns gleam under the golden glow of enchanted chandeliers, their light dancing across polished moonstone floors that reflect like liquid starlight.

At the center, a carved crystal table gleams, surrounded by high-backed chairs upholstered in sapphire velvet that ripples like water, every detail a testament to the regal splendor of this sky-borne council chamber drifting among the clouds. This is a world beyond my imagining, and I can't help but wonder how I fit into any of this.

Standing before me are four of the most powerful faeries in

Aelthar, their presence commanding the room. Thalira, Lady of the Cerulean Dominion, leads the group, her turquoise gown flowing like a gentle tide, silver waves shimmering along its edges. Her long blonde hair cascades like sunlight on water, braided with pearl beads that catch the chandelier's glow, and her bright blue eyes shimmer with a warmth that eases the knot in my chest.

Behind her, Veyrik, Lord of the Crimson Dominion, lounges with a swordsman's grace, his lean frame exuding confidence. His vibrant red hair shines like a flame in the golden light, and his amber eyes glint with cunning, a perpetual smirk playing on his sharp, angular face. He wears regal red and gold threaded attire, echoing the scorched land of his dominion.

Elarion, the Lord of the Aether Dominion, stands apart near a window, his tall, elegant frame held steady with deliberate grace. His ivory hair cascades like silk to his shoulders, pristine against his pale complexion, and his keen light-brown eyes shine with arrogant contempt. His beige robes billow like sails, embroidered with silver swirls of wind, and a sapphire storm-cloud brooch glints at the high collar of his cloak.

Then there's Soren. He lingers a few paces back from the rest, arms crossed, his build radiating quiet menace. His eyes blaze with intensity, cutting through the room's glow like moonlight piercing fog. He's a shadow among the light, and I feel his gaze settle on me, stirring that inexplicable pull I can't shake. He's watching me like he knows something I don't. Is this trust, or a trap?

Veyrik's smirk widens as he leans forward, his voice teasing. "Kiera of Eldwick, I hear you've got a fiery spirit."

I meet his amber eyes, refusing to shrink under his scrutiny. "Let me guess—you're the Lord of Fire?" I challenge, and his grin sharpens, delighted by the spar.

"Veyrik, Lord of the Crimson Dominion," he confirms with a mock bow, his tone dripping with charm. With a flick of his hand, a small flame dances in his palm, flickering beautifully before he snuffs it out with a snap. "At your service, unless you plan to outwit me. Then we'll have some real fun."

Thalira steps forward, her smile soft and genuine, a balm to Veyrik's bravado. "Ignore him, Kiera. We're glad you're here, and I'm truly sorry for what you endured in the Verdant Dominion. Tormen's actions don't reflect the will of this council." Her blue eyes hold mine with a warmth that sparks a fragile trust within me.

Veyrik chuckles, crossing his arms to flex his muscles playfully. "Speak for yourself, Thalira. I won't apologize for my charm." She rolls her eyes, and a slight smile pulls at my lips despite the strain.

I take a steadying breath, my voice softening but firm. "What did Tormen want from me?" I ask, glancing at each of them, searching for clarity.

Thalira's expression falters, and she exchanges a glance with the others. "We're not sure," she confesses, her voice steady yet burdened with worry. "For the past year, Tormen has isolated himself in his dominion, ignoring our councils and refusing to address the rifts or the chaos spreading through Aelthar. Our spies can't penetrate his palace, no matter their skill." Her eyes flick to Soren, who stares at the floor, his silver gaze narrowed as if wrestling with a hidden truth.

"Did he say anything to you?" Elarion interjects, his voice smooth and cold, each word measured with precision. "About the rifts? Dark wielders? The prophecy?"

I shake my head, my tone clipped. "We didn't talk much. He claimed I was marked by the stars to reshape our fate, then tested me to see if I knew magic or felt some stirring power."

"And?" Elarion presses, his eyes narrowing.

"Nothing," I shrug, frustration creeping in. "I'm mortal. I don't understand your dominions or your magic. I don't even know what the prophecy says." Elarion huffs, turning his attention to the window with a dismissive air.

"The prophecy speaks of you, Kiera," Thalira says gently, her words sending a shiver through me. She glances at the others, who nod in agreement, before reciting:

"When protective shields fall from sight,
A mortal soul shall bear their light.
Through rifts that shred the cosmic thread,
She weaves salvation or the dread.
Dark chains in ashen deeps abide,
With ancient secrets, her powers rise.
A Lord she trusts shall crown the skies,
Choose true—or Aelthar's fate demise."

My mind reels, the words sinking like stones. *A Lord shall crown the skies*? Me, choosing someone to rule? I look at each of them—Thalira's gentle gaze, Veyrik's sly grin, Elarion's distant stare, Soren's burning eyes—trying to read their intentions.

"So Tormen thought I'd help him crown the skies?" I ask, my voice sharper than intended. "How am I supposed to save Aelthar when I don't even know what's happening? Where do these rifts come from?"

"We don't know the source," Thalira admits after a hesitant pause, her voice steady but tinged with regret.

I blink, staring at them in disbelief. "You don't know? You're the rulers of these dominions. How can you not know?"

Elarion paces a step, his robes swirling. "It's not so straightforward," he retorts, his voice cutting through my irritation like a dagger. "The rifts are unpredictable, shifting with each occurrence, defying our attempts to trace them."

Veyrik leans back, his arms crossed, his charm tempered by a grim edge. "It started small. Ground shaking, buildings crumbling. Annoying, but manageable. Now the ground splits open, and darkness pours out, like the underworld itself is bleeding. Beasts claw their way up, shredding everything in their path, ancient creatures older than our bloodlines. Lately, dark wielders have joined the chaos, tearing through our realms as if claiming them, though they don't steal or conquer. Just destroy."

My stomach twists with dread. "So how do you stop them?" I ask, needing some shred of hope, but Veyrik's expression hardens.

"The beasts? A good fight can take them down. The dark wielders?" He glances at Soren, who remains silent, staring at the floor. "Only dark magic can match them. And that's a rare skill."

"Few of us have encountered dark wielders in centuries," Thalira adds, her voice soft but heavy with history. "Outside the Umbral Expanse, their magic is a mystery. We don't know how to fight them." Her glance at Soren carries a weighty implication. He's the key they're avoiding.

"Aren't there dark wielders who could help?" I press, my eyes narrowing with suspicion.

Thalira's lips press into a thin line. "They're forbidden from leaving the Umbral Expanse. It's... complicated. A history you'll need to learn in time."

I pace to the window, the shimmering forest below blurring as I piece together the fragments I know. Then it hits me. "When I was taken from Eldwick, there were figures rising from the water. Were those dark wielders?"

Thalira nods once, her expression softening. "Yes. They were stopped before they reached the town. Your people are safe, for now."

Relief floods me, and I glance at Soren, his eyes burning into mine with an intensity that steadies me. He was there, he saved Eldwick after I was taken. I turn back to the window, the weight of their words settling heavy.

Thalira's voice breaks the silence gently. "Perhaps we should discuss your next steps. Is there a dominion where you'd prefer to stay for now, or elsewhere?"

I turn, stunned. "You're letting me choose?" She nods, and I hesitate, my mind racing. Eldwick is home, and I demanded Tormen send me back, but the world is fracturing, and I'm bound to it somehow. Can I go back and pretend this isn't happening?

I glance at Elarion, his arms crossed, eyes distant, annoyance etched in his regal posture. He'd rather not guide me. Veyrik's wicked smirk promises adventure, but a glint in his eyes hints at untrustworthy depths. Thalira's kindness feels like a safe harbor, her Cerulean Dominion warm and welcoming, yet it's Soren's silver gaze that holds me. His Umbral Expanse, gray and brooding, echoes Eldwick's stormy shores more than any sunlit beach.

"I'd like to stay in the Umbral Expanse," I say, my voice steady despite the leap of faith it represents. The air freezes, tension crackling. Veyrik's eyes narrow, his smirk faltering as he turns to Soren.

"Let her decide, Soren," he says, his tone sharp, almost accusing. The words suggest there might be more to it.

Soren's eyes snap to Veyrik, his body still as stone. "What makes you think I want a mortal at my palace?" he hisses, the air cooling around us. His words sting, but I recall his gaze on the pier, a flicker of something real beneath the facade. He's playing a role.

Elarion steps forward, his voice cool and regal. "If Soren's palace lacks what you need, the libraries of the Aether Dominion are open. Our history might guide you." His nod is courteous, yet it feels like a polite dismissal.

"Thank you," I reply, meeting his gaze before dipping my head in respect.

Thalira smiles warmly. "You're always welcome in the Cerulean Dominion, Kiera. If you need anything, my door is open." Her glance at the males carries a silent promise of support, and I nod gratefully.

"Shall we?" Rennor says, stepping to my side and offering his arm.

I nod, gently placing my hand in the crook of his elbow, and glance at the others one last time. My eyes linger on Soren, his gaze burning into me, holding me steady as the star-drift's light begins to swirl. The chamber, the prophecy, this fate. They pull me into the unknown, but for the first time, I feel the stirrings of a purpose, a place I might claim as my own amidst the chaos.

CHAPTER EIGHT

The black swirl of the star-drift fades, depositing me back in the heart of the Umbral Expanse's great hall, where Rennor's steady hand lingers on my elbow, grounding me as the world steadies beneath my feet. My thoughts swirl with memories of the Aether Dominion. Thalira's gentle blue eyes, Veyrik's cunning smirks, Elarion's frosty scorn, and the prophecy's eerie chant: *A mortal soul shall bear their light*. Rifts tearing through realms, dark wielders rising, Aelthar's fate teetering on the edge, it's a storm I can't escape, and I'm caught in its eye. What am I supposed to do with this burden? I'm no hero, just a girl from Eldwick.

Rennor steps back, his eyes catching the dim glow of the hall's light, a spark of warmth softening his sharp features. "Still with me, Kiera?" he asks, his voice smooth yet gentle, a faint smile tugging at his lips. "If you'd like, I can show you the rest of the palace. Give you a tour to clear your head."

I shake my head, my thoughts too tangled to unravel in anyone's company. "I need to breathe," I say, my voice low but edged with a quiet resolve. "Can I have a moment alone?" I need space to think, to figure out what this place means for me.

He nods, a flicker of concern shadowing his face. "A terrace lies just beyond that passage," he says, gesturing toward an archway edged with coiling vines of black stone. "But don't stray far, Kiera, and whatever you do, avoid the forest alone. The Umbral Expanse has a hunger for those who wander too deep." His tone loses its usual playfulness, turning serious, and the weight of his warning settles into my bones.

"Thanks," I murmur, turning toward the archway, my boots echoing softly on the stone as I leave him behind.

The terrace opens before me, the cool air sharp with the briny scent of salt and the mud undertone of cedar, a stark contrast to the palace's interior. The view halts me mid-step, stealing my breath. Beyond the palace's edge stretches a shadowed forest, its black and silver-barked trees twisting upward under a sky heavy with brooding clouds, their leaves glinting like shards of moonlight caught in a storm.

In the distance, the ocean roars, its black and silver waves crashing against jagged cliffs with a relentless rhythm that mirrors Eldwick's stormy shores. My chest tightens. This is the home I chose, a gray expanse that feels both familiar and foreign, a dream that could shatter me if I let it. It's like Eldwick, but darker, wilder.

"Enjoying the view?" a voice cuts through the silence, low and smooth, sending a jolt through me.

I spin around to find Soren leaning casually against the archway, hands tucked into the pockets of his dark tunic. His eyes glow with a softness I've never seen, like moonlight filtering through mist, and his hair falls slightly over his brow, framing a face that seems almost approachable in this unguarded moment. My heart stumbles, and I turn back to the forest, unwilling to linger on the warmth his presence stirs.

He steps beside me, the silence stretching between us, heavy yet oddly comforting. "Am I a prisoner here?" I ask, my voice sharp.

"Your quarters should have clarified that," he responds, his tone soft yet resolute, offering reassurance I'm hesitant to trust. "No, Kiera, you're not a prisoner. You're free to do as you please within these walls, and beyond, if you choose."

I meet his gaze, searching for the truth beneath his words. "So I can walk out those gates and leave?" I challenge, knowing full well the perilous magic and unknown threats beyond the forest would likely claim me.

"If you wish," he replies calmly, his eyes holding a weight that acknowledges the unspoken reality. "Are you planning to make a run for it?"

"I don't think I'd make it far," I admit, my voice dry with self-awareness. "Do you think Tormen will come after me?"

"No," Soren says lightly, his gaze steady as he meets mine. "The other Lords avoid the Umbral Expanse, even for what they claim as theirs. You're safe here." His words are steady, but after Tormen's treachery, trust feels like a fragile thread, and I'm hesitant to weave it with Soren just yet. Safe? Maybe. But safe with him? That's another question.

"Does the sun ever show up here?" I ask, shifting my eyes to the mist-shrouded sky, seeking a distraction from the intensity of his presence.

"Yes, though not often," he replies, tilting his head as if peering through the clouds. "No more than in Eldwick, I'd assume."

"That's one reason I chose this place," I admit. "I don't know if I could handle blue skies and crystal waters every day." It's the grayness, the storm. I feel it in my bones, like home.

He glances at me, his eyes tracing my face with a curiosity that makes my pulse quicken. "The Cerulean Dominion's beauty is unmatched, a palace of dreams," he says, his voice softening with a hint of longing, as if he's lost in memories of other realms, much like I once was with my father's tales.

"You sound like you envy it," I observe, studying the fleeting wonder that softens his sharp features.

He shrugs, turning his gaze back to the forest. "Beauty fades, even in dreams," he offers, his eyes meeting mine. "I assume you have more questions," he adds, his voice calm but laced with an edge, as if bracing for the storm of inquiries I might unleash.

My mind races. His appearance in Eldwick, Tormen's schemes, the beast that saved me, the prophecy, the rifts, all swirling in a chaotic dance. He knows more than he's saying, and I need to understand why he's involved.

"I don't even know where to start," I admit, huffing out a breath as I glance at him. "Would you even tell me the truth if I asked?"

His eyes lock onto mine, neutral yet piercing, holding a depth that unsettles me. "Concealing the truth merely accelerates Aelthar's ruin. I have no interest in that." His voice carries the weight of the rifts, the destruction tied to my presence, and a pang of responsibility tightens my chest.

"Then why wait so long to bring me here?" I press, frustration bubbling up. "If you knew about the rifts, the prophecy, me. Why now? What if I could have stopped this already?"

His jaw tightens, his tone clipped but honest. "Because no one knew how to help you. You're mortal, Kiera, lacking magic and training. Bringing you here felt like a death sentence, until we had no choice." His eyes soften, a flicker of regret breaking through his stoic facade.

"Great..." I mutter, swallowing the sting of his words, the implication that my ignorance might doom us all.

He leans forward slightly, his eyes holding mine with a steadiness that feels almost personal. "If you fail, then we've failed you. We'll guide you as best we can." His voice is kind, and a warmth I don't want to acknowledge flickers within me. "Perhaps we should start with some history. My study might give you the foundation you need."

"Okay," I agree with a gentle nod, and he extends his hand to guide me back into the palace, his touch light but firm, sending an unexpected shiver through me. I can't deny he's different here. Less guarded, more real. But trusting him? That's a line I'm not crossing yet.

The door swings open, revealing Soren's study, a chamber that feels like a vault of hidden truths. The walls are dark stone, lined with shelves groaning under the weight of tomes. Some in the common tongue, others in a flowing script I can't decipher, their spines glinting with silver threads. A single window filters faint light through stained glass depicting black wings, casting violet and silver prisms across the room. A sleek desk rests at the center, bordered by two chairs.

I drift toward a shelf, my fingers brushing the spines, titles leaping out at me: *A Chronicle of Umbral Pacts, Shadowed Oaths: Aelthar's Fate, Lost to Ancient Binds: Aelthar's Forgotten*

Artifacts. My stomach twists with unease. I've never studied anything in Eldwick, where fishing, mending nets, and weathering storms defined my days. This feels beyond me, and my hands tremble slightly as I touch the leather.

"What language are these others in?" I ask, turning to find Soren leaning against the desk, arms crossed, his eyes watching me with an intensity that makes my breath catch.

"Vethralis," he replies, his voice flat. "One of Aelthar's ancient tongue. Few can read it now." He remains still, his gaze steady, as if gauging my reaction. "Do you know how to read?" Soren asks, his voice calm as he leans against the desk.

I whirl to face him, a menacing glare hardening my features. "Yes, I know how to read," I snap, the words sharp with defiance, though he remains unflinching, his steady gaze unnerving me. His assumption stings, though I seethe inwardly, knowing he has a right to ask.

"I figured most in Eldwick have little need for literature," he continues, his tone neutral, and I clench my jaw. "Who taught you?"

"My father," I mutter, the words catching in my throat with a bitter edge as I turn back to the shelves, seeking refuge in the tomes. "He had a book of Aelthar's tales and legends. He'd read them to us on long winter nights, insisting we learn what lay beyond Eldwick. So we could dream of a world larger than our own." The memory burns, a lump rising as I recall his voice, his passion, now tied to this place.

"Sounds like a wise man," Soren says, his voice softening with a respect that catches me off guard.

"He was," I reply curtly, the lump thickening. My father's tales of the vyrskal he encountered in the forest, creatures I now suspect hail from the Umbral Expanse, link him to this darkness. This place might have driven him mad, led to his disappearance, left us abandoned. I could blame Soren for it all if I let myself dwell too long, but I push the thought aside, focusing on the books. "Is there a pattern to the rifts?"

Soren raises a hand, and the air hums as four books drift from the shelves, settling gently on the desk. "They emerge at the borders of our realms, then strike their targets like lightning, each location unique, but the creatures and dark wielders concentrate in one place at a time," he explains, his voice steady as I move to an armchair and he takes the head of the desk.

"So if the Umbral Expanse were hit, the other realms would be safe?" I ask, leaning forward, my voice tight with hope.

"Safe, perhaps, but not unscathed. The ground splits open across all dominions, a natural destruction we can't avoid," he replies grimly, and I wince, picturing the world fracturing, darkness seeping through.

"Got it," I murmur, turning my attention to the books spread before me: *The Dragon's Forge: A Chronicle of Aelthar's Dawn, Umbral Oaths: The Legacy of Aelthar's Makers, Shadows of the First Flame: Aelthar's Lost Histories.* His gaze lingers on me, watchful, as if anticipating my next move, and I ponder the rifts, the attacks, the origin of this dark magic. Why is Aelthar unraveling? Where did this darkness begin?

"The dominions are terra, water, air, and fire," I say, meeting his eyes with a newfound intensity. "Why is your home called the Umbral Expanse and not a dominion?"

He waves his hand, and the books shift, *The Dragon's Forge* opening to a page depicting a majestic black dragon. "Centuries ago, this land was ruled by a dragon named Aethryion, who wielded light, darkness, terra, water, air, and fire—the essence of life itself. He turned day to night, shaped the seasons, and nurtured the land's growth. But mortals grew restless, always demanding more, and Aethryion, weary of their pleas, created four dragons to share his burden: Dravokar of Terra, Sylthara of Air, Lyrisene of Water, and Vyrathax of Fire. He entrusted them with aiding mortals, then vanished."

I lean closer, tracing the dragon's scaled form as he continues. "The four dragons fulfilled their duty, granting requests—rivers for struggling villages, trees for shade, richer soil for crops—fostering a thriving land. Yet some mortals craved more, approaching the dragons to share their powers, arguing it would ease their lives and reduce the dragons' workload. After years of consideration, the dragons agreed, gifting the power of terra, water, fire, and air to the mortals."

Soren flips the page to show mortals wielding magic. "It took months to master the basics, years to refine their skills, and the land transformed. Seeing the benefits, the dragons invited more to bear their gifts. Over time, these empowered mortals evolved—living longer, healing faster, their senses and strength heightened—becoming faeries, immortal beings. But as generations passed, the blending of powers with corrupt hearts birthed darkness. Faeries emerged who bent shadows, infiltrated minds, and forced unspeakable acts. Powers never meant to exist."

He turns to a map of five glowing realms. "To curb this, the dragons created the dominions: Verdant for terra, Cerulean for water, Aether for air, Crimson for fire, and mortal lands to limit magic's spread, preserving some of Aelthar's original state. Each dominion strengthened its native power to discourage wandering, and for a time, peace reigned under appointed rulers. But the dark wielders, unbound by territory, roamed freely, spreading chaos and plotting to dominate Aelthar."

The page shifts to Aethryion soaring overhead. "Aethryion returned, his flight a reminder of his rule, and he crafted the Umbral Expanse beyond the Crimson Dominion. He mind-linked the dark wielders, drawing them—whether by force or will remains unknown—and raised the Ironspine Mountains, sealing them with fog, wind, and water to create a prison where they could live but never leave."

"Why can you and Rennor leave?" I ask, my curiosity piqued.

"Only the Lord, his family, and chosen members may depart, and only at the Lord's command," Soren explains, flipping to a page with a single line of Vethralis.

"What happened to Aethryion and the other dragons? Where did they go?" I press, my voice tinged with urgency.

"No one knows," he says, his tone somber. "He departed with the four dragons, and since then, no trace has been found. The tale leans more toward legend than fact, with no living soul to confirm their existence."

"Do you believe they exist?" I ask, searching his face.

He pauses, his eyes drifting into the distance. "I don't know. If they do, why permit this death and destruction to persist?" He meets my gaze, and I slouch back, grimacing at the weight of his question.

"Maybe they'll return," I offer, a flicker of hope in my voice.

"Maybe," he replies, waving his hand as the books close and stack neatly. He pushes them toward me, and I gather them into my arms, their weight grounding me. "Since you're delving into our history from the beginning, you might uncover truths I've never reached."

"What if the truth doesn't save us?" I ask, a thread of fear weaving through my words.

"Then we're all damned soon," he says, his eyes unflinching. I stand, my hand resting on the books, a warmth toward him stirring within me. He's offering me a path, a purpose. Maybe I can trust him, just a little.

"Thank you," I begin, my voice softening as I meet his gaze, letting that warmth settle. "For everything."

"Think nothing of it," he replies, leaning back with his hands folded on the desk. "I'm at your disposal." His eyes burn into me as I turn, and I take a steadying breath, stepping into the hall's dim light, the books a heavy reminder of Aelthar's fate resting on my shoulders.

CHAPTER
NINE

I wander the halls of the Umbral Expanse, a book clutched under my arm, its weight a quiet companion as I trace my fingers along the silver-threaded spine. The palace feels eerily silent today, the usual hum of life muted, until distant sounds pierce the stillness. Clashing steel, grunts of effort, and sharp bursts of banter echoing through the stone corridors. Curiosity pulls me forward, my boots tapping a steady rhythm as I follow the noise, emerging through a back opening into a vast plaza.

The ground gleams with slick black marble, framed by towering silver trees. In the center, Rennor and Soren dance with swords, their movements a blur of gentle grace and lethal speed, sweat glistening on their taut frames. My breath catches, my eyes widening as I struggle to keep my gaze from lingering on Soren's powerful form, the way his silver eyes flash with focus.

"Enjoying the show, Kiera?" Rennor calls out, his mischievous grin gleaming as he deflects a blow, and warmth rushes to my cheeks.

"More like it's distracting me from a peaceful read," I retort, my voice snapping with irritation. Rennor's laughter rings out, bright and unrestrained, while Soren pauses, his gaze sweeping over me with an intensity that makes my pulse quicken. He mutters something low to Rennor, who nods, then flips his sword with a flourish and stalks toward me.

He stops before me, hand extended, and I hesitate before passing the book nestled under my arm. Rennor glances at the cover, then casually chucks it back through the door, where it skids across the floor and vanishes from sight.

"What are you doing?" I protest, and he turns the sword in his hand, offering me the hilt with a challenging smirk. I stare at it, then up at him, shaking my head. "Funny," I say flatly, crossing my arms.

"You must defend yourself," he asserts, his tone grave now, and I squint, acknowledging his truth. A mortal among faeries with magic and beasts of brute strength, I'm little more than bait waiting to be devoured. I can't deny it. I'm vulnerable here.

"I've never held a sword in my life. What makes you think I want to start now?" I challenge, my voice laced with defiance.

Rennor reaches behind his back and unsheathes a small dagger with an intricate design, its hilt adorned with swirling obsidian vines inlaid with silver, a beautiful yet deadly weapon. "You know how to use one of these, don't you?" he asks, holding it out.

"So what?" I snap, crossing my arms tighter, though I feel Soren's presence burning in the distance, a distraction I fight to ignore.

"Then this should come naturally," Rennor says, lifting the sword again. "Show me what you know." He spins the dagger, offering the hilt, and without thinking, I snatch it and flick my wrist. The blade soars through the air, embedding itself perfectly in the trunk of a nearby silver tree with a satisfying thud. Both of them snap their heads toward it, and Rennor's grin widens, his eyes gleaming with approval as he holds the sword out once more.

"I'm not sparring with either of you," I declare..

"Why not?" Rennor asks, tilting his head.

"Because you'll mock me the whole time," I say, pointing at him, "and he'll lose his patience, storm off cursing under his breath. I won't subject myself to that humiliation." My sharp tone draws a loud laugh from Rennor, his head tilting back in amusement.

"You're not wrong," he admits, resting the sword's tip on the ground and leaning on the pommel. "What if we find someone more patient and straightforward to teach you?"

"Let me know when you find them," I reply dryly, turning back toward the palace to retrieve my book. I scoop it up from the floor, dusting off the cover with a scowl.

Later, I stride down the hall with the book under my arm, muttering Rennor's words under my breath, my mind drifting to Soren's sweat-slicked form in the plaza. As I reach for my bedroom door, a dagger whizzes past, lodging into the wood frame with a sharp thunk. I spin around, heart pounding, to see a figure at the far end of the hall, unfamiliar, cloaked in shadow. Before I can react, another dagger flies, and I duck, the blade embedding where my head had been. The figure, a female in black, steps closer, her movements deliberate, and I bolt, sprinting down the hall as panic surges. Who is she?

Glancing over my shoulder, I register her long black braid and lithe frame, the black attire marking her as from the Umbral Expanse, yet no one I recognize. I slow down and fling my book with all my might, then race toward the main entry's staircase.

"Soren! Rennor!" I shout, my voice echoing unanswered, and panic flares.

I leap down the stairs two at a time, my heart pounding in my ears, each step a desperate bid for distance. But a sharp thunk halts me mid-stride. A dagger embeds itself into the banister inches from my hand, the vibration humming through the wood.

I glance back quickly and find her at the top of the stairs, her grin wide and lethal, eyes gleaming with the promise of violence. Instinct surges through me and without thinking, I hop onto the railing and slide down. I tumble off at the bottom, rolling onto my shoulder to absorb the impact, the world blurring for a split second before I crouch low, my muscles coiled for whatever comes next.

She descends with effortless elegance, gliding down the stairs, her voice laced with dark humor that sends a chill racing up my spine. "Are you going to keep running, Kiera?"

I take off down the hall towards the training plaza, my boots slamming against the stone floor in a desperate rhythm. I grab the doorframe, using it to launch myself into the open air, the cool breeze whipping my hair back as I burst into the courtyard. The sword lies abandoned in the center of the ring, glinting mockingly under the fading light, and my earlier dagger remains embedded in the tree trunk. But Soren and Rennor are nowhere in sight. The plaza is empty, their absence a gnawing void that fuels my panic. So I sprint to the tree and yank the dagger free with a sharp tug.

"There you are." The words drip with predatory satisfaction, and I whirl around, flinging the dagger in a desperate arc. She dodges with unnatural speed, the blade grazing the doorframe inches from her eye, embedding itself with a resounding thunk.

She plucks the dagger free without flinching, inspecting it with a mix of shock and twisted amusement, her lips curling into a smirk.

"Impressive aim," she acknowledges, twirling the blade between her fingers. "But you'll have to do better than that if you want to survive what comes next." My mind races. Run, fight, scream for help? But her eyes lock onto mine, daring me to make my move, the tension coiling.

"What do you want from me?" I demand, my voice trembling despite my efforts to sound defiant, the words echoing off the palace walls.

"Nothing, really," she shrugs casually, her shoulders rising and falling with an ease that only fuels my frustration. I glance between her and the sword lying in the center of the ring, calculating my odds.

"Who are you?" I press, my heart racing as I try to buy time, my mind whirling with confusion and anger.

"Your trainer," she says with a wide grin, spinning the dagger effortlessly between her fingers. I hunch over, hands on my thighs, gasping for breath as realization crashes over me. A test? She chased me through the palace, threw daggers at me, nearly killed me. All for this?

"You must be joking," I rasp, glancing at the dagger. "You could have killed me."

"I would have healed you," she replies nonchalantly, as if it's the most obvious thing in the world, and I straighten, staring at her in disbelief, my chest heaving.

"What was the point of all this?" I snap, frustration boiling over into my voice, my hands clenching into fists at my sides.

"I think you know," she says calmly, and I know she's right. It was to prove how desperately I needed to learn to fight. The chase left me winded and exposed, a stark reminder of my vulnerabilities.

"You could have just asked me to train with you," I retort, my anger flaring as I cross my arms, trying to mask the lingering shake in my limbs.

"Rennor said you're stubborn," she counters, tossing the dagger up and catching it with a flourish. "Is this yours?"

"Rennor's."

"I don't think he deserves a dagger this pretty. You should keep it," she insists, offering the hilt to me. I take it hesitantly, studying the intricate design etched into the metal.

"It's not mine," I say, then fling it back toward the tree with a sharp throw where it strikes with a thud. She grins widely, planting her hands on her hips in a firm stance.

"I'm Zyra, by the way," she introduces, and I watch her cautiously, my instincts still on high alert after the chase.

"How will you train me?" I ask warily, my eyes flicking to her hands for any sign of another attack.

"We'll start with basics. Strengthening your arms, legs, core. Then balance, coordination, strikes, kicks, tackles. Finally, weapons," she explains, her tone matter-of-fact, as if she's outlining a simple routine rather than a grueling regimen.

"I'm not doing this."

"You're out of breath from running through the palace. You need the training," she points out bluntly, and I shoot her an annoyed glare, hating how right she is. My lungs still burn from the sprint.

"Soren said I'm safe here. Why bother?" I counter, grasping at excuses, though a part of me knows the truth.

"Do you plan to fulfill the prophecy by hiding in this palace, hoping answers leap from these books?" she challenges, her tone shifting to something more serious, her eyes locking onto mine with an intensity that makes me pause. "There's much to learn, but books won't teach you survival."

"When?" I ask, relenting with a sigh, the fight draining out of me.

"Every day at dawn."

"No," I reply instantly, shaking my head at the absurdity of the hour, and she laughs, a genuine sound that eases some of the tension.

"I'll be in this circle tomorrow morning, and only tomorrow if you don't show," she warns, her eyes sparkling with a dare I can't ignore.

"Who are you to them? Why were you chosen?" I ask, curiosity overriding my caution as I study her, trying to piece together her place in this palace.

"I'm the Lady of the Umbral Expanse," Zyra declares, and a torrent of emotions crashes over me. Shock hitting first, followed by a sharp pang of betrayal, and a creeping dread that settles like ice in my veins. The Lady? Soren's wife?

"You're… you and Soren are…" I stammer, my voice fracturing under the weight of the revelation, my world tilting as the implications sink in.

"Yes," she confirms, her expression solemn, and my eyes widen further, my breath hitching as I struggle to process it all. But before I can drown in the turmoil, Zyra's laughter erupts, her head tilting back with unrestrained mirth that echoes through the plaza. "I'm sorry, I had to," she gasps through her chuckles, and my instincts flare to life, a mix of relief and irritation surging through me.

I stride to the tree and yank the dagger free with a furious tug and hurl it at her, my anger blazing hot. Shadows twist in the air, seizing the blade mid-flight before it can connect, and she brushes her eyes, still smiling through the remnants of her laughter. "No, I'm not Soren's Lady. He's a brooding bachelor, through and through. Rennor's my brother, we grew up together in this palace."

Heat rushes to my cheeks as I shake my head, embarrassment mingling with a flood of relief that leaves me lightheaded. "I should've known," I mutter, then turn sharply toward the palace doors, my steps quick and resolute as I seek escape from the whirlwind of emotions.

"Back to your reading?" Zyra calls after me, her tone teasing and light, following me like a playful shadow.

"Yes," I snap, then step inside, away from the truth I can't escape—I'm unprepared for this world, yet I have to rise to meet it, no matter the cost.

"See you tomorrow!" she shouts, her voice echoing as I retreat into the shadows of the hall, muttering a string of frustrated curses under my breath.

CHAPTER
TEN

A week has passed since my initial grueling training session with Zyra, and my muscles are just starting to feel familiar again. The first day left me barely able to walk, each step a struggle to rise from bed or descend the stairs. Zyra's claim that she'd 'ease up' on the second day was the final time I trusted her promise of mercy. Now, as I step into the sparring ring for my tenth session, I pause with hands on my hips, surveying the scene.

Rennor stands at the center, his sword sweeping through the air in a smooth, captivating motion, and I shake my head, part amused, part annoyed. He finishes with a swift stop, turning to face me, his trademark grin already plastered across his face.

"Good morning, Kiera," he greets, his voice laced with mischief.

"What are you doing here?" I ask, narrowing my eyes as

suspicion creeps in.

He spreads his arms wide, feigning innocence. "What? I'm not allowed to train with you?" His tone is playful, but I shoot him a glare.

"No. Where's Zyra?" I scan the plaza, noting the absence of her usual gear—leather satchel, worn boots, the dagger she sharpens obsessively. "Please don't tell me you're training me today."

"Zyra's tied up with other business. She sends her regards," he says with a mock-apologetic bow, and I tilt my head back, staring at the gray sky with a groan. Letting out a long breath, I step forward, shedding my light jacket and rolling my shoulders to loosen them. If I'm stuck with him, I might as well make it worth my while.

"Do I at least get to punch you with full strength?" I ask, a wry edge to my voice.

"If you can manage," he replies with a wicked grin, and we begin circling each other at an even pace. "Zyra says you're surprisingly fast for a mortal." His words jab at me, and I block him out, launching a flurry of punches and kicks. He deflects them effortlessly, pushing back with gentle counters that still force me to stagger. "She also says you've got deadly precision with a dagger."

"Are you gonna talk the whole time?" I snap, frustration bubbling as he laughs and returns a series of soft kicks and punches. I block them, but the force sends me stumbling further than I'd like.

"Where did you learn your skills?" he probes, his tone curious.

"Lots of downtime in Eldwick," I reply curtly, throwing a succession of punches—left, right, right, left, left, left, right—muttering Zyra's combinations under my breath. Until they're second nature, as she insists, I'll cheat my way through. Left right, keep moving, don't stop.

"Are all mortals good with daggers?" he asks, evading effortlessly.

"I wouldn't know," I retort, and he sweeps my ankle with his foot. I topple, catching myself with my hands and pop up quickly.

"Nice," he says smoothly, and I falter, surprised by the genuine compliment, only to realize my mistake too late. He grabs my wrist, spins me, and flips me onto my back with a thud. I groan, closing my eyes as I try to catch my breath, feeling his smug smile without needing to look. Of course he'd turn that against me.

"You know I'm mortal, right? You could actually kill me," I mutter, opening my eyes to see his hand extended.

"I have my doubts," he says with a smirk, and I grab his hand, letting him pull me up. A groan escapes as my back aches, and I huff out a breath.

"You have doubts? About what? Killing me?" I demand, narrowing my eyes as I study him fully. "Rennor, I'm from Eldwick. The furthest thing from magic. What makes you think I'm one of you? I can barely take a punch."

"You can barely take a compliment," he teases, throwing a punch that I block instinctively. "But you can take a punch."

"If this were a real fight, I'd be dead," I counter, frustration spilling over as I unleash a relentless barrage of punches. My arms burn, and I stop, hands on my hips, panting. "Why are you here?"

"To train," he says simply, but his evasive tone irks me. I'm mortal. Kiera of Eldwick, nothing more. What's he hiding? I open my mouth to demand answers, but the ground trembles violently, cracking open before us.

I drop low, heart pounding, as a deafening crack splits the air above, a sound hauntingly familiar from Eldwick. A veil of shimmering light cascades down, revealing a dome-like shield over the palace. A shield? Like the one in Eldwick the day I was taken, or has it always been there, unnoticed? The ground groans, the palace behind us shuddering with a screeching wail, as if in agony.

"What's happening?" I yell over the rumble, and Rennor throws his arms out. He conjures an invisible shield around me, and I fight to steady my breath, my balance teetering.

"What do we do?" I ask urgently, but Rennor draws his weapons, adopting a battle stance, his eyes locked on the forest.

"Don't move," he warns, his voice low. "Don't even breathe if you can manage." A cold dread seeps into me, my hands trembling as the ground stills and an eerie silence falls.

Beyond the forest line, black ghostly figures hover just above the ground. Cloaked in tattered robes, their hoods revealing swirling pits of smoke where faces should be, trailing wisps of whipping black mist. I've read of forest creatures, but nothing like this.

"What are those?" I whisper, my voice barely audible.

"Soul Drifters," Rennor replies, lowering his sword into a confident stance as they reach the plaza's edge, halted by an unseen barrier. Their eerie voices murmur among themselves, dismissing me as the Chosen One, calling me weak, a lesser threat than rumored. I clench my fists, shame burning. They're right. I'm a liability.

"You have been summoned," they intone in a rasping, guttural whisper, and I freeze, staring in terror.

"Who has summoned her?" Rennor demands, stepping between me and the creatures, but they press closer, their presence making the shield shimmer like lightning-struck glass. It cracks with a thunderous explosion as Rennor retreats, and I mirror him, the air growing frigid.

A figure emerges from the palace door. Soren, moving with calm authority, shadows flaring from his body like a dark storm. His features remain cool, unfazed. "Go inside, Kiera," he commands sharply, and though I open my mouth to protest—to warn him, to beg him to be careful—I bite it back, refusing to undermine them before these beings. I retreat to the door, pausing at the threshold to watch.

"Took you long enough," Rennor quips as Soren takes his side.

"The Cerulean Coast is in shambles," Soren states, his voice grim, and my eyes widen. He was in another dominion—facing what, I wonder?

"Give us the girl," the Drifters rasp, but Soren and Rennor stand unflinching.

"Who sent for Kiera?" Soren asks evenly, and the Drifters respond with a riddle.

"A ruler from the Obsidian Depths, where shadows weave and silence reigns, calls for the Chosen One." Their words twist in my mind, meaningless yet ominous.

"We will not return without the Chosen One," they hiss.

"Then you won't be leaving at all," Soren declares.

The Soul Drifters surge forward with blinding speed, their tattered forms a blur of black smoke and malice. Before I can blink, Soren's shadows erupt like a living storm, lashing out with serpentine precision. Tendrils of darkness whip through the air, coiling around the nearest Drifter, binding its smoky limbs as it screeches, a sound that grates against my bones. The shadow tightens, crushing the creature into a dissipating wisp, its cloak fluttering to the ground in tatters.

Rennor moves in tandem, his sword flashing as he slashes at a second Drifter, but then he raises his free hand, and shadows of his own explode from his fingertips. They twist like living vines, snaring the Drifter's form, pulling it toward him as he drives his blade through its core. The creature shrieks, its smoky essence fracturing, and Rennor spins, shadows flaring to deflect a retaliatory tendril that lashes back. The fight ignites into a chaotic dance of power and steel, the plaza trembling under the onslaught.

Three Drifters remain, their movements synchronized as they counterattack. One hurls a wave of chilling smoke, forcing Soren to erect a barrier of writhing shadows, the impact sending sparks of dark energy crackling through the air. He counters with a sweeping arc of shadow, the tendril slicing toward a Drifter, but it dodges with unnatural agility, its form splitting and reforming.

Rennor leaps into the fray, shadows coiling from his hand to ensnare the evasive Drifter, pinning it long enough for him to plunge his sword downward, the blade piercing through smoke and cloth. The creature collapses, its wail echoing as it dissolves.

The two remaining Drifters converge, their smoky tendrils weaving a net of cold death. Soren roars, unleashing a torrent of shadows that crash like a tidal wave, slamming into one Drifter and pinning it against an invisible wall. He clenches his fist, and the shadows compress, crushing the creature with a sickening crunch, its form imploding into nothingness.

Rennor dances with the last Drifter, his shadows spiraling like a whirlwind, clashing against the creature's defenses. He thrusts his sword, the blade grazing its side, but the Drifter retaliates, a tendril slashing across his chest, tearing a deep gash. Blood stains his tunic as he staggers, shadows flickering weakly.

Rennor, panting and ragged, fights on, his shadows lashing out in desperate arcs, each strike weaker than the last. The Drifter closes in, its claws raking across his arm, and he drops to one knee, his sword clattering to the marble.

Soren's eyes blaze with fury, and with a guttural shout, he unleashes a colossal blast of shadow, the force shattering the shield in a burst of crackling energy. The raw power surges forward, engulfing the Drifter, tearing it apart in a violent explosion of smoke and shadow. The plaza falls silent, the air heavy with the scent of ozone and defeat.

I rush to Rennor, where Soren is already crouched, layering shadows over the wound. Court members pour through the door, an older faerie pushing forward, raising his hands to levitate Rennor.

"Careful," Soren growls, and they hurry inside.

Rennor is laid on the corridor's center table, three healers hovering their hands over him as shadows weave around him tightly.

"It's a deep wound."

"His organs are slashed."

"Heal him," Soren snaps, his voice a whip crack. The healers focus intensely, one shaking their head in doubt. Soren paces to the door, staring into the void where only cloak fragments remain, then raises his hands. Energy crackles as a new shield domes the palace.

Then, Rennor's eyes flutter open, his breath shallow. "Told you I'd outlast you," he rasps with a weak grin, breaking the tension. He closes his eyes again, and Soren turns to me, his gaze locking with mine, hardening.

"No one will ever summon you," he vows in a low, resolute rasp, and I nod. The weight of his promise, and my place in this chaos, settling deep within me.

CHAPTER ELEVEN

I've been training every day since the Soul Drifters' attack two weeks ago, and every muscle aches in unexpected spots—my shoulders pulse, my calves wail, and some mornings I can hardly haul myself from the twisted sheets. Yet, with each grueling day, the pain ebbs. My muscles no longer ignite with fire when I rise, and a strange resilience creeps in, softening the burn into something manageable. Maybe I'm stronger than I thought, I muse, though the idea feels foreign.

Zyra keeps me tethered to the basics. Arms flexing with punches, legs steadying with kicks, core tightening with every stance, balance tested on wobbling platforms, and a relentless rhythm of strikes. The more I push, the faster I move, energy surging through me like a hidden current. I hate to admit it, but I feel... better, alive in a way Eldwick's quiet docks never allowed.

Standing before the full-length mirror in my chamber, I run my fingers through hair still damp from a warm bath, the steam lingering like mist over the sea. I smooth the silken fabric of a new outfit—black, a color that once felt too daring against Eldwick's muted grays and browns.

The maids here, with their tender smiles, have stocked my wardrobe with these offerings, their threads so delicate they gleam faintly even in the muted light seeping through the arched windows. Weeks have passed since I last wore my threadbare Eldwick clothes, and the thought of returning to them feels as distant as the stars I used to trace.

I push open the heavy oak door, its hinges creaking softly, and freeze. Zyra stands before me, a vision in a deep violet dress that cascades to the floor in elegant waves, the fabric catching the light like a twilight sky. My eyes widen, and she waves me back into the room with a playful shooing motion, her grin wicked and full of secrets.

"Why are you so dressed up?" I ask, stepping back into the warm glow of my chamber.

"We're going out," she declares, her tone brimming with mischief.

"Out where?" I ask, incredulous, as she flicks her wrist. My wardrobe flies open, revealing a cascade of dresses—black, gray, blue—materializing as if by magic, their fabrics shimmering with an otherworldly sheen. "Where did these come from?"

"Stop asking so many questions," she chides, flipping through the options with a practiced eye. I reach out, drawn to a dark indigo dress laced with what might be stardust, its light catching like sparks against the gloom.

"Okay, but where are we going?" I press, holding the dress up to the light.

"To the Crimson Dominion."

"The what?" I gasp, my voice rising as I stare at her, wide-eyed. "Why?"

"They're holding the Emberheart Festival, a celebration. You've been formally invited by Lord Veyrik himself," she says, her eyes gleaming with excitement.

"Of course," I mutter, a knot tightening in my stomach.

"What? Did something happen between you two? You have to tell me," she rushes, her voice bubbling with curiosity.

"It's not like that," I assure her, slipping out of my clothes and stepping into the dress as she holds it open, zipping the back with a gentle tug. The act feels oddly normal. Never in Eldwick did I have someone to dress with, to gossip about males or braid hair. This could be nice, I think, a flicker of warmth breaking through my nerves. "Veyrik is a bit... how do I say it—"

"Charismatic. Arrogant. Impulsive?" she supplies, her smile widening as if she knows him intimately.

"Yes, exactly," I laugh, meeting her gaze in the mirror. The dress dips low in the back, thin straps crisscrossing to a deep V at my sternum. Beautiful, yet unfamiliar to my rugged self. "Is this too much?"

"Too much? It's perfect," Zyra insists, her reflection beaming. "You're stunning. I can't wait for them to see you."

"Who's going?" I ask, my tone clipped, a flush creeping up my cheeks at the thought of Soren's eyes on me in this.

"Soren, Rennor, and me. Veyrik was insistent you come, and Soren wouldn't let you go alone," she says, her voice softening. Alone? Because he thinks I'll flee? Because of Veyrik? Or Tormen? I wonder, my mind racing. "Try not to overthink. If anything goes wrong, we won't let harm come to you."

I haven't left the Umbral Expanse since arriving, barely spoken to anyone beyond these walls, and now I'm headed to a festival where I'll likely be the center of attention. Can I handle this? I question inwardly, but Zyra's outstretched arm pulls me from my spiral. I study myself one last time before taking her arm, and we vanish into a swirl of darkness.

We land on a balcony carved into the rugged side of a mountain, the air hitting me like a furnace blast, warm and thick, stealing my breath. Peering over the edge, I see we're perched midway up a jagged range, and in the distance is a volcano glowing red and smoking, a molten heartbeat pulsing against the night. The heat clings to my skin, and I take shallow breaths, willing my lungs to adjust.

I gaze down at the capital city of Ignarath. Sandstone buildings sprawl, their warm hues glowing under torchlight, streets teeming with faeries in formal reds, oranges, and browns—attire befitting for a festival.

"You may find the faeries here are tough. They pride themselves on enduring harsh conditions, as they should. It's not an easy place to live," Zyra murmurs, her voice low and reverent. I nod, turning to the open entryway, my gaze drifting back to the volcano.

"Doesn't seem like a wise place to build a city," I remark, tracing the mountain's rugged lines.

"It would take an abnormal amount of lava to reach the town below. With so many fire wielders, the flow's easily redirected if needed," she explains matter-of-factly. I follow her gaze down to the city, its energy palpable even from here.

"Would you like to go inside?" she asks, and I nod eagerly, falling into step beside her as we cross the threshold.

The grand hall unfolds like a regal inferno, its walls of polished obsidian veined with molten gold, reflecting the flickering light of chandeliers forged from volcanic glass that hang like captured flames. The floor is a mosaic of blackened stone and ruby tiles, warm underfoot. Faeries glide through the space, their laughter and chatter a vibrant hum that fills the air with a heady, celebratory vibe. The heat presses against me, my heart pounding as if ready to burst, but I lift my chin, refusing to shrink under their curious stares.

A pull tugs at me, and my eyes find Soren and Rennor in the crowd. Soren leans casually against a pillar, his black suit tailored to his lean frame, top buttons undone to reveal a hint of chest, his jet-black hair a contained mess. His eyes lock onto mine and I force myself to look away as we stop before them. Rennor, equally striking in black, offers a gentle smile.

"You two look lovely," he says.

"Thank you. So do you," I reply, my voice tight, then meet Soren's gaze. "You as well."

"Thank you," Soren murmurs softly, nodding as if unsure of his next move.

A loud commotion erupts, chatter swelling like a wave. I turn slowly, feeling Soren's gaze burn into me, the heat amplifying my flush. Across the room, Veyrik strides through the crowd, his rugged ease commanding attention in his signature crimson and gold attire. He waves, calling faeries by name with a sharp, authoritative tone, his grin unwavering. Then his eyes land on me, and he halts, jaw clenching as he takes me in, a devious smile spreading as he saunters over.

"Kiera of Eldwick. I almost didn't recognize you," he says, leaning to brush his lips against my cheek.

"You, on the other hand, are difficult to miss," I snap, intending fierceness, but his smile softens my edge.

"Can't keep your eyes off me, huh?" he teases, and a grin cracks my lips. His gaze flicks to them, then back to my eyes, before turning to Zyra. "You're looking as beautiful as ever, Zy." He kisses her cheek with more force, wrapping an arm around her waist. They do know each other well, I think, noting her earlier description.

"Rennor," Veyrik nods.

"Veyrik," Rennor returns quietly, a respectful but cool acknowledgment.

"Try not to look so drab, Soren. I thought you'd enjoy the change of scenery," Veyrik jabs, but Soren's eyes flicker with a deadpan stare.

"Don't you have someone else to charm?"

"I do, actually," Veyrik says, turning to me with an outstretched hand. "Shall we?" My eyes widen, darting to Zyra and Rennor, then to Soren, whose shadows flare faintly, his tension palpable.

"She's not going anywhere with you," Soren growls low.

"Oh, relax. Do you really think I'd let something happen to her in my palace?" Veyrik laughs, raising his hand higher as he meets my eyes. "I promise to behave."

"I doubt that," I quip quickly, earning a wide grin. I glance at Soren one last time, his seething restraint barely contained, then follow Veyrik into the crowd.

I tilt my head upward, my gaze tracing the grand staircase Veyrik has led me to, its steps carved from volcanic obsidian that gleams with a deep, molten sheen under the flickering torchlight.

Glancing sideways, I catch his wide, roguish grin, his arm extended toward me with an air of challenge. Can I trust him? I wonder, my instincts warring with the strange ease I feel in his presence.

"Don't trust me, Kiera?" he teases, his voice a warm rumble that echoes faintly off the stone walls.

"I don't trust anyone," I reply, keeping my tone steady, though my heart beats a little faster.

His smile widens, flashing white teeth against his tanned skin, and I take his arm, lifting the hem of my indigo dress with my free hand. Thank the winds for Zyra's training, I'm grateful my legs won't betray me with every step.

"I was never told what the Emberheart Festival is for," I say softly, my breath already quickening as we ascend. Veyrik slows his pace, sensing my struggle, his grip on my arm firm yet gentle.

"The festival marks the autumn equinox each year," he begins, his voice taking on a reverent cadence. "At dusk, faeries gather in the heart of the capital below, and the pyre is lit with a spark from the Everflame—a sacred fire said to have been kindled by Vyrathax himself. It's a night of passion, renewal, and reverence for fire's dual nature: creation and destruction." His words hang in the air, and my mind races. Creation and destruction. Does he mean it literally?

"Do you believe the dragons truly existed?" I ask, curiosity overriding my caution. His eyes snap to mine, sharp and assessing.

"Vyrathax is one of our creators. His flames bind us all, just as the other elements bind the rest. So yes, I believe he exists," he says with conviction, studying me as I keep my gaze forward. "You don't?"

"I've only read about them. I'm not sure what to believe," I admit, glancing at him. The distraction costs me, my foot catches a step and I stumble. His arm braces me instantly, his free hand covering mine to steady me, and heat floods my cheeks with embarrassment.

He'll mock me now—call me a clumsy mortal—I brace myself, but no jest comes. Instead, he guides me upward with quiet assurance, leading me to an outdoor balcony as we reach the top.

CHAPTER
TWELVE

The evening glow bathes us in a warm, amber light, the city sprawling below like a living tapestry of sandstone and fire-lit streets. Chatter, laughter, and music rise from the capital, a symphony that stirs memories of Eldwick's market days, though this vibrancy dwarfs anything I knew.

"Have you made any sense of the prophecy yet?" Veyrik asks quietly, leaning forward on the rail with elbows propped, ankles crossed behind him.

"I don't think I've stopped the rifts by reading books, so no. Not yet," I reply, my tone edged with frustration, expecting him to chide me for my lack of progress. But he surprises me, his posture relaxed, his face softened by the fading light. He doesn't look so jagged here, I note, tracing the sharp lines of his profile.

"We've been grappling with these rifts for years. Our best scholars, historians, and alchemists haven't deciphered them either. Don't be too hard on yourself," he says matter-of-factly, and I study him, the sincerity in his voice catching me off guard.

"It doesn't sound like you have much faith in me," I say honestly, meeting his gaze.

"I've placed all my faith in you," he counters, his eyes holding mine with an intensity that makes me look away, my cheeks warming again.

"I really don't know what to do from here," I confess, the admission burning with embarrassment, yet talking with him feels surprisingly natural. He nods, turning back to the view.

"Fate has a strange way of revealing itself," he muses, his tone cryptic.

"Is that the only advice you have for me?" I ask, a hint of exasperation creeping in.

"Try not to get killed," he says with a shrug, and I roll my eyes.

"That's the most straightforward thing you've said yet," I retort, and he chuckles deeply, standing straight to lean against the rail, facing me fully. The weight of his presence presses in, both comforting and unsettling.

"If you like reading, I could send some books back with you. I imagine Soren's library is stuffed with dark creatures and mystic mind-bending spells," he teases, the familiar edge returning.

"It seems you might be jealous of Soren," I fire back, catching a flicker in his eyes like I'm treading a fine line.

He opens his mouth to reply, but a brilliant flash erupts off the balcony, followed by a booming shockwave that rattles the stone beneath us. I stumble back toward the door, reaching instinctively for a dagger that isn't there.

Veyrik turns, a grin on his face that fades to concern when he sees me. "You have nothing to fear," he says, hand extended as a sphere of flame materializes in his palm. "We call it a Starvox. It's part of the celebration tradition."

I watch, mesmerized, as the flame hardens into a sphere like crumbled lava, which he tosses into the air. It arcs upward, and just as it begins to fall, it explodes into a cascade of vibrant light—reds, golds, and blues—fanning outward in a dazzling display. My eyes widen, and I step closer, drawn to the beauty.

"That's incredible," I murmur.

His gaze follows me as I approach, and he extends his hand once more. Five more Starvox form, each tossed higher than the last, erupting in synchronized bursts as he flexes his fingers. Then, shifting into a new stance, he thrusts both hands forward, unleashing a wide stream of flame that dances in the air. With fluid motions, he shapes it, and my breath catches as a fiery rendition of Vyrathax takes form—its wings flapping, sending waves of heat toward us.

He guides the dragon upward, then dives it toward the city below. I lean over the rail, watching as faeries cheer, children and adults alike chasing its path through the streets, weaving between buildings. It soars back toward us, circling just before me, and I study its jagged spikes, horned head, and dagger-like tail—almost identical to the sketches I've seen, save for its flaming body. Then it rockets into the distance, curling into a ball before exploding into a shower of embers that glimmer like starlight against the fading sun.

"I think I've started a chain reaction," Veyrik says, and I smile widely as booms and cheers echo across the skyline. My eyes linger on the display before turning to him, his shoulders squared, eyes sparkling with wonder.

"That was beautiful," I say softly, awestruck by the magic I never imagined.

"I have something for you. A gift, if I may present it," he offers, reaching into his pocket.

"I don't need any gifts," I reply, taken aback, but he unwraps a small burgundy cloth, revealing a necklace. A simple gold chain with a black, jagged pendant that reminds me of a fish scale.

"For you, Kiera of Eldwick," he declares with formality. I lean closer, intrigued yet wary.

"What is it?"

"I'm not sure," he admits, grinning at my skeptical look. "It was passed to me in exchange for a promise. I've held it for centuries, trying to discern its purpose and owner. But I believe it's meant for you."

"I don't think I can accept this," I say, suspecting a trick, though his warmth beneath the arrogance catches me off guard. "Is it cursed?"

"It's made of black. All things made of black are cursed," he says with a shrug.

"What is it with you and darkness?" I mutter, rolling my eyes as he spins his finger, signaling me to turn. I move my hair aside, feeling his fingers brush my neck as he fastens the chain. Turning back, I glance at the pendant resting against my chest.

"It suits you," he says, and I raise an eyebrow.

"Do you know why you had to give it to me?" I press, fishing for more, but he shakes his head. "Does it do anything? Will it hurt me? Is it dangerous?" I rush out.

"We all have our own fates," he replies cryptically, his eyes hinting at withheld knowledge. "Shall we head inside?" I hold his gaze, nodding once, and follow him back.

The grand hall of the Crimson Dominion pulses with life as we descend the staircase, the air thick with the heat of the Emberheart Festival and the resonant clang of music that assaults my ears. The dance floor whirls with faeries in vivid reds and golds, their motions a blur under volcanic glass chandeliers that spread a warm, wavering light across crimson-streaked walls. I scan the area, searching for Soren, Rennor, and Zyra, but they're swallowed by the crowd, lost amid the sea of elegance and revelry.

When we make it to the bottom, my gaze drifts to the musicians at the room's heart—harps strumming delicate strings that tug at my chest like a homesick lullaby, horns of brass blaring with bold triumph, and soft violins weaving a melody so beautiful it aches. This is nothing like Eldwick's rough shanties, I think, a pang of longing mixing with awe.

"I've never heard music this beautiful before," I whisper, more to myself than to anyone, but as I glance back, Veyrik hovers a step behind, a cunning smile twisting his lips. His hand extends toward me, an invitation wrapped in mischief. I shake my head quickly, stepping back, my pulse quickening. "I don't dance."

"I won't let you fall," he assures, closing the distance. I glance around, desperate for an escape, but without my companions in sight, wandering alone feels reckless. I'm stuck, I realize, so I lay my hand in his palm with a resigned breath. "Just follow my lead," he says, guiding me into the crowd.

Eyes trail us as we weave through the dancers, whispers and murmurs rising. At first, I focus on my feet, terrified of tripping, but as Veyrik moves with confidence, I let my body loosen, surrendering to the rhythm. His grip tightens around my waist, matching the tempo, and I dare to lift my gaze, trusting him to keep his word. I've never danced with anyone, I marvel, the intimacy of his touch foreign yet thrilling. If Eldwick heard this tale, they'd call me mad. Dancing with the Lord of the Crimson Dominion.

The music slows, and he sways me gently, his voice low. "Soren is lucky to have you."

"I'm not his," I retort, meeting his eyes with a firmness that surprises me.

"You reside at his palace, don't you?" he counters, his grin smooth.

"Yes, but I'm free to leave if I choose," I snap, and he chuckles, turning me with a flourish. My eyes catch Soren and Rennor at the room's edge. Soren's silver gaze fixed on me, a storm brewing behind his stoic stance, shadows flickering at his fingertips. "He's not holding me captive, if that's what you're insinuating. He's not as terrible as everyone makes him out to be," I defend, feeling Veyrik's hand squeeze mine lightly.

"Oh, I understand Soren more than you realize," he says, his tone thoughtful. "When fae think of terra, they see grounding. Water, serenity. Air, lightness. But fire? Destruction. Shadows and darkness? Fear. It's natural to dread what can ruin. Yet fire is life, warmth. It can heal as it harms, just like the other elements."

"And what about shadows and darkness?" I ask, intrigued despite myself.

"You should fear them above all. Shadows are alive. Always present, listening, feeling, creeping where they shouldn't. They can twist your thoughts, stir feelings you'd never embrace otherwise," he warns, his grin fading.

"I don't fear Soren," I say quietly, and he shrugs.

"Soren isn't shadows and darkness. He commands them; they

91

don't rule him. If they did, he'd be fearsome. But fae know his power. If he chose, he could slaughter us in minutes. That's why they fear him." My eyes flicker to Soren, now deep in conversation with Rennor, and I look back at Veyrik.

"He doesn't have reason to do that."

"I can think of a few reasons why he might," Veyrik says, and I study his eyes, searching for meaning. "It seems our time has run out," he adds evenly, halting our dance. I glance past him to see Soren striding toward us, his pace brisk and purposeful. "Just know, if you ever need me, I'm on your side," Veyrik whispers, leaning to kiss my cheek with a sly grin. I roll my eyes, a mix of amusement and unease swirling within.

Soren reaches my side, and Veyrik passes my hand to him with a nod before stalking away. Soren turns me into his embrace, his hand resting gently on my lower back as we sway. "I wasn't sure if you needed rescuing. He can be a bit much sometimes," he says, his voice a low hum.

"He talks in riddles most of the time. I'm not sure I understand even half of what he says," I reply lightly, noticing his gaze drop to my chest.

"A gift?" he asks, his eyebrows furrowing as he studies the pendant, suspicion etched in his features. "Do you trust him?" His hand pulls me closer, a protective edge to his touch.

"I do," I admit honestly. Veyrik's arrogance masks a kindness, and though his motives linger like a shadow, I sense no deceit. At least not yet. "Did Zyra already leave?"

"She's mingling. We don't often attend such events," he says, his eyes scanning the room. "Do you like it here?" he tests, his tone cautious.

"It's a bit hot," I say, and a grin cracks his lips, mirrored by mine until a sudden jolt breaks it. His arm stiffens, pressing me against him as screams erupt around us. I brace myself, too afraid to look, but I glance up—Soren's silver eyes swirl, jaw clenched, smoke tendrils flaring from his clothes.

I turn slowly, and my breath catches when I see a steel spear wrapped in black smoke hovering inches from my face. I press back against Soren's chest, and he steps forward, placing himself between me and the threat. A few feet away, a fae hangs suspended, frozen mid-sprint, his face contorted in terror.

Soren strides forward, snatching the spear, twirling it with deft precision before holding it at his side.

"Kiera," Veyrik calls from my side, his hand outstretched, concern etched in his features. "Are you okay, dear?" I nod, but shadows flood the floor, swirling like a dark ocean, wrapping the room's occupants. Shrieks pierce the air as I step back, heart pounding.

"Don't move," Veyrik commands, his hand halting me. "Soren," he says sharply, advancing. "Is it necessary to frighten my subjects?"

Soren spins, raising his hands, shadows creeping up Veyrik's legs. "What part did you have in this?" he demands, his tone menacing.

"What makes you think I have motive to kill Kiera?" Veyrik retorts, hands raised.

"Why were you insistent on her coming tonight?" Soren presses, and I glance at Veyrik, puzzled.

"I have my reasons, as you have yours," Veyrik counters. "Look in my mind, Soren. If you need convincing, go ahead. I know you can."

He can read minds, I realize, my thoughts spiraling. Has he looked inside my mind? Seen my feelings for him, the pull I can't explain? My cheeks burn, recalling Veyrik's earlier words about reasons Soren might act. My eyes flash to Soren's power, the lives he holds in his grasp.

"What else do you want from me, Soren?" Veyrik asks smoothly. The shadows recede, slithering back to the corners, and the hall empties quickly. "Did you kill him?" Veyrik asks, stepping toward the faerie, nudging him. He twitches but doesn't resist. Veyrik waves his hand, and ropes of fire bind the faerie's ankles, wrists, and neck, hardening into restraints. Why would someone try to kill me? To stop the prophecy?

"Did you take what you needed from him?" Veyrik asks Soren, who stares at my pendant, mirroring Veyrik's earlier scrutiny. Are they waiting for it to do something? I think, unease growing.

"We should go," Rennor breaks the silence, and Soren nods, his eyes meeting mine.

He steps close, raising his arm, but I hesitate, glancing at Rennor and Zyra approaching, then Veyrik. His eyes hold a desperate plea, a silent request to stay, but I take Soren's arm, knowing it would only worsen things. This night was meant for celebration, not this.

CHAPTER
THIRTEEN

We materialize in the grand hall of the Umbral Expanse Palace, the air thick with a stifling tension as the shadows of the star-drift fade. I turn slowly, my eyes scanning the gathered faces—Soren, Rennor, Zyra, and a few court members—each marked by an intricate weave of emotions: curiosity, anguish, panic, and bewilderment. The silence that settles over us presses against my chest like a physical weight, heavy and suffocating.

Soren paces with a deceptive calm, dark smoke drifting idly from his frame, his hands flexing and relaxing as if wrestling an invisible battle within. Yet his face betrays him. Pale and hollow, his eyes clouded with a profound weariness, as if vitality has been sapped from his core. He looks as if he hasn't slept in days, teetering on the edge of collapse. What toll did that encounter extract from him? I wonder, a pang of concern threading through my unease.

"Well?" Rennor's voice cuts through the silence, tight with tension, breaking the hush that had bound us.

Soren shakes his head, his response a low mutter that barely reaches my ears. "It's out of his control." My brow furrows, a hunger for clarity gnawing at me as I wait.

"The Elite?" Rennor urges, his tone persistent, and Soren rubs a tired hand across his face as he nods.

"Apparently, they've been making themselves known in the Crimson Dominion," Soren elaborates, his voice heavy with frustration. "Veyrik's spies are scouring for their base, but he's had no luck so far."

"Excuse me. What?" I blurt, disbelief rising as every gaze in the room shifts to me. "What are you talking about?" I demand, their quick, sidelong glances suggesting a silent debate over how much to unveil. "Is there more you're hiding from me?"

Soren's voice sharpens, a rare edge cutting through his usual restraint. "Just because you've skimmed a few books doesn't mean you grasp it all." The sting of his words throws me off balance, a stark departure from the patience I've come to expect, leaving me momentarily speechless.

"Soren," Rennor warns, his tone stern, but Soren waves a hand dismissively, turning away as if to shield himself from the confrontation. "The mixed-blood fae, born from unions across dominions, inherit a blend of elements," Rennor continues, stepping in to fill the void. "Water and air, fire and terra. Their power can manifest as a single dominant force or both, a volatile gift shaped by the resonance of their lineage. But such unions are forbidden, as they often lead to instability, and the Elite are those who embrace this forbidden path, seeking to overthrow the divided order."

"How do dark wielders fit into this?" I ask, my mind racing to connect the dots, eager to understand.

"When the essences of parents conflict, particularly if corruption hovers near their union, a child might inherit dark powers," Rennor clarifies, his voice even yet somber. "Shadows, voids, chaotic energy, these emerge as a natural byproduct, not a mark of evil. It's a potential, not a destiny, though it adds an inherent instability to their core. The Elite rally these mixed-bloods, promising freedom from persecution, but their agenda is darker. Blending the dominions by force to amplify their power."

"And only fae with dark powers can turn corrupt?" I venture, my gaze shifting between them, searching for reassurance amidst the uncertainty.

"Corruption isn't inherent," Rennor clarifies, his tone deliberate. "It can strike any fae, singular or mixed, when the lust for power overtakes them. Mixed-blood fae face a greater risk due to the conflict of their dual essences, and dark wielders, with their volatile magic, are even more susceptible. But it's a choice, a gradual slide into obsession. The Elite exploit this vulnerability, luring those on the brink with visions of supremacy."

"What happens when fae turn?" I press, my voice trembling as the implications sink in.

"Corruption begins with an insatiable craving for power," Rennor continues, his words painting a grim picture. "Their magic distorts—fire darkens to black, water turns acidic—and they become jaded, preferring disorder over harmony. Over time, their minds twist into something almost bestial, driven to kill and dominate, their identity consumed by that relentless hunger. The Elite see this as a tool, a weapon to dismantle the dominions."

I glance at Soren, the faint tendrils of smoke rising from him a silent testament to his own power. "Can you turn corrupt?" I ask, the question escaping before I can restrain it.

"Any fae can," he replies flatly, his voice devoid of emotion. "The risk looms if we let power rule us. Our control over our destiny is our only shield."

The air grows heavier as I muster the courage for my next question. "So then, what do the Elite want?"

"They've lingered since Aelthar's division, aware of their own instability," Rennor says, his gaze distant as he recounts their history. "For centuries, they've secluded themselves, their mixed lineage a closely guarded secret. But recent gatherings, rifts, attacks—they hint at a plan. Their dual powers could tip the balance, and after tonight, it seems as though you might be the key they seek to disrupt the existing order."

"They don't want me to fulfill the prophecy," I murmur, the realization dawning as much to myself as to them. They nod in unison, their silence confirming my fear. "Why would they want that?" No one answers, and I pace across the hall, my mind a whirlwind of speculation.

If they oppose the prophecy, are they planning an attack? An escape? No. Perhaps their goal is to liberate the dark wielders, reviving an ancient scheme to wage war and seize control of Aelthar. That has to be it. They've never relinquished that ambition.

I turn back to the group, my eyes wide, breath ragged as the realization mirrors the dread etched into their faces. A truth they've likely suspected but hesitated to voice. "Has anyone ever escaped the Umbral Expanse?" I ask quietly, a chilling unease gathering in my stomach.

"No. It isn't possible," Soren replies, but a flicker of doubt taints his tone, unsettling me further and planting seeds of suspicion.

"Can you ensure that?" I plead, desperation creeping into my voice. With rifts spawning ancient creatures and dark wielders, the threat of war looms large. How can we possibly survive this?

"Many have tried, and all have failed," he says evenly, but a gnawing instinct tells me we're overlooking a critical detail. Something they're blind to or deliberately withholding.

"Can these rifts be the cause of dark wielders?" I ask, and the silence that follows drops like a stone into the pit of my stomach. Why are they concealing this? What else do they know that they're keeping from the rest of us?

I exhale shakily, panic clawing at my chest, and pace toward the nearest door. Are they the enemy? Is Soren orchestrating this death and destruction? Have I been a pawn in his scheme to dominate Aelthar? "I want to go back to the Crimson Dominion," I blurt, then correct myself. "Anywhere else. I don't want to stay here."

"You will not be going anywhere else," Soren declares bluntly, his words a firm barrier, and my breath catches in my throat.

"They gave me a choice to pick where I stay. Take me somewhere else," I urge, shifting to Rennor and Zyra, who share a wary look. "Zyra, please."

"I'm sorry, Kiera. It truly is for the best," she says softly, her voice laced with regret.

"The best for whom? Why am I here?" I press, their silence stoking my frustration to a fever pitch. "If I'd chosen Eldwick or another dominion, would you have let me go?" I lock eyes with Soren, challenging him to respond.

"No," he admits without flinching, and a surge of rage ignites within me.

"Why am I here?" I ask again, my voice edged with desperation, needing to understand if my presence here seals our fate.

"I am the only one who can protect you," Soren says, his tone resolute, and my hands clench at my sides in frustration.

"Protect me? That's what you're trying to do?" I challenge, catching Rennor's wary glance at Soren, a silent plea for restraint.

"If you went to the Crimson Dominion and dark wielders attacked, no one there could protect you," he explains sharply. "We're the only ones who can fight them, the only ones who can kill them. If I'm not there in time and they take you, I can't save you." His words hit hard, forcing me to wrestle with my spiraling thoughts.

"Are you causing the rifts?" I ask, searching his face for any sign of deceit.

"No," he answers without hesitation, his gaze steady, and I study him, testing his resolve.

"Do you know who is?"

"No."

"But you think it's dark wielders?" I press, glancing at the others, their expressions reflecting a shared dread. If the dark wielders did escape, and Soren is the sole barrier, the other dominions would fall. Not to war, but to a merciless slaughter.

"How am I..." I begin, but fear chokes the words. How can I, a mere mortal with fledgling powers, stop this?

"We're here to help you, Kiera," Zyra says, her voice sincere yet tinged with uncertainty, her eyes betraying their lack of a clear path forward. They believe in me, but even they don't know how to help me.

"Despite what you may think now, we are not your enemies," Rennor adds, his tone earnest, and I can only stare between them all. Their revelations convince me they're not behind the rifts. Especially given their efforts to protect fae from them. Yet the sting of their withheld knowledge lingers, a sharp ache that they've kept me in the dark. They're meant to guide me, but it feels as though they don't fully trust me with the truth.

"I need to think," I say, stepping back toward the door. My gaze locks with Soren's, searching for any final reassurance, but he remains silent, his eyes softening with a vulnerable intensity. It makes me wonder, what does he see in me? A beacon of hope, or a burden he's sworn to bear?

CHAPTER
FOURTEEN

Hours earlier, I had sunk into bed, certain that the profound fatigue from today's challenges would draw me into a long-overdue rest. Yet, as the minutes stretched into a restless eternity, my mind refused to quiet. Vivid images flickered behind my closed eyelids—the Crimson Dominion's chaotic streets, the chilling attempt on my life, and the staggering weight of the knowledge now resting on my shoulders. Perhaps they withheld it to shield me, a mortal floundering in their ageless world, or maybe they doubted my ability to comprehend it.

Unable to bear another moment of this mental storm, I slid from the twisted sheets, my bare feet gliding over the cool stone floor of my chamber, careful to avoid the paths that might betray my midnight wanderings.

I turn down a shadowed corridor, tiptoeing past the heavy

wooden doors where scholars typically murmur over ancient tomes, their voices now stilled by the late hour. With a swift lunge, I ease into the study's threshold, halting mid-stride when I realize the fae lights are already ignited. At the desk, Soren slumps forward, his hands gripped firmly, his narrowed eyes fixed on an open book in front of him. I hold my breath and step back quietly, my heart thudding with the intent to retreat unnoticed.

"Did you need something?" His deep, smooth voice whispers gently, stopping me in my path with a nearly magnetic draw.

"I was just..." I begin, but my words dissolve as my gaze locks onto him. The fae lights envelop his features in a refined radiance, highlighting the crisp contours of his jaw and the brilliant silver of his eyes, making him nearly too stunning to grasp.

When his gaze lifts to meet mine, I notice a transformation; compared to the drained husk he was upon our return, color has returned to his face, his sunken eyes now glimmering with a fragile vitality. He's been restored, but only just, as if teetering on the edge of his reserves.

"I was hoping to find a new book," I manage to say, my voice steadier than I feel. He raises an arm toward the towering shelves, his focus drifting back to his tome with that same intense, almost haunted expression.

I step sideways, my heart fluttering as I approach the books, the mage lights brightening to guide my search. My eyes trace the spines: *The Veil of Aethryion, Echoes of the Obsidian Depths, Chronicles of the Lost Orbs, The Shattered Dominion*. I don't know what I'm seeking, but the need for distraction gnaws at me. I'm lost, adrift in uncertainty, desperate for something to ground me.

"Looking for anything in particular?" His voice comes softer now, closer than before, and I freeze. I turn to find him leaning casually against the desk, arms crossed tightly, legs crossed at the ankles.

"Just seeing if anything catches my eye," I reply, forcing a steady tone as he shifts his weight, stepping toward the shelves. He tilts his chin up, his sharp jawline and aquiline nose catching the light, and I quickly avert my gaze, my face burning under the intensity of his nearness.

He pulls a book from the shelf, flipping through its pages with deliberate care before sliding it back, his movements a quiet dance of precision. I try to focus on the titles before me, but my mind fizzles, overwhelmed by the charged air between us.

"Try this," he suggests, and when I glance over, he's closer still, holding out a volume titled *The Luminous Fracture*. His proximity sends my pulse racing, and I reach for it with trembling fingers.

"Thanks," I whisper, clearing my throat as I take the book, flipping through pages I barely register with him so near. I should leave now, retreat to read or attempt sleep, but my feet refuse to move.

"I'm sorry for how things unraveled earlier," he admits, his tone quiet and genuine. "I was caught up in the moment after everything that happened, clearly not thinking straight." I nod slowly, my eyes tracing the lines of his face, searching for meaning. "We've been dealing with this for so long, sometimes it's difficult to discern what information you may need to help you."

"How long have you suspected the rifts are being caused by dark wielders?" I ask, my voice steady despite the turmoil within.

"Since the beginning," he confesses, and my eyes tighten, examining him closely. "When the rifts happen, I can feel the energy being drained, like it's being pulled from the air around me.

It's how I'm able to know which Dominion is being attacked." His explanation hangs between us, a revelation that shifts my perspective.

"Do the others know?" I ask, holding my breath for his response.

"They may suspect it, but none have mentioned their theories, at least not to me," he says after a pause, and I nod, the pieces beginning to align. The rifts spew dark creatures and wielders, I'm certain the other dominions suspect the Umbral Expanse's involvement by now. "Do you feel like a prisoner here?" he asks gently, his voice a soft probe into my thoughts.

"That's essentially what this place is, isn't it?" I respond, my tone laced with acceptance as I hold his unwavering gaze. "It's hard to know who to trust. Everyone knows more than me, and I'm lost on what to do... I get why I'm here, though. I just feel like I'm already failing." I trace the edge of the book with my thumb, vulnerability seeping into my words.

"Our destiny will unfold in its own time," he answers, his voice a serene contrast to my irritation.

"Veyrik said something similar," I note, and his gaze drops to the necklace resting against my chest. "Do you know what this is?" I ask, touching the pendant lightly.

He shakes his head and reaches towards me. I brace for the warmth of his touch, but he pauses, his eyes softening before flicking his wrist. The necklace unclasps and the pendant floats to his hand.

"Fifty years ago, Veyrik brought this here," he begins, and I recall his earlier claim that other lords avoid this place. "All creatures of black stem from the Umbral Expanse, so he thought I'd recognize it. But I've never seen its like."

He pinches the pendant between his fingers, tracing its jagged edges with a look of wonder. "I offered to have alchemists test its material and study its patterns, but he was reluctant to part with it. When I was in his mind today, he showed me why."

He extends the pendant, so I take it gently and clasp it around my neck. "He doesn't know its purpose or power, but it's tied to his fate. To discover its owner."

"What do you mean?" I ask, frowning as I process his words.

"There are many prophecies. Some overlap, some stand alone. Some bind to beings, others to objects. Veyrik's prophecy compels him to uncover this necklace's owner."

"And if he doesn't?" I ask warily, a knot forming in my stomach.

"If he fails before his lifeline ends, it passes to another. That's how he received it," he says, and I glance at the black pendant, its weight suddenly heavier.

"He said he's had it for centuries," I murmur, and he nods. "I don't think I have centuries to save Aelthar," I admit, meeting his gaze with a mix of fear and resolve.

"Perhaps you don't need centuries," he counters softly, and I exhale shakily, the burden lightening slightly under his reassurance.

He extends a hand, his finger raising my chin softly, directing my gaze to his. His hand moves with care, tucking a stray strand of hair aside, his thumb brushing just above my cheekbone, trailing down my jaw. His gaze follows, lingering on my lips before returning to my eyes, and a rush of heat floods my blood. I should step back, create distance. But I'm paralyzed, caught in the intensity of the moment.

"Do you wish to go back to Eldwick?" he asks, his voice a

tender probe. "I'll take you anywhere you want, as long as you don't mind the company."

"I like it here," I whisper, my voice trembling with emotion, and I catch a faint grin tugging at the corners of his lips.

"You're more important than you realize," he says softly, dropping his hand and stepping back, leaving a void where his warmth had been.

Before I can question him further, he turns and waves his hand towards his desk. The book he'd been reading closes with a soft thud, then he stacks them neatly with two others before they float toward him. He grabs them and holds them out. Burnt red and burgundy covers, a vivid contrast to the library's usual black and gray.

"Veyrik sent these," he says, and he flicks his wrist again to produce a note. I take it, reading: *Hopefully these add a little color to your life while living in shadows.* A grin escapes me as I flip through—*The Crimson Veil, Vyrathax: The Ember Sovereign, and The Great Feats of the Crimson Dominion*—then look up.

"Are you and Veyrik friends?" I ask, a playful curiosity lacing my tone.

"Hardly," he replies, crossing his arms with a skeptical look. "Why would you suggest that?"

"He acts like he despises you, but I think he might admire you," I say with a smile, and his expression hardens slightly.

"Well, he definitely admires you," he says tightly, and I laugh, the sound breaking the tension.

"Oh, really?"

"Yes. Painfully obvious," he insists, and I huff, amused by the underlying jealousy.

"Were you planning to give me these books, or keep them?" I

tease, and his jaw tightens in response.

"I hadn't decided," he says curtly, and I bite my lip, suppressing a grin.

"Well, thank you for handing them over," I say, his gaze sweeping over my face, reigniting the heat in my cheeks. "I should probably go." He stares, his silence a challenge. "You should rest too. You look like you need it."

"I'll do my best," he replies, and I nod slowly, turning toward the door.

Clutching the books to my chest, my mind races, my heart pounding with a mix of anticipation and restraint. If I turn back now, I might act on impulses I'd later regret. Forcing my legs to move, I disappear into the shadows of the hall, the weight of the encounter lingering.

CHAPTER
FIFTEEN

When I reach my room, the faint glow seeping around the edges of my curtains signals dawn's approach. I've been awake all night, lost in thought. Instead of collapsing into bed, I settle at the desk by the window, the cool marble pressing against my forearms as I set the books down.

I flip through the black tome Soren gave me, *The Luminous Fracture*, its pages a blur of cryptic text. Then I pull the vibrant red-bound books closer with a smile tugging at my lips.

The Crimson Veil, Vyrathax: The Ember Sovereign, and The Great Feats of the Crimson Dominion—Veyrik's touch of color amid this shadowed realm. I choose *Vyrathax: The Ember Sovereign*, its leather spine worn and creased, suggesting it's either a beloved relic of the Crimson Dominion or a volume Veyrik revisits often.

I run my fingers along its edges, then open it to the first page and find a detailed drawing of Vyrathax. The red dragon sprawls across the parchment, its scales a blazing crimson dotted with molten gold, twin horns arching backward from its skull, and vast wings extended, their membranes threaded with ember-like traces. I study its piercing amber eyes, its sinewy body, struggling to reconcile these beasts with mortals.

Flipping further, I land on a page about armor. Shields and body plates designed to mimic dragon scales, their overlapping patterns shifting fluidly beneath clothing, offering flexibility without stiffness. A sketch of the original designs catches my eye, and I lean forward, squinting at the pointed tips and jagged edges. My gaze darts to my necklace, and I pull it off, placing it next to the book. The shape matches perfectly. Veyrik claimed ignorance, or has he simply forgotten this connection?

I turn to a page depicting all four dragons. Vyrathax, Sylthara, Lyrisene, and Dravokar, then line up the pendant. My breath quickens as realization dawns: a dragon scale, black as the Umbral Expanse itself. Why give me this? A black dragon scale.

I lean closer, staring at the illustration. If they're still out there, why abandon us? If they know how to stop the rifts, where are they? Did they die? Can they die? Too many questions swirl, and I drop my head into my hands.

"Where are they?" I whisper, and a long breath escapes me, the room brightening with dawn's light. Zyra will expect me soon, but I'm drained—mentally, physically. Can I even train like this?

"What am I even doing..." I mutter, leaning back. My eyes widen as the pendant trembles on the open book, a soft rumble vibrating through the desk.

I lean forward, hovering my hand over it, heart pounding. It's shaking—vibrating with energy. What if it explodes? Releases smoke? Draws dark wielders here? My gaze flicks to the dragons on the page, their eyes almost expectant. Ignoring my doubts, I grab it, and light engulfs me.

I close my eyes tightly, gripping the pendant as my body surges through time and space, the feeling disorienting. Then I stop and sink into something soft. Warmth washes over my face, sunlight penetrating my closed eyelids. A novelty in the Umbral Expanse or Eldwick.

I open my eyes slowly, my breath catching in my throat as a breathtaking vista unfolds before me. An expansive meadow of green grass extends infinitely, surrounded by lofty verdant trees standing like guardians, their leaves murmuring in the wind. Vibrant flowers pepper the ground in bursts of color while small creatures, their forms a blur of fur and feathers, skitter away into the underbrush.

This is no familiar landscape—no stark shadows of the Umbral Expanse, no rugged cliffs of Eldwick, nor the fiery plains of the Crimson Dominion. The abundance of green sets my heart racing. Could this be the Verdant Dominion?

Panic surges through me, a cold spike of fear that Tormen might lurk nearby, ready to drag me back to that suffocating cell. I take an instinctive step back, muscles tensing as I poise myself to flee, when a loud crack from a tree splits the air behind me—too resonant, too deep to belong to any faerie or beast I've encountered.

I turn slowly, bracing myself against the unknown, my hands trembling as luminous white eyes gaze through the thick foliage. My mind blanks, unable to process the scale. No creature I know could cast such a presence. My gaze rises, widening in awe as a majestic white dragon emerges. Sylthara, her scales shimmering under the dappled sunlight, her wings folded with a graceful elegance.

I stumble back. Do I run? Hide? Bow? Instinct drives me to bow, dropping low as she approaches, a decision born of necessity. One misstep, and she could devour me or crush me beneath her immense weight. I'm defenseless if I choose wrong, my fate hanging by a thread.

Kiera of Eldwick, a gentle, fragile voice resounds in my mind, and I jerk my head upward. It can speak…directly into my thoughts.

To the right, another dragon emerges, its scales cascading in shades of blue like a living ocean. Lyrisene, her presence serene yet commanding. Then, overhead, I spot Vyrathax, his crimson bulk dwarfing the others, his amber eyes glinting with an ancient fire as he circles above. The elemental dragons—here, in this moment? My hand instinctively clutches the scale cutting into my palm, and I loosen my grip. This scale must have brought me here.

"Where am I?" I whisper, my voice barely audible over the rustling grass, my eyes darting between the towering figures. The two dragons lower their heads, their gazes piercing as if assessing my very soul.

You are in the Skyward Expanse, Sylthara's voice resonates within my mind, her tone carrying a weight of authority. My brows furrow in confusion. An Expanse, not a Dominion, and certainly not marked on any map I've studied.

"Are the other dragons here?" I ask, my curiosity overcoming my fear, and they lift their heads in unison.

Dravokar does not wish to deal with fae, Lyrisene's melodic voice flows, her tone cool and measured.

"And Aethryion?" I choke out, the name slipping from my lips as a desperate plea, but all I'm met with is silence. Soren had said he disappeared after imprisoning the dark wielders, perhaps he sought solitude in another Expanse he created for himself.

"Where, exactly, is this place?" I press, and a sudden rush of wind answers. I look up to see Vyrathax hovering above, his massive wings beating with a thunderous rhythm. Before I can react, he snatches me in his claws, his grip firm yet surprisingly gentle. "No, no, no!" I cry, pushing against his claws, but my efforts are futile. He holds me effortlessly, his strength unyielding.

He ascends higher, the treetops receding below us, and my breath halts as the scenery transforms. We're above Aelthar, not tethered to connected land or a coastal island, but a floating expanse suspended high above the jagged peaks of the Ironspine Mountains. We descend swiftly, and when my feet hit the grass, I stumble, the impact jarring my knees.

Vyrathax lands with a heavy thud, his wings still flapping, the gust knocking me to my hands and knees. "Gods. That's something Veyrik would do," I mutter, wiping my hands on my pants as I stand.

Never compare me to a fae again, Vyrathax growls in my mind, his deep rumble vibrating through my bones, and I roll my eyes, a flicker of defiance rising despite my predicament.

"He's part of your bloodline, isn't he?" I retort, a smirk tugging at my lips. He grumbles, a low sound of displeasure, the exchange feeling oddly reminiscent of my sparring with Veyrik. "Not my fault if you're alike."

Do you realize we decide your fate? He intones ominously, his amber eyes locking onto mine, and I fall silent, the weight of his words sinking in. Would they kill me if they deem me unworthy?

Is this a test of my resolve, my purpose?

"What do you want from me?" I demand as sternly as I can muster, then turn to Sylthara and Lyrisene for answers. "Why am I here?" My voice trembles slightly, but I hold my ground, needing to understand my place.

So we can weigh your worth, Sylthara replies, her voice smooth.

"You don't get to decide that," I snap, a surge of defiance flaring within me, and she tilts her head, her glowing eyes studying me with renewed interest.

There is light in you, she says, her tone softening. *Do you think you are worthy?* A test. Her words hang in the air, a challenge to my self-perception. What do they expect? Worthy of what—life, death, saving Aelthar?

I pause, my mind racing through a whirlwind of memories. In Eldwick, I was never deemed worthy, a simple mortal overlooked by those around me. Yet, since arriving in these realms, I've stayed out of duty, driven by a desire to make a difference despite the overwhelming odds stacked against me.

"No," I say firmly, taking a steadying breath. "But I might be someday." The admission feels raw, a confession of my imperfections paired with a flicker of hope.

Lyrisene steps forward, her blue scales glinting as she parts her jaws. I brace myself, expecting a torrent of flames, but instead, a frosty breeze flows out, a wet fog seeping into my skin with an icy caress. My veins glow beneath my flesh, the cold water infusing me with a strange, invigorating energy.

"What did you do?" I gasp, my voice rising in alarm.

You must learn the elements, her melodic voice flows again, calm and resolute. Before I can protest, a flash of white light envelops me, blinding and disorienting. I squeeze my eyes shut, the unknown pulling me forward into its embrace, my fate now intertwined with the dragons' enigmatic purpose.

CHAPTER SIXTEEN

As I open my eyes, the golden sunlight and vast green fields of the Skyward Expanse disappear in a flash, replaced by the cold obsidian floor and the silvery, skeletal trees of the Umbral Expanse's training ring. My shoulders, tensed into a tight hunch during my otherworldly encounter, relax as I lean forward, hands resting on my knees, a wave of relief washing over me. They spared me. They let me live. But what does that decision mean for me now? The weight of their judgment lingers heavily, unanswered questions swirling in my mind.

Black smoke erupts from the ground around me, curling upward in dense, ominous tendrils, and I lift my gaze to find Soren forming before me. His hands are clenched into fists, his silver eyes swirling with a stormy rage that seems to mirror the chaos within. His body trembles faintly, dark tendrils flaring from his shoulders like a storm poised to erupt, a stark contrast to the calm facade he usually maintains. I step forward instinctively, concern overriding the caution that should keep me at a distance.

"What's wrong?" I ask softly, my voice a tentative bridge across the tension, and his expression softens slightly, though the intensity in his gaze remains undimmed.

"Where did you go?" he demands, his voice sharp and edged with urgency, catching me off guard. My eyes widen, a jolt of surprise coursing through me. I should confess everything. The Skyward Expanse, the dragons, their cryptic words about my worth, but the truth lodges in my throat, an invisible barrier sealing my lips as if bound by some unseen force.

"Where did you go, Kiera?" he seethes, stepping closer, his presence towering, and I retreat a step, shaking my head in helpless denial. Did the dragons impose this silence upon me? Is this why the words refuse to form?

My gaze darts toward the arched doorway behind him as the heavy sound of footsteps echoes through the hall. Rennor and Zyra burst into the training ring, their urgency palpable in the rapid rhythm of their strides.

"Kiera!" Zyra calls, halting before me with a mixture of relief and alarm. She reaches for my arms but pauses, her eyes widening as they trace over my form. "What happened? Are you okay?" she asks, her voice laced with genuine worry, her hands hovering uncertainly.

I glance down, a gasp escaping me as I notice long, jagged gashes tearing through my shirt along my arms and torso. Wounds I hadn't felt amidst the adrenaline and terror of Vyrathax's claws lifting me into the sky. How did I not notice the pain, the blood seeping through the fabric?

"I'm fine. Don't worry about it," I say, forcing a confident tone despite the dread of the sting I'll face in my next bath, the thought alone making me wince inwardly.

"Don't worry? We were terrified," Zyra insists, her voice trembling with the echo of their fear. "Soren couldn't find you anywhere." My eyes flicker to him, noting how the smoke has thinned to delicate tendrils, his hardened expression easing slightly, though I sense he still demands answers. Especially now, seeing me battered and bloodied.

"Where did you go?" Rennor tries, his tone gentler, an attempt to coax the truth from me, but I shake my head, the barrier holding firm. "How did you get back here?"

"I don't know," I reply honestly to his second question, the mystery of my return as baffling to me as my sudden departure, my mind grasping for any clue that might explain it.

Rennor exchanges a sidelong glance with Soren, their uncertainty palpable as they weigh how to pry more from my sealed lips, then steps back, conceding for the moment.

Beyond him, I notice the fae court members huddled in low, anxious murmurs, their whispers a soft undercurrent to the tension. To the right, a figure in vibrant red stands with arms crossed, his presence commanding attention.

"Veyrik?" I question, and he lowers his arms, approaching with an expression I can't quite decipher, a mix of concern and guarded reserve. "What are you doing here?"

As he nears, he raises a hand, a shimmering shield of crimson energy forming around us, muting the outside world in a cocoon of silence. I glance past the barrier. Soren speaks sternly to Rennor, Zyra mediating with calming gestures, their words lost to the soundproofing, their faces a blur of emotion. Veyrik's eyes trace the gashes on my arms, lingering on the scale nestled against my chest before meeting my gaze.

"I had to know if my actions caused your demise," he murmurs, his voice low and weighted with guilt. "Are you okay?"

"Yes," I nod, studying the amber intensity in his eyes. An echo of Vyrathax's gaze that sets my nerves alight with unease. "Have you given this to others before me?" I ask, touching the scale, its edges rough against my fingertips.

He meets my eyes solemnly, nodding. "I shouldn't have. But I was eager to pass it on," he admits, his confession carrying the burden of past mistakes.

"I assume there's a reason it always returned to you," I say, my voice steady despite the tremor of doubt within, recalling the dragons' words about my fate. They judged others unworthy. Am I next to face that verdict?

"I didn't want to give it to you," he confesses, his grimace deepening. "The thought of what it might do terrified me, but this time, I was certain. Too much was at stake not to try." The weight of his choice settles in my gut like a cold stone, a realization of the gamble he took with my life.

"How did you know to come here?" I ask, my curiosity piqued, and he grimaces again, as if the admission pains him.

"I was with Soren when he felt you return," he reveals, and my brows lift in surprise.

"Why?"

"He asked for my help to find you," he says, and I glance at Soren, skepticism threading through my thoughts.

"That doesn't seem like something he would do."

"Well, he showed up and blew my terrace apart. So there is that," Veyrik adds with a casual shrug, as if such destruction is a mundane occurrence. "I think he feared someone captured you. And after Tormen, I suppose I was the next guess. He said when he tried to find you, you were nowhere. Like you didn't exist."

"What do you mean, tried to find me? How would he do that?" I press, my mind racing with questions, and his jaw tightens, a flicker of reluctance crossing his face. Before he can answer, the barrier cracks with a sharp sound, shattering the fragile privacy.

I snap my attention to Soren, his hand outstretched, black smoke seeping from his fingers as he dismantles Veyrik's shield.

"His powers irk me," Veyrik mutters with a hint of distaste, and I can't suppress a small grin, the tension easing for a fleeting moment.

He studies me a moment longer, as if weighing his next words, but with the barrier down, he seems reluctant to continue. "If you need me, find me," he says, his tone carrying a promise, and I nod slowly, wondering if I will need him, and if there's more to this scale's mystery yet to unfold.

"Thank you for the books," I tell him, and the corners of his lips turn up as he bows, then steps back to face Soren. They lock eyes, a silent exchange passing between them, and with a swirl of flames, he vanishes in a flash of crimson light. My gaze lingers on the spot where he stood, then shifts to Soren.

"We should get you to a healer," he says evenly, his voice steady, and I nod once, grateful for the reprieve.

He leads me down the palace halls, his footsteps the only sound against the polished obsidian floor, his silence heavy with unspoken questions. Does he resent me for this disappearance, for the wounds I bear?

"How often do prophecies overlap?" I ask, breaking the quiet, glancing up at his graceful stride, seeking a distraction from my churning thoughts.

"Very rare," he replies, glancing sideways but keeping his chin forward, his profile sharp against the dim light.

"Do you know what his prophecy is?" I probe, curious about the secrets Veyrik guards.

"No," he says simply, sliding his hands into his pockets with a casual air. "He's bound to silence, as I assume you are now."

I narrow my eyes, understanding dawning. No wonder Veyrik was evasive, he couldn't speak of it. Am I trapped by the same magical bind, my silence a price for the dragons' judgment? Will it ever break, allowing me to share this burden?

"I'm sorry I can't tell you more," I offer, my voice soft with regret.

"Is it safe?" he asks indirectly, perhaps hoping a vague question might loosen my tongue, his concern threading through the words.

"I think so," I answer honestly, recalling the Skyward Expanse's serene beauty. Aside from the dragons' enigmatic assessment, it felt safer than the Umbral Expanse's shadowed halls.

"Will I ever be able to find you?" he presses, his voice carrying a note of vulnerability, and I shake my head, the scale's unique power my only link to that realm, unless another path exists.

He stops before an unfamiliar door, its dark wood carved with intricate details. "The healing will hurt at first," he warns, his tone gentle but firm. "Some cuts look deep, but once the initial layer is cleaned and mended, the rest should be easy."

"Okay…" I mutter, my hands trembling as the adrenaline fades, the gashes' sting now a sharp, insistent ache. I've never been this hurt, or healed with magic.

"Do you want me to stay?" he asks softly, his eyes searching mine, and I force an even breath, preferring he not witness me break whether I pass out or cry out in pain.

"That's okay," I manage, offering a small smile. "Thanks though." He nods, stepping back with a lingering glance, and I push the door open, stepping into the unknown.

Inside, an older faerie stands beside a vacant leather chair, his silver hair catching the faint light. He rises, bowing slightly with a reassuring grin, and gestures to the seat.

"Please," he says calmly, his voice a soothing balm. "Have a seat. This won't take long."

CHAPTER SEVENTEEN

I stand before the mirror, tracing the long scars still healing across my arms with a blend of wonder and discomfort. The pink lines, especially those slashing across my stomach, are beginning to blend with my skin, though I doubt they'll ever fade completely. They're a reminder of the pressure to save Aelthar. A burden etched into my flesh.

I've been wrestling with Lyrisene's cryptic words—*You must learn the elements*—revisiting every tome on elemental mastery in Soren's library, seeking a revelation. But the collection is sparse beyond the Umbral Expanse, and the texts offer no new insight, the words blurring into static noise in my mind.

Soren offered to take me to the Aether Dominion's libraries, but the idea feels wrong. Instead, I asked him to bring me to the Cerulean Dominion. Lyrisene spoke to me. Perhaps Thalira, her dominion's ruler, can unravel this puzzle.

A soft knock interrupts my thoughts, and I cross the room to open the door. Soren stands at the hall's end, his eyes already fixed on me, a quiet intensity in his gaze.

"Do you need more time?" he asks, his voice low.

I shake my head, adjusting the dagger at my hip and the scale pendant around my neck. "No, I'm ready." I step toward him, and he extends his arm. When I grasp it, black smoke envelops us, and in a flash, we're gone.

We land on a terrace, and I spin around, breathless, taking in the view. Soren described the Cerulean Dominion as a palace of dreams, but the reality surpasses imagination. The palace perches on a high bluff, its spires twisting like spiraling seashells, encrusted with abalone that mirrors the ocean's hues—turquoise, sapphire, and deep indigo, shimmering under the relentless sun.

Below, the capital city of Sypheris sprawls across a crescent bay, its buildings crafted from coral and driftwood, roofs tiled with shimmering scales that mimic fish. Narrow canals thread through the streets, faeries gliding in sleek boats. And in the distance, smaller islands dot the sea, their white beaches glowing under the sun.

"Is it always this sunny?" I ask quietly, awed.

"Yes, the light here is quite blinding," Soren replies, stepping beside me and sliding his hands into his pockets.

"The lack of doom is quite disturbing," I tease, feeling his glance and catching a hint of a grin—a rare crack in his brooding facade. I look up, my own smile irrepressible, then shift my gaze past him to the palace interior.

The circular room unfolds like a dream, its walls of translucent aquamarine stone. The floor is a mosaic of polished shells and sea glass, swirls with wave patterns and sea creatures. The domed ceiling, a stained-glass masterpiece, depicts Lyrisene. Her blue scales glinting as she coils through a starry ocean, filtering sunlight into cascades of blue and green that bathe the room. It's like standing inside a living wave.

"Whenever you wish to go, we will go," Soren says, and I nod slowly, drawing a deep breath. He offers his arm, and I hesitate, studying it, before wrapping mine around his. He leads me inside.

"This is incredible," I whisper, my voice soft with wonder. At the room's end, Thalira's eyes light up, her smile radiating warmth.

"Kiera! I'm so happy you're here!" a voice rings out with unrestrained joy, her cerulean robes billowing like waves around her. I release Soren's steadying grip and grasp her outstretched arms in greeting, her infectious energy washing over me like a warm tide. "How have you been? You look great!" she exclaims, her eyes sparkling with genuine delight.

"I'm doing good, thank you," I reply, surprised by the genuine cheer that colors my voice, a stark contrast to the weight I've carried lately. "How have you been?"

"I've been great!" she beams, her enthusiasm practically radiating from her. "I'm so excited to show you our dominion, you'll love it," she adds, casting a quick glance toward Soren, who stands a step behind me. "Do you mind if I take her for a tour, Soren?" she asks, her tone playful yet probing. His face hardens instantly, a shadow of displeasure settling over his features. "Oh, don't look so glum. If something happens, I'm sure you'll find us," she teases lightly, trying to ease the tension.

"It's up to Kiera," he says sternly, his voice firm as his silver gaze locks onto mine, a silent question lingering in his eyes.

I pause for a moment, weighing my options, the allure of exploration tugging at me. "I'd love to see the palace," I decide, and Thalira claps her hands together, her beam widening into a radiant smile.

"Fantastic. This way!" she chirps happily, her excitement a buoyant force that lifts my spirits. I grin at her infectious enthusiasm, feeling a lightness I hadn't realized I'd lost, and catch Soren's reluctant stare from the corner of my eye. A soft chuckle escapes me under my breath before I turn to follow her down the grand hall, the echo of our footsteps blending with the distant murmur of the sea.

She loops her arm through mine with a graceful ease, her step light and bouncy, her presence exuding a charm that begins to unravel the knots of tension coiled within me. As we walk, she turns to me fully, her expression softening with a hint of concern. "Tell me," she says gently, "how have you been? Really." Her question prompts a deep, steadying breath, opening a door to the turmoil I've kept locked away.

"I've been..." I begin, but my thoughts overflow with the recent months. "I've actually been good... all things considering," I manage, forcing a smile as her sympathetic gaze meets mine. "Back in Eldwick, I never imagined a life like this. Or that any of this existed," I confess, the words carrying a mix of wonder and disbelief.

"Have you been back to Eldwick?" she asks, her tone gentle, and my chest tightens at the thought of home.

"As much as I'd love to, I think it's best to stay away. For now," I admit, my voice lowering as I wrestle with the decision. If I return, Ma and Rory would face a barrage of questions. It's better if they think I've disappeared until it's safe and I have answers to shield them from the chaos. "I have my reasons," I add, leaving the details unspoken.

"I'm sure you do," she says kindly, her understanding a quiet comfort, and my eyes drift toward the vast ocean view stretching beyond the palace windows, its turquoise waves glinting under the sun.

"I never knew the ocean could be this beautiful," I marvel, the sight stirring a sense of peace I haven't felt in months.

She chuckles softly. "What's Eldwick like?" she asks, her curiosity piqued, and I grimace, earning another laugh from her.

"Imagine the Umbral Expanse, but less elegant," I say with a wry smile, picturing the muddy lanes and weathered cottages of my village.

"And you miss it?" she probes gently, tilting her head as she studies me.

I stare out the window, the memory of Ma's warm hearth and Rory's mischievous grin tugging at my heart, the simplicity of my old life a distant echo. But do I truly miss it, with all its limitations and ignorance of this magical world?

"I'm not sure if I do," I confess, glancing at her encouraging smile, the admission feeling like a step toward understanding myself.

"There's an even better view up ahead," she says, her voice bright with anticipation as she gestures down the hall.

We reach a circular room that juts from the palace like a glass bubble, offering a near-360-degree panorama. To the left, the city of Sypheris gleams with coral-tiled roofs, a vibrant tapestry against the coastline. Straight ahead, sea cliffs rise majestically, their edges softened by lush forests that intertwine with shimmering rivers carving through the land. To the right, the distant Crimson

Dominion volcano looms, its peak a stark contrast to the serene blues around us.

"I didn't realize how close we are to the Crimson Dominion," I say, my voice tinged with surprise as I take in the proximity.

Thalira steps to the edge of the room, pointing toward the horizon with a graceful sweep of her hand. "The Crimson Dominion has a reservoir east of our border. Each season, we provide fresh water to their major cities. Their harsh climate demands it, and we do what we can to support them," she explains, her tone reflecting a sense of duty.

"I had no idea," I murmur, tracing the tree line with my eyes, imagining the river's path as it flows toward their arid lands. "I never thought about their water source."

"Most Dominions trade resources," she says thoughtfully. "A singular element has its perks, but it also imposes limits. Trade balances our strengths and keeps us interconnected." The logic clicks into place, a revelation of the delicate harmony that sustains these realms.

"This view is stunning. I could sit here for hours," I add, drawn to the ocean's clear blue expanse, its waves a hypnotic dance under the sky.

"But I assume there's a reason you came to the Cerulean Dominion?" she asks, her voice softening as she turns to face me fully, sensing the shift in my demeanor.

"There is, actually," I say, exhaling deeply as I gather my courage. "I was wondering if you could tell me about Lyrisene."

"Lyrisene?" she echoes curiously, her smile widening as I nod eagerly. "What do you wish to know?"

"Anything—everything," I reply, my voice tinged with urgency. "What was she like? What's she known for? How did fae view her then versus now? I've read every book on elements and dragons in Soren's study, but I feel the real knowledge lies with fae. Stories passed down through generations," I explain, and she nods confidently, her eyes lighting up with the prospect of sharing.

"To us, Lyrisene is no mere myth but the ocean's living heart— serene yet fierce, nurturing yet wild," she begins, her voice taking on a reverent tone. "Fae once wove tales of her gliding through the depths, her frosty breath calming raging storms or summoning tides to shield our shores from invaders. Fisherfolk swore she guided their nets to abundance, their catches a testament to her favor, while water mages felt her essence woven into their spells— healing with gentle mists or crafting shimmering barriers to protect our villages. Yet some feared her wrath; they spoke of tidal waves swallowing those who defiled her waters, ships lost to whirlpools that sang her name in mournful tones.

"We still draw life from her power, her influence lingering in the currents that sustain us, but it's been centuries since anyone laid eyes on a dragon. Few worship as they once did, offering respects for bountiful catches or pure water, their rituals faded into memory. Some say the dragons abandoned us. Granting us their powers, watching as we teetered on the brink of self-destruction, then vanishing into the ether. If you hoped for their aid in these dark times, I'd suggest seeking another path," she concludes, her words carrying a wistful note.

"I see," I murmur, my breath shaky as I absorb the depth of her tale, the image of Lyrisene swimming these very depths vivid in my mind. "Would you say most faeries question their existence?"

"Yes," she replies with a nod, her expression sobering. "It's been this way for centuries. Many long for their return, but after countless trials when we need them most—they never come. The silence has bred doubt, even among the faithful."

I gaze at the water, imagining Lyrisene's graceful form beneath the waves, her absence a void that echoes through time.

"What can you tell me about water wielding?" I ask, my curiosity rekindled, a spark of determination igniting within me.

Her smile widens, a gleam of pride in her eyes. "I think Korvis, our Master Water Wielder, should teach you. He knows everything you'd want to learn. Every nuance, every secret of the craft," she says, gesturing back the way we came with an inviting wave of her hand. I nod, following her lead, my steps quickening as curiosity and a newfound sense of purpose propels me forward.

CHAPTER EIGHTEEN

As we step into what appears to be the palace's central plaza, I pause to take in my surroundings, my gaze sweeping over the bustling scene. More faeries populate this area than any other we've traversed, their ethereal forms moving with a grace that feels both foreign and mesmerizing. Some cast curious glances our way, their luminous eyes lingering for a moment before they return to their own affairs, leaving us to our purpose.

"This way," Thalira says, her voice a gentle guide as she leads us into a vast chamber that resembles a ballroom, or perhaps a space reserved for grand formal events. At the far end, a male faerie stands silhouetted against a towering window, his figure framed by the soft light filtering through. He seems to be older than most fae I've encountered, yet calculating one's age I centuries remains illusive.

"Kiera, this is Master Korvis," Thalira introduces, her tone warm yet formal. The faerie turns slightly, his expression sharpening into one of mild annoyance. "Korvis, this is Kiera of Eldwick."

"Ah, yes. The savior of Aelthar. How delightful to meet you," he remarks, his words threaded with sarcasm that bites, causing my fists to tighten reflexively at my sides, a reaction sparked by irritation.

"Be kind, Korvis. We are all doing our best," Thalira chides, her voice carrying an undercurrent of authority that compels him to offer a slight bow, though his demeanor remains tinged with defiance.

"What can I do for you?" he asks, his tone softening marginally.

"I was wondering if you could tell me more about the essence of water wielding," I say, my voice steady despite the nerves fluttering within. "I'm trying to learn all I can about the elements." His head tilts, his gaze sharpening as he studies me with an intensity that makes my skin prickle.

"You want to learn how to wield water?" he inquires, and I shake my head quickly, a flush creeping up my neck.

"No, I have no magic abilities. I'm simply trying to understand it," I clarify softly. He regards me for a long moment, his eyes narrowing as if peering into my soul, before nodding.

"Very well," he concedes, raising his hand with a fluid motion. A long, shimmering tendril of water materializes, weaving between his fingers as he guides it back and forth with effortless control. "Water wielding is about understanding and mastering the flow of water in all its forms, tapping into the natural energy that drives the tides and dances to the moon's pull. It's a delicate balance of give and take, a constant interplay between calm control." The water swirls in a gentle circle, serene and hypnotic, "and unpredictable force." With a flick of his wrist, it transforms into a rapid vortex, mimicking a storm on the horizon.

"The moon's sway is crucial," he proceeds, his voice adopting an instructive tone. "Its gravitational tug shapes the tides, and we learn to sense that same pull in the air, in the ground, even within our own bodies. Water can be liquid, flowing freely, or solidify into ice, rigid and unyielding." A spear of ice forms in his grasp, its surface gleaming with cold precision. "It can shift to mist for concealment or gather into clouds to nourish parched lands." A small cloud coalesces above us, releasing a gentle rain that patters against the floor. "Our task is to harness these transformations, using water's versatility to adapt to any challenge."

The rain ceases abruptly, and with a swift gesture, all the moisture clinging to my clothes and dampening my hair, evaporates into the air, leaving the room as pristine as before. I blink, awestruck by the seamless display.

"Water's strength also resides in its capacity to nurture life," he notes, and from the floor, fragile flowers formed wholly of water rise, their petals gleaming with an ethereal luster. "The key is balance: knowing when to let it flow freely, when to hold it firm as ice, or when to disperse it as mist." The flowers harden into ice, then shatter into glittering fragments that dissolve into the air. A sight both beautiful and haunting, revealing capabilities I could never have imagined.

"Once a wielder senses the tides' energy, they're ready to call upon water's strength. Whether to shield, strike, or heal. The possibilities are endless," he concludes, and the room falls still, the air thick with the echo of his demonstration. My heart pounds, a mix of awe and unease at the power this faerie commands with such ease.

Veyrik once told me most fae view fire as destruction, yet it offers warmth and life. A perspective that could apply to all elements. Only now, watching Korvis, do I begin to grasp the darker edge of this power. The line between good and evil feels perilously thin. How easily these forces could be turned to death and destruction if the will demanded it.

"How long does it take to master an element?" I ask, my curiosity overriding my trepidation.

"Centuries," he replies, his voice clipped, and I nod slowly, the weight of his age settling over me. He must be ancient, a repository of stories about Lyrisene and the dragons. Perhaps even knowing those who walked with them. "You claim to be mortal?" he probes, snapping my attention back.

"Yes," I answer, unsure if he expects me to justify my lack of power, my voice tinged with defensiveness.

"Interesting," he muses, the word echoing the first time Zyra spoke it after I threw a dagger at her. The memory lingers as I feel Soren's presence before I see him. The dark, vibrating power he carries pulsing through me like a heartbeat.

Korvis's eyes flash with alarm, quickly masked as Soren enters, his stride purposeful. "That's right. Where the young lady goes, the Lord of Shadows follows," Korvis says, his tone reverting to its earlier snideness, though I detect a flicker of fear beneath it.

"Korvis," Soren acknowledges flatly, positioning himself between us all with a commanding presence.

"I'm surprised you haven't felt a shift in her power," Korvis remarks, drawing our collective attention.

"What do you mean, Korvis?" Thalira's voice cuts through,

sharp with concern.

He raises his hands, and a slow drizzle begins falling from the ceiling. We stare upward, transfixed, until the drops gather and plunge downward—fast, forming spears of ice in every shape and size, aimed directly at me. My eyes widen, and I brace myself, raising a hand instinctively as my heart hammers, expecting the end. But it never comes.

Peeking through half-closed lids, I see Thalira with her hands raised, her expression a mix of shock and awe. I straighten, staring at the suspended shards before my hand. Lowering it, the ice clatters to the polished floor, and I turn to Korvis. He's wrapped in dark shadows, lifted off the ground, yet sporting a knowing grin.

"Either you tried to deceive us, or you truly didn't know," he rasps, dropped unceremoniously as he stumbles, rubbing his neck.

"You can wield water," Thalira states, her voice a blend of wonder and wariness, and I glance at my hands, expecting the glow from the Skyward Expanse, but they appear unchanged.

You must learn the elements, Lyrisene's voice echoes in my memory, her cold mist washing over me. Did she grant me this power? Is this how the first fae were born?

"Did you know?" Thalira asks, her tone probing, as if weighing whether I'm a threat. I shake my head quickly, my face likely betraying the fear and panic swirling within. Then she turns to Soren. "Did you?"

He studies me intently, his gaze searching, perhaps questioning his own oversight, before shaking his head gently. We all turn to Korvis, who surveys us deliberately.

"Water is energy flowing through all natural beings, even our bodies. There's an energy to magic, and the surge within you seems more than you can contain," he explains. My hands tremble, and I clench them to hide it.

I wielded water, stopped the ice without thought—magic lives within me. Does that make me fae now? The realization spins my head, and I stumble back a step, my identity as Kiera of Eldwick fracturing. My fate has shifted irrevocably.

Soren and Thalira departed, likely to confer about my newfound abilities. Now, Korvis leads me to a small chamber within the palace. One side opens to a cascading waterfall, its mist cooling the air, though he hasn't yet agreed to teach me fully. Instead, he proposes a test to determine if I'm worth his time.

"Create water in the palm of your hand," he instructs simply, his tone leaving no room for elaboration. I stare, dumbfounded. Is that all the guidance he'll offer? No pointers, no encouragement?

I huff, extending my hand and focusing on the sensation of water, willing it to appear. But the harder I concentrate, the more frustrated I grow as nothing happens, and my effort is met with silence.

"You're trying too hard," he observes, and I glance up with a skeptical tilt of my eyes. "In the other room, when I sent the ice at you, what did you do?"

"I didn't do anything," I snap, annoyed, but he remains impassive. "I held up my hand," I add, and he gestures for me to repeat it.

I lift my hand higher, showing him I'm already doing so, yet nothing stirs. Muttering under my breath, I shake my head and raise it again. This time, I let my thoughts drift, willing the water to rise without force. A prickling sensation blooms under my skin, as if water seeps through to reveal itself. Focusing on that feeling, a surge of power rises so swiftly it nearly dizzies me.

"You're using too much power," Korvis warns, and I lower my hand in frustration.

"I don't even know what I'm doing. I know nothing about magic!" I exclaim, and he crosses his arms, his posture suggesting I'm at fault.

"You must not allow emotions to dominate when wielding magic. Particularly water," he retorts firmly.

"Can you give me some direction I can actually follow?" I plead, and he exhales deeply.

"Eldwick borders the sea, yes?" he asks, and I nod. "What does it feel like when a storm approaches? What do the tides do, what does the air feel like?"

"Like everything is pushing and pulling," I say, the memory of standing on the pier, the sea churning, vivid in my mind.

"You must learn to feel that push and pull within yourself. Draw the energy out, push it back in. The more you pull, the more you push. Everything has energy; with water, you must find balance within," he explains. I raise my hands, studying my veins, and repeat his words silently: *push and pull*.

Taking a deep breath, I exhale slowly, imagining Eldwick's tides before a storm. The pulse of waves, the motion of clouds, the charged air. I picture that storm within me, a dance of calm control and unpredictable force. Water pools in my hand, spilling over the edges in a steady flow, and my eyes light up with wonder.

"Now imagine that tide, pushing and pulling it into a sphere," he instructs, and I visualize it, willing it into being. "Good," he says, a hint of surprise in his voice, and I glance up to catch his expression.

"What now?" I ask, eager for more.

"You can make anything you want," he replies, incredulous,

and I look at the water turning in my hand.

Recalling the flowers he created earlier, I think of the Umbral Expanse's gardens, the silver petals glinting like moonlight. I push the tides within, crafting an exact replica. The water breathes new life into it, beautiful and fragile.

Water can be liquid, flowing freely or solid as ice, his earlier words echo. I curl my fingers, imagining a storm turning to rain, then hail, and the flower solidifies, crystallizing at the tips. Catching it as it falls, I grin widely.

"What flower is that?" Korvis asks quietly, and I shrug, holding it out. He pinches it between his fingers, spinning it smoothly, frost flaking off toward us.

"Will you teach me?" I ask, my voice steady as I meet his gaze, the weight of the question hanging between us.

"Yes," he replies with a firm resolve, releasing the flower to dissolve into a cascade of sparkling dust that drifts away on the air. "But I suspect you'll have much to teach me as well."

His words linger, a recognition that ignites something within me. For the first time since stepping into these enchanted realms, a sense of purpose takes root, its tendrils weaving through my uncertainty, revealing a clear path stretching out before me.

CHAPTER NINETEEN

When I finished my first training lesson with Korvis in the Cerulean Dominion, I found Rennor waiting patiently to escort me back. He mentioned that Soren was tied up in a meeting with the dominion rulers, deliberating the newest turn of events. A development I could only assume revolves around me now possessing powers that defied the norms of my mortal origins.

As we made our way back to the palace, Rennor took the time to give me a thorough rundown of how magic operates within this world. He explained that I was likely to feel worn down for a while, a natural consequence of my novice status.

"As you begin mastering magic, it demands an immense amount of energy," he stated, his voice firm with wisdom. "You have to be mindful of your energy levels, or you can find yourself in a precarious position. But with more training, as you become more skillful and resourceful, you'll build up your magical stamina over time. The stronger you get, the easier it becomes to harness that power."

As soon as my head hit the pillow on my bed, exhaustion claimed me, the trials of the day fading into a deep, dreamless sleep. But I woke this morning to the most hauntingly beautiful music, a melody that seemed to weave through the air like a spectral thread.

It's nearly dawn now, I can tell by the faint silver lighting of the clouds beyond the mist and fog that clings to the palace, and the halls stretch long and dark, still cloaked in a quiet hush as I walk along the cool stone walls.

Every now and then, I catch sight of dark shadows flitting by or slipping swiftly into the next room, and I know they are the other court members going about their secretive business, staying hidden in the shadows as is their custom. They don't bother me, and I don't disturb them, a silent agreement that has held since my arrival—and likely will persist now that I wield powers that belong to another dominion, marking me as an outsider in their eyes.

When I reach the central corridor, I push through the grand front doors and stop suddenly, my breath catching at the sight before me. Sitting alone on the steps is Soren, his figure a solitary silhouette against the dim predawn light. He's wearing the same black tunic from yesterday, the sleeves rolled up to his elbows, revealing his strong forearms. His hair shimmers faintly under the soft glow, a silver cascade that catches the eye.

I debate whether to continue forward or slip back into the palace's safety, my heart thudding with uncertainty, but he turns his head slightly, acknowledging my presence with a subtle tilt, as if he sensed me all along.

I step forward, my footsteps hesitant, and move down a few steps to sit beside him on the same cold stone stair. Together, we stare out into the dense forest that surrounds the palace, its stillness wrapping around us like a blanket. It's quiet, just as it always is in these early hours, and then I hear it—the song. A haunting melody drifts from the trees, its notes weaving through the air with an ethereal grace.

"What is that?" I ask quietly, my voice barely above a whisper, and he grips his hands together tightly, as if bracing himself against the sound.

"It's known as a Duskwing," he murmurs in a gentle tone, his voice bearing a depth of reverence. I keep listening, the music unfolding with a low, melodic tone that stirs deep emotions within me. It sings as if it has lost its way, a lament that can't find its path back to peace.

"It sounds sad," I say, because the more I listen, the more my heart aches for the creature behind the song, a pang of empathy tightening my chest.

"We call it The Final Mourning Prayer," he explains, and I glance at him, my curiosity piqued by the solemnity in his voice. He lets out a soft breath and turns to look at me fully, his eyes meeting mine. "Do you know what soul-bound means?" he asks, his tone almost hesitant.

I shake my head, the term unfamiliar yet intriguing. "Soul-bound is when two souls are intertwined," he continues, his voice steadying. "Two halves of a whole. One cannot exist without the other. The Duskwing's entire life revolves around their Soul-Bond. So when one perishes, the other mourns its death until its own soul is lost."

"It dies of heartbreak..." I murmur under my breath, the

realization sinking in as I look down at my feet. I can feel Soren's glance shift toward me, but I don't dare look up, the vulnerability of the moment too raw.

"Have you lost someone?" he asks timidly, his voice gentle, and I take a deep breath, the question unlocking a door I've kept closed.

"My father," I say, the words slipping out as I've been ignoring the facts, trying not to piece together the pain I've carried since arriving here. The admission hangs between us, a quiet confession.

"What was he like?" he asks, his tone encouraging, and I turn my gaze to the forest as the Duskwing's song fades into the distance, its mourning a fading echo.

"He was smart. And incredibly brave..." I begin, my hands gripping together as memories flood back. "People say he was the best fisherman in Eldwick. But he told stories of magic and creatures and fae, and they deemed him mad." The words carry a mix of pride and sorrow, the weight of his legacy pressing against my heart.

"Was Eldwick against magic?" he asks curiously, his head tilting slightly as he listens.

"I wouldn't say they're against magic," I reply with a shrug, my thoughts drifting to my village. "But Eldwick is so far south, with little to no reason for outsiders to visit. So for him to claim he fought with faeries and vyrskal was unheard of. They couldn't justify his story," I tell him, and he looks down at the ground, his expression thoughtful, as if he wants to say more but holds back.

"What happened to him?" he asks, his voice soft, and I shrug gently, the uncertainty still a wound that hasn't healed.

"Soon after his incident in the forest, he went out to sea and never came back. There was no storm, no treacherous current, no reason for him to not return. So when my mother went looking for help, all the fishermen told us he was the best captain, and there's no way he would have gotten lost at sea, so they never went looking for him," I explain, the memory bitter on my tongue. He nods along to my story, his silence a respectful acknowledgment, offering no judgment.

"I'm sorry that happened," he says, and I look over at him, my heart aching not just for my loss but for the burden I know he carries—a weight far greater than my own.

I've poured over the books, sought out his history, traced his family line through dusty tomes in the palace library, but so far, I haven't been able to find anything concrete. It's as if everything about him has been wiped away, a blank slate shrouded in mystery.

"What about you? Do you have a family?" I ask quietly, my voice barely rising above the morning stillness.

He looks up, his gaze drifting to the forest with a longing that tugs at my chest. "I've lost everyone," he says, the words heavy with a sorrow that mirrors the Duskwing's song. I follow his eyes to the trees, noting the quiet now that the Duskwing has found its own peace of sorts.

"What about Rennor?" I ask, a faint hope in my tone.

"He just won't die," he says with a hint of sarcasm, a rare glimmer of lightness breaking through, and I can't help the grin that starts at the corner of my lips.

"I don't think you've tried hard enough," I say playfully, turning to him, hoping to see a spark of amusement in his eyes. But the lightness I seek isn't there, his expression still shadowed. "What about the others? Your true family?" I ask quietly, and he grips his hands together between his legs, his jaw clenching tight as if bracing himself.

"It's a story full of tragedy. One I don't think you would wish to hear," he tells me, his voice low, but I lean forward toward him, drawn by the need to understand.

"I would like to know your history," I say, my voice firm yet gentle. "Please," I add, and he nods once, a resolute movement that signals his willingness to share.

"I had a mother and father—the Lord and Lady of the Umbral Expanse—along with an elder brother, an elder sister, and a younger sister," he starts, his tone deliberate. "When I was about a century old, I had amassed enough power and abilities that I was chosen to be the next Lord. My older brother and sister, who were years ahead of me, were raised with the expectation that one of them would succeed, and when they weren't chosen, their souls turned corrupt." His words hang heavy, and my breath hitches in my throat at the implication. "The darkness overran them, and due to our lineage, that made them more powerful than they should have been. So my father, the Lord, had to do what was written. He had to slay them."

"No..." I can't help but mutter, my heart breaking at the thought of such familial betrayal, tears welling in my eyes. "Did he do it?"

"He had to," he says, his voice steady but laced with pain. "My mother was devastated, so she did what she could to protect what was left. She took my younger sister and fled the palace, leaving me behind to be the next Lord... but my father and mother were soul-bound. So when my mother left, my father lost his mind."

"Is she still alive?" I ask, my voice trembling, and he glances down again, his hands gripping tighter as if to hold back the grief.

"When two faeries are soul-bound, there's a tether between them—a line connecting one to the other. That means if the other is

144

alive, you can find them no matter where they are," he explains, and I shut my eyes, shaking my head at the cruelty of it. "He gave her the chance to come back, and when she refused, he brought her back anyway. But she was not herself and was eventually taken away by her heartbreak."

"What about your sister?" I ask, my voice barely a whisper, dreading the answer.

"Sonja… My father never told me what happened to her. I can only assume he slayed her when he found my mother," he says, and I let out a shaky breath, every turn of this story growing darker, almost too painful to bear. I'm almost too afraid to know the rest.

"And your father?" I ask quietly, and I can see him chew the inside of his lip, his silver eyes swirling gently like a breeze rustling through the trees.

"A Soul-bond affects everyone differently. Some can move on with a broken heart, but others are bound so deeply it makes it impossible to go on. So after my mother died, my father quickly lost control. It was clear he was no longer himself. And he, himself, became corrupt," he tells me, and I hold a hand to my mouth, horrified. "So as the next Lord, I had to do my duty to protect the Umbral Expanse from his destruction." A tear slides down my face, the weight of his confession pressing against my chest.

"I'm so sorry," I manage to say, my voice thick with emotion, but he only shrugs, a gesture that belies the turmoil within.

"As the Lord of the Umbral Expanse, I have to rid it of any soul that has turned corrupt. It's an order that was set in place when this land was created," he tells me in a flat tone, as if it's a mantra he's rehearsed to bury the guilt. But then his shoulders sag, the facade cracking. "In the end, I think he was ready for it. He was no longer himself, and I don't think he could live with himself after what he had done... I had my siblings killed, he killed my mother and sister, and I killed him..."

"It's not your fault," I tell him, my voice firm with conviction, and he looks at me fully. His eyes are filled with pain, regret, and sorrow—emotions laid bare, unshielded by the hardened darkness that usually contains them.

"If I hadn't been chosen to be the next Lord, they wouldn't have turned," he says, his voice heavy with self-blame.

"But you don't know how corrupt they already were before you were chosen," I counter, leaning closer. "That doesn't seem like something that just happens overnight," I tell him, and he holds my gaze like I'm a lifeline. "If they had been chosen, who's to say they wouldn't have turned corrupt over time? You were chosen for a reason. Maybe that's because they knew your soul is pure."

"But what if it's not..." he says, his voice trailing off, and I blink, the question echoing in my mind.

What if he's not pure? I ask myself, but deep down, I know the fae before me has done nothing but act with integrity for the sake of others. A corrupt soul would have taken sides long ago, bending the world to its will.

"It is," I tell him, my voice steady with certainty, and his eyes flicker between mine gently before he looks to the forest again, the vulnerability lingering.

"I hope you're right," he says solemnly, and I follow his gaze.

The clouds are shining brighter now, signaling that it must be well into the morning, but the trees remain as still as ever—like they're listening to every word, reliving the pain just as Soren does. As if they remember the destruction that once ravaged this land, their silence a testament to the scars that remain.

CHAPTER TWENTY

This morning, Soren guided me to the Cerulean Palace, and for the last two hours, the atmosphere has been heavy with irritation, fiery debates, and loud exchanges as I sparred with Korvis. He urges me to tackle challenges that appear hopelessly out of reach, yet when he showcases them with seamless elegance, the tasks feel nearly effortless.

His expectations have escalated rapidly—first, crafting a frozen flower yesterday, and now he demands I flood our training room with water up to my hips, summon a cascading waterfall from the ceiling, and sculpt an ice replica of Eldwick's pier from memory alone. The leap from a delicate bloom to such grand displays of magic left me reeling, a stark reminder of how far I still have to go.

Frustrated, Korvis was the first to storm off, throwing his hands up in exasperation and ordering me to remain within the palace walls. Yet, the more I paced from room to room, the tighter my confinement felt, until curiosity overpowered my obedience. My feet carried me to an outdoor balcony overlooking the sprawling city below, its vibrant life beckoning me. Drawn by an irresistible pull, I navigated a winding staircase and discovered a gate leading into the heart of Sypheris.

Two guards stood watch on the city side, their blue tunics a stark contrast to my black attire. As I pushed the gate open and stepped past, they exchanged a glance before stepping aside, as if uncertain whether I was a threat or merely a lost soul. In their eyes, a girl clad in Umbral black must have been an enigma—neither fully friend nor foe.

No one halted my departure, though a pang of guilt nags at me. I should have informed someone of my intentions, but the suffocating pressure of forced wielding in that room had become unbearable. I've always thrived in solitude, especially by the sea, where water feels like an extension of myself. That connection, that freedom, is what I crave now.

The city unfolds before me with a chaotic beauty. Wide roads intertwine with narrow passages, crisscrossing in no discernible pattern. Water canals serve as the lifeblood, their gentle tides carrying small boats and crafts that glide to and from various docks with a rhythmic grace. Fae board and depart, their movements blending seamlessly with the flow of the water, as if the entire dominion pulses in unison, a living, breathing entity. It's mesmerizing, a stark contrast to the rigid structure of my training sessions.

Few passersby pay me much heed, and those who do offer kind nods and warm greetings—a novelty after weeks of being shadowed and guarded since leaving Eldwick. I understand the necessity, but this unescorted wanderlust rekindles a forgotten sense of liberation, a chance to be myself amidst the wonders I choose to explore.

"Good afternoon," a shop lady calls as I pass, her voice bright. I return a gentle nod, my gaze drifting over her display of exotic flowers. Tall blooms droop with vibrant colors, while others, bundled tightly, hint at imminent blossoms under the rising sun casting golden hues over the buildings.

"These are beautiful," I say, pointing to a radiant yellow flower with long, elegant petals. "What are they called?"

"Stars of the Veil," she answers, raising one and offering it to me. "They only bloom when the sun shines more than ten hours a day, taking months to grow but lasting just weeks at their peak. Worth every moment of their beauty, don't you think?"

"That's incredible," I whisper, taking the stem and spinning it gently between my fingers. In Eldwick, we have humble dandelions and lilyleapers, but nothing compares to this exquisite creation.

"You may take it, if you wish," she suggests with a grin.

"Oh, no, that's okay," I reply, offering it back to her. "Where I live, the flower would likely be withered by shadows." She smiles warmly, placing it back on her stand.

"Are you from the Umbral Expanse? I assume so, given the black attire, though I thought no one was allowed to leave unless the order has changed," she inquires, her curiosity gentle.

"I'm not from there, but that's where I reside now," I explain, a half-truth easing the conversation.

"A traveler?" she probes, her eyes twinkling.

"Of sorts," I reply with a grin, unsure how to encapsulate my chaotic journey. "Is the beach much further from here?"

"Keep going down, then turn left on a narrow road just past the bread shop. It'll lead you straight there, much faster," she directs, pointing along my path. I look in that direction, gratitude warming me.

"Thank you."

"Good luck in your journey," she calls as I turn away, stealing one last look at the Stars of the Veil before continuing.

The heat creeps up my back, a reminder I should have dressed more practically than in skin-tight pants, though my light, airy tunic catches the breeze filtering through the narrow roads. Spotting the bread shop, I take a sharp left, the passage far narrower than I expected. If someone recognizes me here, this could easily be an ambush point. Glancing over my shoulder, I hold my breath, imagining Soren's wrath if he knew my reckless venture.

The crashing waves and salty tang of the air reach me before I emerge, and when I step into the clearing, I halt, wide-eyed. The beach stretches endlessly, its sparkling white sand glistening like finely ground crystals, dotted with vibrant, glossy shells that catch the light almost blindingly.

Unlike Eldwick's rugged coastline with sharp rocks and fractured shells, this sand cushions gently beneath my feet as I near the water's brink, staring out to the horizon's limit. The sky blazes a brilliant blue, the sun's glare triggering a headache from narrowing my eyes, yet the panorama behind me is just as awe-inspiring. The city rises ahead, the palace towering like a sand-castle fortress, its blue spires blending seamlessly with the landscape, as if every drop of water in this dominion animates its life.

I lift my hand, remembering the water I can call forth with

focused intent, feeling the power stir within me, water and energy merging into a single, pulsing force. A sense of possibility swells. Here, by the sea, I might finally harness it.

"Pardon me," a voice breaks in from behind. I spin quickly, lowering my hand to my side, my heart jolting at the sight of a tall, lean male faerie with golden skin, dressed in sea-green robes that shimmer faintly. The green triggers warnings in my mind. "Forgive me if I'm mistaken, but are you Kiera of Eldwick?"

"I am," I answer, my tone firm as I retreat, his closeness unnerving.

"It's a pleasure to meet you. My name is Maren," he declares with a subtle nod, but I squint, observing his every gesture for concealed motives. "Are you enjoying the palace so far?"

"I am. In fact, I was just about to head back," I say, eager to retreat.

"Back to the palace?" he inquires, his hands joined with slightly excessive formality.

"Yes," I admit, his inspection hinting he grasps more than I'd like.

"Would you mind if I accompanied you?" he asks, and I gulp deeply, my nerves unraveling. The city's blues contrast sharply with his green attire, and his poised demeanor raises red flags.

"If you wish," I state, and he motions for me to guide us back toward the city, distancing us from the sea. "Are you a member of the court?"

"Not of this court, but yes, of sorts," he replies ambiguously. I exhale sharply, glancing at him, trying to decipher his meaning or how he found me. I'd been certain no one followed, but fae senses likely outstrip mine.

"The Verdant Dominion?" I ask, a hitch in my voice, and his sly grin suggests he knows my trials, though he remains silent. "Are you part of the Elite?" I whisper, and his smile widens.

"Clever girl," he says, and my hands clench at my sides. Mixed blood—sent to kill me, like the Crimson fae? Does he see me as a powerless mortal, or does he know my wielding strength?

"What do you want from me?" I demand, watching him closely for any sign of a weapon as he keeps his hands behind his back, eyes forward.

"Have you been enjoying your visits to the Cerulean Dominion?" he counters evenly as we weave through the streets. "I can only imagine how different it must be from your home in Eldwick." The mention of my hometown sends my nails digging into my palms, a surge of anger rising.

"What do you want from me?" I seethe, turning to face him more directly.

"No need to bare your teeth, Kiera," he remarks with a mocking tone that heats my blood, as though I'm a piece in his scheme. "Soon, our vision for a blended Aelthar will come to fruition."

"A blended Aelthar?" I repeat, my mind racing. The Elite, hybrid fae from two realms, exiled since the land's split, now concealed. The rifts weakening borders—would they collapse them all?

"Indeed. United, we shall eradicate the prejudice against hybrid faeries, shaping a new regime where our kind governs, liberated from the Dominions' elemental divisions," he proclaims. I gape, eyes wide. Why disclose this to me, when my purpose is to halt their devastation?

"Why would you think I'd ever help you?"

"When you were in Eldwick, didn't you ever dream of more? The freedom to leave, to travel Aelthar and see its wonders?

Shouldn't we all dream that way? Why must we be divided, our kind reprimanded for choosing our lives?" he asks, his words stirring a tumult of thoughts. Why confide in me? Why assume I'd align with him? What's his motive? My mind spins, questions drowning my response.

"Friend of yours?" he asks, nodding upward. I follow his gaze to a black bird, its large wings flapping elegantly, glinting in the sunlight above the rooftops. "Soon, this will all become clear," he remarks, pausing.

I turn, memorizing his features—every line, every nuance. "Aelthar will remain as it should. We will stop the rifts," I assert, and his grin suggests amusement at my defiance.

"We'll see," he replies, gesturing for me to continue. "It was a pleasure to meet you, Kiera of Eldwick." I pivot, eyes on the ground, listening for any sudden move. But when I glance back, he's vanished.

A blended Aelthar, I echo in my mind, doubt creeping in. Once, faeries lived in peace on unified lands, free to love and roam. Yet dark wielders emerged from those unions—reason enough to divide, to isolate? Do the Umbral fae deserve their exile, never to leave? Who do I trust? The Dominion rulers upholding division for peace, or the Elite promising a new, blended order?

I glance upward and spot the bird exactly where I anticipated. It swoops down towards me and I take a deep breath. I know I'm close to the palace. Not because I can see it, but because I can feel who's waiting at the end of the bird's flight path.

CHAPTER TWENTY-ONE

Soren stands before me, arms crossed over his broad chest, his face etched with that familiar annoyance I've come to expect these days. I halt in front of him, bracing for the inevitable reprimand—words about my recklessness, pleas to prioritize my safety. Yet he remains silent, his silver eyes glinting with a storm of unspoken thoughts, and the weight of his stare unnerves me more than any lecture could.

I brush past him, my shoulder grazing his arm, and stride through the towering gates, their iron creaking faintly in the stillness. He follows close behind, his footsteps a quiet echo at my heels, while the black bird soars overhead, its wings slicing through the pale sky as if it anticipates a sudden dash for freedom. His refusal to speak gnaws at me. Perhaps this muted disapproval stings worse than the sharpest rebuke.

The grand double doors to the palace entrance swing open of their own accord, revealing Korvis and Thalira waiting within, their presence a stark contrast to the tension coiling in my chest. Thalira's face lights up with relief.

"Oh, praise the creators," she exhales, rushing toward me, her azure robes rustling gently. "I came to check on your training and found those two at each other's throats."

"Sorry," I whisper, my tone hushed as I look at Korvis, whose frown reflects Soren's with startling accuracy. "I just wanted to see the city."

"That was a reckless choice," Korvis retorts, his tone keen and stinging. I meet his glare with a defiant tilt of my chin.

"You're the one who left me alone. What did you expect?" I retort, my patience thinning.

"I instructed you to stay within the palace walls," he corrects, his arms crossing tighter. "With the rifts widening and threats lurking, you're not nearly strong enough to wander unprotected."

"I'm not a child," I insist, my nails digging crescents into my palms as frustration surges.

"No, but you don't think with logic, do you?" he counters, his words a deliberate jab that fuels my growing anger.

Thalira steps between us, her presence a calming wave amid the storm. "No one got harmed," she says gently, though her eyes flicker with concern. "At least take a guard next time." Her compassion irritates. I'm tired of being seen as delicate, a burden requiring perpetual protection

"We're done for the day," I declare, turning away from Korvis's smug expression.

"Done?" he laughs, the sound cutting like glass. "You can barely summon a puddle." His sneer ignites a deep, simmering

156

rage, heat rising through me until I feel I might steam.

"Yet you demand the impossible—flooding a room, crafting waterfalls—while you lose your temper and abandon me at every turn!" I fire back, meeting his narrowed eyes with my own defiance.

"You shall remain here until your training concludes," he commands, his voice a deep rumble echoing off the stone walls.

"I'd rather face the Umbral Expanse's darkest woods than stay here," I retort, and from the corner of my eye, I catch the faintest quirk at the edge of Soren's lips. A rare hint of amusement that sends a flicker of pride through me.

"He asked you to make a waterfall?" Thalira interrupts, her forehead creasing as she faces Korvis. When silence meets her question, her focus sharpens. "Isn't that somewhat advanced for Kiera? I thought we settled on beginning with the fundamentals."

"I believed she might be capable of more," Korvis replies dismissively, his tone threaded with arrogance. "Clearly, I overestimated her." The insult snaps something within me. I raise my hands, summoning the power I've suppressed since standing at the ocean's edge. Power churns within, a storm craving liberation, and I unleash it in a wild, forceful surge.

Water cascades from the ceiling, flooding the hall in a rush of cold liquid. I extend my hands toward Korvis, the torrent engulfing him as he stumbles back. I sweep my arms from left to right, drawing on the memory of a storm at sea—ferocious winds howling, waves crashing over the boat's edge, lightning splitting the sky, thunder shaking my bones, and the primal fear of survival clawing at my chest. I direct that feeling, that fury, into the water, morphing it into an unyielding stream, a power no mortal could withstand.

"Kiera…" Thalira's voice trembles with warning, but I see Soren step forward, raising a hand to halt her interference, his expression unreadable yet steady.

Within the chaos of my storm, Korvis creates an air sphere around himself, a delicate barrier holding him steady and alive. I raise my hands, and the water crashes into the ceiling, spiraling left and right under my control.

His sphere falters but restores quickly. I rotate my hand, summoning a twisting vortex of water, increasing pressure until his air dissipates completely. With a firm thrust of my hands to the floor, the water tumbles in a shower of droplets, and Korvis's form falls to the ground. He groans, struggling to his hands and knees as the last of the flood evaporates into the air.

Soren drops his hand, and Thalira hurries to Korvis, kneeling beside him with a concerned grimace. "Are you okay, Korvis?" she whispers gently. I stand frozen, watching as he wheezes and coughs up water, Thalira's gaze shifting to us with a mix of concern and a flicker of fear.

"We're finished," I state, my voice a low growl. Korvis peers up through wet, tousled hair, his eyes shadowed with an inscrutable emotion.

Soren moves to my side, offering his arm. Without hesitation, I loop my hand around it, and the world fades into darkness.

Cold air brushes my face as I find my balance, my breath hitching as I calm my frantic thoughts. "If you're about to tell me I need to be more careful, I'd rather not hear it," I snap at Soren, who steps back and slips his hands into his pockets. I wait for the familiar reprimand, but his quietness surrounds me, a gentle wave easing the adrenaline's intensity.

"Did you know you could do that?" he asks, his voice gentle and tinged with curiosity, surprising me. I shake my head once, turning to take in our new surroundings.

We stand atop the palace's tallest rooftop, the wide stretch of treetops extending below us, the main entrance visible far down— a landing site I recall from my first arrival with the beast. He brought me here for a reason.

"You shouldn't possess that much power," he states, his gaze locking with mine. Instead of the fear I saw in Thalira and Korvis, amusement flickers in his eyes, a gleam that relieves my strain.

"What did you feel when you summoned it?"

"I felt angry," I confess in a hushed tone, retreating from the edge, the echo of that fury still lingering.

"Good. You should be angry." His words hold my gaze, a stark contrast to Eldwick's endless demands to smile and soften. Soren validates my rage, a revelation that steadies me. "Higher faeries like Korvis often forget their place. They deem themselves above all others."

"I probably shouldn't have lashed out like that, though," I whisper, doubting the force of my reaction.

"If you hadn't, I would have thrown him out the window myself," he replies with a seriousness that startles me. I stare, then a grin breaks through my guarded expression.

"Now that's irrational," I tease, and he shrugs, unfazed.

"Perhaps," he replies plainly. I breathe out fully, leaning my head back to the faint, drab sky, sensing my muscles relax as the adrenaline fades. He's giving me space to process this.

"I'm guessing you want to know where I went when I left the palace?" I ask, lowering my eyes to meet his.

"I'm only interested in the fae you were speaking with," he

159

says, a quiet rage brewing beneath his composed exterior.

"He was a member of the Elite," I reveal, feeling the tension tighten within him. "He spoke of a blended Aelthar... and honestly, I'm not sure why that would be so terrible." The confession tumbles out, a knot of reflections I've grappled with since the shore.

"Fae can cross borders and dwell in other realms if they wish. The borders are in place to confine darkness, to halt corruption from spreading," he explains, his voice firm and deliberate.

"But it doesn't seem fair to assume all dark wielders will turn corrupt. Rennor, Zyra, and others in your court live in the Umbral Expanse, punished for past mistakes. Why should they be denied the freedom to leave?" I argue, my voice rising with conviction. His eyes narrow, a subtle warning flickering in their depths.

"Careful, Kiera," he cautions, and I turn away, frustration escaping in a sharp breath. Nothing makes sense anymore. Knowledge overwhelms me, and I can't distinguish right from wrong.

"I don't know who I'm supposed to trust anymore," I admit, gazing into the far-off horizon. Corrupt dark wielders pose a threat, but why can't they enjoy the same freedoms as others?

"You don't need to trust anyone," he says, stepping closer until I turn to face him. "As long as you trust yourself, you'll never make the wrong decision."

"It's not that easy, and you know it," I challenge, my heart racing as his eyes shift from mine to my lips and back, his nearness sparking a heat I can't dismiss.

"Listen to what individuals say. Understand their perspectives, their origins. Then withdraw, allow yourself to choose based on your own reflections, your own emotions. There's no definitive right or wrong," he advises, his words sinking deep, a gentle tide washing over my doubts. He's never dictated my path, always leaving me to forge my own way.

"What if Aelthar falls?" I ask quietly, vulnerability threading my voice.

"Then that is what fate intends," he answers with a shrug, stepping even closer, his breath blending with mine in the crisp air.

"Are you not afraid?" I whisper, and his hand lifts, his thumb stroking down my cheek, tracing my lower lip with a gentleness that takes my breath away.

"I'm afraid of many things, Kiera," he admits, and at the sound of my name, I lean into his touch. His hand cradles my face, warm against my skin, but as I lean toward him, he retreats, allowing it to drop to his side.

"Think about what you need to know, then come find me," he says, turning toward the ledge.

"Soren," I call impulsively, and he turns gracefully, his gaze questioning. I falter, realizing all I want is for him to stay. "Why does that bird follow me?" I ask, and for the first time, a broad smile spreads across his face, illuminating his features.

"So I can keep an eye on you," he says, and my eyebrows knit in confusion. *Keep an eye on me?* What does that mean? "Good luck getting down," he adds with a mischievous glint, then turns and jumps off the edge, descending gracefully by shadows until he reaches the ground.

I rush to the ledge, watching his descent with a mix of admiration and annoyance, then whirl around, understanding his purpose. He brought me here to train me, in his own twisted, challenging way. A chuckle breaks free, laced with frustration.

"Damn bastard," I mutter to myself, yet I lift my hand, allowing water to stream from my fingertips, its coolness anchoring me as I prepare to navigate this unexpected lesson.

CHAPTER
TWENTY-TWO

It took two full days for the fog of exhaustion to lift, my energy returning in slow, tentative waves, a stark reminder of how vital it is to wield magic sparingly—especially since I'm still learning to harness its depths. The experience humbled me, sharply conscious that overextending could exhaust me completely, a lesson ingrained in my bones after testing my boundaries.

Soren has been leading me through minor training drills to enhance my endurance—creating water spheres that float and twirl, evoking mist that eddies around us, molding ice into fragile fragments, and calling rain in soft cycles throughout the day. Each task tires me by nightfall, a satisfying ache that tests my endurance without shattering it completely, a balance he maintains with care.

Then came word from Korvis that he wishes to resume my training. The news stirs a nervous flutter in my chest, an unease I can't quite shake. I made a spectacle of my powers back at the Cerulean palace, and I can't help but assume Korvis now expects grand feats from me—or at least a quick grasp of the skills he'll demand. But what if I falter? What if the dragons entrusted me with their power only for it to amount to nothing, a flicker snuffed out by my own inadequacy?

"Are you nervous?" Soren asks, his voice soft beside me, pulling me from my spiraling thoughts. We've been waiting on the beach of Sypheris, and the longer I stand here, the more my nerves tighten.

"I just don't want to disappoint anyone," I admit quietly, shifting my weight as I avoid his gaze, the burden of expectation pressing down.

He turns to face me fully, his expression steady and reassuring. "You don't have to worry about disappointing anyone. Especially not Korvis. Just do your best. And if he's not the right trainer for you, we'll find someone else." His words ease the knot in my chest, and I meet his eyes, nodding as I let out a deep, cleansing breath.

My gaze drifts to the sea, its vast expanse stretching before us, and I feel its power. The steady ebb and flow of waves washing over the shore, an energy Korvis once described as the heartbeat of life itself. Tapping into it feels like connecting to the very essence of existence, a hum that resonates within me.

"I'm afraid you won't be able to join us, Lord Soren," a voice cuts in from behind, crisp and commanding. I turn to see Korvis gliding toward us over the sand, his light blue tunic and pants a stark contrast to the heavier robes I've seen him wear before, throwing me off with his casual attire.

"Where will you be going?" Soren asks, his tone pinched with concern, and I hold my breath, sensing the tension between them.

"Out to sea. And you will not be able to join us," Korvis repeats, his voice firm. I glance at Soren, giving a slight nod to assure him it's fine, though my heart pounds with doubt. He holds my gaze for a long moment, his eyes searching mine, then turns to Korvis.

"I have no doubt she'll try to drown you again if you cross her," Soren states, and my eyes lift in astonishment, connecting with Korvis's equally shocked look. "I'll be here the moment I sense she needs me."

"I understand," Korvis replies, but my mind reels with questions. How can Soren sense when I'm in danger? "We will be safe," Korvis adds, and Soren vanishes into a swirl of black smoke.

Turning to Korvis, I watch as he raises his hands, pressing them together before lifting them in a graceful arc. From the water's depths, two forms rise. Not vessels in the usual sense, but small rafts fashioned from aged wood planks, each equipped with a plain sail fluttering gently in the wind.

"For such a noble Dominion, are these the only boats you have here?" I ask, arching an eyebrow as I take in the modest crafts.

Korvis gives me a sideways glance, a flicker of amusement in his eyes. "We'll propel them using the water. It's simpler to master with a raft that's lightweight and maneuverable—and easier to flip back over."

"Such little faith," I mutter under my breath, wading into the water. Expecting the icy chill of Eldwick's shores, I'm surprised by its warmth, as if the sun has kissed it all day. I board the raft, securing my balance effortlessly, and observe as Korvis sits cross-legged at the front of his own. Imitating his actions, I unfurl the sail and fasten it, checking the ropes without his cue—a skill refined from boat outings in Eldwick during lean times, though I'm no seasoned sailor.

"To glide through the water, you must sense the currents," Korvis directs, extending his hands to his sides and moving them in a smooth, rhythmic pattern. "Just like the waves roll in and out, push and pull—you must do the same."

I copy him, trying to mirror his grace, but feel nothing. His raft rocks gently with the tide, while mine drifts closer to shore, stubbornly resisting.

"You must consider the ocean's natural rhythm," he continues, his voice patient. "If you're pushing forward against the waves, you won't get far." I pause, closing my eyes to sense the rhythm beneath me, then move my hands in harmony with the tide's pulse. A faint push and pull awakens within, connecting me to the water.

"Good," Korvis says, transitioning to longer, sweeping arm motions that propel him forward steadily. I watch, a flicker of panic rising as he pulls ahead, doubt and fear creeping in. "Come on, Kiera. If you can conjure a storm inside, you can maneuver a raft on the sea," he barks, his words a shock that sharpens my concentration.

I move my arms with determination, channeling the energy flowing through me, and my raft lurches forward slowly. Feeling Korvis's gaze, I pour more strength into my will, closing the distance between us.

"Very good," he notes, a trace of surprise in his voice, though I push the thought aside. "We're heading to an island a few miles out. Pay attention to the currents. Usually a strong maneuver can correct your path, but at times it's wiser to follow them."

"Can't we just star-drift to the island?" I ask, squinting at the horizon, seeing nothing but endless water.

"If you can master the ocean on a small raft—feeling its changes, overcoming the unknown—you can master almost all aspects of water wielding," he responds, his voice bearing the burden of experience.

"Is this basics training?" I venture, curious about his approach, and he studies me for a long moment.

"I think everyone can agree you've surpassed the basics," he says, and I nod, shifting my focus to the water. "Despite what you might think of me, these rifts are tearing our world apart. If you're our chance to end this, I'd like to do it swiftly."

"Let's get on with it then," I reply, his rare encouragement settling like a stone in my gut. They have faith in me, or wish to. And still, some days, I find it hard to trust in myself.

"Onward we go," he says, moving his arms with expert precision, his raft sailing forward at a steady pace.

I look back at the Cerulean Dominion's coastline, the palace perched on its hill, then take a deep breath. Concentrating on the currents beneath me, I move with greater ease this time, adjusting my drift when it veers right, then overcompensating to the left with a groan of irritation. I press forward, anticipating the currents before they tug me off course, and watch as Korvis pulls ahead, too far for my voice to reach, leaving me no choice but to keep going.

When I finally catch up, I lean back on my hands, tilting my head back with closed eyes, the sun's warmth on my face. The Cerulean Dominion's shoreline is a hazy smudge on the horizon, the expanse immense.

"Please don't tell me you're going to make us sail all the way back," I say, leaning forward to meet his gaze.

"I don't imagine you'll be able to once we're done out here," he replies, and my eyes widen in disbelief.

"You mean we're not done?" I glance around—nothing but water stretches in all directions. "Where's the island? There's nothing out here?"

"It's below us," he states serenely, and I gaze into the pristine water, its depths shifting to deep blue with the ocean's vast depth. "I want you to dive down using an air bubble and tell me what you see."

"How deep is it?" I ask, drawing a deep breath, my throat tightening.

"About 100 feet," he replies, and my eyes widen further.

"Do you really think I can do that?" I ask, staring into the ominous depths, imagining lurking creatures and the unknown below.

"Concentrate on the water encircling your head, press it outward, and collect the air inside it," he directs. "Should you lose air, reduce the bubble and enlarge it again." My hands tremble lightly, dread seeping in. I've never feared water, I've jumped from boats and cliffs in Eldwick, but this is different, a plunge where one mistake could mean drowning or being trapped.

"When you're ready," he prompts, but I hesitate.

"I can't do this," I admit, my voice small.

"You won't know if you don't try," he counters, his gaze unwavering.

"What if I drown? What if I can't get back in time?"

"You won't drown," he says with absolute certainty.

"You don't know that," I argue, but his confidence holds firm. "Will you pull me up if I can't make it?"

"Such little faith," he echoes my earlier words, a subtle challenge. I shake my head lightly, scooting to the raft's edge and dip my feet in. Lighter clothes and no shoes would help, but this mirrors real survival scenarios. I have to trust my new abilities.

I shove myself over the side, clinging to the raft with one arm, then dunk under without overthinking. Submerging, I focus as Korvis instructed—pushing the water outward, but nothing happens. Panic sets in as my oxygen dwindles, and I try again, but I'm forced to surface when it fails.

"That was a poor attempt," he remarks, and I tread water, regaining my breath before diving again. Over and over, I try, until finally, air envelops my head. Gasping in the air, I expand it as it shrinks, and the bubble stabilizes.

Glancing around, the water is clear, fish darting harmlessly. I add more air and descend, but the pressure grows heavier as the surface recedes. Panic flares as my bubble shrinks and my body freezes. *Air. I need air.* I swim upward quickly, but the quick movement shrinks it further until it disappears completely. Desperate, I kick up as hard as I can, but I feel like I'm getting nowhere and panic sets in. Would Korvis save me, or was this his plan? I need to get back to the raft. Now.

Then, in an instant, I'm back at the raft, the wooden edge biting into my palms as I haul myself halfway over it, coughing up seawater that burns my throat. My heart pounds in my chest, my head spinning with disorientation and the lingering panic of drowning.

Then, a loud caw jolts me fully alert, and I force my eyes open to see Soren's crow perched nearby, its sleek feathers ruffled, staring at me with those unnervingly intelligent eyes. Right beside an annoyed-looking Korvis, who shifts uncomfortably as if the bird's presence is a personal affront.

"Friend of yours?" Korvis asks dryly.

"Something like that," I manage, resting my head on my arms. The crow caws loudly in Korvis's face, and he flinches and moves aside.

"I'd appreciate if you sent it away," he says, irritated.

"I can barely wield water. What makes you think I can command animals?" I retort, chuckling as the crow hops closer to him, making him retreat. Wiping my face, I slip back into the water and let out a long breath. "Thanks for bringing me up."

"You did that yourself," Korvis says, and I study him, the silence stretching. "Apparently, you can star-drift now."

"How?" I glance at the crow, then back. "I didn't do anything."

"To star-drift, you have to focus all your energy on your desired location. You wanted the raft, and here you are," he explains. I nod slowly, the revelation sinking in. I can star-drift.

"And I can go anywhere?"

"Yes, though your range may be limited as your magic strengthens. You might be able to reach the bottom," he admits, but his look warns caution. "But without knowing the limits or seeing the place first, you could end up lost."

"Oh," I say, exhaling. "So only places I can visualize, or those I'm connected to."

"Exactly. But we're not done until you reach the bottom," he warns. "So don't even think about leaving."

"I doubt you could prevent me if I chose to," I probe, and he sighs in irritation. Looking into the water, I admit, "There was too much pressure. I couldn't keep the air."

"You'd be faster if you used the water to propel you, not just your arms," he suggests.

"Oh," I realize, unused to swimming and thinking about water in this way. "That makes sense."

"Try again," he urges, and the crow flies off.

I sink into the water, form the air bubble, and push the water to propel me downward. Speed and distance come easier, using less physical and mental energy. And when I reach the depth where my air bubble begins to weaken, I expand it, descending confidently, ready to star-drift back up if needed.

As I get further, the light fades, but it's not total darkness. And just beneath, the silhouette of a structure appears. I reach out, touching a spire's tip, then notice other structures around it— pergolas, statues, a temple. Swimming down, I find a grand statue of Lyrisene, so realistic it stuns me. I touch its snout, marveling, then spin to see houses. Fae once lived here. And by the looks of it, it's been recently submerged, with little overgrowth.

I kick upward, letting the water pull me, and the light grow brighter until I surface and climb onto the raft. I turn to Korvis, who holds a distant expression on his face.

"A tragedy to lose such a monument," he murmurs, his expression shadowed with memory.

"What happened?"

"A rift, powerful enough to shatter half our city, dragged this temple beneath the waves," he explains, his tone heavy. "The island's residents managed to evacuate, but we lost everything tied to that sacred place. Our history, our faith, swallowed by the depths."

"I'm sorry," I say, the words feeling inadequate as I meet his eyes, seeing the quiet sorrow etched there.

"Too many lives have been lost," he replies gravely, his voice carrying the burden of a leader who's seen too much. "Some refuse to call it a war, but that's what we're facing. A relentless struggle tearing our world apart." Does he know of the Elite's plans, their vision for a blended Aelthar? As a master of water wielding, he must sense the currents of change, the hidden threats stirring beneath the surface.

"Are there temples for each dragon?" I ask, shifting the focus, my curiosity piqued by the sacredness of what I've just witnessed.

"Yes," he confirms, his gaze steady. "Each Dominion holds a sacred temple dedicated to their creator, a testament to their lasting legacy."

As he speaks, I lift my arms, water dripping from my soaked clothes. With a focused push of my arms, I draw the moisture away, letting it flow back into the sea until I'm dry, a grin spreading across my face at the small triumph.

"Now, you're thinking like a water wielder," Korvis says, a rare note of approval in his voice. And this time, my smile feels genuine, a warm spark of pride igniting within me, reinforced by the sense that I'm finally beginning to grasp the power I've been given.

CHAPTER
TWENTY-THREE

For the past week, star-drifting to and from the Cerulean Dominion for training with Korvis has become my daily ritual, a rhythm carved into the fabric of my existence. The act grows smoother with each journey, the void of star-drifting feeling less disorienting, though it still leaves a faint hum in my bones. Today marks the first day Korvis grants me a reprieve, a rare pause in the relentless grind, but his reasoning lingers. He warned that the next week will intensify, demanding every ounce of my energy. From now on, he plans to guide me to the training fields to practice water wielding alongside the Cerulean Legion—a decision that hints at his growing concerns about war.

I shared this news with Soren this morning over a quiet breakfast of bread and tea, and he vanished almost instantly, likely to confront Korvis about the shift in my training. I wonder what they'll decide. Will Soren push back, or agree it's necessary?

With the day to myself, I embrace indolence as my act of rebellion. I lingered in bed until the sun climbed high, a long, warm bath followed as I washed away the week's tension, the scent of lavender oil soothing my frayed nerves. Now, I sit in Soren's study. I've spread several books across his polished wood desk, hoping to uncover something, anything, useful within their pages. The quiet crackle of the hearth fills the space, casting a warm glow over the dark wood and velvet drapes.

I've skimmed *The Umbral Pact*, a dense chronicle of bargains struck between the Umbral Expanse and other realms, its ink faded but its tales of diplomacy and betrayal still sharp. *Tales of the Saltcrag Clans* recounts the Cerulean Dominion's internal wars centuries past, a saga of blood and ambition inscribed in every line.

But *The Scale of Eternity* grips me most, its cover embossed with dragon-scale patterns that drew me in. It recounts a grim era when mortals captured Dravokar, the only dragon I've yet to meet, and drained his power for their own gain. The story resonates deeply. If mortals he trusted enslaved him, it's no surprise dark wielders arose. Some powers were never meant for mortal hands.

A gentle knock breaks my thoughts, and I look up sharply. The door eases open, revealing Soren, his hand resting on the frame, his silver eye scanning the room before settling on me.

"May I join you?" he asks, his voice a low rumble that carries a hint of warmth. I nod, quickly gathering the scattered books to move, but he halts me with a smooth, "You can stay there." His tone softens my guilt, and I settle back into the chair, realizing I should have sought permission. Though I hadn't anticipated his presence.

"I should have asked to use your desk," I murmur, my voice

barely above a whisper.

He shakes his head, stepping closer to the armchair across from me, resting a hand on its headrest. "You may use anything of mine as your own," he says, the words bearing a weight that tightens my chest.

"I'm guessing you spoke to Korvis?" I venture, shifting the focus, and he nods. "Should I worry about joining their legion?"

"Many in the legion question the prophecy," he explains, shifting to sit at the chair's edge, his posture alert. "To them, pinning Aelthar's fate on one person diminishes their role in the dominion. They're a collective force, believing wars are won by many, not one."

I lean back fully, the chair creaking softly. I never considered their perspective. Am I a threat to their pride? "It's not like I'm truly alone. I have many helping me," I counter, and he tilts his head, considering.

"Yes," he acknowledges. "But they will still likely resent you for it."

I exhale a long breath, the weight of their potential hostility settling on my shoulders. "Will you be going too?"

"I doubt my presence would help," he says, and I nod slowly, though I'd feel safer with him. His authority often silences dissent. "What are you reading?" he asks, leaning forward with interest.

"*The Scale of Eternity*," I reply, sliding the book toward him. He nods, recognizing it instantly.

"Ah, the story of Dravokar's capture," he says, leaning back with a rare slouch, his relaxed pose catching me off guard. "What drew you to it?"

"The cover looked intriguing," I admit, turning the book to trace the scale-like embossing. "I didn't expect such a sad story."

"It marked a pivotal moment in our history," Soren reflects, his voice bearing the weight of centuries as he leans back in the chair, firelight casting flickering shadows over his sharp features.

"I didn't get far," I confess, a flush of embarrassment warming my cheeks as I shift. My fingers fidget with the edge of the worn book in my lap. Soren rests his hands on his stomach, his fingers lacing together in a thoughtful gesture.

"Would you like me to tell you?" he offers, his eyes locking with mine. A spark ignites between us. A fleeting connection that sends a shiver down my spine. I nod, drawn in by the promise of unraveling more of this ancient tale. "Where did you leave off?"

"Mortals found a scale to reach the dragons and forced Dravokar to give them his power," I recount, settling back into the plush chair as Soren's gaze drifts upward, lost in the recesses of memory. The room seems to fade, leaving only his voice to guide me through the past.

"When Dravokar was captured, they bound him with ancient magic. An unbreakable bond, defying both strength and spell," he begins, his tone steady and resonant, as if reciting a sacred chant. "They carved a treacherous path through the rugged mountains in the Verdant Dominion, and chained him deep within a cavern."

"What's ancient magic?" I ask, my curiosity flaring.

"Magic taught by the dragons themselves, then twisted and reshaped by the first fae," he explains, his jaw tightening as if the memory stings. "Once chained, they brought others to be turned, seeking to harness his essence. But Dravokar refused. So they drained him by force, nearly stripping all his power in a single, ruthless blow." He shifts in his seat, a flicker of discomfort crossing his face, as though the brutality still lingers in his mind.

"That's horrific," I breathe, my voice trembling. "How could

176

they take someone's power like that?" I meet his intense stare, searching for answers in the depths of his eyes.

"No one knows the technique. They say there's a book that holds all the secrets of ancient magic, but not even the Aether Dominion's wisest historians have deciphered that secret," he admits, his gaze softening with a trace of regret. I glance upward, my mind whirring as I absorb the implications, the room's warm glow contrasting with the coldness of the tale.

"So how did he escape?" I press, leaning forward slightly, my heart quickening with anticipation. A long pause stretches between us heightening the tension.

"Why do you assume he escaped?" he counters, his voice low and probing. I lower my eyes slowly, a flush creeping up my neck. I never saw Dravokar in the Skyward Expanse, and the stories haven't hinted at his death. Only absence. "No one knows how he escaped, but rumors suggest a sixth dragon, a dragon of light, who freed him, her radiance severing the chains of ancient magic."

"Is that in the book?" I ask, intrigued, my fingers tracing the book's spine as if it might reveal more secrets.

"It's suggested," he replies, a cryptic smile tugging at the corner of his mouth. I look aside, my thoughts spiraling around this enigmatic sixth dragon.

"What happened once he was free?" I ask, drawn deeper into the narrative.

Soren grimaces, the lines of his face hardening. "After the first mortal-fae war, an order was forged, forbidding dragons from choosing sides or harming mortals or fae, a fragile peace to prevent further bloodshed. But freed, Dravokar defied it. In a fury, he killed his captors, collapsing the mountain range in a cataclysmic rage. Aethryion, understanding his wrath yet bound by duty, banished him from Aelthar, exiling him to a realm beyond our reach."

No wonder he shuns us, I think, recalling the dragons' distant words. "And then the dark wielders forced Aethryion to banish the rest," I add, echoing our first lesson, the pieces of the puzzle clicking into place.

"And no one has seen them since," he says, a speculative edge sharpening his tone, as if he's considering possibilities beyond my understanding.

"What happened to the book on ancient spells?" I ask, my curiosity unrelenting.

"They say it's buried in the mountain's rubble," he replies, his voice tinged with melancholy. "Some have searched, motivated by greed or desperation, but none have found or claimed it. Its secrets remain lost to time."

I bite my cheek, pondering the lost knowledge, then tilt my head. "Why is it called *Scale of Eternity*? Is the scale mentioned?"

"The mortals used a dragon scale to locate Dravokar, nicknaming it the Scale of Eternity," he explains, his voice softening. "It is said whoever holds the scale is taken to a dragon, who then grants them power—a power that gives them eternal life." My breath catches, my heart pounding under the pendant at my neck. Could this be that scale?

"Only one scale existed?" I ask, leaning forward.

"Two are said to exist—one black, one gold," he continues, his eyes holding mine, deliberately avoiding my necklace though I sense he recognizes its importance. "The gold, used on Dravokar, was destroyed in the chaos. They say the black scale lies hidden in the volcano's pit."

"I see," I say, my voice steady despite the tumult within. He studies my face, searching for a reaction, though I trust he won't pry into my thoughts uninvited. "Is this book common among fae?"

"I'd be shocked to find a copy in another dominion," he says evasively. "Dravokar's story is widely known, a cautionary tale handed down, but this book was made for my father. He relished tales ending in chaos and destruction, reflecting his own nature."

"May I borrow it to finish?" I ask, hope threading through my voice. He nods once, a gesture of trust. "Thank you," I say softly, resting my hand on the cover, feeling the weight of its history.

"I think you'll like this too," he says, waving a hand with a flourish. A dusty tome floats down from the top shelf, landing gently before me. I wipe the cover with care, revealing the title etched in faded gold.

"*Lost Origins of Auralyth,*" I read aloud, glancing up at him, my pulse quickening. "What's it about?"

"The sixth dragon," he replies, his voice dropping to a conspiratorial hush. "Aethryion created her to wield light, her scales gleaming like the dawn. But her beauty was so profound that he hoarded her, shielding her from mortals, a treasure concealed from the world."

"Sounds like another tragedy," I murmur, my mind painting the image of a radiant dragon caged by her own creator.

"Perhaps," he says mysteriously, a glint of amusement in his eyes. I flip open the book, revealing a shimmering illustration. A golden dragon with radiant yellow eyes that seem to glow from the page. I trace the image with a fingertip, lost in its elegance.

"I'll leave you to it," he says, rising with a grace that masks the weight of our discussion. I watch him move toward the door, my thoughts a whirlwind.

"Soren," I call, the word slipping out before I can reconsider. He turns, his gaze intense, pinning me in place.

"Yes, Kiera?" he asks, his voice a deep rumble that sends warmth rushing to my cheeks, a blush I can't hide.

"Thank you..." I say shyly, my voice barely audible, the gratitude mingling with something deeper I can't name. After a pause, he nods, a slight grin flickering across his lips. Like a rare glimpse of warmth, before he vanishes in a swirl of shadow.

I slump back in the chair, resting my head against the cushion, its softness a sharp contrast to the turmoil in my mind.

"What's wrong with me?" I mutter inwardly, huffing a deep breath as my eyes drift closed.

My heart races, not from fear or fatigue, but from the unexplained pull I feel toward him. A bond strengthening with each shared moment, every glance. The books lie heavy in my lap, their secrets a distraction I cling to, yet my thoughts keep circling back to Soren, to the way his presence lingers even after he's gone. I press a hand to my chest, willing my pulse to steady, but the warmth there refuses to fade.

CHAPTER
TWENTY-FOUR

We land in an expansive field blanketed with vibrant green moss, its soft texture easing my feet as I step away from Korvis, releasing his arm with a faint tension. A prickling sensation creeps over my skin. I sense eyes on me from all sides, a silent scrutiny bearing down heavily. Those I meet shake their heads and turn to each other, their whispers spinning a web of judgment around me. My stomach tightens, but I force myself to stand tall.

Soren accompanied me to the Cerulean Palace to see me off to the Legion of the Cerulean Dominion, his presence a steadying force until he and Korvis exchanged heated words. Before departing, Soren pulled me aside, his voice low and sincere.

"If anyone comes after you, strike them down first," he said, his eyes blazing with a seriousness I'm not yet used to. I thought he might be jesting at first, dark humor to ease my nerves, but the intensity in his gaze told me otherwise.

Korvis quickly assured him that no one in his Legion would attempt to harm me, yet the flicker of uncertainty in his own eyes betrayed his confidence. Killing someone… I don't know if I can do that. It clashes with everything I was raised to believe. Life is sacred, not to be snuffed out. But as these fae stare at me like I'm an intruder, a disgrace to their world, I realize I may need to rethink my principles, to adapt to this unforgiving realm where survival demands a different code.

"This way, Kiera," Korvis says from my side, his tone firm yet guiding. I turn and follow him through the tall grass, my boots sinking slightly with each step. As I take in the surroundings, my throat tightens. This doesn't feel like the Cerulean Dominion I know—the air hangs heavy with the scent of mud and damp foliage, trees laden with cascading greenery, moss and vines draping from branch to branch, blocking the sky above. Soren had mentioned we'd be near the Verdant Dominion's border, but I hadn't expected it to mirror that lush, wild landscape so closely.

"How big is your Legion?" I ask quietly, though I suspect these fae, with their heightened senses, can hear me from a mile away. My voice feels small against the vastness of the field.

"In the thousands," Korvis replies indirectly, his gaze sweeping the area.

Everyone instinctively steps back from Soren when he's near, yet his presence never unnerved me. These fae, however, with their cold glares and whispered disdain, makes me feel uneasy. I fight the urge to shrink, to let my gaze drop like a coward. No, I must show strength. However I can muster it.

"This is where you'll begin," Korvis explains as we round a bend in the trees, revealing a large clearing bustling with at least a hundred fae. They're clad in identical uniforms—dark blue tunics and pants, paired with sturdy gray boots—a sea of disciplined figures moving in unison. "We call it the Lirivox Ritual. We perform this exercise every morning as a warm-up. I'd like you to participate."

"This counts as a warm-up?" I ask, my voice laced with awe as I watch them. The sight is mesmerizing. Each fae performs a series of fluid motions that resemble a dance, wielding long orbs of water with graceful precision. They lunge and step in all directions, their arms pushing and pulling to elongate the water into streams, then shrink it into tight balls, spiraling it above their heads, just above the ground, and even weaving it through their legs. It flows like a winding river, seamless and hypnotic, a testament to their mastery.

"You expect me to do this? Today?" I say, glancing sideways at him, doubt creeping in.

"Yes. You'll stand in the back and do your best to follow along. You don't need to wield water until you've mastered the motions," he instructs. Relief washes over me. If I had to manipulate water now, I'd likely drench everyone around me in a clumsy mess. Yet not wielding it might draw more attention to my inexperience, leaving me caught between two undesirable outcomes. There's no easy win here.

"Go on," he says, and I clench my hands to stop their trembling, forcing my legs to move. I circle to the back, avoiding the gazes of the others, and take a wide stance. My eyes lock onto the fae before me, but I freeze, overwhelmed. Where do I even start? How do I move? How can I memorize this intricate dance? What am I doing here, thrust into a world I barely understand?

"Just move," a voice calls from in front of me, firm yet encouraging. I mimic the fae ahead, lagging a step behind, my arms and legs awkward and uncoordinated. "Repeat," she says after a while, and I mentally latch onto the motion she emphasizes, committing it to memory. I stumble, feeling awkward and misplaced, each misstep a silent urge to give up. But quitting would be worse than trying, so I press on, repeating the sequence —up, down, right, right, spin, twist—until it becomes a mantra echoing in my mind.

As the moves start to sink in, my arms and legs burn from the repetition, but I focus on the fluidity, letting my body find its rhythm. The fae before me make it look effortless, as if it's woven into their very blood, and I wonder how long it will take me to wield water with even a fraction of their grace.

"Done," the voice announces, and I stop, mirroring the group as they raise their arms to the sides, lifting them above their heads with a deep inhale, then lowering them with a slow exhale. A pause follows, then the crowd disperses, the air shifting with subtle tension.

The fae around me drift as far as possible, but one lingers, turning to face me. Her eyes are a striking blue, her skin warm and glowing despite the shade, and she studies me for a long moment before nodding. "Not all of us view you as a threat," she says, her voice carrying a trace of reassurance, before she turns and strides away swiftly.

A threat? I hadn't considered myself one. Yet as the chosen one to save Aelthar, I suppose I jeopardize their purpose, their role as protectors against opposition.

I make my way to Korvis, who stands with arms crossed, and he nods toward another path. I follow, my arms aching but not as sore as I'd feared—though I suspect wielding water alongside this would drain me completely.

"Hey, you!" a voice calls, clearly aimed at me. I glance at Korvis, who continues walking, seemingly unconcerned, so I lower my eyes and match his pace. Would someone really confront me with him nearby? Do they care so little for his authority?

"Prophecy mortal," the voice sneers, and that title ignites a fire in my blood. I turn sharply, facing three fae striding toward me, a small crowd trailing behind. Korvis walks a few steps ahead, deliberately leaving me to fend for myself, testing me perhaps. The trio closes in, the largest looming over me.

"You're smaller than we thought," one mocks, but I hold my ground, staring them down. I've seen Soren handle such encounters with silence, so I channel an inner darkness to intimidate. Maybe I can emulate that.

"What? You have nothing to say?" another challenges, and I shrug, keeping my tone even.

"I don't like to waste my breath." A few chuckles ripple from the crowd, but the three grin wickedly, stepping closer.

"How about I cut off your breath, sparing you the worry?" the largest threatens, and I glare, my heart racing. Together, they outmatch me in size and skill.

"You can try," I reply simply, mimicking Soren's cool detachment. It seems to stall them—they hesitate, unsure. "You're lucky I'm not interested in fighting right now."

"You might not have a choice," one scoffs loudly, and before I can process further, I raise my hand. Water erupts from the ground, wraps around his leg and freezes solid. He breaks free quickly, but it buys me time to step back, creating distance.

The other two unleash a tidal wave, knocking me back several feet. I hit the ground hard, but a surge of power flows through me, rage igniting as I clench my fists. These fae are trained killers, honed by years of daily combat, advanced in every way I'm not—stronger, smarter, more experienced. But that's their weakness—they think alike. I'm different, unpredictable, and that might be my edge.

A whip of water lashes out, grabbing my leg and yanking me toward them. I undo the binds with a quick twist and scramble to my feet.

Raising my hands, I flood the area up to our shins within a circular barrier, isolating our fight. I consider trapping them as I did Korvis, but they'd likely counter it. Freezing the water might work, yet they could undo it too. I need something new, something they've never faced.

Water whips strike from all directions, snapping me out of my planning. Instinct takes over. I raise my hands and visualize Lyrisene: her serpentine body, long wings, the fins along her spine for gliding, her spiral horns, and sharp teeth. I conjure her before their eyes, and a moment's pause grips the clearing as they stare, distracted.

Seizing the opportunity, I open her mouth, releasing a volley of sharp ice daggers. A few hit their mark, but they react swiftly, erecting an ice shield.

I transform Lyrisene into solid ice and crash her into their defense, the impact hurling them backwards. I raise a wall of water to soften their crash against the trees, anticipating a stronger retaliation. Instead, as the water recedes, they rise to their knees, wide-eyed and stunned, the fight draining from them.

Power surges through me, overwhelming and uncontainable, my hands trembling violently.

"You're done for the day," Korvis states, stepping forward. I whirl to face him, hands poised to strike, but I hold back, breathing heavily. "You may leave," he adds quietly.

I turn back to the group, now standing, and assess the aftermath. Ice shards protruding from the ground, lodged in tree trunks, even piercing some fae. I did this. I hurt them. Guilt crashes over me, and I close my eyes. I star-drift to the one place I know offers sanctuary—the Skyward Expanse—where no one can find me.

CHAPTER
TWENTY-FIVE

When I land in the meadow, my legs give way beneath me, and I sink to my knees in the soft grass, staring at my trembling hands as if they belong to someone else. What have I just done? What's wrong with me? I didn't intend to summon such power—it erupted like a tidal wave, wild and furious. If I hadn't stopped, if I'd let it keep building... I could have killed someone.

I press my palms into my eyes, hard enough to see stars bursting behind my lids, and force myself to breathe until the world stops spinning quite so violently. I shouldn't have used Lyrisene's essence to scare them, to harm them. But in the heat of the moment, with their sneers and threats closing in, what other recourse did I have? I haven't seen much wielding yet, nothing beyond the basics, and Veyrik's fire dragon was the only thing that flashed in my mind. A spectacle turned weapon.

You did well to defend yourself, Lyrisene's voice echoes in my mind, calm and steady, cutting through the chaos of my thoughts. I perk up, twisting around quickly, my heart leaping.

She bounds toward me with effortless grace, leaping through the air and drifting down like a falling leaf until she's before me, her massive form somehow not overwhelming in this sacred space.

"I'm sorry, I didn't mean to," I blurt out, my voice breaking. She circles me slowly in a wide arc, her scales shimmering faintly in the sunlight, before settling down with her head lowered to the ground. Her blue eyes blaze into mine, piercing right through to my core, as if she can see every doubt and fear swirling within. "I don't know what I'm doing."

Protecting yourself, she replies simply, her voice unwavering. I huff out a breath, shaking my head. She can't mean that. I was chaos incarnate, destruction given form. Everything I'm not supposed to be. *You did what was necessary*, she adds, as if sensing my turmoil.

"I could have killed someone," I whisper, the words tasting bitter on my tongue.

Yet you didn't. She counters swiftly, without pause. I glance up to the sky as Sylthara appears, circling wide above us like a guardian spirit, her white form a stark contrast against the blue expanse.

"I don't want them to fear you," I say, my voice small. The dragons are ancient, revered—or they should be. Not tools for my reckless outbursts.

Fae have not seen us for many centuries, Lyrisene explains. *Most believe we abandoned them. Perhaps your summoning us can restore faith, remind them of the old bonds.* I shake my head, unconvinced. *You hold too much power within you now. You must learn to draw only what's needed, when it's needed.*

"How do I release it?" I ask, raising my arms again, staring at my trembling hands, the residual energy burning like fire.

Still your mind and return it to its source, she instructs. I try, closing my eyes and focusing, but my thoughts are a tangled mess. *You visited my temple, did you not?* she prompts, and I nod, recalling the serene depths of that sacred place. *Create a temple in your mind, buried deep where it is hard to reach at the bottom of the ocean. Then send your energy there. Let it drift down, layer by layer.*

I comply, eyes tightly shut, picturing the Temple of Lyrisene in vivid detail—its cool stone walls, the echoing chambers plunging into endless shadow. I make it fathomless, surrounded by inky darkness in the recesses of my consciousness. Then, I focus on the light of my power, that surging blue-white force, and push it away gently. I watch in my mind's eye as it drifts downward, sinking into the abyss, and slowly, the shaking in my hands subsides, the hum fading to a whisper.

Hopefully it's deep enough that you can't draw it all up at once, she says, her voice approving. I slump forward onto my hands in the grass, suddenly depleted, as if the release has drained me to my core.

"What if I lose control?" I murmur, fear escaping before I can restrain it. "What if I turn corrupt? What if my soul is already tainted?"

The exercises you practiced today will help with control, she assures me. *Water flows through all living things. You must attune to its rhythm—the pulse of life in every vein, every river, every drop of rain. Once you master the flow of energy through water, wielding will become instinct, without conscious thought.*

"I don't think I should have this power," I confess, looking up as she lifts her head. I have to crane my neck just to meet her gaze, but she opens her mouth, exhaling a breath of icy mist that cools the air around us, grounding me.

I've seen fae commit far worse with lesser abilities, she says, her tone matter-of-fact. I close my eyes, letting the words sink in. *Defending yourself and proving your strength to doubters will benefit you more than you know.*

"It won't change anything in the Legion," I mutter, slumping down further, the weight of their judgment pressing on me.

You will be surprised how fae value power over status, she replies. I suck in a deep breath, holding it as the idea takes root. Power over status. Could someone truly surpass a Lord or Lady through sheer might? Is that the path I'm on?

"What is this all for? Why me?" I ask, turning my eyes to her, pleading for clarity. "Why did you choose me?"

Because you have the makings of worthiness, she says, offering no further explanation. It echoes what I once boldly claimed to them, in a moment of misplaced confidence. I'm not worthy yet. That much is clear. *You should go. Rest is needed.*

"Thank you," I whisper softly, gratitude mingling with exhaustion. I let myself star-drift, the meadow fading as I teleport away.

When I materialize in my room, the first thing that hits me is the overwhelming urge for a warm bath to wash away the day's grime and the lingering chill of misused power. But as I reach out with my senses, probing the palace's shadows, I feel something new. A familiar presence, like a spark in the darkness. Intrigued, I follow it, drifting to the front gardens where moonlight filters through the leaves.

There, among the blooming night flowers, stands a figure with a fiery mane of red hair atop broad shoulders. "Veyrik?" I ask, surprise lacing my voice.

He turns quickly, his eyes raking over me in that appraising way of his, then breaks into his signature wicked grin.

"Hello, Kiera. I'm glad you found me." He approaches with a measured stride, radiating effortless charm. I glance around the garden, half-expecting Soren to materialize in a swirl of smoke, ready to intervene, but it's just us. "I heard you stole my party trick," he says, amusement dancing in his eyes.

"How did you know?" I ask, tensing as he leans in, pressing a light kiss to my cheek in greeting. "Let me guess— Soren."

"As always," he replies smoothly, offering his arm in an invitation to walk. I hesitate but take it, and we stroll along the winding paths. "Soren mentioned you could wield water now, but I don't think any of us anticipated just how powerful you'd become so quickly."

"I don't think I did either," I admit, my voice quieter than intended. He glances sideways, studying my face with an intensity that makes me shift uncomfortably.

"What you did to those fae, I'm certain they deserved it," he says, but I keep my gaze on the flowers we pass, their petals glowing softly in the moonlight. Guilt twists in my stomach; deserved or not, the fear in their eyes haunts me. "The fae realm differs, Kiera. Lingering too long on what troubles you will lead to an unhappy life, and we live for a very long time."

"I don't want to hurt anyone," I murmur, the words heavy with truth.

"You're likely to at some point during this war," he says matter-of-factly. I glance up at him sharply, recalling Korvis' similar words.

"Are we all admitting we're in a war now?" I ask, an edge creeping into my tone.

"We've waged a silent war for ages," he explains. "It's only now becoming more apparent." I roll my eyes, frustration bubbling up.

"You fae with your secrets. Don't you think I deserve to know these things?" I snap, drawing back slightly. He stops abruptly, turning to face me head-on. I halt just short of colliding with his chest, looking up into his intense gaze.

"I'm revealing what I can without endangering your fate," he says, his voice low and grave.

"What the hell does that mean?" I demand, my temper flaring as his eyes dart between mine, searching.

"You have a mortal mind. You don't know what we know. We're protecting you from being swayed by falsehoods."

"Like the Elite's desire for a blended Aelthar?" I challenge, and he tilts his head, surprise flashing across his face. I shake my head, rolling my eyes as I push past him, nudging his arm. He falls back into step beside me.

"I didn't know you were aware of that," he admits. "Who told you?" I stay silent, lips pressed tight. "What do you think of it?"

"I don't know what to think," I confess honestly. He grabs my arm gently, turning me to face him again.

"You can't trust what they say."

"So I should trust you instead?" I retort, pulling free. "What if they have a point?" His expression hardens slightly, but he shakes his head. "Why are you here, Veyrik?"

"Because I'm your friend. Isn't that enough?" he asks, and I give him a skeptical sideways glance. "I had to ensure you were okay."

"But why? Why do you care?" I press, searching his face for the truth. He sucks in a deep breath, releasing it sharply.

"There's a lot at stake when you disappear," he says cryptically. It makes me pause. He's hinting at something, I can feel it, but the words are veiled, like everything else in this world.

"Did something happen I should know about? Or are you not telling me that either?" I say, sarcasm dripping. His lips press into a flat line, confirming my suspicion. "Great. This has been productive. Thanks for stopping by."

I turn down the next path, but in a blink, he star-drifts in front of me. I shove at his chest instinctively, stepping back, but he's as immovable as stone.

"I'm only going to say this once," he warns, his eyes locking onto mine with an intensity that holds me in place. "I am not your enemy, Kiera. Do you understand?"

"Why does it matter?" I shoot back, then push him aside and continue down the path.

I listen for his footsteps, bracing to stop if he blocks me again, but nothing comes. When I reach the end of the trail, I scan the garden. No sign of him. He disappeared without a trace, like a flame extinguished.

He does seem to care, perhaps more than he should, given my tangled role in this prophecy. But with everything at stake, trust feels like a luxury I can't afford. Maybe I do know too much about the Elite now. Their vision of a borderless, blended Aelthar.

It might have been easier to fight blindly, without questioning the cost, but that's not my reality anymore. I have to be cautious with every word, every alliance, every step I take.

CHAPTER TWENTY-SIX

Since mastering the Lirivox Ritual, it has become an essential part of my mornings, a quiet discipline I undertake with increasing reverence. Every other day, I travel to the Cerulean Dominion for intense training in wielding and combat, sharpening my skills under Korvis's watchful eye. On my off days, I double my efforts. Once at dawn, when mist still shrouds the world, and again at dusk, when shadows deepen and the air cools.

Initially, the ritual felt awkward, a task I resented, but with each repetition, I feel a transformation stirring within. My powers feel more controlled, more aligned, as if I'm finally finding a rhythm amid the chaos of my new life. Starting each day with it steadies me, helping me find balance amid the swirling uncertainties that threaten to overwhelm me.

I've begun performing the ritual in various corners of the

Umbral Palace, drawing inspiration from the diverse landscapes for my contemplation. Today, I chose the front gardens, where the fragrant blooms and the gentle rustle of leaves provide a soothing backdrop.

Midway through my session, Soren appeared with a book tucked under his arm, then took a seat on the steps to read. For the first few minutes, he appeared engrossed in the pages, but his focus shifted. Now, he watches me intently, his eyes tracing every fluid motion as I weave through the garden, my movements a dance of grace and power.

"Did you want to join me?" I ask calmly, breaking the silence, though I continue my routine uninterrupted. When he doesn't respond immediately, I glance his way, catching the flicker of a smile before returning my focus to the ritual.

"You should try it with water this time," he suggests smoothly, rising from the steps and approaching with a measured stride. "You've improved remarkably."

"I don't think I'm ready," I admit, a hint of reluctance in my voice. I've tried it with water before, and it ended in disaster. My movements jerky, my balance unsteady, the water slipping from my grasp. I figured I needed more time to master the basic forms before adding that layer of complexity.

"I think you might surprise yourself," he counters, a spark of encouragement in his tone.

He conjures a ball of dark shadows between his hands, rolling it back and forth with effortless ease, a demonstration of his mastery. I watch closely as he begins the sequence from the start, his limbs moving with a fluid elegance that makes my breath catch. The way his shadows twist and swirl around him, dark tendrils coiling like living smoke, captivates me. A stunning symphony of power and precision.

"Did you want to join me?" he teases, his voice laced with amusement, snapping me out of my reverie.

I take a deep breath, centering myself, and summon water between my palms, letting it hover there for a moment as I feel its weight, its coolness. I push it back and forth, mimicking his motion, finding the rhythm. When he reaches the end of the sequence, I step away slightly and begin anew, determined to match his pace.

The water flows more smoothly with each motion, but I notice I'm overthinking. Focusing on the next step, what to shape the water into, how effortlessly Soren beside me seems to perform it. I push him from my thoughts, trusting my body to recall the sequence, and focus solely on the water. Gradually, a sense of peace settles over me, my breathing evening out, the flow of my body through each motion feeling more natural than ever before.

Yet, what pulls at me most is Soren. It's as if we're in sync, body and mind, moving through the ritual together. Our elements differ, water and shadow, but something about him resonates with me on a deeper level. Perhaps it always existed, but since becoming fae, that connection has deepened, evolving into something more significant.

Whenever I'm near him, every muscle and bone in my body seems to ache to draw closer, to understand him deeply, to weave our fates together. Now, performing this ritual with him, our magic synchronized so closely, an unbearable pull ignites within me, impossible to ignore.

He slows his motions as we near the end of the sequence, and when we complete the next set, he stops entirely. I watch as he stands, his posture rigid yet commanding, and when he turns to face me, my breath catches in my throat.

His eyes burn with an intensity I've never seen. Fire and longing blazing through the silver, making my body quiver with a mix of nerves and desire. Is it the ritual, the shared energy, or something deeper? A flame crackles between us, undeniable, a line we both teeter on the edge of crossing.

"You make that look easy," I say softly, trying to break the charged silence, though my voice trembles slightly. My gaze flickers to his sharp jawline as it clenches, then lingers on his lips before I force my eyes back up, heat rising to my cheeks.

He takes two long strides, closing the distance between us, and my body instinctively leans toward him, anticipating the touch of his hand on my cheek or his arm around my waist. But it doesn't come. We hover there, suspended in a moment of unspoken tension, both of us on the brink of crossing a boundary that looms large and fragile.

My lips part, a bold question hovering on the tip of my tongue, but a shadow shifts at the edge of my vision, breaking the spell. "Soren," a sharp voice calls, slicing through the air like a blade.

I turn to see Rennor standing in the doorway, his expression more serious than I've witnessed in some time. My mind races. Has an urgent matter emerged, or is he intentionally interrupting, shielding us from whatever might transpire? I glance back at Soren, noting the smoke flaring from his shoulders, a sign of his barely contained frustration. His hands clench tightly, as if restraining an impulse to lash out, but then he exhales, and the shadows ease.

"Are you heading to the Cerulean Legion today?" he asks, his voice steadying as he studies my eyes, the silver depths swirling with unspoken thoughts.

"Korvis wants me for the afternoon training," I reply, shifting my gaze to Rennor, who stands poised and waiting. "I'll probably head there now." Soren's stare intensifies, a silent weight behind it.

"Stay safe," he says softly, his words laced with tenderness that makes my heart skip.

"I'll do my best," I assure him with a firm nod. After a long pause, he returns the gesture and turns, brushing past Rennor, who sidesteps quickly to avoid a collision, before vanishing into the palace.

I want to ask Rennor what's happening, if there's something critical I should know, but the words stick in my throat. Deep down, I suspect he's trying to keep us apart, and I'm not sure I'm ready to face the reason why. Rather than dwell on it, I let instinct take over, drifting to the Legion's base without a second thought.

I haven't returned to the Legion since unleashing a water dragon on those fae, so I land where Korvis first led me, swiftly scanning the area to ensure no ambush awaits. A few heads turn. Some with recognition, others with annoyance, but most glance and look away with indifference, their blue tunics blending into a sea of unfamiliar faces. I search for Korvis, expecting his long blue robe to stand out, but he's nowhere in sight. I could ask someone for directions, but nerves twist in my stomach, holding me back.

I set off in a familiar direction, weaving through the crowd of towering figures, their broad shoulders and blue attire making it impossible to see far.

"Hey," a voice calls, its tone familiar enough to make me pause. I turn, scanning my immediate surroundings until I meet a pair of eyes I recognize. The female fae who once told me to move, who insisted not everyone sees me as a threat.

"Hi," I say cautiously, meeting her halfway as she approaches. "Any chance you've seen Korvis?"

"Not today," she replies, scanning around. "I assumed he'd escort you here." Her curious gaze lingers on me. "You can stardrift?"

"Yeah," I answer shortly, and she nods, a hint of admiration in her expression. "Korvis mentioned an afternoon session. Is there a specific place I should go?"

"You can join me if you'd like," she offers. "We're heading on a run through the forest to another training field for close combat. There's an obstacle course too, depending on which group Korvis assigns you to." I let out a breath. Great, an obstacle course to stumble through.

"Thanks. I'll just wait over here," I say, pointing to an open patch, but she scoffs.

"Because you'd rather not be seen with me, or because you think I'd avoid being seen with you?" she challenges, and a slight grin tugs at my lips. "I don't care who you are. I've never seen anyone summon Lyrisene at the scale you did, let alone take down three of the toughest fae here."

"I don't want to cause trouble," I murmur, shifting uncomfortably.

"I feel like trouble follows you wherever you go," she says with a laugh, drawing a few curious glances our way, though she seems unbothered. "I'm Nivara."

"Kiera," I reply without hesitation, and she nods. A sharp whistle pierces the air, reminiscent of the sea captains' calls from Eldwick, and I turn my head quickly.

"This way. Quickly," Nivara says, breaking into a jog toward where the group is lining up. They stand with hands at their sides, eyes fixed on the front podium, so I mimic them, trying to stay still. "That's Syron, General of the Legion," she whispers.

"Thanks," I murmur back, spotting Korvis step beside Syron. At least he hasn't abandoned me. "To those of you who know the training ground, you know the way. To those who don't—good luck," Syron intones mysteriously. I mentally roll my eyes at the cryptic fae encouragement.

As the group moves forward, I lock eyes with Korvis as we pass the podium. His steady nod confirms I'm where I belong, and I exhale in relief. But Syron's gaze burns with fierce hatred, forcing me to look away and focus on the path ahead.

"It's a five-mile run," Nivara whispers, and my stomach drops. *Five miles*? I've been running, but that distance feels daunting.

The group ahead jogs off, and my group follows, leaving me no choice. I focus on my breathing, finding a steady rhythm, trying not to dwell on the unknowns. What if I can't finish? I could stardrift, but my black attire makes me a glaring target; everyone would notice.

Time drags on, an eternity of burning lungs and legs turning to liquid. I distract myself by gazing at the endless trees, but every clearing teases only more forest. Slowing my pace, my pendant aches against my chest, and Nivara matches my step.

"You okay?" she asks quietly, her tone laced with concern, as if she fears I might collapse.

"Something's off," I admit, the pendant's warning bells ringing in my mind. She scans the area, and others follow suit, a ripple of unease spreading. I slow further.

"We have to keep going," she urges, but just as I try to pick up speed, the ground shakes. Trees groan, leaves whirl like a storm overhead, and the group halts abruptly. Shouts and commands to gather ring out.

"Is this part of training?" I ask Nivara as we huddle, but she shakes her head. No, this feels personal. Because of me, I'm sure.

"Oh, Kiera," a sing-song voice croons, sending a cold chill deep into my bones. *No. It can't be.* "Kiera, darling. You've finally broken free of your escorts."

"Who is that?" someone whispers behind me, and my hands tremble. *Tormen.* Did he know I'd be here? Is he allowed?

"It's Lord Tormen," the whisper spreads, the crowd shifting uneasily. He wants me, not them. If I don't go, he'll fight them all to reach me, and I won't bear their blood on my hands.

"Don't," Nivara warns as I step forward, but I pull my arm from her grasp.

"You don't need to suffer because of me," I say, my mind flashing to the battle in his palace—how close he came to strangling me, killing the beast. He'd do the same here.

"You shouldn't have to sacrifice yourself," she insists, but I push through the crowd anyway.

"Here she comes," Tormen announces cheerfully. The group parts, revealing him in his green tunic and glinting emerald crown, more unhinged than I remember.

"What do you want, Tormen?" I snap, glaring at his sly grin.

"I'm surprised anyone lets you out of their sight these days," he taunts. "I heard you wield water now. I had to see it for myself. How does it feel to shed your mortality, to abandon the family you once clung to?"

"You're on Cerulean land. I'd think you'd know better than to start a fight where you have no jurisdiction," I seethe.

"Ah, and you've been reading books," he mocks, and my fists clench.

"What do you want?"

"You'll be coming with me," he declares, throwing up his hands to create a shield around us, trapping everyone inside.

I hold out my hands, reaching deep into my mental temple to draw my magic. I leave half at the surface, ready to access, and let the rest flow through me. Not with rage, but with a protective resolve for those caught in this mess.

"I doubt you'll make it back to your palace in one piece," I warn.

His smile turns menacing, a harbinger of death. "Still so spirited," he says, reaching up to summon vines from the trees above.

CHAPTER TWENTY-SEVEN

I stand frozen as the vines snake out from the ground, their thorny tendrils lashing toward the fae at the edges of my group. One by one, they're seized and tossed aside, their efforts to deflect the assault weak and futile. They don't fight back. Why would they? This isn't their battle. No, this is between me and Tormen, a personal vendetta playing out in the Cerulean Dominion, but I can't let them suffer for my sake.

With a deep breath, I pull moisture from the air, shaping it into sharp, slicing arcs that I hurl toward the vines. The blades cut through a few, severing them with satisfying snaps, but Tormen counters with ease, brushing my efforts aside with a casual wrist flick. I grit my teeth. My mind races, urging me to think faster, to outwit him. I draw water up from the saturated ground, coaxing it to climb the remaining vines like a living tide. Freezing it in segments, I shatter the ice in bursts, aiming to break his grip, but he summons more vines with alarming speed, their growth relentless.

A seismic wave spreads outward, the ground quaking beneath me as roots and jagged boulders rush toward me. Panic flares, but before I can react, a few fae from my group surround me, lifting me off the ground with a cushion of water to shield me from the onslaught. When they set me down, Nivara rushes to my side with three others, their faces etched with urgency. A shield of ice and water springs up around us, a fragile barrier against the chaos.

"You must leave," Nivara says, her words tumbling out in a rush. "We can't fight Tormen. It would be an act of war against his dominion."

"He wants me," I counter, my voice firm. "I'm not abandoning you to be attacked in my place."

"He won't kill us," another fae interjects, a stranger with a stern gaze. "He's just taunting you. You must go." I shake my head, unwilling to flee while they're at risk.

"He's blocked anyone from leaving," another says as they run up, and I scan the panicked faces around me. Their eyes flicker with uncertainty—a clear indication no one leads here, no guide to steer them through this ordeal. "Even if she wanted to, she couldn't. None of us can."

The ground rumbles again, and the ice shield fractures under the pressure. Tormen's vines continue their assault, tossing fae aside, though he avoids killing them. If murder were his aim, their bodies would already be impaled. That restraint tells me I need to draw his focus back to me, to spare them further harm.

I form a tornado of water as wide as the barrier allows. It roars to life, sucking up debris, rocks, and brush in a swirling vortex, and I send it hurtling toward him. The funnel sweeps over where he stood, a surge of triumph in my chest. Until it fades, exposing his absence. A tense silence settles as everyone searches the area, anticipating his reappearance behind us. Then, with a wicked grin, he bursts from the ground, unscathed.

"It'll take far more than that to get rid of me," he taunts, his voice thick with mockery.

A sudden crack splits the air, followed by a booming explosion that shakes the ground and fractures the shield around us. Black smoke coils around its base, wrapping upward, and the sky darkens to an oppressive gloom. My heart flutters with a spark of hope, though the panic rippling through the surrounding fae is evident.

"What was that?"

"What's going on?" their mutters rise in a chaotic chorus. Even Tormen looks momentarily taken aback, his confidence wavering.

A massive storm of black swirls high above, forming a pointed tip that curves downward, streaking toward the shield's peak. The fae around me duck, raising their own shields, but I remain spellbound as the dark force crashes into the barrier, shattering it with a seismic blast. A grin spreads across my face, but Tormen swiftly erects new shields, layering them one after another, shrinking our confined space.

"Holy hells," someone gasps as the fae begin to rise, their voices trembling. I glance aside, catching Tormen's gaze fixed on something beyond.

"He's not as powerful as he once was, Kiera," he says, a trace of strain in his voice. "He's lucky he brought backup." I follow his line of sight and spot Soren, flanked by Rennor, Zyra, and two court fae I recognize, their presence a beacon of dark power.

"It's the Lord of Darkness."

"Lord Soren."

"Why is he here?"

"Which side is he on?" The whispers ripple through the crowd. Tormen raises his hands, and the ground around Soren's group clumps together, forming a towering creature of rock, trees, and debris. It tears a tree from the ground, wielding it like a club. Soren and his allies unleash dark tendrils, but my focus shifts. I must target the source.

Seizing the distraction, I guide water up the trees encircling Tormen. The ground and flora are his arsenal; my best chance lies in dismantling it. I freeze the water around several trunks, then lift the ice, uprooting the trees and their tangled roots. Tormen's attention snaps to them, his hand rising to counter, but I act swiftly, sending the frozen mass crashing into him. The first two strike his chest, bursting into a shower of bark and limbs that scatters toward us. I follow with more trees, embedding them with ice shards and daggers. He grabs his arm with a wince, but spins toward me, the ground splitting with alarming speed.

A swarm of thorn-laden vines erupts, wrapping around my legs and lower body, dragging me toward him. But water from my allies pulls me back, stretching my body painfully. I grit my teeth, slipping water between me and the vines to loosen their grip, and break free, tumbling back to the Legion's side. Scrapes and deep cuts sting from the thorns, but I push the pain aside. There's no time for weakness.

Closing my eyes, I sense the water saturating the air and ground, drawing a deep breath to steady myself. I exhale slowly, picturing every water particle expanding, turning the air into a dense mist like Eldwick's morning fog. The ground trembles, a roll pulsing through the dirt. His magic counters mine at every turn. He controls the ground, the roots, the nature around us. How do I fight that?

A series of explosions draws everyone's attention to Tormen's creature outside of our shield. Zyra lies sprawled, another fae motionless, while only Rennor and Soren face the beast, their defeat seeming imminent. The creature unleashes a torrent of vines, trapping Rennor and squeezing until his pained scream cuts through the barriers.

No. This is my fault, my burden to bear.

I plunge into my mental temple, summoning every drop of water and magic I can gather, my body trembling with the overload. Focusing beyond the shield, I pull water from every direction, crafting a towering tidal wave that hovers menacingly. I push it down, swirling it around the creature to blind it, forcing water into every crevice and crack. When no more can fit, I freeze it solid, immobilizing the beast with a single step.

I break into a jog, forming a ramp of water and freezing it beneath me. Each step builds my momentum as I maneuver around the shield's edge. Tormen's gaze locks onto me, and he hurls rocks and debris, but I counter with a continuous ice shield, reforming it as each breaks until I'm mere feet away. He crafts a jagged wooden sword, and I mirror him with an ice blade. He swings as I pass, but I duck, sliding on the ice, and trap him in a swirling vortex of my own creation.

Dropping to his level, I swing my sword, not to strike but to test him. He counters, and as roots and vines grip my feet, I thrust my hand sideways, unleashing an explosion of ice shards that pepper the barrier. Tormen ducks, glancing at his shattered creature—my distraction. I slice my blade across his arm, disarming him, then hurl ice daggers at his legs and shoulder, avoiding lethal strikes.

He cries out, sending vines my way, but I blast water down the center, exploding them as they emerge.

I let the water rise, wrapping around his lower half to lift him from the ground, severing his connection to his element. Vines retaliate, pulling me downward, but I flood the area to my knees and freeze it, trapping them.

"You won't kill me," Tormen snarls, unleashing leaves like razor-sharp knives that slice into my clothes and skin.

Water flows through all living things, Lyrisene's voice echoes in my mind. I raise my hands, and time seems to still. The leaves, trees, air, every drop of water under my control freezes in place. Tormen's eyes narrow, his jaw clenching as he struggles against my hold.

"Where did you get your power from?" he seethes through gritted teeth. I grin.

"Why? Are you afraid?" I expand the water, bursting through every living thing in a shockwave, then freeze his prison and the surrounding area, transforming our bubble into an icy winter fortress. His face pales as he surveys the scene, meeting my gaze with a mix of defiance and dread.

"The Elite will come for you," he warns, and my head tilts instinctively. What does he know?

"Why do you want me? To crown the skies, or for your own plan?" After a pause, he bites down hard.

"For protection," he admits, his voice laced with a desperate edge I can't decipher. "You won't get another chance to kill me."

"Neither will you," I mutter, and in an instant, he vanishes. I stare at the ice that held him, expecting a trick, but the shields fall, leaving only my frozen creation.

I press my hands down, melting it back into the ground, half-suspecting another of Tormen's deceptions. After a long silence, I turn to assess the damage—trees stripped of leaves, many reduced to splinters, the ground cracked with dead vines strewn about.

A warm surge floods my veins, and I turn to see Soren racing toward me, unscathed despite the battle. He cups my cheek, and I lean into his touch, the warmth easing my battered soul and quieting my racing mind.

"Get away from her," Nivara snaps from behind, her voice thick with rage. Soren lowers his hand slowly, and I turn to face her.

"He's here for me," I explain, her wary gaze shifting between us. "I reside at the Umbral Expanse."

"But you're a water wielder," she says after a pause, and I shrug.

More fae approach, and I scan the area—where are Korvis, Syron, or any Legion commanders? Shouldn't they be here by now? Their absence fuels a dark suspicion. Were they complicit? How did Tormen know I'd be here? Soren's expression mirrors my thoughts, and Nivara's silence suggests she shares our doubts, though her rank forbids her from challenging it.

"Will you turn back or keep going?" I ask her. She surveys the group, but no one steps forward to decide.

"Turn back," she says, her tone stern, and I nod once.

"Stay safe," I reply, and she glances at Soren before locking eyes with me again.

"You too," she says, then turns to the Legion, issuing a command to regroup. They organize swiftly.

"Let's go home," Soren says, his eyes still simmering with silent fury. I let out a long breath, studying his gaze, then take his arm, letting him guide me back to the Umbral Expanse.

CHAPTER
TWENTY-EIGHT

The moment we materialize in the center plaza of the Umbral Palace, Rennor's voice cuts through the air, sharp and demanding. "What was that?" he snaps, his eyes blazing with frustration. I instinctively step aside from Soren, needing a moment to collect my thoughts, but his arm coils around my waist, drawing me back with possessive firmness. "How did Tormen, of all fae, know Kiera would be there? Who's feeding him this information?"

"I don't know," Soren replies, his tone resolute as he glances down at me, his expression unreadable yet tinged with concern.

"It was Korvis' idea to have me do this training today," I interject, my voice steady despite the inner turmoil. "Whether he knew about Tormen's plans or not, I can't say for sure."

Zyra steps forward, her presence drawing my attention. I scan her up and down, recalling her crumpled form on the battlefield, yet she stands now with an air of unshaken resolve, her composure a stark contrast to the chaos we've endured.

"There's someone in the Cerulean Dominion working with Tormen," Rennor asserts, his words igniting a storm in my mind. It could be anyone. Korvis, Syron, even Nivara, for all I know. The thought twists my gut, planting seeds of distrust in every corner of my thoughts.

Before anyone can respond, the room lurches violently, the floor trembling beneath us. We all drop into a crouch, instincts taking over as Soren and Rennor raise their hands, summoning a tight shadow shield that envelops us. Windows shatter with a deafening crash, paintings tumble to the ground, their frames splintering. And then just as abruptly as it began, the shaking ceases, leaving a heavy silence in its wake. I glance between the three of them, my hands and body trembling with the anticipation of what might follow, but their faces betray no immediate urgency, a calm that unnerves me further.

"There's no way," Zyra breathes, her voice laced with disbelief. "A rift? Right now? After that fight with Tormen?" We exchange wary looks, a shared realization dawning that this is no coincidence. There's a deeper design at play.

"It has to be the Aether Dominion this time," Rennor suggests, his tone measured. "They haven't been targeted in months." All eyes turn to Soren, awaiting his judgment.

"Cerulean," he mutters, his voice low and decisive, though a shadow of doubt lingers.

"This isn't a coincidence," Zyra whispers, her words mirroring my own suspicions. I nod faintly, the pieces beginning to align in my mind.

"Tormen is allied with the Elite," I venture, my voice barely audible, strength fading as their gazes fix on me. "He said he wanted me for protection." When my eyes meet Soren's, I search for a reaction, but his expression remains an enigma, guarded and impenetrable.

"We'll have to figure that out later," Rennor interjects, turning to Soren with focused intensity. "Is it creatures? Or dark wielders?"

"Both," he confirms, locking eyes with Rennor. "I can't ask you two to risk your lives."

"We're coming with you," Rennor declares, standing alongside Zyra unwavering. "You don't have to ask."

"If your life is in immediate danger, retreat without hesitation," Soren instructs, his tone resolute.

"I'm going with you too," I announce, meeting Soren's gaze. His eyes darken with a seriousness I've never seen, a silent command brewing.

"You will remain here within my shield," he counters, his voice stern and demanding. "That's not up for discussion."

"It's not your decision to make," I retort, squaring my shoulders as his jaw clenches, his scrutiny intense. I feel Rennor and Zyra tense, awaiting his next move, but he turns to them with a neutral expression.

"To the palace gates," he orders, and they nod, dissolving into shadows. He steps to me, halting inches from my face, his gaze traveling over me with a mix of concern and resolve. "Don't wield unless you have to. After today, I'm not sure how much more energy you can expend."

"I'll do what I can," I promise, my voice softening. For a moment, he's so close that every fiber of me yearns to bridge the gap, but he raises his arm. I grab it, and a swirl of black whisks us

213

away.

We arrive at the Cerulean Palace's front gates, greeted by chaos. Screams pierce the air, panic reigning supreme. My initial impression hits like a visceral blow: half the palace lies in ruins, crumbled stone scattered across the ground, while guards scramble with drawn swords, guarding what's left. Beyond, the city suffers more, a massive crack in the ground bleeds dark shadows, suggesting terrors already released. Rennor and Zyra have their weapons ready, so I draw my dagger, its weight a small comfort.

"We do what we can, but we won't risk our own lives," Soren commands, his voice slicing through the clamor. We nod in unison. "Zyra, Rennor, stay close together. Watch each other's backs. Take out the creatures, but direct everyone possible to the palace."

He raises his hands, summoning shadows from every corner, sending them swirling down the streets like a dark tide. Screams erupt, then fade into an eerie silence, as if fear itself has consumed their terror.

Zyra and Rennor dart down a street, and Soren turns to me. I sense his urge to send me back, but instead, he cups my face, his touch grounding.

"Stay near the palace. If anything happens, retreat here. Don't search for us. We'll find you when we can." His voice softens. "There will be many fatalities in times like this. You'll see things you wish you hadn't. Help everyone you can."

"Where will you go?" I ask, my voice trembling slightly.

"To find the dark wielders," he replies. I nod, watching more fae flee past us. "I'll be back," he adds, brushing my cheek before turning. I catch his wrist, stopping him. He pivots, his gaze expectant, and my heart aches more than it should at his departure.

"Don't risk your life either," I manage, and his eyes soften before he nods and vanishes into smoke.

I stand in the plaza, frozen, trying to process the madness. Faeries of all ages rush toward me, and I feel rooted, unprepared despite my recent fights. Soren, Zyra, and Rennor are out there, ready to kill if necessary. Can I do the same? The doubt gnaws at me, a lingering uncertainty about my capacity for such acts.

Steeling myself, I step toward the chaos, focusing on steady breaths. I've been the one saved and defended time after time, but now I have powers. I can't stand idly by. I break into a light jog, screams urging me forward, though every logical instinct screams to flee. Yet, as Korvis often noted, I rarely choose the sensible path.

I round a corner and recognize the street. It's the same one from before. The image of the flower shop owner flickers in my mind, her vibrant blooms cultivated over months. Now, amid this destruction, a new rage ignites in me. If the Elite is behind this, pushing for some blended new order, what's the point? Slaughter, ruin, fear. Why unleash this among innocents?

I skid to a halt as two creatures come into view. Monstrosities I've never encountered, not even in Soren's library of dark creature tomes.

They're towering beasts, easily twice my height, with sinewy limbs covered in iridescent black scales that shift like oil on water. Their heads are stretched long and snakelike, with jagged horns curling back from their brows. Eyes glow crimson, slit pupils fixating with predatory hunger, and their mouths gape to reveal rows of needle-sharp teeth dripping with viscous saliva. Claws like obsidian blades scrape the stone as they move, tails whipping behind them with barbed ends that could impale a body in a single strike.

One lifts its head, turning slowly toward me. My breath catches as it locks eyes, then squares its shoulders, muscles rippling under impenetrable scales. I step back, instincts urging retreat, but I know it's futile. This thing could outpace me in seconds. This is a fight I have to face.

"Run!" a voice yells. My gaze darts to the female faerie trapped beyond them, cornered against a shattered wall, her eyes wide with resignation. "Just run!"

I hold my hands out to my sides, palms downward, feeling rage swell like a storm coursing through my veins—hot, unyielding, driving every heartbeat. This fight is nothing like the ones in the forest, where I could unleash raw power without a second thought, letting explosions rip through trees and ground with no innocents in the crossfire. Here, in the heart of this crumbling city, surrounded by terrified faeries huddled in doorways and behind debris, I have to be precise, every move calculated, every burst of magic controlled. One wrong surge, and I could drown the very ones I'm trying to save.

I let water pool at my feet, and my breath comes steady as I stalk forward. The creatures focus on me entirely, their heads snapping in unison, low growls rumbling from their throats. The trapped female faerie plea echoes in my ears, but I block it out; if I run now, they'll tear her apart before turning on the next victim.

I raise my hands high, then slam them down with all the force I can muster. The street erupts in a flood, inches of water surging beneath us like a living tide, foaming and churning as it spreads. My fingers grip tight, knuckles white, as I recall Tormen's vines. Those thick, unbreakable thorns that had bound me once, unbreakable in their grip. Water is fluid, slippery, but I can adapt it, shape it into something deadly.

Tendrils erupt from the flood like serpents rising from the deep, thick and ropy, coiling around the creatures' limbs and necks with a wet slap. I tighten my mental hold, willing them to constrict, to crush. But the beasts roar, muscles bulging under their scales, and break free with raw, brute power. I conjure more tendrils instantly, faster this time, my mind racing through frantic calculations. Water alone won't hold; I need something stronger.

Wrapping them again, I multiply the strands into a writhing mass, then clench my fists hard enough for my nails to dig into my palms. The water hardens in an instant, freezing into jagged ice that crackles and groans under the strain. The creatures crash down, pinned low to the flooded street, their bodies slamming against the stone with bone-jarring thuds.

They're massive up close, towers of muscle and scale, their armor knit so tight that vulnerable spots seem like a myth. But Tormen wounded the vyrskal, piercing through to draw blood; if he could do it with his twisted magic, then so can I.

I focus on the nearer one, its crimson eyes locked on mine with feral hate, its claws scraping furrows in the ice. More tendrils take shape at my command, their tips honing into jagged ice shards that gleam like daggers in the dim light. They slice down in a barrage, carving small gashes across its hide. Shallow at first, but drawing black ichor that hisses as it hits the water. The creature thrashes, bellowing in pain, but the farther one leaps over its companion in a blur of motion, charging straight at me with ground-shaking strides, its barbed tail whipping the air.

I whirl on my heel, heart slamming against my ribs, and hurl a volley of ice spears. Long, razor-sharp projectiles that whistle through the air. It swats them aside effortlessly, the impacts exploding into frosty shards that rain down harmlessly. I have to go for the soft spots. Eyes, mouth, maybe the underbelly, but it's too agile, dodging and weaving like a shadow given form. Sweat beads on my forehead, mixing with the mist in the air; I can't keep this up forever. I need to think of something new.

Orbs. The word flashes in my mind. Tormen had used them, dark spheres of energy that burst on impact; Veyrik too, with his flashes of light. Mine would be ice, frozen fury. But spears first, I need to buy some time.

I summon a storm of them, ice spears and arrows raining down from above like Korvis' merciless attack on me during training, a deadly hail that blankets the street. The creature dodges wildly, leaping from wall to wall, claws digging into stone and sending chunks flying. But not all miss. Some pierce through gaps in its scales, embedding deep, drawing more ichor that stains the water black. It slows, just a fraction, but enough to give me hope.

In desperation, my hands trembling from the effort, I form spheres of compressed ice. Then I launch them forward. They explode in its face with concussive force, unleashing blinding bursts of ice dust and freezing vapor that blanket the air like a blizzard. The beast rears back, shaking its head, momentarily stunned. Seizing the moment, I craft a sleek ice dagger. Smaller, lighter, faster than the spears, and launch it with everything I have, a streak of lethal frost cutting through the haze.

The final orb bursts right in its eyes, then the dagger embeds deep with a sickening squelch. It staggers, roaring in agony, ichor gushing as it yanks the blade free with a claw, the wound bubbling and steaming. Blinded on one side, it advances anyway, slower but no less terrifying.

But then, a cascade of spears hurtles from above. Not mine, but from the rooftops. Real spears, forged of metal and wood, impaled by faeries standing tall against the chaos, their faces grim and determined. They pin the creature to the ground in a hail of strikes, its body convulsing as life ebbs away, finally still.

I hunch over, hands resting on my knees, breath coming in ragged gasps that burn my lungs. My body trembles uncontrollably, exhaustion crashing over me like a wave. I close my eyes, willing the shakes to subside, the world spinning around me.

"Look out!" The shout pierces the haze, and I duck on instinct as the second creature vaults over me in a blur of scales and fury, its bleeding form landing with a thud that cracks the street. It's wounded from my earlier slashes, ichor trailing behind it, but still vicious, blocking my path back to the palace gates with its bulk.

Spears fly from the rooftops again, a desperate volley, but the beast charges through them, shrugging off the hits like annoyances.

"Run!" the voices echo, urgent and fearful.

I sprint, legs pumping, summoning a dense mist—swirling fog that wraps around me, obscuring my form in a veil of white. Over my shoulder, I fling an array of ice weapons backward—spears bursting from the ground in a chaotic surge, targeting the pursuer. My lungs burn like fire, each breath a knife; I can't kill this one, not now, not with my energy fading. Just halt it, slow it down.

Ahead, the bread shop looms, its sign swinging wildly in the wind. I skid into the narrow alley the flower seller told me about, the walls closing in like a trap. Shouts from above warn me—too narrow, too dangerous—but that's exactly the plan. Slow it down, force it to squeeze where its size becomes a curse.

Halfway in, the alley's shadows swallowing me, I turn, pressing my back to the cold stone. The creature squeezes through, shoulders scraping walls with sparks and grating stone, its eyes fixed on me with unrestrained fury. My heart pounds so hard I can feel it in my throat, but I force long, steady breaths, summoning every drop of water I can manage to pool at my feet, rising like a tide in the confined space.

"Come on!" I shout, my voice raw, echoing off the walls. It lunges, jaws snapping, claws extended.

I raise my hands in a sweeping arc, raising a wall of water that surges upward, flooding from cracks in the buildings above until it's a towering mass, roaring like a waterfall. The creature barrels into it, but I lift its entire body suspended in the air, a churning prison of liquid fury. It swims fiercely, powerful strokes propelling it toward me, teeth bared in a snarl.

With a guttural cry, I pour every shred of will into the effort, and the mass solidifies instantly. It crackles like a thousand breaking bones, trapping the beast mid-motion, its form sealed in an icy tomb, eyes wide with frozen shock.

I wait, body rigid, breath held in anticipation, expecting it to shatter free any second. But it doesn't stir, doesn't even twitch. The ice holds.

Lowering my shaking hands, I feel the uncontrollable tremors spread through my limbs, my vision blurring at the edges, spots dancing like dark stars. I need air. I need out. The alley feels like it's closing in, suffocating.

I stumble forward, legs like lead, forcing my way through the narrow passage until I emerge at the other end. The sun hits me full in the face, blinding and warm, and a waft of salt and seaweed fills my lungs, sharp and familiar. Eldwick. It smells like Eldwick. The sea, the docks, it's all I can think as the world tilts, darkness closing in from the sides, claiming me utterly.

CHAPTER TWENTY-NINE

My mind wakes before my eyes open, a haze of consciousness cutting through the fog. My whole body feels like it's on fire. Every muscle throbs with a deep, persistent ache, my lungs raw and dry as if filled with sand, and my head pounds so intensely that thoughts scatter. Pain is all I know right now.

I place my hand flat against whatever lies beneath me, feeling the soft give of fabric and padding. A bed, then. But where? Still in the shattered ruins of the Cerulean Dominion, or back in the familiar shadows of my room in the Umbral Expanse?

My eyelids flutter open, adjusting to the dim light filtering through until I see black walls and shadowy drapes. Relief washes over me as I let out a soft breath, then sink deeper into the mattress. Home. Somehow, I made it back.

Soren leans forward from a chair by the bed and I glance over.

His face is pale, eyes more hollow than ever, and shadows cling to him like weary ghosts. He must have expended too much magic. But he's here, those silver eyes fixed on me with a mix of worry and frustration that makes my chest tighten.

"Before you say I should have stayed at the palace," I begin, my voice raspy, closing my eyes against the pounding behind them, "just know you were probably right." Admitting it stings, but the exhaustion makes denial pointless.

His hand rests over mine, warm and firm, squeezing gently. "You should get more rest," he says softly, his tone laced with concern rather than anger.

"You should too," I murmur, turning my hand to press our palms together, lacing our fingers. The simple contact soothes the edges of my pain, and I drift back into a heavy, dreamless sleep.

I roll over with a groan, pressing my face into the pillow. My body still hurts, but the pain has lessened—a bearable throb in my muscles, a faint echo in my lungs with each breath. The headache lingers like a stubborn fog, but I can think through it.

Rolling onto my back, I gaze at the ceiling. The room is quiet and empty. No footsteps, no voices. Only a lingering sense of absence. I glance to the chair anyway; it's vacant. My fingers twitch, remembering Soren's touch, a sensation that warms and aches in equal measure.

Propping up on my elbows, I scan the room. Everything is as I left it—books stacked haphazardly, wardrobe slightly ajar, the faint scent of shadows and ink. My hand flies to my chest, fingers brushing the cool, jagged scale necklace. Still there. I exhale deeply, relief mingling with a strange pull. In just a few months, this thing has upended my world: dragons, water wielding, battles with dark creatures. Maybe Veyrik was right—objects of black carry curses.

I swing my legs out of bed, wincing at the stiffness, and head to the wardrobe. I slip into fresh clothes and perform light stretches until I feel the knots in my muscles loosen. How long was I out? A day? Two? My body feels stagnant after too long. Frail, yet resilient in ways it never was.

I catch my reflection in the mirror and I pause. I barely recognize myself: toned muscles from training, hair longer in its braid, standing taller and stronger. More fae than mortal, with powers liberating beneath my skin. It's exhilarating and terrifying. Am I still me, or something reshaped by fate?

My gaze drops to the scale, that insistent pull tugs at me like a whisper calling me back to the Skyward Expanse. I touch it, letting the sensation guide me, and the world shifts.

A gentle breeze caresses my skin, soft grass cushioning my feet. I know this place before I open my eyes—the vast meadow, the endless sky. Breathing deeply, the fresh air fills my lungs, easing aches I hadn't noticed lingered. My body relaxes, mind clearing with each breath.

Fingers brushing the necklace, I scan the horizon. No dragons in sight. Toward the forest where Lyrisene and Sylthara emerged last time, I head that way, trailing my hands through the tall grass, a grin sneaking onto my face. This realm is breathtaking—vibrant greens, wildflowers swaying in the wind, more alive than any Dominion I've visited. And it's mine, a sanctuary untouched by creatures or dark wielders, free from suspicion and shadows.

Pushing through the trees, I reach a small lake, its crystal-clear waters reflecting the sky. Lyrisene lies curled on the sandy bank opposite, her scales shimmering like polished sapphires in the sunlight. She's even more stunning than I remember, perhaps the light off the water enhancing her glow, or maybe it's her element embracing her.

I stop at the edge, gazing into the depths where colorful fish swim in lazy circles. Crouching, I dip my hand, the cool water rippling as they scatter. Cupping some up, I let it trickle through my fingers, feeling its familiar essence.

You wield water as if it's second nature, Lyrisene's voice echoes in my mind, calm and resonant. I look up to find her head lifted, those blue eyes fixed on me with ancient wisdom.

I lean back, settling onto the soft sand by the water's edge, gazing through the clear surface at the darting fish below.

"I spent most of my life in Eldwick near the sea. It's easy for me to imagine water's strength," I say aloud, my voice carrying across the lake. Then she uncurls her long, serpentine body, stretching with a fluid grace that ripples across her scales. "When you said I must learn the elements, do you really mean all of them?"

Yes, she replies simply, her form gliding along the lake's edge before easing into the water. I watch, mesmerized, as she moves through it like the legends Thalira once shared—effortless, as if the lake is an extension of herself.

"What if it takes too long to learn the others?" I ask as her head breaks the surface, droplets falling like jewels. I grip my hands together, knuckles whitening. "What if it's still not enough to make a difference?"

Then we have chosen wrong, she says, her tone stern yet not unkind. I huff out a breath, staring deep into the water—not truly seeing the depths, just letting my swirling thoughts exist in the quiet.

"If I do learn the other elements…" I begin, but falter, my mind slipping into shadows of unvoiced fears.

You will be mixed-blood, she finishes, as if plucking the thought from my head. I meet her unflinching gaze, steady and profound.

"What does that make me, then? The Elite aims to blend Aelthar, but if they're tied to these rifts—the death, the destruction ripping through the realms—I don't want any part in that."

She swims to the shore, emerging with water sheeting off her scales in sparkling cascades. *Not all mixed-bloods align with the Elite*, she explains, and I tilt my head, absorbing this new revelation. *The Elite seek to erase borders for greater power. But many mixed-bloods desire no such thing. Most live in quiet peace, keeping to themselves, forging their own paths. As long as they avoid disrupting the established order, the Lords and Ladies have never forced them otherwise.*

"So, when I learn the other elements, there's no decree that will send them hunting me?" I ask, hope threading my words. She lowers her head to the ground, bringing her eyes level with mine.

No, she answers plainly, and I release a held breath, tension easing slightly.

"And Soren won't need to kill me?" My voice tightens with vulnerability, a pause stretching between us like a fragile thread.

As Lord of the Umbral Expanse, Soren is tasked with slaying the corrupt, she says evenly. *Being mixed-blood alone does not invoke that order.*

"Unless I become corrupt…" I whisper, more to myself, the lingering silence unsettling me, stirring doubts like ripples in still water. "What if I do turn? Will I sense it happening, or does it just… consume you?"

You will probably be too lost to realize what you're becoming, she admits. I rub my temples and eyes, frustration mounting. *Yet it appears you have allies to steer you from such a path.*

"But what if it does happen?" I plead, staring directly into her eyes, desperation edging my tone.

Then that is what fate has decided, she replies simply, without pity or comfort. I roll my eyes, slouching forward in defeat.

"That's exactly what Soren told me," I mutter, pressing my palms into my eyes. "Can I trust Soren? Truly trust him?"

That is not for me to decide, she says, her voice a soft echo.

I grunt, irritation flaring hot. "You can't just give a straight answer? Everyone here speaks in riddles, circling the truth like it's forbidden."

When she remains silent, I glance at her. *If someone asked you about the scale,* she counters, *wouldn't you speak in riddles to protect its secrets?*

I grunt again, staring at the water's serene surface, alive with hidden currents and life below. Frustration builds like a storm inside me, needing release. I grab the nearest rock and fling it across the lake, watching it skip impossibly far, faster than any throw I've made before, vanishing into the distance.

You are fae, her voice resounds in my head.

I take a deep breath, my reality sinking in. I'm gaining their qualities—speed, strength, height, ethereal beauty, even immortality. But is this the life I wanted? Trapped in eternal conflicts, forever changed?

"Why did I feel like the scale was calling me?" I ask, the words hanging in the air. Suddenly, a noticeable shift ripples through the breeze, making me look up. I duck instinctively as a massive, white-clouded form soars through the trees, graceful yet immense.

Sylthara lands with ethereal grace on the lake's far side, her presence commanding. I shift uneasily in my place; Lyrisene has stayed low to the ground, minimizing her intimidation, but Sylthara towers at full height, her form awe-inspiring and overwhelming.

I was testing if you would listen, her wispy voice drifts into my mind. I let out a slow breath, steadying myself. *The Cerulean Dominion will require time to rebuild after the attack. You must press onward.*

"You expect me to learn another element so soon?" Disbelief tints my words as she leaps across the water, landing before me with a gentle gust. "Do you really think I'm ready for that?"

You will never be ready for what lies ahead, she says sharply, the truth landing like a heavy stone on my heart. *You will learn to wield air. It flows much like water, so the beginning may come easily, but its essence differs. You will need a teacher who is flexible and creative.*

"Did you have someone in mind?" I press, but silence meets me. "That is not for you to decide," I mutter, recalling Lyrisene's earlier words. I nod resolutely. "Elarion doesn't strike me as flexible or creative, so I suppose I'll have to find someone else."

Elarion is bound by oaths to protect his knowledge, she explains. *His libraries hold secrets even we dragons do not possess.*

"Which means more riddles," I sigh, exasperation creeping in. Sylthara lowers her head until it's inches from mine, her nostrils flaring as white smoke curls out like mist.

When you go, you must seek the Galehaven Temple, she instructs, her eyes piercing. *You will need to be clever, to prove your worth.* Then she opens her mouth, tongue curling in a deliberate motion.

I turn away, bracing for a blast like Lyrisene's mist, but only a gentle breeze brushes me. Opening my eyes, I see beautiful swirls of white air weaving around my limbs, my veins glowing with a bright, ethereal light. The power surges within me immediately, alive and invigorating.

I lift my hand, focusing on the rhythm of air flowing in and out of my lungs, summoning a swirl to mimic the veil Sylthara wove around me. A wisp spirals from my palm, trailing in graceful loops before fading. It's mesmerizing, lighter and more whimsical than water's steady force, yet undeniably there, coursing through my veins like a fresh wind.

"Thank you for this gift," I say sincerely, bowing slightly to her. Turning to Lyrisene, I bow again. "And for yours. I hope these powers let me save more lives, protect those who can't protect themselves."

They exchange a knowing glance, then bow in return, their movements synchronized and respectful.

We are here if you need us, Sylthara says elegantly. And with that, she bounds into a powerful leap, wings unfurling as she takes off in swift flight, vanishing through the canopy.

I watch her disappear among the trees, then turn to Lyrisene, who's wading back into the lake's embrace.

"Why don't you ever leave this place?" I ask, curiosity overriding the moment's calm. After a long stretch of silence, she glances over her shoulder, her eyes holding depths of untold stories.

We are unable, she replies simply, then dives beneath the surface, vanishing without a ripple, leaving me alone with the whispering wind and my racing thoughts.

CHAPTER THIRTY

I land in the central hall of the Umbral Expanse and the familiar chill of the palace wraps around me. The vast chamber is empty as expected. My boots echo softly on the polished obsidian floor as I navigate the halls, the weight of my new powers—water and air—seeping into my bones like an untested promise. I need to find a trainer in the Aether Dominion, seek out this mysterious Galehaven Temple. I could have pressed Lyrisene or Sylthara for answers, but their silence forms a wall I've learned not to challenge—questions answered with riddles are sometimes more frustrating than helpful.

As I pass a few faeries creeping along the corridors, their eyes flickering away from mine, I keep my head down, lost in thought. My mind churns with plans—how to navigate the Aether Dominion, who might guide me there, and why this temple calls to me with such urgency. But before I can unravel it, a sudden shift in the air stops me mid-step. Black smoke swirls at the far end of the hall, solidifying into Soren's tall, commanding form. He stands motionless, his eyes locking onto me with an unreadable expression, a mask of control.

"Welcome back," he says, his voice sharp with an edge of annoyance as I approach. A grin pulls at my lips despite myself—his tone, so predictably exasperated, feels almost comforting.

"Thank you," I reply simply, brushing past him. My arm nudges his gently, a brief contact igniting a spark through me, and I continue down the hall, pretending nonchalance.

I feel him turn, his presence aligning with mine, his arm maintaining that subtle pressure against mine as we stride together. I keep my gaze forward, but my eyes flicker sideways, noticing his intense gaze upon me, quickening my pulse.

"Where do you go?" he asks, his tone steady yet laced with curiosity. I shrug, reluctant to reveal the Skyward Expanse's sanctuary. "I haven't been able to sense you in any of the realms. It's as if you vanish."

"Are you stalking me?" I tease, glancing up with raised brows, a grin playing on my lips.

"My inability to trace you worries me, so yes, I might be tracking you," he admits, his voice lowering. I turn my eyes ahead, forcing my breathing to stay even under his gaze. "You're not going to tell me?"

"No," I say flatly, and he huffs, a sound of mild frustration. "Did you really search every realm for me?" I ask, glancing as we round a corner. "Did you go to Eldwick?"

"Yes," he confirms, and my step falters, but his arm urges me forward. "I thought that's where you might be going."

"Did you see them?" I ask softly, my voice betraying a longing I've buried. His gaze meets mine, steady and searching.

"Are you referring to the kid with the black eye?" he asks. I scoff, picturing Rory's lopsided grin, perpetually paired with a fresh bruise or cut from his rugged dockside life.

"Yeah, probably," I murmur, a wave of homesickness pulling at me. They're so close yet so far. Now that I can travel alone, nothing should stop me from visiting, but so much has changed. I'm fae now, wielding powers they'd never understand. What could I possibly say?

"They're both doing fine," Soren reassures, his voice gentle, and I nod slowly, the knot in my chest loosening slightly. "I need to know where you go," he says firmly, drawing me back to the moment. His eyes sweep across my face, assessing, deciding.

"If you ever read my mind to find out, I will hate you forever," I warn, the warning spilling out with more heat than intended. He blinks, momentarily taken aback.

"Then try to tell me," he counters, his hand brushing mine lightly. My fingers twitch, instinct urging me to grab his, but I resist, clenching my fist instead.

"I'll answer your question if you answer one of mine," I propose, and after a pause, he steps forward, stopping abruptly to face me. I jolt, nearly colliding with his chest.

"Where do you go?" he asks, his tone serious, demanding.

"A place you've never been," I say with a grin, watching his eyes narrow, a storm brewing behind them as if he might dissolve into smoke any second.

"That hardly qualifies as an answer," he growls, towering over me. I tilt my head back, meeting his gaze fully.

"Now my question," I press, gathering my courage. "How do

you keep yourself from kissing me all the time? I might need practice with that kind of restraint."

His eyes widen for an instant, dropping to my lips before snapping back up, a hungry spark igniting.

"You're deflecting my question," he mutters, his voice a low growl, yet there's a crack in his composure, a tremor revealing his inner struggle.

"Maybe I just want you to kiss me," I whisper, leaning in, near enough to sense the warmth emanating from him, challenging him to close the distance.

He moves with startling speed, hands gripping my waist, fingers digging in with possessive strength. His lips crash into mine, fierce and relentless, a whirlwind of heat and desire. I kiss him back just as fiercely, hands twisting in his tunic, pulling him closer as if I could anchor myself in this chaotic moment. His mouth is warm, and every nerve ignites, craving more.

My fingers slide up, tracing the firm contours of his chest, and he deepens the kiss, a deep, primal sound escaping his throat, sending shivers coursing down my spine. The hallway, my abilities, the impending rifts of Aelthar—all fade into oblivion, leaving only the pressure of his body, the roughness of his stubble against my palm, the way his grip tightens as if I might vanish.

But he pulls back, breath ragged, eyes dark with desire, locking onto mine. My hand lingers on his abdomen, feeling the taut muscle under his tunic, every instinct screaming to pull him closer. But he steps away, breaking the contact, and the cold air rushes in, sharp against my flushed skin.

"Looks like I need work on my control too," he says, his voice teasing yet rough, a half-smile curving his lips. I laugh—a short, breathless sound laced with frustration—because I want more, and the way his eyes linger tells me he knows it.

Footsteps interrupt, a familiar rhythm that makes Soren step back slowly.

"Hello, you two," Rennor calls, strolling toward us with a sly grin, as if he's caught us in some secret game. I tilt my head back, rolling my eyes with a slight shake.

"You don't have anyone else to bother?" I retort, turning to face him. His casual stride and knowing smirk annoy me. He's too perceptive for his own good.

"Nope. Just the two of you," he says, grinning wider. "Am I interrupting?" he teases, and instinctively, I thrust my hand out, unleashing a blast of air toward him. His feet lift off the ground, and he flies down the hall, landing with a loud thud.

"What in heaven's name!" he shouts, scrambling to his feet, rubbing his back. I chuckle quietly, the sound escaping despite myself.

"You can wield air?" Soren asks, his tone a mixture of disbelief and curiosity. I turn to him swiftly, my eyes scanning his face for a hint of his emotions—anger, annoyance, worry? Yet his features hold an unreadable mask, a seamless expanse of silver eyes and taut jawline revealing nothing. My heart thuds erratically in my chest, a drumbeat of uncertainty.

"I…" I begin, my voice wavering as I grapple for words. How do I explain when I can't even decipher his reaction? The silence stretches, heavy with unspoken questions.

"How?" he presses quietly, his gaze intensifying, and I sense the burden of his expectation bearing down on me. What can I say when the truth forms a tangled web I hesitate to untangle? My mind scrambles for an answer, a safe diversion.

"Because I've been somewhere you've never been," I reply, the words emerging like a riddle, a veiled allusion to the secrets I protect. It dawns on me. This is my own cryptic key to the mysteries I hold, a divide between us I'm unprepared to bridge.

"Somewhere I've never been," he echoes softly, his eyes flickering over my face as if piecing together a puzzle. Each glance seems to weigh a different possibility, a different meaning behind my words. Before he can venture a guess, Rennor stomps toward us, rubbing his neck with a grimace, his presence breaking the moment.

"That was unfair," he grumbles, his tone a mix of irritation and mock indignation as he faces me.

"You deserved it," I retort, a faint smirk tugging at my lips despite the tension.

"For what? All I'm doing is asking what you're up to today?" He protests, raising his hands in exasperation. I roll my eyes, his dramatic flair a stark contrast to the gravity of our situation. He really is something else—unpredictable, yet oddly grounding.

"I'm going to assume we're heading to the Aether Dominion," Soren interjects, his voice steady as he glances down at me. His eyes meet mine, and a grin spreads across my face. His intuition about me, even without full understanding, warms me unexpectedly.

"Do I have to go?" Rennor complains, his tone shifting to a petulant whine as Soren regards him with a serious look.

"You're my advisor, are you not?" Soren replies, his voice carrying a quiet authority. "You understand their politics better than I do. And Elarion irritates me."

"Fine," Rennor sighs, his shoulders sagging in defeat. "But there's no way we're going to another Dominion right now. Not after what just happened. The both of you need to rest." His concern lingers in the air, a practical counterpoint to my restless energy.

"What do you want to do?" Soren asks, turning to me, his eyes searching mine. The anticipation gnawing at me drives me to push ahead, to dive into the Aether Dominion's mysteries, yet Rennor's argument resonates. We have to regroup, to untangle the threads of the last events.

"We can wait," I concede, the words tasting of reluctant wisdom. Soren nods once, then shifts his gaze to Rennor.

"Then we'll call a meeting with the other Lords and Ladies," Soren decides, his tone resolute.

"I would suggest holding it here," Rennor adds, his voice lowering with caution. "To see who has the will to show up. I'm not sure who we can trust at this point." My eyes widen at the suggestion. Invite them to the Umbral Expanse?

"Set it up," Soren commands, his voice admitting no argument. Rennor turns to me, his steady gaze piercing.

"Do you plan on learning all the elements?" he asks, his question taking me by surprise. He's the first apart from Soren to directly question my powers, and the inquiry stirs a wary unease. The potential of this power, what it might make me, looms large.

"I suppose so," I admit, my voice hesitant. Rennor's jaw clenches, a trace of concern crossing his features. "If I start to turn corrupt… you would tell me, right?" I ask, my eyes darting to Soren, every part of me begging for their watchfulness should it come to that.

"You are not corrupt," Soren says firmly, his hand squeezing my hip reassuringly. Yet, if he fears his own potential for corruption, what of my own? "It won't come down to that."

"Okay…" I murmur, releasing a shaky breath. The uncertainty

gnaws at me, but Soren's gaze shifts to Rennor, a silent cue they need to consult. I step away from his side, needing space to process. "I'm gonna get some rest. Since that's what the advisor advises."

"Smart," Rennor quips, a hint of a smile breaking through.

"We'll let you know when we hear from the others," Soren adds, his voice softening. I nod and turn, my shoulders heavy with an inexplicable weight. Why does my heart feel so weighed down? Perhaps it's the relentless uncertainty, the way each step forward encounters a setback, pulling me back into the unknown.

CHAPTER
THIRTY-ONE

After a few days of exchanging messages with the Lords and Ladies across the dominions, they've all finally agreed to convene in the Umbral Expanse. It's a small victory, but one laced with tension. Veyrik was the first to confirm his attendance, his reply swift and laced with his signature dry wit. Thalia took longer— understandably so, given the recent devastation in her realm, where dark wielders and monstrous creatures had torn through her lands like an uncontrolled storm. And Elarion? He declined at first, only to relent once he learned the others were committing.

The meeting hall in the palace's west wing overlooks the sea, though "overlooks" feels generous today. The view is more of a shrouded veil than a vista, nothing like the crystalline expanses of the Cerulean Dominion. To outsiders, this place might seem stark and uninviting, with its shadowed stone walls and the constant hush that clings to the air like mist. Yet to me, there's a strange comfort in it. A reminder of Eldwick's rugged isolation.

I stand at the window, taking a deep breath. The fog is unusually thick this morning, swallowing the horizon whole, but the rhythmic crash of waves below filters through, soothing the knot of anxiety twisting in my chest. After debriefing with Soren, Rennor, and Zyra about the brutal clash with Tormen, we've reached an uneasy consensus: he's allied with the Elite, or whatever shadowy force is orchestrating these rifts. The true question troubling us is whether Thalira and Korvis pursue their own agendas. Trust feels like a delicate thread these days, one wrong pull from breaking.

"Remind us to teach you how to make a shield," Rennor says as he enters the room, his voice light yet carrying that hidden undercurrent of concern. I turn slightly, meeting his gaze. He positions himself beside me, arms folded across his broad chest, staring out into the opaque white expanse as if it holds answers.

"Remind me to apologize for beating you up in the ring this morning," I reply flatly, though a hint of a smirk tugs at my lips. Training with him has become a ritual, a way to release the restless energy building inside me.

Rennor chuckles softly, the sound rumbling low in his throat. "You're going to need a more skilled trainer soon," he admits, glancing sideways at me with a mix of pride and resignation.

I shrug, flexing my fingers absently. "Kinda feels nice to win sometimes."

"You've won nearly every wielding fight you've been in," he points out, his tone matter-of-fact.

"Doesn't really feel like it though," I murmur, my mind wandering to the scars—both visible and concealed—from those conflicts.

He nods slowly, understanding without needing words. I ball my hands into fists, releasing them repeatedly, trying to shake off the nervous buzz humming under my skin. It's futile, of course. For the time being, we've agreed to conceal my air-wielding ability during this meeting. Let them reveal their hands first—see what slips in conversation. If anyone harbors hidden motives, it's better they underestimate me. Yet that requires me to stay composed, concealing the suspicion gnawing at my thoughts, and prevent any unintended power surges from exposing us.

"Try not to act too suspicious of them," Rennor whispers, his voice barely audible, as if the walls themselves might betray us.

I dart my eyes toward him, ready to retort, when soft footsteps echo from behind. I turn fully, and there stands Thalira, her presence as warm and composed as ever.

"Kiera!" she exclaims, her tone bright and seemingly genuine, or at least it seems so. I force a smile, willing it to reach my eyes. "I heard what happened in the forest, and I feel devastated. And then the rift struck... I never had the chance to speak with you properly."

"That's okay," I reply, matching her kindness as best I can. "How is the rebuilding going? I'm sorry I haven't visited."

She approaches, wrapping me in a gentle embrace. I return the gesture, careful not to stiffen, though my mind races as I analyze every nuance, every shift in her stance.

"We are doing what we can to clear everything out," she says, pulling back slightly. Her words carry a weight; 'everything' undoubtedly encompasses the rubble and the fallen bodies, the lives shattered by the chaos. "It will take time, but we're managing. And I can't thank you, and all who helped here, enough."

When her gaze shifts to Rennor, a subtle spark flickers in her eyes, something almost flirtatious. It catches me off guard, and I squint at him with a questioning look, but he keeps a neutral expression, turning his attention to the far end of the room as if nothing happened.

"I wasn't expecting everything here to be quite so... dark," Elarion interjects, his voice dripping with distaste as he examines the hall. The contrast with his own luminous palace in the Aether Dominion must be jarring— all gleaming spires and perpetual light against this somber elegance.

"Each dominion varies; we must honor each other's choices," Thalira responds diplomatically, nodding toward him.

Elarion holds my gaze for a long, assessing moment before moving to another window, murmuring under his breath, "I would rather not spend the rest of my day in this dreary weather."

I lift my eyebrows at Rennor, who mirrors the expression. The first time I met Elarion was in a similar gathering, and I attributed his sharpness to a bad day. Now, I'm starting to wonder if this rigid demeanor is his default—surprising for someone ruling a realm of light and air, where I'd expect more... levity.

My thoughts disperse as a flash of red hair draws my attention. Veyrik enters, and an involuntary grin spreads across my face. Our last conversation in the garden had veered into tense territory, revolving around the Elite without resolution, yet his presence always injects a spark of humor into the gloom.

"Naturally, Soren would be the last to arrive in his own palace," Veyrik quips, striding toward me with that effortless confidence. He reaches out, leaning in as if to kiss my cheek, but wisps of smoke curl across the floor, compelling him to step back. "The last to arrive, yet right on time," Veyrik adds smoothly, unfazed. I brush his arm lightly, squeezing in welcome, and he offers a playful wink.

Amid the whirlwind of recent days, Soren and I haven't had a private moment to unpack what happened in the hall, and that charged encounter hangs between us like unspoken words. A part of me wonders if we're both avoiding it, assessing emotions before diving in.

Soren's eyes swirl with restrained annoyance as they fix on Veyrik, smoke fading from his shoulders as he strides to the table, his posture rigid. "Please, take a seat," he commands, his voice sharp.

We comply, the air thickening with anticipation. Soren takes the head of the table, while I position myself between Rennor and Veyrik. Across from us, Thalira and Elarion take their seats, the arrangement feeling like a delicate balance of alliances.

"So, who wishes to begin the discussion?" Veyrik asks without preamble, his bluntness cutting through the silence like fire through fog. I scan the faces around the room, but no one jumps in. "We're all aware of the sequence of events in that forest. And someone here knows something."

Thalira leans forward, her hands clasped on the table. "I realize everyone likely suspects the Cerulean Dominion's involvement, but I can assure you—neither I nor Korvis understand how Tormen learned of Kiera's presence there."

"They were on your territory," Veyrik counters sharply, "so it's reasonable to suspect your involvement now."

"I have never intended harm to anyone," Thalira insists, her voice steady but edged with frustration. "Especially not Kiera. If I were involved, why would I unleash a rift to devastate my own home?"

"Because you were unsuccessful," Elarion states flatly, drawing every eye to him. The simplicity of it hits like a cold wave—failing to capture me might justify the retaliation. But the Cerulean Dominion has been targeted before; this isn't their first brush with destruction.

"Could it have been one of the Legion fighters?" I venture, the notion rising from my own experiences. Heads turn toward me.

"Why would it be one of the fighters?" Elarion asks, his annoyance laced with genuine curiosity.

"A few attacked me on my first day there," I explain. "They weren't thrilled about me being there." I turn to Thalira. "How do fae enlist in the Legion?"

"There's a standard assessment and physical test for all our legions," she replies. "I can't fathom why anyone would target you in that manner."

I shift my gaze to Veyrik, aware that his extensive knowledge of the Elite often reveals hidden layers. He meets my eyes, reading my unspoken question. "You're wondering whether the Elite could infiltrate the Legion," he says, leaning forward. "It's possible. Someone might wield both terra and water yet disclose only water. We'd have no way of knowing their true abilities."

"How would we confirm it?" I press.

Veyrik's eyes flick to Soren, and the room's attention shifts accordingly. Mind-reading—Soren's talent, one I often forget amid the chaos.

"If I'm allowed," Soren says, his gaze locked on Thalira, "I'd like to get to the bottom of this."

After a tense pause, she nods. "You have no justification to kill one of my subjects."

Veyrik scoffs. "Good thing Soren has a strong will."

Before anyone can object further, Soren dissolves into smoke, vanishing from the room.

The ensuing silence feels oppressive, like the fog outside bearing down. I glance at Rennor, suddenly aware of the vulnerability in Soren's absence, but Veyrik leans in, breaking the stillness. "How do you maintain such clean robes, Elarion? Do you summon a gentle breeze to prevent them from trailing on the floor?"

I suppress a grin, the levity offering a welcome relief.

"Do you always have to make jokes?" Elarion retorts.

"It soothes others' tensions. You might consider trying it sometime," Veyrik fires back, then rests his cheek on his hand and faces me. "Can you heal with your water powers?"

"I didn't know that was possible," I admit, angling toward him, intrigued.

"Healers exist across all magics. It's a skill worth exploring— perhaps worth attempting." His meaning is evident: another tool in my arsenal, one I should test soon. "Do you actually enjoy living here?" he asks next, his tone transitioning to a more personal note.

"Believe it or not, it reminds me of Eldwick," I say with a short scoff, and he smiles. His eyes sparkle despite the dim light.

"Sounds like a dreary place."

"It is," I concede, sensing his gaze trace my features, probing for more.

A sudden crack breaks the moment, followed by piercing screams resonating through the hall. Two Legion fighters appear on the floor, grasping their heads, writhing in pain. Soren towers over them, expressionless, then encases them in a shield, silencing the noise. He disappears once more in a puff of smoke.

We all rise, my heart racing as I instinctively retreat. Veyrik's hand rests gently on my lower back, steadying me, and I lean into the support without thinking. These fae are unfamiliar to me, but their Legion attire is unmistakable. My suspicion was right—and it's terrifying.

"Well, I suppose that settles it," Veyrik says dryly.

Elarion crosses his arms, his face a mask of disappointment and dread. Thalira stands frozen, hand to her chest, as if the betrayal has physically struck her.

Another crack splits the air, and Korvis and Syron materialize, their expressions changing from confusion to shock.

"I swear by all the creators, if you slip into my mind, I'll—" Korvis begins, but he hesitates at the scene before him. "Thalira? What are you doing here?" He scans us one by one. "What's going on?"

"It appears you've recruited some Elite members into your Legion," Elarion says deadpan, shaking his head as if it's the ultimate disgrace.

"We've committed no such act," Syron retorts sternly, his gaze fixed on the writhing fae with a mix of horror and denial. "What have you done to them? Release them at once!"

Soren raises a hand in a controlled gesture, dissolving the translucent shield with a subtle shimmer, but the screams continue, raw and piercing. The fae claw at their ears in desperation, their bodies contorting in relentless torment, while Soren observes without emotion, his expression etched in stone.

"Soren, that's enough," Thalira commands, her voice rising to a stern shout that echoes through the hall. She steps forward, her brow creased in alarm. "You're going to kill them."

"Killing and torture are two very different things," Veyrik

remarks coolly, a hint of wry detachment in his tone as he watches the scene.

Suddenly, the room falls into heavy silence, the cries cutting off abruptly. The fae collapse like limp rags, their bodies seized by violent convulsions, chests heaving erratically. Soren's gaze meets mine briefly before shifting to Korvis and Syron. "These fae are to be disposed of," he declares, his tone unwavering, allowing no dissent.

Syron steps forward, color draining from his face, yet his posture remains resolute. "You lack physical evidence they are as you claim."

Soren kicks one fae with precise, forceful motion, rolling him onto his side. The broken figure struggles to rise to hands and knees, staring blankly at the floor, stripped of will.

"Wield," Soren orders, venom saturating the command.

The fae extends a shaky hand toward the window, summoning a small rock that hurtles inward and lands in his palm. He levitates it briefly, then crushes it to dust. A clear demonstration of terra magic, undeniable.

"Physical proof," Soren declares curtly, his stare challenging Syron.

Syron blinks slowly, processing the incriminating display with clear difficulty.

"That doesn't prove they're Elite," Korvis argues desperately, his words tumbling out in a rush of denial.

Soren kicks the other fae, turning him over with clinical efficiency. "How do the Elite travel between dominions?"

My breath hitches. Has anyone ever drawn this from an Elite before? Or is this revelation new to all of us?

"Underground tunnels," the fae mutters, the confession flat and resigned. Korvis steps back, horror carving stark lines across his face.

"How long have you been in the Elite?" Syron demands, his voice cracking with raw anguish.

Their fists clench convulsively—silent confirmation of guilt. "76 years." "42 years," they confess sequentially, the revelations falling like stones.

"And is the Elite working with Tormen?" Soren presses, zeroing in on the central suspicion.

"Yes," they say in unison, the affirmation chilling the air.

Thalira gasps, her fingers trembling to her lips in dismay.

"If you don't kill them, I will," Soren says flatly, wisps of smoke coiling at his edges.

Syron stares down at them, betrayal raw in his eyes—as if they were wayward sons who have destroyed his world. "We will handle the situation," he says finally, facing Thalira and Korvis. "And we will investigate the others."

"Thank you, Syron," Thalira murmurs, though doubt lingers in my mind. Is he truly innocent?

Syron and Korvis seize the fae's arms in iron grips and disappear without a trace, the space they filled now eerily empty.

I exhale deeply, my mind spinning from the onslaught of revelations. Soren crosses his arms, his piercing gaze locking on me with fierce protectiveness before snapping sharply to Veyrik's proximity.

"Thank you all for meeting here at our palace," Rennor interjects diplomatically, easing the lingering tension. "I'm sure you have much to discuss in your own dominions. We're more than willing to assist with any future developments."

Thalira nods briskly. "Thank you," she says, then she fades into a soft glow.

Elarion offers a curt nod before dissolving into nothingness.

That leaves Veyrik, his gaze on me—watchful, deep, charged with unspoken emotions. Overwhelmed, I call upon my power to star-drift to the cliffs, the solitude a fragile refuge amid the growing turmoil.

CHAPTER THIRTY-TWO

I linger at the threshold of a small sitting room on the main floor, my gaze settling on Soren and Rennor seated inside. For a moment, I hesitate, debating whether to disturb their quiet retreat. The air feels thick with an unspoken truce between them, and I wonder if they notice my awkward presence lingering at the door. Knowing their heightened awareness, they've likely detected me from halfway down the corridor, explaining their silence as they wait for my next move.

"Will you come in already?" Rennor calls out, his voice breaking the stillness with a hint of exasperation.

I step inside quickly, glancing around the unfamiliar area. The door is usually closed, shrouding this room in mystery, but now I find it's a cozy lounge—perhaps a meeting room—with plush armchairs circling a low table, its edges worn from countless discussions. Sunlight filters through a tall window, casting soft patterns on the stone floor.

"I wasn't sure if you two were actually busy," I say, taking another cautious step forward, my boots scuffing lightly against the rug.

"Did you need something?" Soren asks, his tone clipped as he looks up, his dark eyes meeting mine with a hint of impatience.

Days have passed since our last strained meeting with the Dominion rulers, and I know both he and Rennor have sent messages to Elarion, requesting another audience. Yet, no reply has come, leaving me restless. I've been practicing my air magic in stolen moments, testing its limits, but it mirrors water magic only superficially. The power eludes me, especially when I try to attempt an attack—something stronger, more decisive.

"I was wondering if you had heard anything from the Aether Dominion," I admit, my voice faltering as I shift my stance. "It's not a big deal. I'm just... restless, I guess." The truth gnaws at me —I'm struggling, unsure how to wield this new element, and Elarion's silence only heightens my unease.

"I haven't heard anything," Soren mutters, his words heavy with a mood I can't quite place—irritation, perhaps, or fatigue. I take a step back toward the door, sensing his distance.

"That's fine. I'll just be around then," I say, turning to leave, but a subtle shift in the room stops me. The creak of a chair, the rustle of fabric.

"Would you like to go now?" Soren's voice cuts through, low and deliberate. I freeze, turning to face him, my heart fluttering.

"What do you mean? Just show up? Is that allowed?" I ask, my brow furrowing as I glance between him and Rennor.

"No, it's not. And Elarion would be furious if we did," Rennor interjects sternly, his tone a warning as he fixes Soren with a hard stare. "We are not going to the Aether Dominion without an invitation, Soren."

"Since when have I cared about invitations, *Rennor*?" Soren counters, emphasizing his name with a defiant edge, earning an eye roll and a head shake from Rennor. "Days have passed, and all we receive is a directive to wait. If it's important to Kiera, then we should go."

"I don't want to make it a big deal," I protest, my voice soft, though the weight of my need presses against my chest.

"It already is," Rennor snaps, his frustration surfacing as he turns to me. "Do you want to go, or no?" His question hangs, and I hesitate, caught between Rennor's counsel and my own desperation to master air magic. He's the advisor, the voice of reason, yet I can't keep stalling.

"I would like to go," I say finally, my determination solidifying. Soren nods and rises with ease, while Rennor grunts, adjusting his tunic with a resigned sigh.

"Then we shall go," Soren declares, a spark of determination in his eyes. Rennor steps forward, his expression stern.

"Please, just send us somewhere near the throne room or a meeting place. Don't make this worse than it already is," he pleads, but Soren's rare grin tells me he has no intention of playing by the rules.

"We'll see you there," Soren says, approaching me and extending his arm with a gallant tilt of his head.

My feet land smoothly, the familiar black smoke swirling around us in a thick dome, lingering longer than usual. I let go of Soren's arm and look up, noticing a flicker of annoyance tightening his features.

"What's wrong?" I whisper, unease prickling my skin.

"They've drawn their swords," he murmurs, his voice low and tense. Rennor appears beside us, mirroring Soren's grim expression.

"Likely because you placed us into their private chambers," Rennor says sharply, and I cast Soren a look of disbelief.

The smoke clears, revealing our surroundings—a lavish chamber with high ceilings adorned with intricate silver filigree, tapestries portraying swirling winds flowing down the walls, and a long table laid with delicate porcelain teacups and a steaming kettle.

As expected, guards encircle us, swords glinting in the dim light, two closing in to tighten the circle and block any escape. Yet, with Soren's power, Rennor's skill, and my developing abilities, I doubt they could hold us if it came to that.

"Elarion," Rennor calls out with a hint of humor, raising his hands in a gesture of peace. "We apologize for the intrusion. We were unaware you were preparing for afternoon tea."

My eyes sweep the room—elegant yet austere, with a massive arched window framing a vista of endless sky, the air humming with a faint, ethereal breeze. Elarion stands rigid, flanked by an unfamiliar female fae, both guarded by the tense posture of the sentinels.

"You ought to know better than to arrive without notice," Elarion snaps, waving a hand to summon a gust of wind that pushes against us, forcing us back a step. "You are to leave at once."

"We only wish to talk," Rennor replies, his tone softening into diplomacy, though even his charm seems to wane against Elarion's anger. I feel the female fae's gaze on me, intense and searching, so I meet her eyes, maintaining composure under her scrutiny.

"You must be Kiera of Eldwick," she says, her voice a soft melody contrasting the tension. "I've heard so much about you. Your battle against the creatures in the Cerulean Dominion is a story deserving praise."

"Thank you," I reply with a curt nod, stealing a glance at Elarion, whose teeth grind audibly in fury. I quickly turn back to her. "I'm sorry, but I don't believe I know who you are."

"My name is Serith," she says, stepping forward as the guards move aside to let her pass. "I serve as Lady of the Aether Dominion." My eyes widen—Lady of the Aether Dominion? That makes her Elarion's wife, a detail no one mentioned.

"I'm sorry. I didn't realize," I stammer, but she waves it off with a kind smile.

"It's no fault of your own," she assures me, gesturing toward the table. "I'd be delighted for you to join us for tea. And if you still wish to talk, we can discuss it."

"Serith," Elarion interjects firmly, but her glance quiets him, a subtle command that makes him relent.

"Aren't you interested in what they have to say?" she asks, and he nods curtly, gesturing to the table with a resigned wave.

I glance at Rennor and Soren, their expressions reflecting my own surprise, before we approach the table and take the offered chairs.

Maids glide in silently, placing cups, spoons, and sugar bowls before us. I lean forward as steaming tea pours from a ceramic kettle, the aroma of jasmine and honey rising to meet me.

"Thank you," I murmur softly, wrapping my hands around the warm cup, closing my eyes to inhale it, the heat a fleeting comfort.

"You seem like someone familiar with tea," Serith observes, and I feel all eyes on me.

"My mother was an herbalist. In Eldwick, tea was a luxury unless you knew how to cultivate it," I explain, a surge of longing hitting as I inhale again, the scent stirring memories of home—my past life, my mother's gentle smile.

"I've heard the stories of you in the Cerulean Dominion, but is it really true?" she asks as I take a sip, setting the cup down gently. "Can you wield water?"

I lift my hand over my cup, drawing the liquid up in a smooth arc, then shape it into the Star of the Veil flower, freezing it upright. Serith leans forward, awe lighting her face, while Elarion's hands clench on the table, his stare piercing.

"Incredible," she breathes. "What flower is that? Does it come from the Umbral Expanse?"

"It originates from the Cerulean Dominion. It's known as Star of the Veil. It only blooms when the sun shines more than ten hours a day," I say, waving my hand to form a flower in her cup. She reaches out, hesitating as if afraid to disturb it. "This one is from the Umbral Expanse. I'm not sure of its name, but it blooms only under a full moon. I've never seen it otherwise."

"I hadn't realized the Umbral Expanse held such beauty," she muses, and I glance at Soren, whose bored demeanor contrasts her wonder.

"It's called a Lunora Sprig," he says flatly, and Serith gives him a timid grin, her caution toward him clear, as with most.

"It's beautiful," she says kindly. I wave my hand, returning the tea to liquid form in our cups, and she leans back, inhaling deeply before turning to Elarion.

"Tell me what you want," Elarion says, his voice slicing

through the fragile peace, and I lean back slightly, my hands tightening in my lap.

"I need a trainer to help me learn to wield air," I state plainly, expecting shock or surprise, yet Elarion's gaze remains steady, unflinching.

"We don't train others, particularly not outsiders to our Dominion," he replies, and I force a steady breath, recalling Sylthara's advice to be smart.

I glance at Serith, then back. "It doesn't have to be someone from the palace or your court. I'm just asking if someone in your Dominion might be willing to train me."

"Are you able to wield air?" Serith asks skeptically, and I nod. "Show us."

I extend my hand, summoning a small wind tornado. The energy pulls at me, stronger here, the air lighter, as if crafted for bending. I let it fizzle out, and Serith's demeanor shifts, her hands folding politely as she turns to Elarion with a stern expression. Wielding two elements, once mortal, must unsettle them.

"We don't train outsiders. It's how it's always been, and will remain," Elarion insists, and I grip my hands tighter, frustration rising. I look down, seeking a new strategy. Sylthara mentioned the temple—perhaps that's where I'll find guidance.

"If you won't train me, may I make one more request, if it's not too much?" I ask, softening my tone to ease into it.

"You're already requesting too much," Elarion snaps, and I fight the urge to roll my eyes.

"Then humor me," I retort, and he gestures impatiently with a hand. "Would it be possible to visit the Galehaven Temple?" He leans forward, eyes narrowing intensely.

"How do you know of Galehaven?" he demands, and I calm my

breath.

"I came across it in a book," I lie, holding his gaze unflinchingly until he leans back.

"We don't permit others to visit Galehaven," he states, and I sigh in frustration, glancing at my hands, then at Soren, who lounges back, picking at a loose thread on his shirt.

"Knowledge in exchange for knowledge—that's your practice, isn't it?" Soren says, his bored tone belying the steel in his eyes as he meets their gazes.

"Yes, that is our usual practice," Elarion concedes, and I look between them.

"Knowledge for knowledge?" I ask, turning to Serith as the others remain silent.

"You must give us something to receive something in return," Elarion explains. "In the Aether Dominion, we hold knowledge sacred. Our libraries are the most extensive in Aelthar, fiercely protected. Bring a gift of knowledge, and we'll assess its worth against your request."

I nod slowly. Knowledge for knowledge. The dragons could have warned me.

"What kind of knowledge?" I press, and Elarion's eye roll ignites my temper.

"Something of worth. Preferably something we don't already possess," he says dismissively.

I arrived in Aelthar with nothing but the clothes on my back. Even if I returned to Eldwick, would anything I have there hold value enough for this? "Thank you. I will try to find something you might find worthy," I say, deflated, exhaling sharply.

Soren pushes his chair back first, followed by Rennor and me in unison. Elarion and Serith rise, standing close as they watch us gather.

"It was lovely to meet you, Kiera. I look forward to speaking again," Serith says, her tone encouraging but her smile fading, the facade lifting.

I nod once, grasping Soren's arm as we vanish in a swirl of smoke.

CHAPTER
THIRTY-THREE

We materialize in the palace's central hall, the grand expanse of marble and arching ceilings greeting us with an almost suffocating silence. The pent-up energy inside me—fueled by quiet rage and frustration—bursts forth as I thrust out my hand, unleashing a powerful blast of air. The force cuts a tunnel of wind through the hall, the sound echoing off the walls like a mournful howl.

I yell out, the shout ripping from my throat, raw and unfiltered. "He's such a prick!" I exclaim, my voice reverberating as I begin pacing the room, my mind a whirlwind of indignation.

Out of the corner of my eye, I notice Rennor give Soren a subtle nod before slipping away, his form fading into the shadows with practiced ease. Soren remains, hands casually tucked into his pockets, his posture exuding an air of indifference. I slow my frantic pacing, stopping directly before him, my chest heaving as I struggle to control my emotions.

"How do you know of Galehaven?" he asks, his voice steady, piercing through the haze of my thoughts. I'd told Elarion I read about it in a book—a book that doesn't exist. The lie sits heavily on my tongue.

"Does it matter?" I mutter, the words escaping as my sole defense, my gaze dropping to avoid his scrutiny.

"Why do you need to go there?" he presses, his tone softening but insistent, searching my face for answers.

I stare at him blankly, shaking my head as uncertainty grips me. "I don't know," I admit, my voice barely above a whisper.

Tilting my head back, I gaze up at the ceiling, where an endless array of glinting stars are embedded in the dark expanse, a celestial map that feels both distant and comforting.

"I just need to go there. And I don't know why." I huff out a breath, the admission leaving me vulnerable.

He studies me intently, his eyes tracing the lines of my face, the depths of my gaze. And for once, I don't feel like he thinks I've lost my mind. That flicker of belief in his expression ignites a fragile hope within me.

"Why do I feel like you already have an idea?" he says, a hint of amusement lacing his words, though his scrutiny remains unwavering.

I meet his gaze, steadying myself. "You can't come with me where I need to go," I tell him, my voice firm despite the tremor beneath it. His eyes narrow, a storm brewing in their depths. "And please, don't try to follow me."

"Where are you going?" he asks, his tone edging with concern, and after a long pause, I gather my courage.

"Eldwick," I say, watching as he nods slowly, his mind visibly working to piece together the puzzle, the implications of my destination sinking in.

"I'm going with you," he declares, his voice firm, but I shake my head vigorously.

"You can't," I insist, my tone stern as I see the fight ignite in his eyes. "As far as I know, they all think I'm dead, so my return is one thing. But if they saw you—of all the rulers—panic would erupt like wildfire. You cannot show up in Eldwick. It would be chaos."

"If anyone harms you, I will burn the whole forest down," he says, his voice dropping to a low, fervent growl, an emotion I've been too afraid to name.

"I'll be safe," I assure him, though the assurance feels fragile. He nods, stepping closer with a grace that contradicts the tension between us.

He lifts a hand to my cheek, his touch warm against my skin, and then presses his lips to mine—soft, warm, intentional. It's the first time since our kiss in the hall, and this time, Rennor doesn't appear to interrupt. The kiss lingers, a silent vow, before he pulls back.

"I will be there if you need me," he murmurs, his breath brushing my skin. "You promise to return?" he asks, his plea pulling at my heart, the vulnerability in his voice a rare crack in his armor.

"Always," I whisper, placing my hand on his cheek, feeling him lean into my touch. I step back, taking a deep breath, and channel all my energy into my powers—toward Eldwick. The rhythmic crash of waves, the briny scent of seaweed and salt, the distant clamor of the town square overwhelm my senses. Then, with a surge of determination, I allow myself to star-drift away.

Mist kisses my face as my feet land on the weathered, lopsided planks of Eldwick's pier. I inhale deeply, the sea salt air filling my lungs, and survey my hometown. After months in the magical realms, with their grand palaces, lush forests, and floating islands, everything here looks faded and worn—decayed, almost.

The buildings lean precariously against one another, their straw roofs fraying in the wind, wood siding peeling and hastily nailed back together. It's hard to reconcile this with the life I once knew —no star-drifting between Dominions, no ethereal beauty, only a narrow cobblestone road, a lively marketplace, and a dilapidated pier stretching into the gray sea.

I turn to face the ocean, the horizon blurring under the mist, and my mind drifts to my last moments here. Dark wielders had closed in, their intent threatening, and I'd been unaware of the true danger. In a twisted way, Tormen might have saved me by whisking me away, yet Soren had been here too. Would he have taken me with him after defeating the dark wielders, or left me to my fate despite knowing my role in the prophecy? So much remains unanswered, a shadow lingering over my past.

Closing my eyes, I focus again, and when I open them, I find myself perched on the rooftops above the town square. The marketplace unfolds below, unchanged. Tents flap in the breeze, voices rise in a cacophony of haggling and laughter, the scent of smoked fish and damp kelp thick in the air. I hear Thom's boisterous laugh somewhere in the chaos and wonder if Rory is among the crowd or out at sea hauling nets.

I move along the roof's edge, my gaze settling easily on Ma. She stands at her usual stall, surrounded by the same group of older women, her hands gesturing animatedly as she discusses herbs—likely one of her latest teas or elixirs. I pause, watching her, the sight stirring a bittersweet ache. She appears older now, or perhaps I'd never noticed the wrinkles around her eyes, the worn fabric of her clothes. Have they repurposed my old clothes, discarded my belongings in my absence?

With a thought, I star-drift into the cramped interior of our old home, the smallness of the space hitting me like a physical blow. The walls seem to close in, almost suffocating, yet everything remains as I left it—untouched by time. The dining table sits crooked in the center, chairs askew, the couch sagging on the left. Picture frames hang unevenly, dishes pile in the sink, and the floorboards creak with every movement. My heart clenches, memories flooding back—laughter, arguments, the quiet mornings —all overshadowed by the months I've missed.

I move to the kitchen, opening a cupboard to reveal my mother's collection of homemade teas. The aroma floods my senses, pulling a grin to my face. We used to share a pot every morning, a ritual now hers alone. Sifting through the leaves, I find the one I seek: a blend of dried sea lavender and wild mint, its deep purple shade and crisp scent a signature of her craft. If the book for Elarion falls short, this might sway Serith, a modest gesture of goodwill.

Next, I approach the bookshelf at the room's end, its torn spines and pages jutting at odd angles catching my eye. It looks more dilapidated than I remember, though back then, I knew no other world.

Crouching, I reach for the book I need, but my hand pauses mid-air. The black binding, embellished with silver detailing, reminds me instantly of Soren's library. I pull it out and trace the silver-inked title: *Tales of Moonshade*. Flipping through, the stories my father read to Rory and me flood back, and my breath catches. Are these from the Umbral Expanse? How did my father get this?

The front door creaks open behind me, and I close the book slowly, the sound of unsteady breathing filling the room. I stand, turning to face the source.

"Kiera?" Rory's voice trembles, and I meet his wide, shocked eyes—perhaps fearing I've returned from the dead. He looks the same, yet different, his youthful frame hardened by time.

"Hi, Rory," I say softly, and his eyes well up, tears spilling down his cheeks.

He rushes forward, dropping his fishing gear with a clatter, nearly knocking me over in a fierce embrace. I wrap my arms around him, burying my face in his chest, the hug a stark contrast to our usual distance. It hits me then—what I've been missing.

"You're alive?" he gasps, pulling back to grip my shoulders, his gaze roaming over me. "You look... amazing. As if you could actually beat me up now." A laugh escapes me, and I punch his arm playfully. "Ow," he winces, rubbing the spot, and I flinch—almost forgetting my fae strength against his mortal frame.

"Sorry," I murmur, my reality becoming more apparent. My powers have already amplified me beyond him.

"You really are strong," he says, stepping back, his expression turning serious. "Why... how... where did you come from? And why are you dressed all in black? It's nice, just... not like you." His eyes search mine, and I see traces of our father in him, his face aged beyond his years.

"It's kind of a long story," I hedge, adjusting the book in my hands. He narrows his eyes at it.

"What are you doing with father's book?" he asks, his tone cautious, a hint of protectiveness threading through.

"I need to use it for something important. I hope you don't mind," I reply, meeting his intense stare with a quiet plea, hoping he'll understand without needing the full truth.

"You're not staying?" he presses, his voice tightening as he searches my face, and I shake my head slowly. "Why? Everyone thinks you're dead. Ma said the ground shook, black smoke rose near the pier, and when it cleared, you were gone."

"I was taken. I didn't have a choice," I begin, pausing as I meet his gaze. The full truth feels too heavy. "Since then, I've been... safe. But there's something I need to do."

"Are you going to wait to see Ma?" he asks, his voice softening, and I hesitate, the image of her tear-streaked face looming large in my mind, a prospect both longed-for and daunting.

"Do you think I should?" I ask, deferring to him, recognizing that he's carried the burden of my absence alongside her, his judgment shaped by their shared grief.

"Maybe not," he says, his eyes shifting toward the door, shadowed with unspoken pain. "It might be best if I just tell her you're alive and safe." He turns back to me, assessing me anew, his brow furrowing. "I can't figure it out, but you seem different."

I breathe heavily, the air catching in my chest as I wrestle with the decision. Should I reveal my fae nature, my command of water and air, the potential for fire and terra that lies ahead? The burden of that confession balanced on my tongue.

"As long as you're being taken care of and not in danger, I'll accept you as you are," he says, his intuition reading my hesitation, and my eyes well up with unshed tears.

"I've missed you," I whisper, my voice breaking with the depth of that truth, and he steps forward, wrapping me in another warm embrace. I cling to him, breathing in the familiar scent of salt and sweat, an anchor to my past.

"Me too," he murmurs, his voice muffled against my hair, and I squeeze him tighter, savoring the moment. "Ma will be back soon. You should probably get going." I nod, stepping back reluctantly, wiping the tears from my cheeks with the back of my hand.

"Don't stay away so long this time," he adds, his tone gentle but firm, and I muster a small, fragile smile, though the promise feels tenuous, stretched thin by the uncertainties ahead.

Is it wrong to shield him from the truth—that Aelthar's fate hangs in a delicate balance, that dark creatures and wielders threaten to engulf these shores? Or is it a mercy to let him fish, to care for Ma, blissfully unaware of the horrors beyond, sparing them the worry that would gnaw at their peace? The question lingers as I take a final breath.

"I'll see you soon," I say, the vow a fragile thread I may not keep, then close my eyes and disappear in a flash, leaving the echoes of my past for the uncharted future that now defines me.

CHAPTER THIRTY-FOUR

I land softly in the tea room, my senses immediately alert as I glance around, the memory of our last visit flashing through my mind—guards with drawn swords surrounding us, tension thick in the air. This time, however, the room stands empty, a stark contrast to that chaos. The long table, once laden with delicate teacups, is now cleared, its polished surface shining under the dim light filtering through the tall windows.

The doors are shut tight, sealing the space in an eerie silence that presses against my ears. I'm not sure of the etiquette for star-drifting uninvited into another Dominion's palace, but I'm sure this could be a breach in protocol that could provoke outrage with Elarion. I could have returned to the Umbral Expanse to seek Soren's assistance, avoiding the inevitable debate with him and Rennor over propriety, but this direct approach seemed like the quickest path to resolve my purpose.

Curiosity pulls me to the door leading to the balcony, and I push it open, stepping out into the cool breeze that carries a faint hum of energy. Leaning against the rail, I examine the palace's outer walls, trying to orient myself, but the view takes my breath away.

The structure rises from the mist, its pale stone and glass walls blending seamlessly into the clouds above. The architecture gleams under the twilight sky, its spires twisting upward like sculpted gusts of wind, their tips catching the fading sunlight in a radiant shimmer of opal and silver. The walls, smooth and almost translucent, are etched with intricate patterns of swirling gusts that seem to dance and ripple, alive with the pulse of air magic. Tall arched windows glow with a soft azure light, mirroring the endless sky that surrounds us.

This palace stands in complete opposition to Soren's—where his is cloaked in shadow and rugged stone, this is a symphony of light and air. Yet, standing here, I find myself at a loss, unsure of my next move.

Closing my eyes, I conjure an image of Elarion—his tall, imposing figure draped in an ivory cloak, his smug expression framed by those enticing light-brown eyes. I concentrate on his presence, willing myself to appear before him, and when I open my eyes, a grin tugs at my lips.

There he stands mere inches away, his features contorted with a look suggesting he'd gladly toss me from the nearest window. I step back, taking in our surroundings—a study, rich with tall bookshelves lined with tomes of every color and size, the air thick with the scent of aged paper and leather.

"Hello, Elarion," I say with a sly edge, watching his fists clench at his sides, a storm brewing in his gaze.

"I should order the guards to throw you into the abyssal cells where you'll rot," he snaps, his voice laced with barely contained fury. I glance around the room, noting the intricate bindings and unfamiliar scripts on the shelves, then shrug with pretended nonchalance.

"That would be unwise," I reply, watching as his jaw tightens into a permanent clench, his irritation palpable.

"Tell me what you want and leave," he demands, his tone clipped, tolerating no delay.

"Knowledge for knowledge. I need to get to Galehaven," I state, meeting his gaze with steady resolve.

"I highly doubt a mortal like you possesses anything our palace might value. You're wasting your time if this is your attempt to convince me otherwise," he retorts, his words dripping with disdain. But I step toward a shelf and pull out the box of tea from my bag and set it on the ledge.

"This is for Serith. From my mother's hand," I say shyly, and adjust it before moving on to the books.

My fingers graze the spines as I read a few titles and notice some are inscribed in a language I don't recognize, its characters foreign and elegant. "This doesn't look like Vethralis," I muse aloud, glancing at him when he remains silent. His expression hardens, but a flicker of interest dances in his eyes, subtle yet undeniable.

"How do you know of Vethralis?" he asks sharply, the intensity of his tone suggesting it's a guarded secret. Soren had mentioned that few fae still master the language, and I wonder how many even know of its existence.

"Knowledge for knowledge," I counter, clutching the book in

my hands closer to my chest as his gaze drops to it.

"It's written in Syltheran," he says, his voice controlled, and I nod slowly, piecing it together.

"I assume it's an ancient language of the Aether Dominion, perhaps originating with the dragon Sylthara," I venture, watching as he tilts his head, his posture shifting like a predator assessing prey. "I've seen a few books in Vethralis during my travels through the Dominions."

"Which Dominion?" he presses, and I shrug, testing his patience.

"I can't remember," I say with a casual turn, facing him fully. "If you're interested in Vethralis, I assume you must be intrigued by the Umbral Expanse. You don't seem to have many black-bound books in your private library."

"Observant," he acknowledges, raising a hand. In an instant, an older fae materializes to my left, and I step back instinctively. His hair is neatly combed to the side, his eyes glazed as if worn by months of studying texts, exuding an air of scholarly wisdom.

"My Lord," the elder fae says with a slight bow, his gaze shifting to me with curiosity.

"This is Kiera of Eldwick," Elarion introduces, gesturing toward the newcomer. "This is Tivren—Master Scribe of the Skyveil. He will determine whether your offer of knowledge is worthy."

"It is a pleasure to meet you," Tivren says, his formal tone even more regal than Elarion's, and I offer a slight bow of my head. "What is the knowledge you seek?"

"I want to go to Galehaven," I reply steadily, and he tilts his head, glancing at Elarion as if seeking guidance.

"Shall we begin?" Elarion prompts, and Tivren nods after a

quick survey of the room.

Tivren extends his hand, and I feel a nervous sweat dampen my palms as I grip the book—my father's book, one of my last connections to him. I hold it up, tracing the worn cover with my eyes, knowing this might be the last time I see it. With a hesitant breath, I offer it forward, and it lifts gently from my hands, floating toward Tivren. But a sudden swirl of shadows beside me stills the air, and Soren appears.

The book stops midair, and I glance at Tivren, who struggles to maintain his composure, his powers wavering. Soren raises his hand, and the book flies to him, landing in his palm with a solid thump. He examines the cover as if recognizing a long-lost treasure, then tucks it under his arm.

"I can't allow Kiera to give you this book," he declares, his voice firm, avoiding my gaze. Tivren and Elarion's expressions darken, their frustration mirroring a desire to eject us both.

"Then I suppose we don't have a trade," Elarion says, his tone pinched with annoyance at the near miss of his prize.

"I believe you'll find this to be more than sufficient," Soren counters, lifting his hand. A black-bound book appears before Tivren, suspended in the air. Its cover displays the elegant script of Vethralis.

"I assure you, this holds greater value than the book in hand," Tivren says, peering up at Soren with a raised brow.

"We seem to prioritize different values," Soren replies deeply, and I look at him, perplexed. Why would he prize my father's book above one in his ancient tongue?

We watch in silence as Tivren turns the pages, his lips curling slightly in private satisfaction. Elarion leans forward, his keen interest suggesting secrets within that he's awaited for centuries.

"You will take Kiera to Galehaven," Soren commands, his authority undeniable. Tivren nods once.

"I would be pleased to take her myself," he says, closing the book as it vanishes from sight. I exhale in relief, though Elarion's gaze shifts between us, perhaps suspecting I'd planned this with Soren—a notion far from my intent.

Soren turns to me, his eyes warming with pride as I look at the book under his arm. Then he grins and vanishes as swiftly as he arrived. I adjust my stance, facing Tivren and Elarion, who look at me as if I hold all the secrets in my grasp.

"If I may ask, what was the other book you intended to present?" Tivren inquires, and Elarion's interest mirrors his.

"*Tales of Moonshade*," I say quickly, noting Elarion's glance at Tivren, awaiting his response.

"Ah, yes. Ancient folklore of the Umbral Expanse. A rare copy indeed," Tivren confirms, and I shift my gaze between them.

"Would you have accepted it?" I ask, and Tivren's grin and nod send a leap through my heart, as if my father's book's value validates something deep within me.

"Yes," he says simply. "When would you like to visit Galehaven?"

"Now," I reply, perhaps too eagerly, and he nods deeply.

"As you wish," Tivren says, stepping toward me with fluid grace.

I glance at Elarion, whose annoyance persists, his eyes flickering between mine as if trying to unravel me.

"Why is it so important for you to reach Galehaven? What do you hope to find?" he asks as Tivren offers his arm.

"I don't know," I admit honestly, a grin tugging at my lips as he rolls his eyes and shakes his head while turning to Tivren.

"Make sure she doesn't wander," he instructs, and Tivren nods, extending his arm further.

I take it gently, aware he could lead me anywhere and claim it's Galehaven. Yet, as an elder fae, his demeanor suggests a respect for tradition. A trade honored with integrity.

CHAPTER
THIRTY-FIVE

When we land, I gently remove my hand from Tivren's arm and step aside, the shift in air pressure leaving me momentarily lightheaded. I spin around, taking in my surroundings with a sense of awe that confirms it in my gut—this must be Galehaven.

The island floats like a dream suspended in the heavens, a vast expanse of pristine white stone platforms connected by elegant, arching bridges that seem to defy gravity. Towering spires of crystal rise from the ground, chiming softly in the perpetual breeze, their facets refracting light into rainbows that dance across the misty clouds below. Lush gardens of ethereal flowers sway gently, tended by invisible winds, while ancient shrines dot the landscape. The air here feels crisp and invigorating, carrying a faint scent of ozone, as though a storm has recently passed, renewing the world.

Tivren stands nearby, his hands clasped serenely in front of him, his scholarly gaze following my every move with polite curiosity. I glance at him, and he offers a warm grin, his eyes crinkling at the corners.

Turning my attention outward, I notice the nearest temple in the distance—a grand structure of swirling marble columns that spiral upward, crowned by a dome that shimmers like captured wind.

"This is Galehaven Temple." He confirms, his voice carrying the weight of reverence. I nod, though inwardly I reprimand myself for not asking Soren more about this place beforehand. My knowledge is limited, pieced together from vague whispers and instincts, leaving me feeling exposed and unprepared.

"Is it sacred?" I ask, my curiosity overcoming caution, and his grin widens, a knowing glint in his eyes. I've just exposed my ignorance. No book I claimed to have read would leave such a basic question unanswered.

"Galehaven is the first island Sylthara created," he explains, his tone patient yet profound. "When she first bestowed her powers upon mortals, she forged a sanctuary for those seeking respite from the chaos below. Since then, it has served as a refuge for the lost and those in hiding. We rarely permit visitors, not due to the temple's nature, but because of its significance to those who dwell here. Their peace must be prioritized above all."

"I see," I murmur, glancing around again, the weight of his words settling over me. Sylthara directed me here, so there must be something—or someone—I'm meant to encounter. I just have to trust her guidance. "Would it be okay if I walk the grounds?"

"I can show you around, if you like," he suggests kindly, but I take a deep breath, sensing his duty to accompany me—Elarion's warning against wandering echoes in my mind.

"If you don't mind, I'd prefer to explore alone," I reply, turning to face him fully. "I promise to respect the residents and the temple. And I won't wander far."

"As you wish," he says with surprising ease, his nod gracious. It surprises me. I'd braced for resistance, an insistence on joining me. Does he know something I don't?

"Thank you," I say sincerely, then turn and make my way down the cobblestone path, its stones worn smooth by centuries of footsteps.

The air here seems almost alive, like a gentle caress on my cheek or fingers weaving through my hair. It whispers secrets, alive and attentive, brushing against everything it touches. Yet the island is eerily silent, as if vacant, despite Tivren's assurance of residents. No voices carry on the wind, no distant laughter or footsteps. Only the subtle symphony of the breeze through the crystals.

I reach the first shrine, a modest alcove of polished stone inscribed with elegant script. Leaning in, I read the tale: a chronicle of Sylthara's triumph over the dark wielders at the Battle of Veil's Edge, where she shattered their forces and raised the floating islands to safeguard the fae from advancing shadows. The words resonate, stirring a connection within me.

Then, a spark of inspiration hits. During my water-wielding training, I'd built a mental temple to contain and direct my power. Perhaps I need something similar for air.

Closing my eyes, I envision this temple elevated in my mind, perched high above the chaos of thoughts and emotions, secure in the clouds. I visualize Sylthara in vivid detail—her iridescent white scales shining, bright white eyes piercing, her slender body and limbs poised with ancient grace, wings folded like sails, and long, swirling horns crowning her head.

With a concentrated breath, I direct the harbored air power upward, channeling it into this sanctuary. Instantly, a lightness washes over me, my mind clearer, my body unburdened, as if a weight has lifted.

Encouraged, I continue to the next plaza, an open expanse overlooking a sheer cliff. Approaching the edge, I peer over, greeted by an endless sea of clouds plummeting downward, obscuring whatever lies below. How high are we really? The isolation feels absolute, invisible from the ground—like the Skyward Expanse, perhaps inspired by this very place.

"I sensed your energy as soon as you arrived," a soft female voice says from behind, sending a jolt through me. I whip around, my heart racing. "What are you?"

The fae before me stands tall and lean, her build reminiscent of Zyra's—athletic, brimming with power, as if she could sweep my legs out from under me without warning. Her skin is smooth and tanned, her jet-black hair flowing like midnight shadows, and her eyes blaze with an intense silver glow. I take her in, my eyes widening as realization dawns.

"Are you..." I begin, hesitating, and she tilts her head, her stance a mix of wariness and readiness. "You're... from the Umbral Expanse?" I ask cautiously, avoiding the direct title, and she crosses her arms, her expression hardening.

"Who are you?" she demands, her tone stern, echoing Soren's commanding timbre so strikingly that it disorients me. Could this really be Sonja?

"I'm Kiera," I reply, steadying my voice. "Of Eldwick." The title feels like a shield, the way others introduce me, and her eyes narrow in recognition.

"The mortal in the prophecy?" she asks, and I nod firmly. "I see." She steps closer, each movement graceful and deliberate, like a shadow unfolding. "Why are you here?"

"I… don't know," I admit, echoing the vague explanations I've given others, but instinct insists she's the key. Tivren and Elarion must have anticipated this encounter. "To meet you, I guess."

"Who told you I was here?" Her question sharpens, suspicion lacing her words.

"No one, technically," I say, and she leans against the rail, tilting her head as if weary of my cryptic responses. "I was told to come here. I wasn't told why."

"Did Soren tell you?" she probes, confirming my suspicion, and I shake my head. "Does he know why you're here?" Another shake, and her gaze intensifies.

"He thinks you're dead," I say, the words knotting in my throat, and she nods after a long pause, acceptance settling over her.

"Then it is as it should be."

"How are you alive?" I blurt, unable to contain the question, and she draws in a deep breath, exhaling slowly, her eyes distant.

"It's a long story. And not one I wish to relive," she replies, her voice carrying the weight of buried pain.

"Soren told me what happened to your family," I venture softly, and her curiosity flares. "About what he had to do. He said his— your father—never told him what happened to you. He assumed he killed you when he found your mother."

"He told you that story?" she asks, surprise softening her features as she gazes into the clouds. "My father told me he was sparing me from a life in darkness, and he left me. I was lucky to find my way here. It was not easy."

"Why not return to the Umbral Expanse?" I ask, and she meets my eyes, her expression resolute.

"Because he vowed to kill me if I did." I swallow hard, the twisted horrors of their family beyond my comprehension, layers of pain I may never fully understand.

"And you know what Soren had to do?" I press gently.

"Yes. I'm glad it was him," she says, a quiet resolve in her tone. I nod, leaning against the rail beside her, mirroring her posture as we stare into the abyss of clouds. She glances at me, her silver eyes tracing my form. "If you're mortal, why can I feel power radiating from you?"

"I used to be mortal," I correct, holding out my hands. In one palm, I summon a gust of air; in the other, a swirling ball of water that I freeze into ice. "I'm not anymore."

"How is that possible?" Her brow furrows, genuine intrigue breaking through her guard.

"We all have secrets," I say with a small smile, and her grin mirrors mine, a spark of camaraderie igniting.

"We do," she agrees, shifting her weight. "Will you tell him what you found here?"

"No," I reply without hesitation, shrugging easily. "That's not my secret to share." She scoffs lightly, a sound of surprised approval. "I actually came here hoping to find someone to teach me air wielding, but I'm assuming you wouldn't be an ideal candidate for that."

"No," she confirms, her gaze serious. "And I wouldn't expect anyone at the palace to agree either."

"Yeah, we figured that out pretty quickly," I admit with a defeated sigh, and she rests her chin in her palm, regarding me thoughtfully.

"Given the black attire, I assume you've been staying at the palace with Soren?" she asks, and I nod. "And what do you think of him? Is Soren as serious as he used to be?"

"He's…" I trail off, my mind flooding with images. His intense gaze, the warmth of his lips on mine, the pull of his hands drawing me close. Heat floods my cheeks, and I push the thoughts away. "With everything going on, he has a right to be the way he is."

"I see," she says simply, but her knowing tone implies she senses more than I've disclosed. If she does, why else would fate lead me here? "Are you two not together?" The question catches me off guard, my eyes widening.

"No, we… we're not… anything," I stammer, feeling my face flush. Her sly grin widens, and I lower my head between my arms, huffing in embarrassment.

"Right," she teases, her voice light. "Not anything." She turns back to the view, a contemplative silence settling. "I'm surprised Soren hasn't told you yet," she murmurs, almost to herself, and I glance at her sharply.

"What do you mean?" I ask, curiosity piqued, but she only shrugs.

"It's not my secret to tell," she replies with a mischievous grin, and I roll my eyes, the irony not lost on me. She glances over her shoulder, and I hear approaching footsteps—Tivren, likely ready to escort me back. "I don't suppose you'll return here soon?"

"Probably not," I say, spotting Tivren lingering nearby, close enough to have overheard, his air magic likely carrying our words on the wind. "I don't know why I was told to come here, but I'm glad I met you."

"Likewise," she says politely, stepping forward to wrap me in a brief, unexpected embrace. I return it, the gesture warm and reassuring. "Stay safe," she whispers as she pulls away, her eyes holding mine for a moment longer.

I nod, then make my way to Tivren, my mind swirling with her words. Hasn't told me what? What other secrets is Soren keeping? The questions gnaw at me, adding a new layer of uncertainty amid the revelations.

"Would you like me to take you back to the Umbral Expanse?" Tivren asks, his voice steady and accommodating.

I shake my head, meeting his gaze. "I can manage my way there, thanks."

"It's quite a long distance from here. Allow me to at least take you back to the Aether Palace."

"I'd like to try," I insist, and he nods once more, stepping aside.

Closing my eyes, I concentrate on the place that has become my sanctuary of shadows and solace. My room in the Umbral Expanse. Home. With a surge of will, my body lightens, weightless, and the world shifts around me.

I land exactly where I envisioned, the familiar shadows of my room embracing me. Yet, something feels off—a change in the atmosphere, a scent that lingers, subtle yet unmistakable. My pulse quickens as I glance around swiftly, confirming I'm alone, the silence pressing against me. Then my gaze settles on the desk beneath the tall, arched window, and a flutter of emotion tightens my chest.

There, on the dark wood, sits a marble vase overflowing with fresh flowers, their vibrant petals splashing color against the somber tones. I can only assume they've been gathered from another Dominion, a gift or gesture I hadn't anticipated, their delicate fragrance mingling with the room's altered air.

I approach the desk, my fingers trembling slightly as I reach out to touch one bloom, feeling the soft petals give beneath my touch. A grin spreads across my face despite the turmoil within, a fleeting moment of joy amid the storm. But then, that undeniable pull surges through me—a force I've struggled to suppress. It pulls at my core, an instinct I can no longer deny, rooted deep in the presence that now fills the room.

Turning, I find Soren standing at the foot of my bed, his tall figure outlined by the flickering shadows. His dark eyes sweep over me with a quiet intensity, no doubt searching for any sign of injury or distress from my journey. The weight of his gaze is both protective and probing, stirring a warmth that clashes with the unease twisting in my stomach.

"Did you find what you were looking for?" he asks, his voice low and steady, a rumble that resonates in the quiet space.

"I think so," I reply, my words cautious as I try to avert my eyes, to resist the insistent pull that draws me to him. But it's useless. His presence demands my attention, pulling me in a way I can't escape.

"I wanted to give you this," he says, his tone softening as he steps closer, extending a hand to present the book—my father's book.

I meet him halfway, my steps hesitant yet drawn, taking the book gently from his hands. The weight of it feels both comforting and heavy as I flip through the pages, my fingers tracing the frayed edges and the delicate script, memories of my father's voice flooding back with each turn. My mind races, questions tumbling over one another.

Lifting my gaze to his, I search his eyes for answers, their depths flickering with something unspoken. "Why is this book so valuable to you?" I ask, my voice barely above a whisper, the inquiry laced with a need to understand.

"Because it's important to you," he answers simply, his gaze steady, though I sense layers beneath the surface, a truth he holds back. I glance down at the book, its black binding and silver details a stark contrast to the chaos in my thoughts, the feeling that there's more to his words gnawing at me.

"Is this book from here? The Umbral Expanse?" I press, my curiosity sharpening, and he nods once, a slow, deliberate motion. "Why did he have it?" My voice drops to a hushed tone, almost afraid of the answer. "How did he get it?"

"You may not accept the truth," he says in a low, cautious tone, his eyes locking with mine as if gauging my readiness. I stare back, unflinching, waiting for the revelation. "I gave it to him," he confesses, and the air rushes from my lungs, my mind fizzing with disbelief, a thousand thoughts colliding at once.

"Time moves differently for fae. We live for centuries while mortals span mere decades. We've known you were the chosen one in the prophecy since you were a child, and we've done what we could to protect you and your family." The explanation unfolds like a tapestry unraveling, each word a blow to my understanding, and I stumble back a step, my balance faltering under the weight. "There were no stories of magic in Eldwick, and I wanted to ensure you were familiar with our world, with what lay beyond. To plant seeds of possibility, dreams of something more."

"Stop," I gasp, stepping away, pressing my hands to my eyes as the world tilts beneath me, the room spinning with the implications. The idea that they've watched me, shaped my life from the shadows, feels like a betrayal of everything I thought I knew.

"I should have told you sooner," he says gently, his voice soft amid my turmoil, but I shake my head, the revelations crashing over me like relentless waves, each one eroding my sense of self.

"Did he know?" I demand, my voice trembling with a mix of anger and desperation.

"No," Soren replies, his tone steady but laced with regret. "I left it where he would find it. I didn't know if he would read the stories to you, but I hoped he would."

"My father saw fae and creatures in the forest. And they called him mad," I whisper, the pieces of my childhood suddenly falling into place.

"I'm sorry he was caught in that." Soren explains, his voice heavy with sincerity. "They were there to protect you, to shield you from threats we couldn't fully control." The admission lingers between us, a bitter truth, and I shake my head, unable to process the depth of their interference. With a surge of frustration, I toss the book onto the bed, the thud echoing in the silence like a final punctuation.

"Get out," I command, my tone stern and resolute, a wall rising between us. He narrows his eyes, concern etching deep lines into his features, a silent plea for understanding. "Get out of my room," I repeat, my voice breaking with the weight of it all. He nods, bowing slightly before vanishing in a swirl of smoke, leaving the room eerily still.

"*This can't be happening,*" I mutter to myself, my footsteps echoing as I pace the room.

They have known who I am since I was a child—watched me grow, shaped my destiny, and waited until the last moment, until I was captured by Tormen, to pull me into this world. I've been tied to magic before I even understood its existence, my life a thread in a tapestry woven by others. And now, I'm expected to magically hold the world together, to prevent Aelthar from crumbling into chaos?

The weight of that responsibility crashes down, a suffocating burden leaving me reeling in the dim light, the flowers on my desk a harsh reminder of the beauty and deception woven into this new reality.

CHAPTER
THIRTY-SIX

I stand at the edge of the palace's highest terrace, my gaze drifting out over the sprawling forest beyond, its canopy a sea of silver and shadowy hollows stretching toward the horizon. The cool evening breeze brushes against my skin, and I draw in a deep, steadying breath, letting it fill my lungs as if it might give me a sense of clarity.

Since Soren abruptly left me here atop the palace, this secluded spot has become my sanctuary. The isolation suits me; no one stumbles upon me by chance, but I've made it clear that if I'm needed, they're welcome to star-drift up, a rare compromise to practicality amid my need for solitude. The terrace, with its weathered stone balustrade and the faint hum of magic woven into the air, feels like a world apart, a place where I can think without the weight of others' expectations pressing down.

Several days have passed since my journey to Galehaven, and the echoes of that experience linger, unresolved. I returned to the Skyward Expanse, hoping to summon Sylthara for guidance—perhaps to uncover what I'd missed or determine my next step toward finding a trainer. But she remained elusive, her presence absent despite my pleas.

Lyrisene, always the loyal companion, found me by the lake's edge, her gentle presence soothing as I wrestled with my thoughts. We sat together, the water gently lapping at the shore, but even her presence couldn't unravel the chaos in my mind. Everything feels broken—Rory knows I'm alive, a secret I've reclaimed in Eldwick; Elarion acknowledges my air-wielding potential yet refuses to assist me; Soren's sister Sonja is alive, her role in my path a mystery I can't yet fathom; and Soren himself... we've barely spoken since the revelation that he's been part of my life far longer than I'd imagined.

The thought of my father gnaws at me. Soren saw him and interacted with him, and this realm, with its hidden machinations, is why he was labeled mad, perhaps even the cause of his disappearance.

Deep down, I'd always held a suspicion, a quiet intuition that something beyond Eldwick had contributed to his unraveling. But hearing it from Soren's lips, his voice, steady yet laced with regret, hurt more than I'd expected. The betrayal stings, not only for the secrecy, but for the years I believed my father's decline was his alone. Can I forgive that? Should I even try? The questions swirl, unanswered, as I lean against the railing, the forest's silence contrasting the turmoil within.

"Hey, Kiera." A soft voice breaks through my reverie, and I turn slightly to see Zyra approaching with measured steps. "Can we talk?"

"Sure," I reply, my tone neutral as she sits beside me, crossing her legs and gazing out at the view. A comfortable silence stretches between us, though I sense her hesitation, as if she's carefully weighing her words.

"Soren's been a pain, I hope you realize," she says at last, her voice carrying a mix of exasperation and fondness. "He doesn't know what to do. Rennor and I don't know what to tell him. I don't even think I fully understand what's going on. Soren can't talk straight anymore, he's so tangled up."

"Then don't worry about it," I say flatly, feeling her eyes roam over me, assessing my demeanor. The weight of her concern is palpable, but I keep my gaze fixed on the horizon, unwilling to delve into the mess of emotions tied to him.

"I am, though," she counters gently. "I care about you, and I care about Soren. And I hate seeing you two so awkward all the time. It's like watching a storm brew and not knowing when it'll break."

Her words stir a pang in my chest. I hate that just as something seemed to spark between us, his revelation shattered it, leaving my feelings a tangled knot.

"I just need time to think about it," I admit, and she nods, her expression softening with understanding. "It's hard to wrap my mind around what this has been like for you all, and what it's been like for me," I continue, my voice quiet but firm. "I've existed in your world a lot longer than you've existed in mine. I'm still learning how to separate everything—the past from the present, my old life from this one."

"I get that," she replies quickly, her eyes flickering as she decides how much more to share. "I think it's challenging for us

287

sometimes to step into your shoes. Our history, all this chaos with the rifts and the prophecy, the secrets we carry. Most of it we've known for years, some for centuries. You've lived twenty-three years, mature for only five. Twenty years to us is a mere blink. We often assume there's only so much you can manage at once, so we end up leaving out details. Our world thrives on information and secrets—it's how we function, how we endure."

"Sometimes I feel like you're not trying to help at all," I confess, the frustration spilling out, and she grimaces, her discomfort evident. "It seems like everything I've learned, you've only revealed after I've discovered it myself—through someone else or some other means."

"I'm sorry..." she says, her voice fading with genuine remorse, and I lower my head, closing my eyes. Her explanation makes sense. The flood of revelations over these months would have overwhelmed me if presented all at once. It probably wouldn't have made sense without context. But the matter with my father— that's a wound between Soren and me, a personal betrayal I have to navigate alone.

"He cares about you, you know," she adds softly, her words piercing the quiet. "And I can tell you do too."

My heart aches at the truth in her words. In my chest, I yearn for the feel of his hand on my cheek, the warmth of his body beside mine. Yet, the shadow of his withheld truths, the time he waited to speak, and the potential secrets still buried, clamp down on that desire, leaving my mind a battlefield of doubt and want.

"But suppose things don't go as planned with the rifts and the prophecy," she continues, her tone shifting to a somber note. "There's a possibility we might not survive."

"Don't talk like that," I interject, my voice sharp with denial, unwilling to entertain the thought.

"It's true, though. And you know it," she insists, meeting my gaze with steady eyes. "You were once mortal. You're likely more accustomed to the idea of a short life, but for us… it's not something we dwell upon. Death arrives only unexpectedly, a rare end unless someone forces it upon us." Her viewpoint alters my understanding—where I've always lived under mortality's shadow, they live in a realm where time stretches endlessly until it's cut short.

"No one is going to die," I assert, clinging to hope.

"But if we do…" she begins, her eyes searching mine, "wouldn't you want Soren to know how you feel?" Her words strike like a dagger, lodging deep in my heart, forcing me to confront the unspoken.

I turn my gaze back to the forest, the Duskwing's final mourning prayer echoing in my memory—*soul-bound is when two souls are intertwined, two halves of a whole, one cannot exist without the other*. Soren had spoken those words back then, a poetic aside I'd dismissed as mere ritual. Now, they carry a deeper meaning.

"Are we—?" I start, the question trembling on my lips, but a deafening crack jolts the palace, cutting me off.

Zyra and I leap to our feet, rushing to the opposite side of the ledge. Below, near the front entrance, a male figure stands with his hands raised in surrender, surrounded by shadow-wrought guards, their black swords gleaming with dark energy pointed at him.

"Lord Soren!" he shouts, his voice carrying urgency.

Zyra and I exchange a glance, then star-drift to the entry hall in a flash. As we arrive, Soren materializes in a swirl of dark shadows, the front doors bursting open with a force that rattles the frame. He strides out with deceptive calm, but the stiffness in his shoulders and tension in his stance reveal a rage simmering beneath.

"Who are you, and what do you want?" he growls, his voice a deep, resonant threat.

"My name is Rhaevor," the fae replies, his tone steady despite the danger. "I have been sent from the Aether Dominion." Zyra and I step toward the doors, but Rennor appears at my side, raising a hand to stop us, his expression wary.

"Who sent you?" Soren demands, his voice cutting through the air like a blade. Rhaevor's eyes shift past him, a bold move, landing on me. He's tall, with shaggy blond hair and bright blue eyes that suggest origins in the Cerulean Dominion, not the Aether.

"Someone from Galehaven," he says, and my eyes widen in recognition. Rennor grunts as I push his hand aside, descending the front stairs with quick, determined steps.

"I need a name," Soren insists, his authority unwavering, and I position myself just behind him, respecting his lead while staying close.

"Why are you here?" I ask, striving to match Soren's commanding tone, though I know my voice lacks the same weight.

"To train you in air wielding," Rhaevor answers calmly, his gaze steady, and my eyes narrow with cautious hope.

I glance sideways at Soren, shadows still flaring wildly from his form, a visual reflection of his inner turmoil. I know there's no way to explain this without revealing Sonja's survival. He'll have to endure the uncertainty, at least for now.

"Do you know this person well?" I inquire, carefully choosing each word to avoid slipping, and he nods affirmatively. "Then tell me something about them," I press, testing his sincerity.

"This person does hope to see their family again someday," he says after a pause, his voice carrying a genuine weight. The sentiment strikes a chord, though it could apply to anyone or be fabricated to sway me. Yet the sincerity in his tone convinces me he speaks the truth.

"When can you start?" I ask, stepping forward slightly, and Soren moves with a long, deliberate stride, turning to face me. His eyes swirl with silver, a telltale sign of his rising temper, but the look he gives me is soft, almost tender, a contrast that tugs at my heart.

"What makes you think you can trust him?" he asks sharply, his voice a challenge, but I meet his gaze, feeling the familiar pull between us—a connection muffled by the chaos but ever-present.

"Because I can," I tell him, holding his stare until he yields, stepping aside to confront Rhaevor again.

"If you betray us, I will kill you so fast, you won't even realize you're in the Abyssra," Soren warns, his tone laced with a lethal promise that even I feel in my bones.

"I would face the same fate returning to Galehaven if I fail to convince you." Rhaevor counters, and I stifle a scoff, struck by the similarity between him and Sonja. Perhaps they share more than blood, a resilience born of their shared history.

"Would you like to take a walk?" I offer, and he glances between us skeptically before nodding.

I look up at Soren, who extends his hand in a gesture of reluctant permission. With a slight nod, I descend the remaining stairs, holding my hand toward the front gates. Rhaevor follows closely, his footsteps light but deliberate, and I notice him glancing back at the palace, assessing its towering spires and shadowed depths before exhaling deeply to match my stride.

I don't know his tie to Sonja, but her influence has clearly compelled him to risk his life, coming here to teach me air-wielding. A chance I can't afford to waste, despite the uncertainties that linger like shadows at my back.

CHAPTER
THIRTY-SEVEN

As Rhaevor and I step into the training ring, he pauses, his gaze sweeping the surroundings with a cautious edge. "Is it safe to speak here?" His voice carries a hint of uncertainty, prompting a scoff from me as I adjust to the familiar weight of the training ground.

"I guarantee nowhere is safe for you to talk while you're here," I reply, my tone laced with a wry edge. The ever-present threat of eavesdropping fae or lurking shadows keeps me guarded. "I'd suggest we avoid mentioning our mutual friend unless you want something to slip."

"I agree," he says with a nod, exhaling deeply as if releasing a burden. We settle onto the ground, crossing our legs in unison, the polished surface grounding us beneath the open sky. "How long have you been able to wield air?" he inquires, his bright blue eyes studying me with quiet interest.

"A week and a half," I answer, reflecting on the brief span since my powers awakened. "I've been adapting exercises I learned from water wielding, but I haven't fully grasped the extent of this power yet. I've been hesitant to test it."

He nods thoughtfully, his hands turning upward on his knees in a gesture of readiness, then tilts his head toward me in invitation.

"We'll start with a breathing exercise," he suggests, his voice calm and measured. I mirror his posture, closing my eyes as he does, the world narrowing to the rhythm of my breath. "Water and air share similarities but diverge in significant ways. Water carries weight—you can mold it into liquid, solid, or gas, shaping it with intent. Air, however, is light, flowing freely, resistant to manipulation in form. It exists as it is, so you must learn to harness it in its natural state. Yet, just as you've used water to move a tree, a boulder, or even your own body, air can achieve the same with enough power.

"Now, focus on your breathing," he continues, his tone guiding me inward. "Inhale and exhale slowly, finding the rhythm of your heartbeat. Everything must be in balance." I follow his instructions, drawing a deep breath, but the moment I try to clear my mind, a flood of thoughts crashes in—Soren's secrets, my father's fate, the prophecy's weight. My concentration wavers, and frustration wells up.

"I can feel your anxious energy," Rhaevor observes, and I let out a sharp breath, shaking out my arms to release the tension. Resting my hands back on my knees, I attempt to restart. "If a thought arises, simply send it away," he advises gently.

"Send it away..." I mutter, the phrase sounding deceptively simple.

Shaking my head lightly, I acknowledge the challenge—far easier said than done. Yet, one by one, I push the thoughts aside, visualizing the temple I crafted in my mind to house my air magic. I allow the energy to vibrate there, a sanctuary above the chaos, and as my mind clears, a surprising peace settles over me. I don't fully understand why this matters to air wielding, but it feels like a release I've craved for far too long.

"Now," Rhaevor says softly, his voice pulling me back, and I focus intently, steadying my breath in anticipation. "Direct your energy to your hands, only your hands, and create a sphere of air. Much like you would a ball of water."

I concentrate, channeling the tingling sensations coursing through me toward my palms. I picture a ball of water first, then imagine air taking shape, but nothing materializes. Instead, I sense Rhaevor's gaze boring into me, his bright blue eyes a persistent presence. Frustration builds, and my eyes snap open to meet his.

"Wait a minute," I blurt. "Your eyes are blue."

"I hadn't noticed," he replies with a hint of mockery, and I roll my eyes slightly, the tension easing into amusement.

"Air wielders from the Aether Dominion don't have blue eyes. Can you actually wield air?" I challenge, skepticism sharpening my tone. In an instant, a burst of air whips from his hand, forming a long, fluid tendril. Then, from his other hand, a steady stream of water flows, and my breath catches. He's mixed-blood, a duality mirroring my own.

"You can wield both," I say, my eyes widening as he disperses his powers with a flick of his wrists. "Just like me." A smile spreads across my face, unbidden and bright, a shared connection igniting hope.

"I don't wield either very often," he admits, his voice steady.

"But I know enough to teach you what you need. Now, make a sphere of air," he commands, and I lay my hands face-up, focusing my energy. Without overthinking, a sphere of air forms, shimmering faintly between my palms.

"I can tell you have a lot of mental blocks," he observes, his tone pragmatic. "You'll need to meditate, focus on your breathing and mental discipline, before you master air wielding." My shoulders slump slightly, the task feeling overwhelming.

"Are you a master?" I ask, curiosity piqued.

"I was once," he replies cryptically, and my eyes narrow. Who is this fae? What's his history, his ties to Sonja, or his role at Galehaven? The questions pile up, unanswered. "Does your mind always race so intensely?" he probes, and a faint smile tugs at my lips.

"Yes," I admit, a reluctant chuckle escaping me.

"What could you possibly be worried about?" he asks, and I stare at him, processing the question. Then I scoff, shaking my head at the absurdity. Where do I even begin?

"How often can you come here for training?" I redirect, steering us back to practicalities.

"Two, maybe three times a week," he answers. "But I can give you exercises to work on as you progress. I heard you picked up water wielding easily. I have no doubt you'll do the same with air, given their similarities." I glance toward the forest, its dense canopy a reminder of my roots.

"Where I'm from, I spent a lot of time by the sea," I explain, meeting his gaze. "I could read the sky like a book—predicting storms, gauging waves. Learning the push and pull of water came naturally. But air feels so distant. I don't know what to secure it to, where to draw that power from."

"When the sea is calm, what is the wind like?" he counters, his voice encouraging. "When a storm brews, how does the air feel? Before rain, does it grow lighter or heavier? It's all the same, just a different perspective." His words sink in, the parallels falling into place, though the sensation remains distinct. "Air isn't primarily an attack like the other elements. It excels in defense, speed, and motion."

"Can I learn to fly? Do fae do that?" I ask, a spark of excitement lighting my voice.

"I wouldn't call it flying, but you can propel yourself with air," he clarifies. "Similar to how you might with water. We can practice that once you master the basics. These trees will be perfect for it."

"The basics," I mutter to myself, leaning back on my hands to stare at the sky, its expanse a mirror to my uncertainties. Perhaps I overestimated my skill after water. "Isn't there a way we can learn it all a bit quicker?"

"In a rush?" he asks, a teasing lilt in his voice, and I sigh deeply. "How about a quick test to see what you can do?"

"Right now?" I ask, and when he nods, I push myself to my feet and he follows suit.

"Right. Form a shield," he instructs, and my jaw clenches. I'd hoped for a simpler start, but perhaps that's his intent—to emphasize my need for fundamentals. "Create a steady flow of air and move it back and forth, similar to how you would with water."

I focus on my hands, isolating the air magic within, then widen my stance. Recalling the fluid motions from the Cerulean Legion's Lirivox Ritual, I figure if it works with water, it should with air. A stream of air forms between my palms, and I guide it through the ritual's steps, ending in the final pose with bated breath.

Expecting critique, I wait, but Rhaevor stares, his eyes alight with an intensity I haven't seen. "Where did you learn the Lirivox Ritual?" he asks curiously, and I shrug.

"I trained with the Cerulean Legion for a day," I reply, skimming over the second day's chaos with Tormen. "I practice it every morning and evening."

"Really?" he says, surprised, and I shrug again. "Maybe try it with air for one session a day."

"That's easy," I say, awaiting further direction, but he only watches me. "Why are you so surprised I can do it?"

"Make a shield," he redirects, and my eyes narrow.

"I don't know how to make a shield," I admit, frustration seeping in.

"Just because you've never done it, doesn't mean you don't know how," he counters. "Put your hand out, imagine any shape you want, and fill it with air. Weave the air together like a knit, pulling it tight to hold firm."

Weave it together... that concept clicks. I extend my hand, picturing the round flag of Eldwick—tattered yet familiar from post-storm repairs. I shape the air into its form, weaving the currents together to mend and strengthen it, drawing more energy from my mental temple with a deep breath.

"Good. Now move it around, keep it close," he instructs. "Imagine a creature before you—it must be strong enough to hold it back." I perform the Lirivox steps, focusing on the shield's thickness, and as I turn, something strikes it. I jolt back, the shield dissipating, revealing Rhaevor with an ice sword similar to mine against Tormen.

"Make a shield," he commands, and I conjure one instinctively as he lunges. It holds, but my powers tremble under the strain. "Weave it together."

He swings repeatedly, each strike testing my resolve, and I resist the urge to counterattack, focusing on defense. If I can't protect myself, what use is any of this? The pressure builds, my arms trembling as I channel more energy, and on his next swing, I push his sword upward. It flies free, shattering on the ground, and I lean forward, hands on my knees, gasping.

"Create a dome of air around us," he says, and I shake my head, exhaustion weighing me down.

"I can't," I mutter, lifting my gaze to meet his.

"If that's all the stamina you have, then I don't want to waste my time," he says, his words igniting a sudden surge of rage. I stand, throwing my arms out, forming a small dome that swirls around us, reminiscent of Soren's dark magic but white. I expand it to the ring's edges, accelerating the air into sea-like waves.

"Stunning," Rhaevor says, and as my attention wavers, the images persist. "I wouldn't doubt your strength."

"I don't even know what I'm doing most of the time," I admit, lowering my hands, the air calming. In the palace doorway, Soren leans against the marble archway, arms crossed, watching.

"I'll show you what to practice while I'm away," Rhaevor says. "When I return, I expect you to demonstrate everything you've figured out on your own." I grin widely, a flicker of pride warming me.

I don't know Rhaevor's full story, but his presence feels significant, perhaps more than anyone here realizes.

CHAPTER THIRTY-EIGHT

The morning unfolds with an unusual calm, the air within the Umbral Expanse carrying a gentle hush as I train alone in the lower courtyard. The upper levels of the palace hum with the muffled voices of a meeting I'm excluded from, its purpose a mystery I'm too drained to unravel. The rhythmic swish of my practice sword against the air fills the silence, a solitary dance preventing my mind from wandering too deeply into the chaos of recent days.

Rhaevor has visited twice more this week, his lessons building on the basics—crafting objects, shaping gusts of wind in varying speeds and sizes, refining my control. Each morning, I pair our breathing techniques with the Lirivox Ritual, alternating between water and air, a ritual that clears my mind and sharpens my wielding. The progress is evident. I cast faster, with greater precision, but an invisible barrier remains, a mental fog I can't clear. I know it stems from unresolved tension, a knot tied to Soren that won't loosen until I confront it.

As I finish my session and move through the palace, I catch sight of Rennor standing with two senior fae near the grand hall. His sharp glance flicks toward me as he senses my approach, his posture stiff with the weight of their discussion.

"Is your meeting finished?" I ask, my voice carrying a hint of curiosity as I approach, and he nods. "Do you know where Soren is?" I press, a hint of urgency threading my words.

"I'm not sure you should disturb him right now," Rennor replies, his tone cautious, and I press my lips together, sensing the undercurrent of warning.

"It's kind of important," I insist, and from down the hall, I hear his deep intake of breath, a sign of his reluctance.

"He's in the training ring. He's not in a good mood," he adds, and I nod slowly, retreating down the corridor. The training ring— where I was moments ago?

"Thanks," I murmur as I turn, my footsteps shuffling against the stone floor, a nervous rhythm to match my racing thoughts. I've longed to speak with Soren, to clear the stifling air between us, to hear his perspective about the book—on my father. Yet, every attempt has been blocked by pressing duties or the presence of others. Now might not be ideal with his temper flaring, but I can't progress with my wielding while he dominates my mind.

As I turn down the hall towards the training ring, a palpable energy fills the space—Soren's essence, raw and turbulent. I wonder what occurred in that meeting to drive him here, whether he needs to vent steam or if something darker fuels his agitation.

Pausing at the doorway, I freeze, my breath catching. Soren

stands shirtless in the center of the ring, his skin glistening with sweat, muscles flexing as he swings his sword in a steady, graceful arc across the floor. His movements are a symphony of ease and power, a beauty I doubt I'll ever replicate no matter how long I train. Smoke swirls around him, flaring into a thin haze that struggles to keep pace with his relentless speed.

"Did you need something?" he asks. His voice breathless yet sharp, pausing mid-swing to face me. My heart pounds as I shrug, words failing me under the intensity of his gaze. He flips the sword in his hand with casual mastery, pacing to the far end of the ring, then back, resuming his routine with a focused intensity.

I watch him closely, noting the fluidity of his arms, the steady legs, the stern set of his face as if envisioning foes to defeat. Usually, he's the one watching my training, so I feel no guilt in studying him now, each motion a lesson in itself.

"How does the bird thing work?" I ask, breaking the silence, and he turns smoothly, tilting his head with curiosity. "You said you watch me with it. Are you the bird? Or are you just using it?"

"I enter its mind to see what it sees," he explains as he steps closer, then rests his hands over the sword's pommel, the point grounded.

"So every time I saw it in Eldwick, it was really you?" I ask, and after a pause, he nods. "Hmm," I muse, glancing past him towards the trees, realizing every chirp or tilt of its head was him listening—responding. "Were you using the beast in the same way? The one that rescued me from Tormen's cell?"

"No," he says simply, his lips pressing together tightly, a barrier to further revelation. "That's a tale for another time." I sense I could argue and perhaps pry it loose, but my mind shifts to a deeper concern.

"Were you one of the faeries my father saw in the forest?" I ask, my voice softening, and he nods again, his expression somber. "Why were you there?"

"Some of the Elite were heading to Eldwick to retrieve you," he reveals, and I breathe quietly, imagining the life I might have led if taken at thirteen—stolen from my family, my world turned upside down. I wasn't prepared when I was brought here a few months ago, I certainly wouldn't have been prepared back then.

"Do you think he knew?" I venture, my heart tightening.

"Who I was?" he clarifies, and I nod. "No. He had a feeling they were after something. He thought it might be the book he found, so he fought with us, unknowingly protecting you." His words hang heavy, and I keep my eyes on the distant trees, processing the irony.

"How did you know he thought they were looking for something?" I press, and he draws a deep breath, letting it out audibly. "Did you read his mind?"

"I was trying to convince him to go back," he admits, "but his thoughts overwhelmed mine. He had a strong mind, just like you." Meeting his gaze with newfound caution, I probe further.

"Have you gone into my mind?" I ask, crossing a line I've guarded to shield myself from too much truth.

"Many times," he confesses, "but only to see if you would let me in." My eyes narrow, a mix of betrayal and curiosity flaring.

"What do you mean?" I demand.

"I can't get through the shields you keep around your mind," he explains, and I shake my head, baffled. Shields? I've built temples for water and air, but this is new.

"I didn't realize I was doing that," I murmur, and he spins the sword under his hands, a thoughtful gesture. "I don't know if I'd want you to read my mind anyway," I add, and he grins, a flicker of warmth breaking through.

"It could be more than that," he says, pausing to elaborate. "If I tried now, I couldn't breach it. But if you lower your guard and project a memory or thought toward me, I can read it. You can shield specific things you don't want seen, locking them away."

"But it seems like you can read minds easily," I counter, recalling the legion fae. "Those two from the Legion—it looked like they were being tortured."

"Ah, yes," he says casually, as if it's a simple trick. "A mind trick to make them believe they are being tortured when they are not." My eyes widen, the casual brutality startling. "It takes years to master mind work, to craft a shield strong enough to block someone like me. Dividing your mind is complex, requiring centuries of training. I wouldn't be surprised if you mastered it sooner."

"Can everyone read minds?" I ask, intrigued.

"Yes and no," he replies, tilting his head. "It's a rare talent to read minds freely. But if you're soul-bound, you and your other half can communicate directly through the mind." His mention of soul-bound sends a flutter through my chest, a question I nearly asked Zyra, but hesitate to voice to him directly.

"I see..." I say softly, clearing my throat as his gaze lingers, glinting in the dull light, a grin tugging at his lips.

"Any more questions?" he asks, and I shake my head quickly, my mind too muddled to pursue further.

"You can go back to your sword if you want," I offer, and he shifts, returning to the ring's center.

He resumes his practice, though his movements lack their earlier fluidity, as if his mind wars with his body's instincts. Part of me clings to my grudge, craving more truth, but a deeper truth—my buried feelings for him—grows tired of suppression.

Glancing at my hand, I envelope it in air, sending a low disc skimming toward him. It hovers under his foot, and as he steps, he nearly slips, losing balance. I stifle a laugh, ducking my head to hide it. Soren, always so poised, stumbling is a rare sight.

Feeling his stare, I glance up as he resumes, but on his next pass, his eyes narrow suspiciously. I offer a coy grin, then whip air to pull his arm back. He spins around with a swiftness that catches the light, his eyes blazing with a mix of frustrated annoyance and restrained fury, yet all I can muster is a wide, unrepentant grin. The air between us crackles with tension.

"I just wanted to try something out," I say, my voice laced with mischief, and without a moment's hesitation, he tosses his sword aside with a clatter that echoes off the stone floor, the blade skidding to the training ring's edge.

"Let's see what you got then," he challenges, his arms spreading wide as he unleashes his shadows fully. The ground trembles as long, sinuous tentacles of darkness erupt, coiling and unfurling to blanket the entire area in an inky shroud.

I step into the ring, my grin unwavering, a thrill coursing through me as I sense this might be the release we both need to purge the strange, electric energy simmering between us. With a determined breath, I unleash a wide blast of air, sweeping the ground clear around me, then whip a stream of water toward him, the liquid arcing like a serpent in the dim light.

He dodges effortlessly, his movements a blur as he counters, sending his shadows spiraling outward in all directions. They strike at me from odd angles testing my reflexes. I deflect most with quick, precise bursts of air, the gusts keeping the tendrils at bay, but one slithers through the mist at my feet, wrapping around my ankle with a cool, firm grip. It tugs gently, pulling me toward him, and I grit my teeth, forcing a wedge of air between my leg and the shadow, sending it outward with a sharp push to break free.

Undeterred, I retaliate with a surging wave of water, the liquid crashing toward him like a tidal force. He reacts instantly, conjuring a dome of darkness over himself, the shadows solidifying into a protective barrier.

I adapt, spinning a water wheel that freezes mid-air, its edges sharpening into shards of ice that spray outward in a glittering arc. The ice shards clink against his dome, but he counters with an explosion of darkness, the force radiating outward to shatter my assault. I raise an air shield just in time, the translucent barrier shimmering as it absorbs the impact, the air vibrating with the clash of our powers.

Our eyes lock across the ring, a brief pause in the chaos—his gaze dark and daring, a challenge etched into every line of his face, while mine burns with defiance.

Then, without warning, he strikes. Shadows coil around my waist, yanking me toward him with a speed that leaves me breathless. I stumble forward, my hands pressing against his chest to halt my momentum, his heart pounding rapidly beneath my palms, his breath warm against my face.

"That's a cheap trick," I murmur, my voice catching in my throat as I channel a sharp gust of air to push back.

The wind ruffles his hair, tousling the dark strands, and he grins, a flash of amusement in his eyes, though he releases me only long enough to launch another attack. I feel his shadows slither up my legs, slow and deliberate, a sensation that's both thrilling and unsettling.

Seizing the moment, I retaliate with a water vortex, the swirling column rising around us, droplets catching the light like tiny stars against the shadowed ring. The shadows weave through the water, a dark dance against my fluid grace, and we're locked in a mesmerizing battle of elements. He pulls me back toward him with his shadows, and this time, I let my hands grip his side and pull him towards me. His breath catches in a gasp, the sound edged with something deeper and I seize the advantage.

"Distracted?" I ask, a wicked grin spreading across my face as I freeze the water I've cast over his feet and ankles, the ice locking him in place. I pull away, leaving him momentarily immobilized, his eyes narrowing as he assesses his predicament.

He glances down at his feet, then, with a swift motion, directs his hands toward me. Shadows lash out, wrapping around my ankles in retaliation, and with a sharp tug, my feet fly out from under me. I land on my back with a short, surprised laugh, the impact softened by his own shadows.

Above me, a spear of shadows forms, descending with lethal intent, and I roll to the side, narrowly avoiding the strike. Scrambling to my feet, I send a series of rapid air bursts toward him, the gusts throwing him off balance, his steps faltering as he struggles to regain his footing.

Undaunted, he unleashes a tidal wave of shadows, the dark mass rolling toward me like a storm surge. I rise, planting my feet firmly, and counter with a towering wall of water. The collision sends a thick mist billowing outward, enveloping us both, the air heavy with moisture as our breaths come in ragged gasps, charged with the intensity of the moment.

Soren closes the distance, his hand rising to brush the wet strands of hair from my face, his touch lingering as the shadows retreat, dissolving into the mist.

"You fight dirty," he whispers, his lips so close I feel the warmth of his breath. I smirk, letting my fingers trace the line of his jaw in a slow, deliberate movement, savoring the roughness of his stubble.

"Only to keep up with you," I reply, my heart pounding as water drips from us, pooling at our feet, a testament to the battle we've fought.

He leans closer, the shadows flickering like a heartbeat, their retreat signaling a shift in the energy between us. The ring falls silent, the mist settling like a veil, and we stand chest to chest, the air electric with a playful yet profound desire that lingers unspoken.

"Call it a draw?" he suggests, his voice husky, his hand resting lightly on my waist.

"Only if you admit I was winning," I counter, leaning in just enough to feel his chest against mine. "I thought you had meetings all day," I add, a teasing note in my voice as I look down at his lips.

"I do," he says, shifting back to create a subtle space between us, though his eyes remain fixed on mine. "But you are more important than anything else I had planned today." His admission sends a warmth through me, and I grin.

I focus on the water cascading down our bodies, then draw it outward with a gentle pull to leave us dry, the droplets evaporating into the air.

"May I say something?" he asks softly, his tone hesitant, almost vulnerable, and despite the nerves fluttering in my chest, I nod, eager yet apprehensive. "I wanted to tell you all this. I know I should have done so sooner. But I knew when I did, you would likely hate me for it. I was being selfish."

"I don't hate you," I say without hesitation, my voice firm yet gentle, and his gaze softens, a flicker of relief crossing his features. "My whole life, I thought I knew who I was. I thought I knew what happened to my father. Then I come here, and little pieces of my past keep unraveling... but I understand why you did it." The words feel like a release, a bridge mending the gap between us.

"I'm sorry you and your family had to endure suffering because of me," he murmurs, his voice thick with regret. "I didn't intend for that to happen."

"It is as fate decided," I reply, recalling the phrase echoed through my journey, and he grins, leaning into the hand I raise to his face, his cheek warm against my palm.

If my father hadn't faltered, if we hadn't been cast aside, I might not be the person I am today. Perhaps this is exactly who I need to be, and where I need to be, standing here with him, the future unfolding in the quiet aftermath of our clash.

CHAPTER THIRTY-NINE

Emerging from my bath chambers, the delicate silk of my nightgown caresses my skin, a soothing contrast to the emotional tempest stirred by my earlier encounter with Soren in the training ring. Since our spar this afternoon, I've sought refuge in ceaseless activity to quiet my racing mind.

Dinner with Zyra stretched into the evening, her lively recounting of their unending meetings a fleeting distraction, though my thoughts wandered to Soren with every pause in her chatter. Later, I retreated to the library, the open books before me a mere prop as I stared blankly, the words blurring into an incomprehensible haze.

In the heat of our fight, as the air thrummed with tension and our bodies gravitated closer, I'd been convinced he might bridge the gap with a kiss. My body ached with a longing so potent it bordered on pain. Yet, he withdrew, leaving me with a playful wink before disappearing into the palace, casting me into a limbo of unfulfilled anticipation.

I'd hoped our shared conversation, the intimacy of our nearness, might herald a deeper connection, but perhaps I should have voiced my forgiveness more explicitly. A missed opportunity that now gnaws at me with regret.

With a subtle flex of my power, I draw the moisture from my hair, watching it rise in a shimmering cascade before releasing it into the air, then glide a comb through the strands, letting them fall in soft waves down my back. I drift toward my bed, lying flat with arms outstretched, my gaze lifting to the ceiling where tiny crystals gleam like captured stars, casting a faint, ethereal glow.

A grunt escapes me as I pull a pillow over my face, exhaling a heavy breath laden with frustration. Maybe we're not soul-bound, I ponder, the thought a quiet ache. Perhaps this magnetic pull toward Soren is a mirage born of my own yearning, a projection of emotions I've harbored in secret for too long.

A faint knock at my door startles me upright, the pillow slipping to the floor. Tension coils in my frame as I summon a flicker of power, a cautious shield against the unknown, but the familiar ache in my stomach softens my guard. A second, slightly louder knock urges me to slide my feet to the cool stone floor, and I hasten to the door, pulling it open with a surge of anticipation.

Soren stands before me, his presence a commanding force despite the disarray of his appearance. His eyes blaze with an intensity that sets my heart racing, his jaw tight and fists clenched at his sides, a storm brewing beneath his surface. Damp hair clings to his forehead, framing eyes that seem to pierce my very soul, while his crumpled tunic hangs loosely, as if hastily thrown on with little regard for its state. The scent of mint and spice envelops me, igniting a longing I can no longer suppress, my heart pounding against my ribcage as if desperate to break free.

I step aside, closing the door with a soft click behind him, and turn to find him standing in the room's center, his gaze sweeping over me with a hunger that mirrors the fire within. Words elude me, trapped in my throat as I close the distance, my hand trembling as I rest it against his chest.

The warmth of him seeps through the fabric, a beacon in the dim light, and in an instant, he pulls me into his arms. His lips crash against mine with a fervor that ignites every nerve, a desperate dance of desire that draws me closer still. My hands clutch at him, fingers digging into his sides as our lips move together, a fusion of urgency and need. His hands roam upward with possessive intent, turning me until the bed frame presses against the backs of my legs, a silent invitation to surrender.

He pulls back, cradling my face in both hands, his eyes searching mine with a depth that feels like a window to his soul. Recalling his earlier lesson—that lowering my mental walls would allow mind-to-mind communion—I retreat inward. I envision the temples of Lyrisene and Sylthara, then construct a palace at their heart, its walls fortified with care. I shield the temples separately, then lower a segment of the outer wall, inviting Soren's presence. A flood of his essence surges into my mind, overwhelming at first, a tidal wave of sensation, before settling into a profound peace that courses through every fiber of my being, a harmony I'd never imagined.

I want you, I project, the thought a tentative thread through the haze, and he leans down, his breath warm against my skin as he kisses me softly this time. My heart stutters, and I rise on my toes, wrapping my arms around his neck, fingers threading through his damp hair, the strands cool against my touch. A low groan rumbles from him, his hands sliding to my waist, lifting me as if I were weightless, a testament to his strength.

With a commanding grip, he lifts me over the bed, setting me gently at the edge where the cool silk sheets brush against my thighs. He reaches for the hem of his shirt, his fingers deftly untucking the fabric, which slides free with a soft rustle. My hands wander up his torso before I tug the tunic over his head, discarding it to the floor to reveal the lean, sculpted expanse of his chest— a canvas of scars that narrate battles fought and survived, each mark a story I yearn to explore.

His hands find my legs, gliding upward with deliberate slowness, his fingers leaving a trail of fire as he lifts my nightgown. The silk pools around my thighs, a delicate frame to the unfolding intimacy, and my breath hitches, a soft gasp escaping as he reveals me fully. His gaze, a potent blend of respect and raw hunger, drinks me in, and I feel exposed yet cherished under its weight. I lie back, the mattress yielding beneath me, and he follows—his body a comforting, solid press against mine, the heat of him seeping into my bones.

"Soren," I whisper, my voice thick with a need that pulses through every vein, and I arch into him. My lips finding his again, the kiss deepening into an urgent, desperate dance as his hands trace the curve of my hips and the dip of my waist.

"*You're mine*," he murmurs against my skin, the words a vow that resonates deep in my core, and I nod, breathless, the world narrowing to the syncopated rhythm of our breaths, the press of his chest against mine.

With a gentle tug, my nightgown slips fully away, the silk

whispering to the floor, and his hands explore with a delicacy that aches in my chest. His fingers trace the lines of my body, each touch a silent promise, a worship of the connection we share. As he lowers himself, his lips capture mine once more, and I feel the promise of an unbreakable bond, forged in the primal heat of Aelthar and the magic that flows between us.

When I wake the next morning, I roll onto my back to find Soren lying beside me, his eyes closed, his breath steady and deep —an image of serene perfection. The lines of his face, usually etched with the weight of command, soften in sleep, revealing a vulnerability that tugs at my heartstrings, a rare glimpse of the fae beneath the warrior. I shift closer, nuzzling into his side, the warmth of his skin a soothing balm against the cool morning air, and his arm lifts instinctively, pulling me tighter against him with a possessive yet tender grip that feels like home.

His hands begin a slow, exploratory journey, trailing up and down my back, grazing the curve of my sides and the dip of my stomach. Each touch ignites a quiet fire beneath my skin, a silent dialogue of affection, and I squeeze him close, savoring the solid strength of his frame, the steady rise and fall of his chest a rhythm I could lose myself in forever.

He rolls onto his side, wrapping both arms around me, his embrace a cocoon of warmth and safety that envelops me completely. I grin as I intertwine my legs with his, the intimacy of the contact sending a thrill through my veins. Yet the steady beat of his heart under my ear calms the lingering restlessness within.

Drifting off on him last night, I'd been uncertain if he would stay. I had convinced myself his departure wouldn't hurt me, but now I can see it was a lie I fabricated as a shield against vulnerability. Realizing he stayed, his presence a constant through the night, shatters that illusion, revealing the depth of my attachment. I would have been heartbroken to wake alone, the thought of distance now a terror that clenches my chest. Having him fully, knowing him in this intimate depth, my body recoils at the prospect of separation, a primal fear rooting itself deep within my being.

I ponder what being soul-bound truly entails—whether this is a fleeting infatuation or a mutual need born of our shared trials—or if it's a deeper connection, a thread woven through the fabric of our very essences. Lying here, it feels as though I've always known him, our souls finally aligning as they were destined to, a recognition that transcends the boundaries of time.

I delve into my mind, checking the fortifications I've built with care. The temples of Lyrisene and Sylthara remain shielded, their secrets locked behind sturdy walls, the palace at their center intact and unbreachable, yet Soren lingers within, a calm and whole presence amid my mental landscape. I wonder if I could breach his mind in return, a curiosity that dances at the edges of my thoughts.

Good luck. I hear his voice rumble through my thoughts, the sound pulling me from my reverie with a jolt of amusement. I lift my head to face him and find a smirk playing on his lips as his eyes drag to mine.

"Can you hear my thoughts all the time now?" I ask, my tone a mix of curiosity and mock indignation. He chuckles softly, the sound a warm rumble that vibrates against my ear, a melody I could listen to endlessly.

"I was worried what you might be thinking," he admits, his voice laced with a teasing warmth, and I roll my eyes, settling back against him, the comfort of his embrace grounding me. "I can only hear them if I want to—or if you want me to. You'll need to shield me like your other mental barriers to keep me out completely."

"I don't want to shield you," I say, splaying my fingers across his chest, tracing the defined muscles of his abdomen with a slow, deliberate touch. He leans closer, inhaling deeply, his breath stirring the hair.

"Are you deliberately shielding these things from me?" he asks quietly, his voice a soft probe. I press my lips together, hesitating as the weight of my secrets presses against the fragile walls I've built.

Maintaining those shields around my temples demands a constant flow of energy, the rise and fall needed to access my powers is a delicate balance that teeters on the edge of exhaustion with added complexity. Yet, the fear of revealing the temples and the dragons within looms large, a shadow cast by the other prophecy's binding silence. It forbids speaking of them, a gag on my tongue, but it never explicitly barred bringing someone to the Skyward Expanse.

"Can I take you somewhere today?" I ask, a moment's pause hanging between us, thick with unspoken possibilities and the promise of revelation. I should consult the dragons first, though asking risks a denial, a chance I might lose my only opportunity to share this with him.

"I've already seen everything Eldwick has to offer," he teases, his tone light but edged with a playful challenge that dances in his eyes. "I have no interest in being depressed today." I pop up again, smacking his chest with a mock scowl, the gesture a playful reprimand.

"I expected more from the Lord of Shadows," I retort, and he laughs fully, the sound vibrating through me, igniting a frenzy that leaves me staring, captivated by the joy that transforms his features. He meets my gaze, a knowing look settling over his face, a silent understanding of the desire that simmers beneath.

"What?" he asks, and I grin widely, biting my lip, the gesture a silent confession of the heat pooling within me. "Ahh, insatiable, are we?" he teases, and I roll my eyes.

I move to lay against him, but he flips me with a swift, fluid motion, guiding me to straddle his hips. I feel him beneath me, firm and ready, a mirror to the desire that surges through me. He grips my hips, his gaze roaming over me with a hunger that suggests our night together was merely a prelude, a chapter yet to be fully written.

CHAPTER
FORTY

The revelation that Soren's chambers are inaccessible unless one star-drifts inside lingers in my mind, a curious detail that adds to his mystique. I've passed the door countless times down the hall from my room, its unassuming frame a silent sentinel, sealed by a spell that alerts him to any unauthorized attempt to enter. The thought of such privacy, enforced by magic, speaks volumes about the life he leads. Guarded, solitary, yet now intertwined with mine.

This morning, after our intimate distraction, we shared a shower in my room, the warm water cascading over us as we lingered in each other's presence, a quiet intimacy that felt both new and eternal. Afterward, he perched at my desk, his gaze following my every move as I prepared for the day.

Opening my wardrobe, I felt his eyes settle on the worn clothes I'd brought from Eldwick, a stark contrast to the finery of the

Umbral Expanse. I braced for a question, a probe into my past, but he remained silent, his restraint a mystery that only deepened my curiosity. I suggested he return to his room to ready himself, hoping to save time, but he insisted on bringing me here, to his private sanctuary, a decision that now unfolds before me with breathtaking grandeur.

When I first arrived at the Umbral Expanse and saw my chambers, I marveled at the luxury. It was lavish beyond anything I'd known in Eldwick. Yet standing in Soren's room now, my own space feels modest, almost insignificant by comparison.

The obsidian walls shimmer with delicate veins of silver, reflecting the soft glow of floating orbs, casting a dreamlike ambiance. A massive bed, draped in midnight-blue velvet, dominates the space beneath a canopy of swirling shadow tendrils that seem to dance in the air. Beyond, a balcony opens to a vista of the endless silver forest, its silvery leaves glinting under a sky tinged with twilight hues.

He disappeared into the bathroom moments ago, leaving me to wander his space, but my eyes are drawn to a smaller bookshelf near his dresser. Glancing toward the open bathroom door to ensure his absence, I wander closer, my fingers brushing the spines as I read the titles between black stone bookends.

Many are inscribed in Vethralis, the ancient language's flowing script a mystery to me, but the few in the common tongue appear old and worn, their pages softened by repeated readings. These must be his favorites, I muse, a window into his soul. The realization that Soren likely commands the rare skill to decipher Vethralis stirs a flicker of wonder—what secrets, what knowledge hidden in those pages, might he possess that others cannot fathom?

"If there's one you're interested in, you can have it," his voice breaks my reverie, and I straighten, turning to find him watching me from the bathroom threshold. He slips a classic black tunic over his head and rolls the sleeves to his elbows with a casual grace that I've come to adore, the look accentuating the strength in his forearms.

"I was just looking," I reply, stepping back from the shelf. "What are these stones? I've never seen them before? They're beautiful."

"Iron," he says simply, and I shift my stance to see the light reflect off them. Then my eyes are drawn back to the books.

"What are the books in Vethralis about?" I press further, and his focus shifts to adjusting his other sleeve before his eyes flash to mine, a guarded intensity in their depths.

"Stories of old," he says evenly, his tone measured, leaving no room for elaboration. I wait, hoping he might offer more, but the silence stretches, and I sense a boundary I'm not yet ready to cross. Part of me yearns to ask why these texts are so coveted by the Aether Dominion, why Elarion and Tivren were so eager to have them, but an instinct holds me back. An unease that the answers might unravel more than I'm prepared to face.

"I'm trying not to slip into your mind to know what you're thinking," he admits, his gaze softening with a concerned edge as he studies me. A grin tugs at my lips, amused by his restraint.

"You look nice," I manage, letting my eyes roam over him again. Compared to the men of Eldwick, he's a vision of masculine beauty, his presence a quiet storm that captivates me.

"You always look nice," he counters, stepping closer to brush a strand of hair from my face. "But I know that's not what you were thinking." I tilt my head, pressing my lips tight in a silent refusal to elaborate, and he nods. "You don't have to tell me," he says, pressing a gentle kiss to my lips, a promise of patience. "But I would like to know where you're taking me."

"I can't tell you," I reply, a nervous breath escaping me. The uncertainty of how the dragons will react to his presence gnaws at me. I'm not even sure if this star-drift will succeed, but the risk feels worth taking, a leap of faith into the unknown.

"Is this a romantic gesture, or just a quick trip somewhere?" he tries, a teasing lilt in his voice, and I scoff softly, masking my anxiety.

"Depends how you wanna look at it, I suppose," I say, and his eyes narrow, sensing the weight behind my words. "There's a fifty-fifty chance we might get eaten. But we can worry about that later."

"What?" he exclaims, but before he can press further, I grab his hand, picture the Skyward Expanse in my mind, and with a surge of will, we vanish from his room.

The transition leaves me gripping Soren's hand tightly as we materialize in the lush green meadow of the Skyward Expanse, the air rich with the scent of wildflowers and mud. Soren turns swiftly, his eyes wide and lips parted as he takes in the surreal landscape, as if he perceives layers beyond my own vision.

"Where are we?" he asks sternly. I release him, stepping back to scan the surroundings. I glance toward the forest where Lyrisene typically resides, then upward where Sylthara often emerges, but for now, only silence greets us. "Kiera. Where are we?" he repeats, his tone insistent.

"Somewhere you've never been," I remind him, and he turns to me, his gaze dissecting every nuance of my expression. A light thud vibrates the ground, and Soren's eyes widen as he looks past me, his composure faltering. A rare sight that leaves me momentarily stunned.

Lyrisene slithers into view, her serpentine body coiling around me in a protective circle, her scales glinting like sapphires in the sunlight. She lowers her head toward Soren, her voice a resonant whisper in my mind.

The others won't be happy you brought him here.

"He can see into my mind," I explain, a defensive edge to my thoughts.

Block him out, she advises, but I shake my head, the complexity of that task weighing on me.

"You know it's not that easy," I argue, and Soren's gaze darts between us, his confusion palpable.

"You can talk to her?" he asks, astonishment lacing his voice.

"You can't hear her?" I counter, turning to Lyrisene. "Why can't he hear you?" She shifts, her gaze lifting to the sky, offering no answer.

A sudden rush of wind heralds Sylthara's arrival, her wings cutting through the air at an unprecedented speed. She lands with gentle grace behind Soren, pacing around him, her nostrils flaring as she sniffs the air above him.

Vyrathax will have his head, she warns, and I glance skyward, my thoughts drifting to the dragon I've only met once, and the elusive Dravokar, whose absence I secretly hope continues.

"Kiera," Soren says, stepping closer, his voice tight with concern. "Please tell me it's only the two of them." I grimace, unable to hide the truth.

"Well..." I begin, my words cut short by a deafening roar from the mountains opposite Lyrisene's lake. "Apparently Vyrathax could be a problem."

"What kind of problem?" he demands, his stance shifting as a red figure soars high above the peaks, diving toward us with alarming speed. Soren raises his hands, ready to defend, but I lay a hand on his arm, my voice firm.

"Don't try to fight him," I say aloud, my voice steady despite the racing of my heart, then shift to a mental whisper, *pretend he's Veyrik.* Soren's curious glance flickers toward me, a silent acknowledgment of the strategy, his mind brushing against mine in that fleeting connection.

Before he can respond, Vyrathax unleashes a wide burst of flame, the fiery ring encircling us with a heat that stops short of burning, a display of dominance rather than destruction. Soren instinctively shields me with his body, his broad frame a protective barrier, but as Vyrathax lands, his mouth agape with a menacing glow, I step forward.

"If you kill him, you kill me," I declare, and the energy in the air freezes, a palpable stillness settling over the meadow. Soren's gaze drops to me, his guard dissolving into a vulnerable softness, but I keep my focus locked on Vyrathax, unwilling to waver.

You have bonded, Lyrisene's voice resonates in my mind, a gentle confirmation, and I nod, the truth of it sinking deep.

Last night, when our souls merged in our intimate union, I felt the certainty that Soren was mine. The realization carries a weight: his death would tether mine, leaving me to sing my last mourning prayer until my own end follows, a fate I'm only beginning to grasp.

Then you will perish together, Vyrathax rumbles, his tone edged with a bluff I can sense beneath the threat, a test rather than a promise. Soren steps closer, his voice cutting through the tension.

"What chance does Aelthar have, if both of us are gone?" I turn to him, startled—he can hear Vyrathax too.

I no longer care, Vyrathax growls, the sound reverberating deep in his chest as he lowers his head to our level, teeth bared and a fiery glow pulsing at the back of his throat. The air grows heavy with the threat evident, yet Soren remains unflinching.

"She is the only chance for all of us to survive this," he says, his words laced with a conviction that tugs at my heart.

She hasn't even decided whose side she's on, Vyrathax murmurs, his gaze narrowing. Does he mean the Elite? The thought unsettles me. I've never fully aligned with them, yet Veyrik's belief that I might sway suggests a divide I hadn't fully considered.

"I'm trying to save Aelthar from these rifts," I counter, my voice firm despite the tremor within. "But I'm struggling alone. Soren knows more than I do. Maybe he can help in ways I can't even imagine. I trust him. I need his help, but I need to tell him everything. Keeping secrets blocks my powers." Vyrathax swings his head toward me, his eyes piercing, and I stand my ground.

You have not earned my power, he retorts, his tone dismissive, and I huff, frustration bubbling up.

"They're the ones giving you your powers," Soren says in a quiet tone, and I nod slowly.

Lyrisene slithers around us both now, her body forming a protective coil, a dual shield against the looming threats. But a shadow flickering across the ground draws my gaze upward, and my breath catches.

Dravokar.

Soren follows my line of sight, and we watch as the massive dragon circles above, his dark form a silhouette against the sky. To my surprise, Vyrathax backs away slowly, his retreat sending a shiver of nerves through me.

"I've never seen Dravokar," I whisper, the tales from *Scale of Eternity* flooding my memory.

"Should we leave?" Soren asks, his voice steady, but I'm transfixed as Dravokar dives with breathtaking speed, landing with a ground-shaking boom that reverberates through the meadow.

I take him in, my breath growing shaky as I study the epitome of terra before us. His dark green scales blend seamlessly with the Verdant Dominion, moss draping his swirling brown horns like a natural crown, and his eyes gleam like emeralds plucked from Tormen's crown. But it's the scars that hold my attention. Deep black indents wrapping his limbs, torso, neck, and muzzle, relics of ancient spells that once bound him, a testament to a pain I can only imagine. A low rumble fills my mind, directed at Soren.

What makes you think you are worthy of our presence?

"I don't care whether or not you find me worthy," Soren replies, his tone calm yet defiant. "All I care about is being worthy enough for Kiera. She has done more for us than you have in the last ten centuries."

Watch how you speak to me, Lord of Darkness, Dravokar's voice thunders, the ground quaking beneath us as if poised to split, a warning that hangs heavy in the air.

"They can't leave here," I interject softly, and Soren's gaze softens as he turns to me. "This place is called the Skyward Expanse. I assume it was created soon after Aethryion made the Umbral Expanse, and he cast them here, just as he did your kind. They're bound, unable to leave, even if they wanted to." Soren's eyes shift to each dragon, a thoughtful intensity in his expression.

"Where's Aethryion?" he demands, his voice carrying an edge of authority, but the dragons remain silent, their stoic forms unflinching. He looks to me, and I shake my head, shrugging helplessly.

"I haven't seen him. And they won't answer me either. I assume he left them here and sought solitude elsewhere," I say, my voice hesitant, the uncertainty weighing on me.

Then Dravokar lifts his head to his full, imposing height, his voice solemn. *We all have much to learn,* he intones, his massive form turning toward the center of the verdant field, his steps heavy yet measured. *Perhaps you will figure it out with his help. Perhaps none of us will survive.*

The prophecy-like cadence of his speech lingers in the air, and I murmur the words under my breath, committing them to memory. If my time here has taught me anything, it's that every utterance from these ancient beings holds a layer of truth, a puzzle piece in the larger mosaic of Aelthar's fate.

"Dravokar," I call out, my voice tinged with a mix of concern and urgency as he flares his wings, the motion stirring the grass around us. But he doesn't pause, his broad back a wall of indifference.

I don't care for your sympathy, he mutters, the words a low growl that reverberates through the ground.

As his wings spread fully, revealing their impressive span, I catch sight of the true burdens he carries—deep scars etched into the translucent membranes, black veins spiderwebbing across them like dark rivers. The sight pierces me; he shouldn't have endured such torment, and yet the darkness within him sparks a troubling thought. Could he be the origin of Aelthar's current strife, the first crack in its foundation?

He lunges forward twice, then lifts off with powerful flaps, vanishing from view in mere moments, leaving a void where his presence once loomed.

I glance at Soren, his expression mirroring my own, his mind clearly turning over the same questions. But my attention shifts as Vyrathax turns, his red scales glinting as he walks away, retracing his path toward the mountains.

"No riddles from you, Vyrathax?" I call out, summoning the last of my courage. My voice carries a challenge, born from the realization that if he shares Veyrik's nature, he's likely a keeper of cryptic wisdom, a trait I've come to both dread and expect.

You will be tested. I hope you choose wisely, he replies, his tone smooth yet enigmatic, and I can't help but huff out a breath, the cryptic nature of his words more frustrating than illuminating.

"You're worse than Veyrik," I retort, a spark of defiance in my voice, and he pauses, his head tilting slightly.

Stop comparing me to your kind, he snaps, a hint of irritation breaking through his stoic facade.

"You created us," I remind him, and his steps falter, a rare moment of hesitation that suggests my words have struck a chord.

It was much simpler back then, he says, his voice a low rumble, before he lifts off in a swift, fiery ascent, disappearing into the distance with a finality that leaves me staring after him.

Sylthara's voice cuts through the lingering silence, her white eyes fixed on Soren with an intensity that commands attention. *You will be bound not to speak of us,* she declares, her words a binding oath. *Should others find out, you must protect her from them.*

Soren nods solemnly, his head dipping in acknowledgment, then shifts his gaze to Lyrisene. "You're bound not to speak of Aethryion," he says, his words more a statement than a question.

Lyrisene lowers her head to the ground, a subtle nod that confirms his intuition, her sapphire scales glinting in the soft light.

"If he's not here, do you know where he is?" I ask, my voice soft but laced with hope, searching their faces for any sign. Their eyes flicker toward me, a fleeting glance that offers no clear yes or no, leaving me suspended in uncertainty. I turn to Soren, who shakes his head, his expression mirroring my frustration.

"We'll figure it out," he says, his voice a quiet vow that steadies me, though a knot of doubt tightens in my chest.

Why does it feel as though we're teetering on the edge of revelation, so close to an answer yet impossibly far from halting the rifts that threaten to tear Aelthar apart.

"Thank you for allowing me here," he adds, his tone respectful, a gesture of gratitude to the ancient guardians.

Do not make us regret it, Sylthara warns, her voice a stern reminder of the trust they've extended.

Soren bows deeply, the motion a silent promise, and as he rises, his eyes meet mine. I offer my hand, my fingers trembling slightly with the weight of what we've experienced, and with a shared breath, I draw upon my power to star-drift back to the Umbral Expanse.

CHAPTER
FORTY-ONE

I guide us back to Soren's room, the obsidian walls and silver-veined sanctuary now feeling like the safest haven for the conversation that looms ahead. As we materialize, I step away from him, my mind buzzes with a chaotic symphony of thoughts. Each departure from the Skyward Expanse leaves me more bewildered than when I arrived, the dragons' words weaving a tapestry of meaning with threads so sparse they unravel into riddles.

Vyrathax's warning that I'll be tested, that I must choose wisely, echoes in my mind. What does it signify? A trial of my powers? A forced allegiance to Tormen or the Elite? The ambiguity gnaws at me, suggesting an impending persuasion from one of those factions, a manipulation I'll need to guard against with every fiber of my being.

Dravokar's solemn declaration that we have much to learn adds another layer of confusion. What knowledge eludes me still? Is it the mastery of my powers? Or the elusive whereabouts of Aethryion? The questions swirl as I try to piece together the fragments they've offered.

Then there's Lyrisene's caution that Soren must protect me if others discover our secret. Of all the enigmas, this one feels the most tangible, the easiest to unravel. I turn to him, his eyes watching me with a careful intensity.

"Why do you have to protect me if the others find out? I'm assuming they mean the other rulers," I ask, my voice tinged with a mix of curiosity and apprehension.

Soren presses his lips together, a moment of hesitation before he speaks. "You are now a direct descendant from the dragons. Not by generation, but a direct lineage from them to you. You have a claim to their thrones," he says, and the air rushes from my lungs in a sharp gasp, the revelation hitting me like a physical blow.

"I don't want their thrones," I protest, my voice cracking with the sincerity of my rejection, but Soren shrugs.

"It doesn't matter," he replies, his tone gentle yet firm. "You will always be a threat to them. Any offspring you may have will also have a claim. Ones you won't be able to control."

The words strike like a punch, a curse etched into my family line, dooming future generations to danger. The thought of my unborn children, entangled in this web of power, sends a wave of dread through me.

"This isn't what I wanted," I whisper, my hands rising to cradle my head as I force air through my tightening chest, the walls of the room seeming to close in with each breath.

"What's done is done," Soren says, his voice quiet, and I feel his hand glide across my back, a warm reassurance that draws me into the solid comfort of his chest. "We'll figure it out," he whispers into my hair, and I squeeze him tightly, clinging to the promise in his words.

"I'm sorry," I murmur, the apology slipping out unbidden, and he gently grasps my shoulders, pulling back to meet my gaze with a fierce tenderness.

"Don't ever be sorry for any of this," he insists, his eyes locking with mine. "Most of it has never been your choice."

I nod slowly and he leans forward, brushing his lips against mine in a soft, tentative kiss. A need flares within me, a burning desire for him to erase the pain, and I pull him down hard, deepening the connection. But he pulls away, his lips parted in a heavy pant, the air between us charged with unspoken longing.

"When you said 'if you kill him, you kill me,' what did you mean?" he asks, his voice low, his thumb tracing the line of my jaw as he cups my face.

"It means you're mine," I confess, the words a vow that binds us, and his eyes darken with emotion. "You're my other half," I tell him, and he pulls me close as his lips crash into mine with a furious passion. His hands press up my back, gripping with a need that transcends want, and I slide my hands under his tunic, craving the warmth of his skin against mine.

"You're mine," he murmurs into the curve of my neck, his voice a deep rumble, and I nip at the stubble on his chin with a grin.

He guides me backward toward the bed, the silk beneath us a promise of solace, but a loud, obnoxious knock at the door shatters the moment. I sigh against his lips, pressing my forehead into his chest with a groan of frustration.

"Let me guess," I mutter, leaning back to glare at the door. "Rennor's here to miraculously pull us apart again."

"How did you guess?" Soren teases, a wry smile tugging at his lips, and I roll my eyes. He pulls his hands away, tucking his shirt halfway in with a reluctant sigh. "He won't leave until I talk to him."

With a wave of his hand, the door swings open just as I smooth my clothes, and Rennor steps in, his gaze darting between us.

"Where have you two been?" he asks, his tone laced with concern rather than accusation, his eyes scanning the room as if it might hold answers.

"We went out," Soren replies simply, his voice neutral, and Rennor's scrutiny intensifies. "What do you need?"

"Rhaevor's been here for hours," Rennor explains, a hint of exasperation in his voice. "I told him I couldn't bother you this morning—well, you know why. And then you both disappeared. I didn't know what to tell him." I wince, the memory of Rhaevor's scheduled training session flooding back, forgotten in the whirlwind of the day.

"I'm sorry. I forgot," I say, moving toward the door, pinching the bridge of my nose in regret. "Is he still here? Did he stay?"

"Yes, I invited him in. He's in the sitting room off the grand hall," Rennor replies, and I glance at Soren, a silent plea for understanding in my eyes.

"I have to go apologize," I tell him, and he nods, though a shadow of reluctance crosses his features.

"Will you do a training session then?" he asks, and I bite the corner of my lip, torn. The desire to stay wrapped in Soren's arms battles with the duty to Rhaevor, whom I see only twice a week now.

"Yes, I think so. Is that okay?" I ask, catching the flicker of need in his eyes, but he nods again, his voice dropping to a dark, envious tone.

"I'll be waiting for you." The promise in his words sends a thrill through me, and I lean toward him, yearning to kiss him, but I pull back, remembering Rennor's watchful presence.

"I'll see you later then," I say, turning to leave, but Soren catches my hand, pulling me back. His caress along my cheek is tender, his lips lowering to mine in a slow, savoring kiss.

"Be safe," he mutters, and I nod slowly, the effort to walk away growing harder with each heartbeat. He's not making this easy. "Better not keep him waiting."

"If you say so," I reply with a reluctant smile, then slip from his arms and pass Rennor with a grin and a shrug. "I tried to spare you."

"Thanks for trying," Rennor says, his tone tinged with annoyance, and I scoff under my breath before star-drifting to the sitting room on the lower level.

Rhaevor lounges in a large armchair, a tea set on the side table and a book in his hands, his focus intent as he turns a page. I approach without masking my steps, allowing him to hear my arrival.

"It's about time," he says, his tone sharp, and I wince at the reprimand.

"I'm really sorry. I got distracted with something," I apologize, and he glances at me, curiosity flickering in his eyes.

"I hope you've been clearing your mental blocks," he says, "because we're going tree jumping again. You'll need all your energy." I let out a low breath, the memory of my last exhausting session dampening my spirits, especially with the thought of returning to Soren too drained to enjoy his company.

"Okay. That's fine. Did you want to go now?" I ask, and he shuts the book smoothly before setting it down.

"Unless you have somewhere else to be," he says. I gesture toward the outdoor balcony, waiting for him to follow me out into the forest.

Hours later, I lean propped against a tree, my arms and legs aching from launching myself between branches. The return journey looms, and I'm uncertain if my strength will hold. Rhaevor insists the trick is to let the air do the work, maintaining a steady current underfoot to propel me forward, but landing on unsteady branches still demands effort and my body protests with every jolt.

"You're doing better today. You seem more focused," Rhaevor says, returning after scouting ahead, a rare note of approval in his voice. He always checks the path before guiding me, ensuring safety. "Your reaction time is on point as well. It seems like you're getting the hang of it."

"My arms are burning," I admit, and he chuckles softly.

"That I can't help you with," he replies, settling back against the branch and looping an arm around the trunk for stability. "When you cast your current, try to feel the wind under your feet. Sense its direction, let it flow through you, not just beneath you."

"Would you believe me if I said I'm trying?" I ask, letting my body sag against the tree, exhaustion seeping into my bones. "Can I ask you something?" I add hesitantly, glancing at him when he shifts uneasily, his posture tensing as if bracing for a blow.

"If you wish," he replies casually, though I catch the faint hesitation in his voice, a subtle crack in his otherwise composed

334

demeanor.

"How did you end up at Galehaven?" I venture, watching his face closely as a rush of emotions washes over it. "You said you used to be a master wielder, but you claim you don't wield often. Are you in hiding?"

He exhales slowly, his gaze drifting to the canopy above as if searching for the right words among the leaves. "It's a complicated past," he admits, glancing at me with a wary edge. "I was in the Cerulean Legion—not a general, but well-respected enough to know the names of the important fae. That is, until they learned I was mixed-blood. I still don't know who outed me, but when they confronted me they gave me two options: be exiled, or become a spy."

"To spy on the Elite?" I ask, my voice sharpening with surprise.

"No," he says, hesitant, his eyes flicking away before meeting mine again. "The Aether Dominion." My eyes widen as the pieces fall into place. "Thalira's father was the Lord before her, and he was a fae of stern means. He thought every dominion was after his resources, his vitality, paranoid to the point of madness."

"So which did you choose? Were you exiled to Galehaven?" I press gently. He lets out a huff, the sound laced with old pain, as if reliving the memory physically hurts.

"I'm not proud of the decision I made, but at the time, it seemed like the right thing to do. I joined the Legion in the Aether Dominion and passed information whenever I could. But after a few decades, I'd had enough. When I asked the Cerulean Dominion to end my service, they denied me—said I had no choice. That's when I found my way to Galehaven. Anyone who takes sanctuary there for a minor offense is safe; they cannot be removed. So that's where I stayed."

"I'm sorry you had to go through that," I say softly, the weight of his story settling over me.

He shrugs easily, straightening his posture. "It led me to Sonja," he says, a faint smile touching his lips, warmth breaking through the regret. "So maybe it was as fate intended." Even through his hardships, he believes in fate. A quiet faith I envy, one I wish I could cling to amid my own uncertainties.

"Thank you for telling me," I say, and he holds my gaze, then nods once.

"We should get going before it gets dark," he adds, glancing at the fading light filtering through the leaves.

I nod, pushing myself upright despite the protest of my weary muscles. Though I've never encountered creatures in these forests, the prospect of nightfall unnerves me. A mystery I'd rather not explore when exhaustion already clouds my judgment.

I launch myself with a blast of air to the next tree, focusing on the current beneath me, and land with a semblance of grace. It's not true flight, but it edges closer than before. Rhaevor lands beside me, and we continue, tree to tree, in a steady pattern. Yet the motion feels choppy, reckless, as if I'm still fumbling in the dark.

Pausing on the next branch, I close my eyes, retreating into my mind. I find my palace, the temples, the walls—and then Soren, a constant pull at the end of a rope, drawing me toward our shared sanctuary.

With renewed focus, I launch again, feeling the air wrap around my legs and torso, a weightless lift in my stomach as I rise and fall. For the first time, I sense the power flowing through me, not just out, a harmony I've yearned to master.

"Nice job," Rhaevor says as he lands, and we press on, the ache in my limbs easing with each leap. "You've got it now," he adds, and I grin, taking off as soon as he lands beside me. But a sudden unease twists in my gut, a sense of something amiss. The pendant at my neck vibrates, and a fae materializes mid-air, seizing my arm with a grip like iron.

"Kiera!" Rhaevor shouts, his voice laced with panic as it fades into the distance, but I'm already torn from his reach, snatched away by an unseen force.

We land abruptly in the crook of a silver-leafed tree, the branches swaying beneath my weight, and before I can steady myself, another hand clamps around my arm, yanking me into another drift.

The world blurs as we materialize in yet another tree, my body passed off like a parcel in a frantic relay. My vision swims, the rapid succession of jumps through time and space leaving me disoriented, my head spinning as if the very fabric of reality is unraveling. And maybe that's their intent, because at the edge of my perception before each drift, I catch dark tendrils of smoke curling through the air—an echo of Soren's power, a sign he's close, perhaps just one jump behind, his soul urging mine to fight, to resist.

Determined to break free, I sense the next landing approaching and unleash a forceful blast of air toward the fae holding me. The gust propels me backward, my body tumbling through the branches until I collide with another tree. The silver leaves glint around me, a reassuring sign we're still within the Umbral Expanse, but after three chaotic jumps, I'm utterly lost.

Before I can recover, another arm seizes me with a bruising grip, and my reflexive air blast backfires, my head slamming against the rough bark of the tree we land in. Pain explodes behind my eyes, leaving me dazed, the world tilting as stars dance in my vision.

"Best not to fight, Kiera," a low, fae voice murmurs near my ear, its tone almost soothing despite the threat. "We're not going to hurt you. Not until you've heard our bargain."

"I'm not making a bargain with anyone," I manage to rasp, my voice trembling with defiance through the haze.

As my vision clears, I catch the glint of a grin on his pale face, his black hair and clothing stark against the silver backdrop, his eyes swirling with a mesmerizing mix of silver and green. Mixed-blood, I recognize instantly, part of the Elite. Their presence is a confirmation of the danger I've stumbled into.

"You don't have a choice," he retorts, his grip tightening, and we land in another tree, my arm passed to yet another fae with seamless efficiency. *No. This can't be happening*, I think, panic rising.

I retreat into my mind, desperate to find Soren, to send a mental cry for help, to let him know I'm still being taken. I trace the familiar paths to my palace, my temples, my walls, seeking that constant pull of his presence. But before I can bridge the connection, the world around me plunges into pitch black.

I lift my hands, stretching them before me, but see nothing—no outlines, no shadows, just an endless darkness. My breathing grows heavy, each inhale thick with the damp scent of sediment and rock. Am I blind? The thought terrifies me, and I curse my lack of fire-wielding skills. If only I had mastered that element first.

"Welcome to Veltharaen," a voice intones, breaking the silence, and I wince as a small flame flares to life before me, its faint glow illuminating the fae holding it.

Maren—the Elite fae I encountered while wandering around the

Cerulean Dominion. His familiar features, now framed by this oppressive darkness, sends a jolt of fear through me as the reality of my predicament settles in.

CHAPTER FORTY-TWO

I picture the gardens of the Umbral palace, Eldwick's rugged cliffs, even the shimmering halls of the Cerulean Dominion. But no matter how vividly I envision those places or how fiercely I will my power to ignite, nothing happens. It's as if an invisible barrier is clamped down on my abilities, smothering them before they can spark. Somehow, star-drifting is blocked here, sealed off by some ancient ward or spell. Which means the only way I can leave is by foot.

I quickly delve into my mind, searching for Soren's presence. But he's gone, leaving behind a hollow ache in my gut that twists sharper with every moment. If he could reach me, he would have by now; I know that with bone-deep certainty. Soren isn't one to hesitate. So if I'm going to escape, I have to do it alone.

The tunnel stretches endlessly, my eyes straining against the void that presses in from all sides. No matter how long we have been walking—minutes? Hours?—my vision refuses to adjust beyond Maren's silhouette. I sharpen every sense, listening for echoes of other fae, the drip of underground water, or the scuff of hidden footsteps. Nothing. It's just the two of us trudging through this labyrinth of damp mud and stone.

When I first encountered Maren, he was clad in a sea-green robe, leading me to assume he is a mix of the Verdant and Cerulean Dominions. But now, with this orb of fire hovering in his palm, my assumption crumbles. Fire? That doesn't seem to fit. Is he masking his true affinity, or is there something more deceptive at play?

We walk in heavy silence, the kind that buzzes with unspoken tension. A million questions swirl in my head, but I bite them back. Revealing my ignorance would only give him leverage. From what I piece together during my capture, we are likely in the underground tunnels the Elite Legion Fighters whispered about. But beyond that? We could be anywhere in Aelthar.

The route they took to bring me here was deliberately circuitous, weaving through paths that blur into one another. Why not a direct path? To disorient me, perhaps, or to evade Soren from finding the entrance? Either way, it worked; I am lost.

We turn a sharp corner into a new tunnel, and the air shifts abruptly—from the thick, stale dampness that clings to my skin, to something crisp and cool. I draw in a deep breath, letting it fill my lungs and chase away the fog in my head.

Ahead, at the tunnel's end, a faint orange glow flickers, promising light and perhaps answers. Relief washes over me, unbidden. I've never feared the dark before—not truly—but this absolute blackness, devoid of stars or even the faintest hint of dawn, sends fear through my core.

"No questions before we arrive?" Maren's voice cuts through the quiet, low and edged with amusement, as if he can sense the storm raging in my thoughts. But I know better than to engage. Knowledge is currency here, and I won't squander mine.

As we near the light, Maren lowers his hands, and the fiery orb dims, then extinguishes entirely. Darkness envelops me once more, but this time it feels different—almost guiding, wrapping around my shoulders like a familiar cloak. It reminds me of Soren, of his shadows that always bring comfort rather than fear. That thought sparks a flicker of strength in my chest, so I lift my chin, drawing on it to steady myself.

We emerge into a vast, domed chamber carved from raw stone, dimly lit by scattered torches that cast dancing shadows across the walls. I scan the room instinctively, my heart pounding as I take in the details. Fae line the perimeter, their clothing a riot of colors—vibrant greens and blues mingling with deep crimsons and even stark blacks, a forbidden hue in many dominions. They stand motionless, their eyes fixed on me with a mix of curiosity and hostility.

At the chamber's head looms a crude throne of jagged rock, and upon it sits a male fae, leaning forward with his elbows braced on his knees. He's older than any fae I've encountered since arriving in the magical realms of Aelthar. His face is etched with the weight of centuries—pale skin stretched taut over sharp bones, dark eyes gleaming with a wild, unhinged hunger. His fingers, long and bony, lace together in a loose grip, but there is nothing relaxed about him. He wears all black, the fabric absorbing the light like a void. And his eyes lock onto mine, predatory, as if I'm prey that's wandered into a trap laid eons ago.

"Kiera, my dear," he rasps, his voice low and gravelly, like stones grinding together after long disuse. "We finally meet."

The words echo the dread I felt when Tormen captured me. But I've learned since then. The fae world is a game of illusions and power plays—every word, every gesture a move on an invisible board. Strength isn't always in brute force; sometimes it lies in subtlety, in holding your motives close. I straighten, meeting his gaze without flinching.

"They say you have a bargain to propose," I say evenly, my voice steady despite the nerves churning inside.

I sweep my eyes around the room, meeting each fae's stare in turn, refusing to show weakness. My breaths come shallow, controlled, as I channel Soren's unflappable calm, imagining his shadows bolstering me. I fortify my mental shields and summon a hum of power to my core—just enough to feel its buzz. A reassurance that it's still there if I need it.

"Let's hear it and get on with it."

"Bold, aren't you?" He leans back on his throne, his dark eyes narrowing with curiosity, a faint smirk twisting his lips.

"You want a blended Aelthar, isn't that right?" I press, keeping my tone neutral, probing for cracks in his facade.

His smirk widens, wicked and knowing. "We wish to live in peace."

He rises from the throne with deliberate slowness, stalking toward me like a shadow unfolding. His presence hits me like a wave—dark, raw power surging outward, but it feels wrong, tainted. Not like Soren's, which is deep and balanced, a force for protection. This is corrupt, hungry, craving destruction and dominance. It slithers against my skin, making my bones ache with the certainty that this fae is the architect of the rifts, the unleashed creatures, the poisoned minds turning fae against their own. Not just the Elite, but something darker—the corrupt heart of it all.

"Isn't that what we all want?" I counter, holding my ground as he circles me.

He scoffs, the sound echoing off the stone walls. "Living divided, skulking in the shadows, confined to places we don't belong—that's not peace. It's barely surviving." His words hang in the air, laced with bitterness, and my mind races. This is it: the motive behind the chaos, the borders crumbling under orchestrated assaults.

"Who are you?" I ask, buying time to think, to weave a strategy from the fragments I have.

He doesn't answer, instead he continues his slow orbit, his eyes raking over me appraisingly. It makes my skin crawl, but I refuse to react. "When I heard of your mixed blood, I knew you were destined for us—to lead us to greatness."

I press my lips together, suppressing a retort. He knows too much about my powers. That knowledge can only come from Elarion or Soren's court, meaning a traitor lurks around me, feeding secrets to the Elite.

"You want me to help bring down the borders?" I ask, injecting a note of feigned interest to mask my hesitation.

He halts in front of me, his glare piercing. "That, I can do alone. I want you to rule with me. To become the most powerful sovereigns Aelthar has ever known." My mouth goes dry at the proposition, the sheer audacity of it. "The moment you were made, I felt your power ripple through the lands like a shockwave. You waste it on mere training. You already possess a wielder's instincts. It's time for you to hone them, and take what is yours."

"What makes you think I want to rule?" I shoot back, my pulse thundering.

He grins, teeth flashing in the dim light. "Don't we all?" He spreads his arms wide, encompassing the chamber and its silent occupants.

Memories of Tormen's capture flash through my mind—my defiance earned me a cell and starvation. If I want to survive this, to gather intel and escape, I have to play along, at least for now.

"I'm surprised you sent Tormen after me," I test, adopting an annoyed tone, as if it was a trivial inconvenience and his lips flatten into a thin line.

"Tormen is being dealt with." The words drip with disdain, like a failed experiment discarded. I wonder what "dealt with" entails. Exile? Death?

"The others don't seem to have much sway either," I continue, dismissing the other Lords and Ladies with a casual wave, as if they are beneath notice.

He studies me intently, searching for bluff. "And what about your beloved Soren?"

My chest tightens at his name, a pang of longing and fear, but I can't falter. "He's not as strong as he used to be," I echo Tormen's taunt from our forest clash, forcing indifference into my voice, and the fae's grin returns.

"No, he's not." He paces a few steps away, hands clasped behind his back. "Though I'll admit, he proves stronger than anticipated. Draining him is taking far longer than planned," he states, and my mind reels. Draining him? Intentionally siphoning Soren's power? Is that what Tormen hinted at?

"What's your plan for him?" The question slips out before I can stop it, too eager, too revealing, and his eyes snap to mine, triumphant, as if he catches my slip.

345

"I don't trust you quite yet. But we'll have time to discuss it." He waves a hand dismissively, and several fae close in, their grips firm on my arms.

Instinct screams to fight—to unleash my power in a blaze of air and water—but survival whispers patience. Outsmart them. I let them lead me toward a side tunnel, my mind frantic. *Think.* Anything to form a plan.

"You know he'll come for me, right?" I call over my shoulder.

"I'm sure he'll try," he replies, unconcerned.

"I wouldn't doubt him yet. If you ask me, he seems determined to be the one to crown the skies." I invoke the prophecy fragment that once unnerved the Lords, sensing the air thicken with pause.

"No one breaches my shields, especially not the Lord of Shadows. I've had centuries to perfect my spells," he states, and any sliver of hope I had dies; this lair is likely warded against Soren specifically. I am truly alone.

As we reach the tunnel's mouth, my eyes dart over the walls. They're slick with moisture, carved with unnatural precision. Then I spot them: large shards of black stone embedded in the rock, glinting like the ones from Soren's room.

Iron.

We have to be beneath the Ironspine Mountains, which is why there are dark wielders here. The Elite terra wielders must have tunneled from the Crimson Dominion, breaching barriers they shouldn't. If the borders fall, this is their invasion point—a hidden army ready to strike at any moment.

CHAPTER FORTY-THREE

I don't know how long I've been confined in this room, the relentless stone walls, floor, and ceiling pressing in like a tomb, unbroken except for narrow vents near the top that tease at freedom but are far too small for me to crawl through. Time blurs here, each moment stretching into the next, and at this point, I feel like I'm teetering on the edge of losing my mind. It's not a brutal torture—no chains, no searing pain—but the isolation gnaws at me, turning every silent hour into a subtle form of torment that builds with each passing day.

This place lacks the ominous dread of Tormen's dungeon, with its dripping shadows and echoes of despair, but it's infinitely less interesting, a bland cage designed for containment rather than cruelty.

They provide the basics: a trickle of water from a spout in the wall, a simple wash basin for minimal hygiene, and silent fae who appear at irregular intervals to deliver trays of food, fresh clothes, or whatever else might pass for comfort in this forsaken hole. If one can call sleeping on a cold stone slab, draped with a thin mat, anything resembling comfort. It's more like a mockery of rest, leaving my back aching and my thoughts restless.

The only spark of intrigue comes from the floating orbs hovering near the ceiling, their soft glow casts a dim, unwavering light over the chamber. I've spent countless hours toying with them using my air and water wielding, summoning gentle gusts to nudge them or tendrils of moisture to encase them, testing if I can extinguish their light or pull them down. But they remain stubbornly aloft, resistant to my efforts, serving as my sole entertainment since they shoved me in here.

I've pleaded countless times to be let out, to stretch my legs in the tunnels beyond, to be anywhere but this suffocating box, but my requests fall on deaf ears. The fae guards meet my words with silence, a sidelong glance of annoyance, or worse, a flicker of pure pity that stings more than any rebuke.

The Underground King—what I've taken to calling the fae in my mind, since he never deigned to share his name—made it clear he doesn't need me to bring down the borders. If I'm not essential to his plans, then I have no real use here at all. I'm useless, a forgotten prisoner who can rot in this cell until the world above crumbles or they decide I'm not worth the food.

I've scoured every inch of this prison, testing the walls for weaknesses, probing cracks with magic, exploring corners where shadows pool deepest. I've even sent bursts of air and streams of water snaking up through the vents, hoping to map what lies beyond or trigger some response, but they reveal nothing. There's no way out unless they choose to bring me out, and that helplessness echoes the despair of Tormen's cell all over again. Even with my powers at my command, I feel just as trapped, just as powerless.

I curl up under the scratchy blanket they provided, its coarse weave a poor substitute for warmth, and stare up at the glowing orbs. Sometimes, I imagine them as the crystals that glint on the ceiling of my bedroom in the Umbral Expanse, their light a comforting reminder of home. But lately, most often, they become the stars I used to gaze at in Eldwick on those rare clear nights, when the clouds parted and the skies revealed themselves. Those were always the most beautiful to me, precisely because they were so scarce. A fleeting gift in a world of gray skies and relentless waves.

A subtle hum vibrates against my hip from the scale hidden there, a light sensation that at first I dismiss as a figment of my weary mind. But after a few moments, the vibration persists, undeniable and insistent, stirring a flicker of curiosity amid the numbness.

I bring my hand to it and stare at the concealed spot, but don't dare to reveal it. If they discovered it and somehow unlocked its secrets, everything would be lost, my last tether to the outside world severed.

You must not lose hope, a voice echoes in my head, gruff and unexpected, jolting me upright as I scan the empty room. Everything appears unchanged, the stone as impassive as ever. *Do not speak out loud,* it adds, and I lean back against the wall, fixing my gaze on the scale, my heart pounding.

Who are you? I think, projecting the question into my mind, and a new presence blooms there, foreign yet not invasive. I

349

hurriedly check my mental defenses—walls, shields, the barriers around my temples—but everything holds firm. "How did you get in my mind?"

Now is not the time for pointless questions, the voice replies in a grumbly tone, laced with impatience, and I pull a face of disbelief, my brows furrowing.

Pointless questions? You're talking to me through my mind, and you won't tell me who you are? I retort mentally, but I'm only met with silence. I huff out a breath, the quiet somehow evoking Soren's brooding demeanor, though I know it's not him. *Okay. So then what do you want?*

For you to find a way out, he says, his tone resolute, and I exhale long and slow, staring at the blank wall opposite me. Doesn't he think I would have escaped by now if it were possible? *You can, and you will get out of here,* he insists, as if reading my doubt.

There's no way out. I don't know what you want me to do, I argue back, pressing my hands to my head in exasperation. I've exhausted every idea, every angle, but unless they let me out...

Then make them let you out, he interrupts before I can finish the thought, and I realize he's not just in my head; he's woven into my very thoughts, anticipating them.

I can't. They come at random times, every visit is unpredictable. I have nothing to offer them, I counter, my mind racing through failed pleas and ignored demands.

A fire is trying to find you. But he will not be able to get you out of this cell, he reveals, and I lean forward, intrigue sharpening my focus.

A fire? My gods, is this a riddle? At a time like this? Why can't you just tell me who it is and save me the hassle of a headache? I demand, rising from the stone bed to pace the narrow confines, my steps echoing softly.

He has masked his powers. I cannot tell who it is, but he is powerful, and he is looking for you, the voice explains, and I shake my head in bewilderment. Masked powers—how is that even possible? *You must reach him. You are running out of time.*

Running out of time? To what? I press, dread coiling in my stomach like a serpent.

To escape, he says simply, the weight of it sinking in. So this rescuer has infiltrated, concealed his essence, but the mask won't hold forever—which means I need to locate him before it's too late.

You said a fire is trying to find me. What does that mean? I probe, my eyes narrowing at the seamless wall where the door materializes.

His soul is made of fire, he replies, and realization dawns. The Ironspine Mountains border the Umbral Expanse and the Crimson Dominion... Veyrik. Of course, the Lord of Fire would come for me. I should have known his loyalty would drive him here.

How do I reach him? Are you here? Can you help me? I ask urgently, grasping for any aid.

I cannot, he responds, his voice fading, distant now, as if each word drains him further, his presence thinning like mist.

Pointless questions, I recall his earlier warning. He can't sustain this for long; I've wasted precious moments on them.

Are you a prisoner here too? How can I find you? I think quickly.

Do not come looking for me, he commands sternly, and I shake my head in refusal. *Do not argue over this matter, young one. Find the fire, and find a way out. They will need you outside of these walls,* he urges, and my stomach drops at the implication. What chaos unfolds above while I remain here?

I wait for more—an answer, a grumble of irritation, anything—but silence reigns, his presence evaporating from my mind. Yet his words ignite a spark of purpose, enough hope to propel me forward.

I lower myself to the ground, then cross my legs and place my hands palm-up on my knees, just as Rhaevor taught me for centering my focus and calming the storm within. I doubt I can speak to Veyrik mind-to-mind, our bond not forged like mine with Soren, but if I can reach out somehow, project my location or a plea, I have to try.

Diving into my mental landscape, I visualize the structures I've built—the shields, the reservoirs of power, the faces of those I've come to trust. Veyrik stands out vividly, his presence like a blaze: piercing eyes that see through facades, a smile that warms even the coldest room. He's always been my guardian, checking on me after every trial, and now he's risked everything to infiltrate this lair.

I conjure his image in my mind—his tall, commanding gait, lean yet powerful stance, broad shoulders and the toned chest peeking from his perpetually open tunic. I roll my eyes inwardly at his fondness for riddles, but as his essence begins to solidify, I push outward with desperation.

Find me. Please. The plea echoes, raw and urgent, but just as I sense him at the periphery, he slips away, vanishing like smoke.

My shoulders sag in defeat as I slump on the floor, exhaustion weighing heavy, then my head snaps up at the faint crack of the door opening. I scramble back, sprawling on the ground with arms outstretched, feigning idle boredom to mask any suspicion, as he steps in: the Underground King, his presence filling the room like a shadow.

"Get up," he mutters, his voice a low rumble, and I push myself up to sit. "What are you doing?" he demands, eyeing me suspiciously.

"Imagining I'm looking at stars," I reply honestly, glancing up at the orbs, yet none appear there now.

He follows my gaze briefly, then snaps, "Get on your feet." I rise slowly, brushing dust and rocks from my pants, my heart racing. "Walk with me," he commands, and a lightness blooms in my chest.

Walk with him? He's actually letting me out? It seems almost too convenient, too timely. Perhaps my mental reach alerted him, or the mysterious voice orchestrated this. Either way, I step through the threshold, drawing a deep breath of the stale tunnel air. It's not fresh, but it's new, a shift from confinement. My chance at freedom, however slim.

"How many days have I been here?" I ask as we navigate the dim tunnels, but he remains silent, his strides purposeful.

I glance at him sidelong. He wears the same dark attire as before, yet it's impeccably clean, his face clean-shaven and groomed, defying the underground grime. Not the ragged under-lord I imagined, but a calculated figure, polished in his menace.

"What's your name?" I press curiously, and he shoots me a glance.

"The world of Aelthar is about to change," he says instead, his words heavy with omen, echoing the voice's warning: *They need me*. "Have you thought of what side you would like to take?" he asks, and my chest tightens, the question a pivot point.

My response could seal my fate, dictating whether I walk free or return to chains. Vyrathax's words from the Skyward Expanse resurface: *You will be tested. I hope you choose wisely.* But what choice? I have already aligned my heart, yet survival might demand deception—or truth, accepting whatever comes.

"I've been to the Dominions, seen their lives, met their kind," I say carefully, drawing on truths to weave my words. "As a mortal, I was despised; now with powers, it's clear I will never be fully accepted." It's no lie. I won't fit their rigid molds, but the Elite's vision of a fractured Aelthar isn't mine. "I don't want to choose a Dominion to live in."

"Soon, you won't have to," he replies, his gaze locking on mine. He studies me, probing for deceit, but my words ring true. I don't want to live in a Dominion. The Umbral Expanse is my home.

We enter a larger chamber, the air thick with savory scents that make my stomach growl—a dining hall, expansive and lit by torches. Fae sit at a long table, hands folded in laps, awaiting their lord, their attire a mosaic of colors defying dominion lines. I scan the exits, tunnels branching into darkness, but escape would be futile. I'd be lost in moments, recaptured in steps.

"Sit," he commands, a chair pulling out to his right at the table's head. I lower myself slowly, eyes sweeping the faces down the line. When one fae meets my gaze, their expression intent, almost communicative, I hold it steady. Not Veyrik, but perhaps an ally. Or a warning.

"Do you have a name?" I ask again, turning to the under-lord beside me.

He grins wide, a chilling flash. "Valthar," he reveals, the name sending a dread coursing through my body. "Let us eat," he declares, raising his hands, and the fae dive into their meals with restrained fervor.

I stare at the plate before me, laden with steaming dishes, my stomach protesting with hunger, yet something holds me back.

"Tell me about your home, Kiera, about Eldwick," he says, taking a deliberate bite, the chew slow and measured. The mention of my village on his lips ignites a spark of anger, my fists clenching beneath the table. "Do you miss it? I'm sure your mother and brother miss you dearly," he adds, and as I glare, a smug tug pulls at his mouth. He knows he's struck a nerve.

"You seem to know everything about me already. Why don't you tell me about yourself instead?" I retort, watching his throat work as he sips from his goblet.

"What would you like to know?" he offers, his eyes locked on mine. Is this genuine, or another test of my defiance?

"When will the borders fall?" I demand sternly, and his brows furrow, caught off guard. Several fae pause their eating, eyes turning toward us, the silence thick and oppressive.

"The borders will fall when the dominions have decided they have endured enough," he answers cryptically, my mind spinning. What more suffering does he plan? Even now, the Dominions struggle against dark wielders; how could they face fae with blended powers?

"Why not attack now?" I press, and he grins, fingers tapping the table as he studies me. "Do you not think you're strong enough?" I test, pushing the boundary.

"I want to prove to you which side is worth fighting for," he says, my heart sinking. He's intent on swaying me. "I want you to see how weak these dominions and their rulers truly are. They lounge in palaces, playing petty games, hoarding knowledge and secrets, barely protecting their own. Aelthar can be so much more. Through chaos, we'll forge peace. A peace I believe you've longed for."

"What makes you think you know what peace is?" I counter, meeting his glare, convinced in his delusion that I'll join him to rule the ruins.

"What do you want?" he says suddenly, breaking our standoff, and I look up to see a hooded figure emerge from a tunnel, steps slow and deliberate. Clad in a black robe that conceals their form and face, they're an enigma, impossible to identify.

"Reveal yourself," Valthar demands more firmly, rising slowly as the figure halts at the table's end. I summon my powers, flooding my core with air and water, bracing for whatever comes —and then a roaring blast of fire erupts down the table, scorching every fae in its path.

CHAPTER FORTY-FOUR

Dark shadows erupt around me, a violent tempest of inky tendrils lashing out with ferocious intent, and in a heartbeat, I react. I summon a surge of air beneath my feet, channeling it with desperate precision, and let it propel me soaring down the length of the table toward the hooded figure at its far end.

The rush of wind fills my ears as I land with a thud, but before I can steady myself, darkness floods the space, coiling around my legs and torso like a living snare. Panic flares, my breath catching, then the floor gives way beneath me and I plunge into an abyss of complete darkness.

No. No. No. The words scream through my mind, my body trembling as fear threatens to overwhelm me. But just as despair begins to take hold, a soft flame ignites before me, its gentle dance casting a warm glow. Through the flickering light, Veyrik's familiar face emerges, his sharp features softened by relief. He reaches out, his hand caressing my cheek with a tenderness that breaks me, and tears well in my eyes, spilling over in a rush of emotion.

"You found me," I whisper, my voice cracking with gratitude.

"I heard you calling," he replies softly, and I release a shaky breath, the weight of my isolation lifting slightly.

"We don't have much time," a voice interrupts from behind, and I whirl around to see the fae who met my gaze at the table, now standing with us, his presence a quiet surprise. His eyes hold a knowing glint—he must be an ally in this treacherous place.

"Let's go," Veyrik urges, and as he and the stranger start running, I don't hesitate to follow. I should have known Veyrik would have insiders. His uncanny knowledge of events always hinted at a network, and now it's clear he's leveraged it to reach me.

Veyrik casts orbs of fire ahead and behind us, their golden glow illuminating the tunnel, but when I glance back, I see the walls closing in, stone grinding against stone to seal the passage behind us to keep anyone from following.

"There's a passage up ahead," the stranger says, his voice steady despite the urgency. "Once you pass it, I won't be able to follow." I study the fae ahead, noting his green and black robes—a blend of Verdant and Umbral, an unusual combination that sparks curiosity.

"Are you a shadow wielder?" I ask quietly, my voice barely audible over our footsteps.

A beat of silence stretches before he answers, "Yes." My eyes narrow in suspicion. Dark wielders have been confined to the Umbral Expanse since its creation, unable to leave. Yet here he is, born perhaps under these mountains. How did Veyrik find him, and what binds them?

"Shadow wielders won't be able to reach you," he continues, "but you'll have to deal with the rest of them." His words sink in— fae with multiple elemental powers, a far greater threat than those wielding a single gift.

"Down this way," he directs as we round a corner, and we skid to a halt, the sudden stop jarring my nerves. A cold dread washes over me as Valthar's voice slithers through the air.

"Did you really think you would escape me that easily?" he taunts, stepping into our light with a devious smile that sends my stomach plummeting. No. This can't be happening, not when we were so close to freedom. His presence looms, a danger I can't fully fathom. If this erupts into a fight, I'm not certain any of us will survive.

"Did you really think I would help you rule your corrupt world?" I retort, my fists clenching as Veyrik's gaze flickers toward me, a silent question in his eyes.

"I hoped you would realize how much everyone is holding you back," Valthar replies, his tone smooth yet insistent, as if he still believes he can sway me. "You're capable of so much more than you know. The world has no place for you, Kiera. Not yet."

"I know my place," I snap back, and shadows begin to close in around us, thick and suffocating.

"You just have to make it to the end of the tunnel," the fae beside me murmurs. "You'll feel a shift." I glance at him, clinging to that sliver of hope.

"You will be the first to die," Valthar hisses at the fae, unleashing a powerful blast of shadows that crafts into a razor-sharp edge, slicing through the air with lethal intent.

The fae raises a wall of stone in defense, but the shadows shatter it like sand, driving forward relentlessly. I send a whirlwind roaring down the hall toward Valthar, and Veyrik unleashes a simultaneous blast of flames, the two forces combining to slow the shadows, though they don't halt. And before I can react further, the shadows pierce the fae.

"No!" I yell, sending a gentle bead of air to cushion his fall as he collapses.

"It's useless, Kiera," Valthar's voice cuts through. "Even with your powers, you're no match for me." Rage ignites within me, energy radiating from every fiber as I step toward him, determination overriding fear.

"Kiera," Veyrik calls quietly, his voice a warning, but he follows my stride, matching my reckless determination.

"I should have known you would come for her," Valthar sneers at Veyrik. "Always so desperate for attention, aren't we?"

Valthar's shadows wrap around him in a vortex of darkness, an image that should intimidate any sane being, but I've already decided I'm getting out of here. I'm not letting him kill anyone else.

The swirling blackness pulses with malevolent energy, tendrils snaking outward like hungry vines, but my determination hardens like steel. I've faced darkness before; this is just another form, corrupted and ancient.

I wrap myself in a thin layer of air, the invisible barrier humming against my skin like a second layer of armor, and conjure a towering wall of water beside him. With a surge of will, I slam it upward, crashing him into the ceiling with a thunderous impact, but a sphere of black energy envelops him at the last moment, cushioning the blow. Then I feel his shadows retaliate, wrapping around me like icy chains, squeezing with relentless force.

I expand the air around me, pushing outward to loosen their grip before they can crush me, and summon ice spears, shaping them in every form I can imagine. They hurtle down the hall, whistling through the dim light, but his shadows knock them aside one by one, shattering them into harmless frost.

When the last spear falls, Veyrik unleashes a roaring cascade of molten flame, its golden-orange brilliance licking the jagged obsidian walls, illuminating the tunnel in a hellish glow. The heat washes over me as the flames clash with Valthar's surging tide of shadow tendrils—their inky blackness swallowing the light, coiling like serpents with razor-sharp edges that hiss and steam on contact.

The shadows explode into jagged spikes, thrusting toward us like deadly thorns, but I dodge with a burst of air, channeling it into a cyclone that shreds them to wisps of smoke. Seizing the brief opening in the darkness, Veyrik slams his fists into the ground, unleashing a river of molten lava that surges forward in a bubbling torrent, forcing Valthar back as the stone floor cracks and melts under its heat. But Valthar surrounds his body in shadows, lifting himself off the ground, hovering like a specter above the flow.

I send a tunnel of air racing through the upper part of the passage, letting it wrap around his shadows. I pull as hard as I can, muscles straining with the effort, trying to drag him away from our escape path, but he remains firm.

I form long spears of ice and launch them down the air current, adding an extra gust for speed. The first one shatters against his shadows in a spray of shards, but the next few slice through the barrier, vanishing into the void. All I can hope is that at least one hits its mark.

Veyrik lifts the lava higher, filling the tunnel with its searing glow, and the black sphere holding Valthar hurtles toward us. I cast a shield of ice above us, thick and glistening, but the lava's heat weakens it, cracks spiderwebbing across its surface in an instant.

Black tendrils hurl toward us as he flies overhead, aiming for the hall's far end. If he's retreating that way, it means we've pushed him close to the border where his power wanes—which means we're almost to the other side.

I turn as the black sphere dissolves, revealing an ice shard lodged in his shoulder, half-melted by Veyrik's lava, blood trickling down his arm. But instead of pulling it out or fleeing, Valthar grins—a sinister, triumphant curl of his lips, as if he's already claimed victory.

"It's too late," he declares, his voice echoing with dark amusement, and the tunnel rumbles and shakes around us, stones loosening from the ceiling. I drop to the ground, throwing up a blast of hardened air to shield us, but when I look at Veyrik beside me, my stomach drops.

His stomach and chest are pierced through with shadows, wicked barbs protruding from his flesh, and beneath his ripped shirt, black spreads through his veins like poison ink, corrupting him from within.

Every limb and muscle in my body vibrates with fury, a raw power surging as if all the dragons' magic is flooding me at once. When I release my clenched fists, black seeps from my hands, shadows spilling forth like liquid night. I stand slowly, staring at the darkness pouring out of me, an unfamiliar yet intoxicating force, and without hesitation, I send waves of it down the tunnel in rapid succession, each one crashing like a tidal wave of oblivion.

Valthar dodges and deflects with his own shadows, countering frantically, but his eyes widen in shock and hesitation. He takes a step back, then another, as I advance, weaving a flurry of ice, wind, and water between my shadows, filling every inch of the tunnel with chaotic power until the walls tremble and crumble. With one last, monumental blast of darkness, the ceiling collapses in a roar of stone, blocking the path between us and sealing Valthar away.

Shadows drip from my body, an overflow I can't contain, trailing like ink from my skin. I turn quickly and see Veyrik propping himself on one arm, his wide eyes fixed on me—not in fear, but in wonder.

I rush toward him and slide to my knees in the dust and blood. I pull open his shirt and I inspect the wounds—red blood pours freely and mingles with oozing black liquid. His face is pale, his eyes dimming like fading embers.

"You have to go," he rasps, his voice strained. "You're the one who has to get out of here, not me. Go before anyone else comes."

"I'm not leaving you," I insist, and I glance at my hands as the shadows begin to dissipate, the power ebbing away. But maybe I can still harness it. "Don't move," I command, and he leans his head against the wall with a grimace.

I hover my trembling hands over his body and focus all my energy on the shadows within him. I sense them swirl through his veins and blood, racing toward his heart like a venomous current, and pull at them. I urge them to me and curl my fists, squeezing my eyes shut as he groans under the strain. I tug harder, drawing the corruption into my grasp, then send it hurtling down the hall with a blast of air, watching it fizzle out into harmless mist.

I look down—his veins are darkened but no longer black, the

taint expelled. Yet the wound in his stomach still bleeds profusely, a relentless flow. I wrap my hands in air, pressing it to the injury to stem the tide. He winces, fingers digging into the ground, but he doesn't flinch away.

I stare at the blood pooling beneath him, a crimson lake too vast. I know it's too much—I was too late to save him fully.

"You have to go," he repeats, his voice weaker, fading like a whisper on the wind, but all I can do is shake my head, denial burning in my chest.

"I'm not leaving you," I say, my voice laced with desperation, and I feel his hand grab my arm, weak but insistent. I open my eyes, tears flooding out unchecked, and meet his gaze. They're pale, drifting, as if he's already slipping away. "I'm not leaving you."

"You have to," he murmurs, pulling my hands from his body. Blood surges forth anew, and when I reach again, his grip tightens, pushing me back. "Soren won't last without you."

"I can't," I choke out, my voice harsh with grief, and he lifts my hand to his lips, kissing it gently, just as he always has—a final, tender gesture. "Veyrik," I whisper, feeling a surge pour into me, something familiar from these depths under the mountain.

Help me, I plead in my head, directing it toward the voice I know lingers there. *Please. Help me.*

In an instant, black smoke surrounds us, and panic shoots through me, dreading another assault—but the shadows envelop like a caress, a welcoming hand guiding rather than harming.

I throw my body over Veyrik's, clutching him tightly as his warm blood soaks through my shirt, and then we're weightless, lifted into the void, carried away from the chaos.

CHAPTER FORTY-FIVE

My knees sink into the soft ground as the scent of fresh air floods my lungs. I lift myself from Veyrik's still form, pressing my hands to his chest, feeling the faint rise and fall of his lungs and the weak thud of his heart beneath my palms. Hope flickers, fragile but alive, until a massive shadow sweeps over us. I glance skyward as Vyrathax dives down, his enormous form landing with a ground-shaking thud that blocks out the sunlight, his scales glinting.

I scoot back instinctively as he lowers his head to the ground, his breath a warm puff of steam washing over Veyrik's body, stirring the air with a hint of sulfur.

Rustling in the trees behind me draws my attention, and I turn to see Lyrisene slithering forward, her serpentine grace swift and silent. In a blink, she's before me, towering with her shimmering scales catching the sunlight, her blue eyes sparkling with an intensity that feels like judgment. She doesn't speak, her silence heavy as if she's weighing my worth in this critical moment. Then, with a quick whip of her head, she moves to Veyrik, exhaling an icy mist that settles over him like a frost-kissed shroud.

I watch his chest, praying for movement, and when it rises and falls slowly, my breath catches. Only for it to stop, and my chest squeezes with dread. I want to scream at them to help, to do anything, but my mind locks, frozen as I stare at his neck, searching desperately for a pulse, any sign of life lingering within him.

Lyrisene leaps upward, spreading her wings in a swift ascent, and my body jolts as the ground trembles again with Dravokar's landing. Vyrathax hovers over Veyrik, snarling with a deep, rumbling growl, his teeth bared in a territorial display. Dravokar juts his horns, shoving Vyrathax's head aside with a forceful nudge, then fixes his burning gaze on me as he passes. This time, I feel the weight of his judgment, a scrutiny that pierces deeper than before.

He leans over Veyrik and vines erupt from the ground, twisting and wrapping around his body with deliberate care. I lurch to my feet, instinct flaring to fight, but Dravokar rumbles a deep warning in his chest, commanding me to stay back. The vines glow faintly, squeezing tighter as small orbs of white light rise through them, shimmering like captured starlight.

I look up at Dravokar's imposing frame, allowing myself a shaky breath as the adrenaline begins to ebb from my limbs, leaving them trembling. Tears well in my eyes, and though I swipe at them quickly, they spill over, unstoppable. My hands, stained with Veyrik's blood, are useless for wiping them away, so I drag my arm across my face, sinking back to my knees as the weight of it all crashes down.

The dragon's gazes linger on me, silent and unreadable. Not even Lyrisene offers a word. Have I broken some unspoken vow by wielding dark magic? Where did that power come from, surging through me like a flood? I'm already a blend of powers. Does this mean I'm turning corrupt? The thought gnaws at me. What if I do? What if that darkness consumes me entirely?

A corrupt mind does not cry, Dravokar's voice resonates in my head, deep and gravelly, and I lift my gaze to meet his piercing eyes, finding a strange reassurance there.

A sudden gasp shatters the tension, and my eyes snap to Veyrik. His eyes are wide open, gulping air in desperate heaves. I rush to his side, hands pressing against his chest, feeling it rise and fall with renewed vigor, his heart pounding beneath my touch like a drumbeat of life.

The vines unravel, sinking back into the ground, and Dravokar strides away without a backward glance, leaving me too stunned to call after him. I meet Veyrik's eyes, a mix of relief and disbelief swirling within me.

"Are we dead?" he asks, his voice hoarse, and a low laugh escapes me as I shake my head.

"I think you might have been," I admit, "but no, we're not." He groans as he tries to shift his body, and I add gently, "You should probably take it easy." He lifts his head, inspecting himself, his brows furrowing at the sight.

"What happened?" he asks, and I sit back on my heels, studying the healed wounds across his chest and stomach. Long scars now mark his torso, and his veins show a dark purple, far lighter than the black poison that coursed through him moments ago. "Did you heal me?" he presses, and I shake my head, uncertainty shadowing my expression.

My gaze drifts past him to Vyrathax, now standing at full height, his head looming above us. Veyrik tilts his head back, then jolts upright, spinning to face Vyrathax, clutching his stomach with a wince. He stares, wide-eyed, at Vyrathax—his creator.

"Now I'm sure I'm dead," he mutters, and I can't help but grin at the irony.

Unfortunately, Vyrathax begins, his tone dry as desert stone, and I roll my eyes preemptively, *we have all decided to save you.* I shake my head, amused despite the gravity.

"You're a grumpy bastard, aren't you?" Veyrik quips, and I scoff, grateful I don't have to mediate between them. Vyrathax's gruffness is beyond my ability to mimic.

Veyrik turns to me, his eyes bright and a teasing grin tugging at his lips. "Is this where you go?" he asks, and I nod slowly, my gaze lifting to Vyrathax for a long moment, a silent acknowledgment of their intervention. They saved him. "Are you a shadow wielder now?" he asks, curiosity lacing his tone, but I shake my head, holding up my hands to inspect them front and back.

"I don't know where that came from," I confess, meeting his eyes. "I don't feel it in me anymore. I don't know what that means."

"I don't know either," he replies, his voice steadying me, "but it's what we needed to survive, so it can't be bad." I nod, though doubt lingers. Rage had fueled that power when I saw him bleeding out. "How long have we been here?"

"With the dragons?" I clarify, and he nods. "A while. Why?"

"You have to find Soren," he says urgently, turning to face me fully. "When you're here, when he can't sense you, he spirals into a frenzy. With you out of reach for so long, I can only imagine the darkness he's lost to."

I hate to interrupt a moment of sincerity, the dragon intones, his form shifting as we both turn to face him. *While you were down there, a rift tore open in the Aether Dominion.*

"What?" I exclaim, the word bursting from me as the memory of the tunnel's violent rumbling floods back—the ground trembling as if it were splitting apart beneath our feet. My heart quickens, dread pooling in my stomach as the implications sink in.

Veyrik sinks to his knees with a soft groan, pausing before summoning the strength to push himself upright. I lunge forward, catching his arm as he stumbles, and support his weight against my shoulder.

"We have to help," he insists, his eyes burning with determination despite his frailty.

"You can't," I counter, my brow furrowing with concern as I steady him. "You need to rest. Now isn't the time to be stubborn." The words feel heavy on my tongue, a mix of worry and exasperation, knowing his spirit outpaces his battered body.

She is right, Vyrathax agrees unexpectedly, his deep rumble catching me off guard. *You are not capable of a fight,* he adds, his tone firm yet not unkind, as if acknowledging Veyrik's courage while enforcing a necessary boundary.

"Is Soren there?" I ask, my fists clenching involuntarily as a surge of power stirs within me, a restless energy begging for release.

He needs you, Vyrathax confirms, dipping his head in a gesture that feels both solemn and urgent—uncertainty giving way to purpose.

"I'll take you back to your palace," I tell Veyrik, my voice steady as I plan our next move, but Vyrathax's deep rumble interrupts, a sound that vibrates through the ground.

He will stay, Vyrathax decrees, his authority unbreakable. *I will send him back when he is ready,* Vyrathax adds, his tone leaving no room for argument.

"Is that... fine with you?" I ask Veyrik, searching his face for any sign of reluctance. But he shrugs, a faint smile tugging at his lips despite the pain etched in his features.

"He seems like good company," he jests, his humor a flicker of light in the darkness. I roll my eyes, now fully convinced these two are kindred spirits in their gruff resilience. Vyrathax shakes his head, a subtle motion, and settles onto the grass.

"I'll be back if I can," I promise Veyrik, my voice softening as I step closer. He moves toward me, his hand brushing the side of my face, trailing down with a tender touch, grounding me in the moment.

"Be safe," he murmurs, his voice thick with concern, a rare vulnerability shining through his usual bravado.

"Aren't I always?" I reply with a grin, trying to lighten the mood, though his tilted head and unconvinced expression tell me he sees through it. "Good luck with this one," I add, nodding toward Vyrathax, who fixes me with a stern look.

"Why do you say it like that?" Veyrik questions, his curiosity piqued.

"I think you'll finally understand what it's like for everyone to talk to you," I tease, and he chuckles deeply, the sound warm and genuine as he settles into a cross-legged sit.

"I can't wait," he says, his grin widening, and I laugh softly, stepping back. My eyes linger on Vyrathax a moment longer, and I nod respectfully.

"Thank you," I say, the words carrying more gratitude than I can express, and to my surprise, he dips his head slightly, a rare gesture of respect.

Do not die, he replies flatly, and I huff a breath, glancing at Veyrik with a wry look.

"I was going to say the same, so…" Veyrik quips, his humor undimmed, and I roll my eyes, a smile tugging at my lips.

"Insufferable," I mutter, and as he laughs, I swear I catch Vyrathax chuffing softly, a sound that feels like an echo of amusement from the ancient beast. "I'll see you," I say, my voice softening as his eyes fill with worry and a hint of dread.

Before that emotion can overwhelm me, I picture Soren in my mind and let myself star-drift, the world fading into shadow as I surrender to the pull of the unknown.

CHAPTER FORTY-SIX

Chaos. Death. Destruction.

That's the relentless pulse pounding through every shattered archway, every crumbling spire, every desperate fae fleeing across the floating isles of the Aether Dominion. The palace I once visited —elegant, polished, a beacon of ethereal beauty—is no longer pristine. The world I've drifted into is a nightmare carved from howling winds and spilling blood, the air thick with a metallic tang and the acrid smoke of rift-born horrors.

I stagger forward through the main entrance of the palace and my boots crunch on debris. The wind whips at my hair, carrying echoes of agony from every direction, raw screams that pierce like daggers. My heart races, a frantic drumbeat urging me deeper into the fray, but doubt creeps in. Am I too late? Has the rift already claimed too much? I tried to star-drift directly to Soren, but something pushed me back and brought me here instead. Maybe that means Soren is in more danger than I realized.

"Kiera," a familiar voice calls, cutting through the din, and I turn to find Tivren sliding to a stop in the middle of the great hall, his scholarly robes disheveled and stained with red. He looks me up and down, his eyes narrowing in assessment. "Are you here as an ally, or to take us down from the inside?" he asks, his tone laced with suspicion that stings more than I expect.

Did they really think I would join the Elite? Is that the true reason they hesitated to train me, fearing my mixed blood might tip me toward corruption? The thought fuels a spark of anger amid the fear. After all I've endured, all I've fought for, this is how they see me?

"Have you seen Soren?" I demand, pushing past his doubt, my voice steady despite the chaos swirling around us.

He shakes his head, glancing over his shoulder toward the distant clamor. "Somewhere in the fray." His words are clipped, and I notice he's moving away from the fight, not toward it. He's probably more concerned about his precious books than the lives at stake in Celestine.

"You're not going to fight?" I challenge, unable to hide the edge in my tone.

"There is much at stake," he replies cryptically, his eyes flickering with unspoken fear. "Much more than you realize." Before I can press him, he adds in a desperate plea, "If you are here to help, then please… help us."

His voice cracks slightly, revealing the strain beneath his composed facade, and I nod curtly, turning my back on him to plunge into the turmoil outside.

Stepping out, the full horror unfolds. A faerie clutches a child to her chest, darting between hovering platforms that sway precariously in the gale, only to be cut down by a shadowy claw ripping through the air like living night.

The dark creatures—twisted abominations spawned from the rifts, their forms a grotesque blend of jagged limbs, void-black eyes, and writhing tendrils—swarm the streets beyond, tearing into flesh with gleeful savagery. There are too many of them, far more than I encountered in the Cerulean Dominion, overwhelming the defenders with sheer numbers and unrelenting ferocity.

I want to help, but I need Soren. His presence tugs at me like an invisible thread, our soul-bound connection stronger now, a lifeline since that night we shared. He's everything to me, the one who keeps me from being swallowed by the void.

I weave through the pandemonium, but it isn't long before a creature spots me. Its form a nightmarish mass of shadows with claws like obsidian blades, and it charges, its maw unhinging to reveal rows of needle-sharp teeth. Panic surges, hot and sharp, but instinct overrides it.

Water answers my call, coiling around my hand like a liquid whip. I lash out, hardening it into icy spikes that pierce its hide, slowing it just enough for me to sidestep and drive an ice sword into its neck. It dissolves into wisps of black smoke, acrid and choking, but more are closing in, their glowing eyes fixed on me with rift-born hunger.

"Soren!" I shout through the pathway in my mind, and the bond flares brighter, guiding me toward a central plaza where the fighting rages fiercest.

Bodies litter the ground, their silver blood pooling in iridescent puddles that reflect the chaotic sky. A male fae stumbles past me, his arm mangled and dangling, muttering frantic prayers before a creature pounces, silencing him in a spray of blood. This isn't Eldwick's quiet docks with their simple struggles; this is war, raw and unforgiving, and I'm thrust into its heart.

There—amid the fray, Soren fights like a storm incarnate. His raven hair whips wildly in the wind, silver eyes blazing with unbridled fury as shadows erupt from his hands, coiling into tendrils that ensnare creatures and crush them into oblivion. He's a whirlwind of motion, his lean frame twisting with lethal precision, but even he can't stem the endless tide alone. A beast lunges at his back, claws extended, and I cry out, summoning a vortex of air to hurl it aside. He spins, his gaze locking on mine through the melee, relief flashing briefly in those silver depths before hardening.

"Are you hurt?" he demands, closing the distance in an instant, his hands roaming my back, checking for wounds even as another beast howls nearby, its cry a guttural promise of death.

"I'm fine," I gasp, clinging to him, my fingers digging into his tunic, drawing strength from his solid presence. "You?"

"Unscathed." He pulls back just enough to search my eyes, his silver gaze intense, filled with a protectiveness that warms me against the chill wind.

Shadows envelop us suddenly, forming a dome of inky blackness that muffles the outside world. The screams fade to distant echoes, the wind's roar dimming to a whisper, leaving only us in this intimate sanctuary, the air thick with his power—a cocoon shielding us from the slaughter. My breath steadies, the chaos outside held at bay by his will alone, and for a fleeting moment, I allow myself to lean into him, the world reduced to the rhythm of our hearts.

He holds me tighter, his forehead resting against mine, his breath warm on my skin. "I felt you arrive, but I couldn't break away. You're really okay?" he asks, his voice a low rumble laced with worry.

"I'm alive," I assure him, and he leans down, crashing his lips against mine in a kiss that's fierce and desperate, pulling our bodies as close as possible. I kiss him back like my life depends on it, like this might be the last chance I ever get to feel his embrace, to taste the salt and shadow on his lips.

"What happened?" he asks as he pulls away, holding my face in his hands, his thumbs brushing away stray tears I didn't realize had fallen. "Is Veyrik with you? Did he find you?" His questions tumble out in a desperate plea, his eyes searching mine for reassurance.

"He found me, but he got injured. He's not able to fight, so he had to stay back," I explain, pressing my lips together against the memory of Veyrik's near-death. When Vyrathax said a rift ripped through the Dominion, he really downplayed the entire situation. "Where's Rennor and Zyra? Are they here?"

"They're helping others to the palace," he replies, his jaw clenching, a flicker of pain shadowing his features. "These creatures… they're stronger than before. There's too many of them."

"We don't have to stop them all. We'll do what we can," I say, trying to infuse my words with conviction, though doubt gnaws at me.

We linger in the embrace a moment longer, his heartbeat syncing with mine, a stolen solace amid the storm. But reality presses in. The dome trembles slightly, his power straining against the relentless onslaught outside.

"We fight together," he vows, his voice low and unwavering. "Protect the survivors, get them to the palace. It's fortified."

I nod, steeling myself against the fear coiling in my gut, then the shadows dissolve with a ripple. The world crashes back in a torrent—screams, clashes of magic, the guttural roars of beasts echoing like thunder.

We move as one, his shadows complementing my elements in a deadly dance. A group of faeries huddles behind an overturned cart, terror etched on their faces as beasts close in. Soren extends his dome briefly, giving me cover as I hurl gusts of air, knocking the creatures off-balance, their forms tumbling.

"To the palace!" I shout, pointing toward the central isle where the grand spires still stand defiant, their barriers glowing with protective magic. "Run!"

They scramble to their feet, dashing across the precarious bridges, and we escort them, fending off attacks with synchronized fury. One beast leaps from a rooftop, claws extended like scythes, but I blast it with a vortex of wind and water, spinning it into the void below.

Soren's shadows lash out, wrapping around another's throat and squeezing until it cracks with a sickening snap. Sweat beads on my brow, my muscles aching from the constant strain, but adrenaline surges through me. The power feels right, an extension of myself, honed by trials I never asked for but survived nonetheless.

More creatures swarm, their numbers seeming endless. Soren grunts as one grazes his arm, drawing a thin line of silver blood that gleams like liquid moonlight, but he retaliates with a burst of darkness that engulfs three at once, their howls cutting short.

"They're targeting the bridges," he yells over the wind, his voice cutting through the gale. "Trying to isolate the islands!"

I spot a family trapped on a fracturing platform, the ground cracking beneath them with ominous groans, chunks already tumbling into the endless drop. Drawing deep from my core, I weave air into a bridge of swirling gusts, solid enough to bear weight, shimmering like a mirage.

"Go!" I urge. They hesitate, eyes wide with fear, then dash across, the child clinging to his mother's neck, glancing back at me with awe-struck wonder.

Then shadows erupt nearby, and Rennor and Zyra materialize from the gloom, their own darkness weaving into the fray like threads in a tapestry. Rennor's shadows form razor blades, slicing through beasts with surgical precision, while Zyra's coil like whips, lashing and pulling them apart with brutal efficiency.

"We thought you might need us!" Rennor shouts, grinning fiercely as he dispatches one with a flourish, its body dissolving mid-air.

Zyra nods, her eyes sharp and focused amid the turmoil. "The palace is holding. We've cleared a path."

Together, we form a tight formation, our powers intertwining seamlessly. Soren commands the bulk with overwhelming force, Rennor's precise strikes carve openings, Zyra's agile defenses shield us, and my elements provide explosive cover and blasts. We carve through the horde, protecting clusters of faeries, sending them sprinting to safety under our guard.

Then finally, a lull descends. The creatures thin out, survivors streaming into the palace like a river finding its course. We gather in a shattered plaza, breaths ragged, bodies slick with sweat and the sticky residue of ichor.

Rennor wipes his brow, his silver eyes scanning the horizon with a wary glint. "Something's wrong. This doesn't seem like it's just a rift assault."

"What do you mean?" I ask, leaning on my knees to catch my

breath.

"There are too many terra wielders," he explains, his voice grim with realization. "They're cracking the foundations. Look."

He points to the edges of the island, where fissures spiderweb the stone, glowing with unnatural green energy that pulses like a heartbeat.

"They're destabilizing the floats. If they keep this up—"

His words cut off as a distant boom echoes, the air trembling with the force of it. We turn as one, horror dawning on our faces. A nearby island—smaller but dotted with spires and homes—erupts in a cascade of rock and magic. Cracks widen rapidly, massive chunks plummeting into the void with deafening crashes, debris raining down like deadly hail. The whole mass shudders, tilting precariously as screams rise in a crescendo of terror.

"No," Zyra whispers, her face paling to a ghostly white, her hands clenching at her sides.

The island explodes outward in a final, cataclysmic roar, terra magic ripping it apart from within. Dust and echoes are all that remain as it begins its fatal descent. Slow at first, then accelerating into the abyss below, crashing into the lower lands of the Aether Dominion with a distant, ground-shaking thud.

Silence falls, broken only by the wind's mournful howl, carrying the faint wails of distant survivors. Soren's hand finds mine, squeezing tight, his eyes dark with a rage that mirrors my own, burning hot in my chest.

"We have to end this," he growls, his voice a low thunder. "Whatever it takes."

CHAPTER FORTY-SEVEN

The palace looms ahead, its towers of swirling ether-glass pulsing with protective wards, a faint beacon amid the ruin that stretches across the Aether Dominion. But the path to safety is a treacherous nightmare. Bridges of woven wind and stone groan under our weight, their structures buckling as fissures snake across them like veins of green terra magic, threatening to snap and send us plummeting into the abyss below.

A creature lunges from a shattered archway—a hulking mass of void and claws, its eyes glowing like embers in the rift's hazy shroud. Soren reacts with lightning precision, shadows erupting from his palms in sharp tendrils that pierce its hide with a sickening squelch. The beast roars, a guttural sound that vibrates through my bones, then swipes wildly and pushes us back with the force of its fury.

I whip air into a vortex that slams into the creature, staggering it long enough for Rennor to strike—his darkness forming a blade that slices clean through its neck in a single, decisive arc. Black ichor sprays, sizzling on the stone like acid, and the thing dissolves into wisps of smoke that curl upward, dissipating into the wind.

"Keep moving!" Zyra shouts, her voice slicing through the howling gale, a command that spurs us onward despite the exhaustion etched into every face.

After securing the fae to safety, we burst into the palace's grand meeting hall. The air inside is heavier, laced with the sweet scent of incense and the faint, metallic bite of blood. Court members mill about in hushed urgency, debating in tight circles around maps of scattered islands, their voices a low hum of desperation.

Elarion stands at the center, his regal form draped in flowing robes of storm-gray silk, his eyes swirling like whirlwinds as he gestures sharply.

"You should not be here. Leave this to the council," he declares, his tone brooking no argument.

We ignore him, pushing through the throng with determined strides. Soren's jaw is set, silver blood still trickling from a gash on his arm, staining his sleeve, but his voice remains steady. "The islands are falling, Elarion. We've seen it. One crashed into the lower lands, an entire city gone. Evacuate everyone to safety before more follow." His words carry the weight of truth, each syllable a plea wrapped in command.

The room quiets, all eyes turning to us, the air thickening with tension. Elarion straightens, his presence commanding. "One small isle, yes, but its inhabitants escaped in time. The larger ones, like this palace, are fortified with ancient wards. Too vast for terra wielders to topple. We hold the line here," he counters, his voice firm.

Soren's fury ignites, his shadows flickering at his fingertips like restless flames. "You're keeping them in a false safety while creatures pour through the streets. Fae are dying—screaming as beasts tear them apart. Evacuate now!" His voice rises, a thunderclap that echoes off the vaulted ceiling.

Before Elarion can retort, the doors burst open with a resounding crash. Tivren rushes in, panting, his face flushed with exertion, eyes darting wildly around the room.

"They have found Galehaven," he gasps, leaning heavily on a pillar, his chest heaving. "Terra wielders, dark wielders too—storming the temple, ransacking everything."

My heart drops like a stone into the void, a cold dread pooling in my gut. Galehaven—the sacred temple isle, repository of Aether's deepest lore—where Sonja lives. The thought of her in danger spurs me forward.

"We have to go," I say, stepping toward the council, my voice firm despite the tremor within. "We have to help them."

"You will do no such thing. Step foot in our temple, and I will banish you from the Dominion forever," Elarion warns, his voice a whip crack of authority.

I close the distance, standing toe-to-toe with him, my voice low and edged. "Your kind are dying while you're up here protecting your books. We're going to help, whether you allow us or not." Whirlwinds swirl in his gaze, a storm of rage and pride, but he says nothing, does nothing as I turn away.

Soren grabs my hand while Rennor and Zyra link arms with us. Shadows swirl around us, a rush of dark ether enveloping our senses, and we star-drift in a heartbeat to Galehaven.

We materialize in the temple's outer courtyard, a sprawling expanse of marble veined with glowing azure lines, surrounded by towering pillars. The temple rises in tiers, mezzanines of polished stone overlooking vast halls, echoing with the distant clashes of battle. Gardens of floating blossoms lie trampled, their delicate stems snapped under the boots of invaders.

I meet Soren's eyes, holding his gaze for a long moment knowing he's about to face Sonja—his sister he believed dead for centuries. His silver gaze questions, searching for answers, but I shake my head subtly.

"This way," I say, leading them through arched corridors. I pause at a shrine to Sylthara and bow my head. I murmur a quick prayer for strength and the air around us seems to hum in response, a faint vibration that steadies my nerves.

We descend to a lower mezzanine, a vast balcony overlooking the central hall, where fae fight fae in a maelstrom of elements. Fireballs arc through the air, the ground rumbles beneath our feet, water crashes in torrents, and air howls in defiance. Powers erupt in bursts of color and destruction. Then below, amid the fray, Rhaevor and Sonja battle side by side, his air flaring into shields around the fae, her shadows mirroring Soren's, dark and steadfast as they fend off the invaders.

"We have to help," I say, starting down the steps, but Soren grips my wrist, pulling me back with a gentle but firm tug. His eyes are wide, fixed on the fight below, his lips parted in a heavy breath.

"Did you know?" he asks, his voice tight, unable to tear his gaze from Sonja. I nod, guilt tugging at me. "Why didn't you tell me?" he presses, his eyes finally meeting mine, a mix of hurt and betrayal flickering within.

"It wasn't my secret to share," I reply softly, and he studies me with a serious look, the weight of my words settling between us.

"Is that...?" Rennor begins, trailing off as realization settles.

"How did you know?" Zyra asks seriously, her voice low, but I keep my eyes on Soren—the only one here who knows the truth of where my powers originate.

"We're wasting time," Soren says abruptly, releasing my wrist, his tone shifting to urgency. "If they've brought down one island already, they intend nothing different with this one."

We star-drift down to the mezzanine, and dark shadows erupt in all directions, casting a shield around the group of fae huddled in a circle, their faces etched with fear. Sonja whips around, hands raised and ready to attack, but her eyes widen in recognition.

"Kiera," she breathes, rushing to me and wrapping me in an embrace that feels like a lifeline. "Thank the creators you're alive. Rhaevor told me what happened. I've been so worried."

"I'm okay," I assure her, pulling back with my hands on her shoulders, offering a small smile. "I brought some backup." Her eyes drift past me, landing on Soren, and she drops her arms, stepping back as if struck.

"Soren..." she whispers, their gazes locking in a moment that stretches thin with unspoken history. "I..." she starts, but words fail her as emotion chokes her voice.

"You're alive," Soren mutters, rushing to her and wrapping her in his arms, his voice breaking with relief. Sonja clings to him tightly, her shadows softening around them.

"I'm sorry I never went back," she says quietly, her voice muffled against his chest.

"It doesn't matter," he replies, pulling back to look at her, their shared history a silent bond. "The Elite aim to take down the islands. We have to evacuate."

"We can't just leave," Sonja protests, and Rhaevor joins her side, taking her hand in a gesture that speaks volumes.

I stare between them, my eyes narrowing. "You're soul-bound..." I murmur, and they nod, confirming my suspicion. "That's why you never went back," I add, understanding dawning. Had Sonja returned to the Umbral Expanse, Rhaevor might not have been able to follow, their bond tethering them here.

Soren looks between them, his breath heavy, then turns to the chaos around us. "We don't have much time," he says, and an explosion erupts in the distance, shaking the mezzanine.

"What do you mean they're taking down the islands?" Rhaevor asks hesitantly, his voice tinged with dread.

"They're falling from the sky..." I say softly, the gravity of the situation sinking in.

"If Galehaven falls..." Rhaevor begins, his gaze shifting to Sonja.

"The repercussions on the lower lands would be devastating," she finishes, her voice steady but her eyes glistening with unshed tears.

"Where, exactly, are we?" I ask, needing clarity amid the chaos.

Sonja shakes her head, her expression grim. "We're a thousand feet above the palace." The reality hits like a physical blow. If Galehaven falls, it will crash straight down onto Celestine, obliterating both in one catastrophic strike. "Are they able to do that? Take down an island?"

"They already have," I reply, and tears flood Sonja's eyes, her composure cracking. "That's why we need to evacuate everyone here," I urge, and she nods this time.

"We have to be quick," she agrees, her voice firm despite the emotion.

We fan out across the isle, shouting warnings through halls of echoing winds and libraries stacked with glowing tomes. Faeries hesitate, their faces etched with uncertainty, but they flee in droves when they recognize us, our presence a rallying cry amid the panic.

Just as I feel we're making progress, two dark wielders materialize, blocking our path in a grand atrium. Its domed ceiling is cracked, sunlight peeking through in jagged beams, illuminating their inky cloaks and void-black eyes, shadows writhing like living smoke around them.

We stand, breaths heavy, then, in a sudden rush of wind, Elarion and Tivren appear before us, their presence a stark contrast to the darkness we face.

"Leave," Elarion commands, his voice a thunderclap, but the dark wielders sneer, baring blackened teeth in defiance.

"Take the others back to the Umbral Expanse," Soren says, turning to Rennor with a decisive nod, but I step forward.

"I'm not letting you fight alone," I declare, my voice steady despite the fear coiling in my chest.

"She's strong," one wielder hisses, its voice a rasp of malice. "Perhaps stronger than all of you."

"Leave this place," Elarion commands again, his voice booming, the winds around him intensifying, howling through the cracks in the dome in a mournful echo.

The wielders sneer, their voices a guttural hiss that slithers through the shadows. "The Dominion falls. Your winds are nothing against the void." The taller one, its cloak absorbing the light, thrusts his hand forward.

Shadows erupt from the ground like black thorns, spiking toward Elarion in a jagged wave, aiming to impale him where he stands, but Elarion doesn't flinch. He sweeps his arms in a wide arc, summoning a gale that slams into the thorns, shredding them into wisps that dissolve like smoke in the wind. Yet the effort leaves him exposed; the second wielder lunges, shadows coiling into a whip that cracks through the air, lashing toward him. Elarion dodges with a burst of speed, his winds propelling him aside, but the whip grazes his side, drawing a sharp grunt of pain.

Soren moves like night itself, his shadows surging to intercept. Tendrils wrap around the whip, yanking it taut, and the wielder stumbles, pulled off-balance. Soren presses the advantage, channeling more darkness into spears that hurtle forward, one piercing the taller wielder's shoulder. A roar echoes off the carved walls, black ichor oozing like tar from the wound.

My heart pounds, fear and adrenaline a volatile mix in my gut. I call on the air first, weaving it into a funnel that spirals toward the second wielder, debris caught in its spin, pelting him like hail. He shields himself with a dome of shadows, the funnel battering against it with a deafening howl, but it buys time.

Water follows, and I shape it into icy blades, hurling them through the gale. One shatters against his barrier, but another breaks through a crack, slicing his arm deep enough to make him hiss and falter.

The taller wielder recovers, its wound knitting with unnatural speed. It retaliates with a blast of shadows that fans out like a wave, knocking Tivren back against a wall with a thud that cracks stone. Tivren slides down, winded, blood trickling from his lip, but he pushes up, summoning a whirlwind that lifts him airborne, diving toward the enemy with claws extended.

Elarion joins the fray fully now, his winds forming a massive cyclone that engulfs the first wielder, lifting it off the ground in a spinning maelstrom. The wielder fights back, shadows clawing at the cyclone's edges, tearing holes that let gusts escape with shrieks.

"You think your breezes can contain the dark?" it mocks, its voice distorted through the roar.

"They don't have to," Soren snaps.

His shadows merge with the cyclone, reinforcing it with inky threads that bind the wielder tighter. Together, they crush inward until the wielder's form buckles, a sickening crack echoing as its defenses shatter. It drops to the floor in a heap, shadows dissipating, but not before lashing out one last time, a tendril grazing Soren's side.

Pain flares through our bond, sharp as a knife at my hip, but Soren turns to the remaining foe. The last wielder, wounded but raging, presses its attack on me. Shadows coil around my legs like damp ropes, pulling me down.

I stumble, the stone floor hard against my knees, and panic surges, threatening to overwhelm me. But I fight it, summoning water to flood the shadows, diluting them into harmless puddles that evaporate with a hiss.

Elarion dives in, his gusts blasting the wielder back, giving me space to rise. "Stay down," he mutters, but his voice is strained, exhaustion creeping into his frame.

"The world of Aether shall be no more," the dark wielder intones in a guttural growl, pressing his fingers to the ground. Dark shadows erupt, burrowing deep, spreading like cracks in ice. The island groans, fissures widening with a sound like the world itself is crying out.

"We have to leave, now!" Soren yells, his voice cutting through the chaos.

"With me," Elarion says, and without hesitation, we star-drift to him, grabbing the nearest body as we're swept away in a whirl of shadows and wind.

CHAPTER
FORTY-EIGHT

We land on an unfamiliar island, the ground firm beneath my feet, and as I glance out toward the horizon, the shattered silhouette of Celestine comes into view, its once-majestic form now marred by ruin. My eyes sweep the surroundings and land on a tall library that stands untouched amidst the chaos. It's a marvel of ancient craftsmanship that rises in elegant tiers. Its walls, hewn from translucent ether-stone, cast a soft, otherworldly glow across the island, bathing the area in a pale, luminescent sheen.

The roof is a dome of spun glass, a mosaic of blues and silvers that refracts the sky above. At its apex, a spire of pure crystal pierces the heavens, its tip crowned with an orb of captured wind that spirals endlessly, a breathtaking display of the air-wielders' mastery. It's a work of art, a sight I never could have dreamed of encountering, and I'm certain this is Elarion's most prized possession.

As I turn to the area, I see fae scattered about. I recognize some from the palace and the city and others from Galehaven, their faces a mix of relief and despair. Yet the island remains untouched, as if shielded by an unseen barrier from the danger that ravages the rest of the dominion. A sense of eerie calm settles over me, but it's short-lived.

"Oh no."

"How could they do this?" Voices mutter nearby, pulling my attention upward.

Through the drifting clouds, rubble begins to fall, then the massive form of Galehaven breaks through at an unnatural speed, its descent a horrifying spectacle. A round of gasps and cries erupts around us, the air filling with the sound of collective anguish. I want to look away from the destruction, to shield myself from the ruin, but my eyes widen, locked on the scene as Galehaven crashes into the edge of Celestine with a thunderous impact, obliterating half the palace in a shower of crystal debris and dust.

A chunk of the island breaks off, dragging the temple down with it, and I feel Soren's hand grasp mine, his touch a lifeline amid the chaos. Sonja turns into Rhaevor's embrace, stifling her cries. Everything she once knew is gone, reduced to rubble in moments.

Soren glances at them, then lowers his eyes to the ground, his jaw tight with grief. I watch, helpless, as more of Celestine fractures, chunks breaking off and plummeting to the lower lands of Aether, crumbling into dust upon impact. A shockwave ripples through the ground, pushing the trees back with a violent blast, the force traveling miles until it's no longer visible. I wonder how many cities below were struck by the devastation, how many lives snuffed out in an instant.

I pull my hand from Soren's and step back, the rage building within me too potent to contain. I walk away from the group, staring off at the distant clouds, my mind a storm of frustration and guilt.

"Are you okay?" Soren asks gently, and I shake my head, the weight of it all pressing down.

"What's the point of any of this?" I say sternly, my voice cracking with the pain of the question. "The destruction, the killing —it hurts my head to think this will keep happening. What's the point of me being here, learning these powers, if I can't do anything about it? I'm failing. And fae are dying." The words spill out, raw and unfiltered, the prophecy's burden crushing me.

"It's not only you that is failing," Soren counters, but I shake my head fiercely. It is me. I'm the one spoken of in the prophecy, the one tasked with unraveling this nightmare, and yet fae keep dying, their blood on my hands.

I can feel the fae around us staring, their eyes and ears intent on our exchange, but I couldn't care less. The weight of their gazes only adds to the pressure bearing down on me, a suffocating mantle of expectation.

"There's nothing you could have done to prevent this," Rhaevor says, his voice gentle but firm, and I turn my eyes up to him, glaring with a silent fury that burns in my chest.

He doesn't know what I know. I stood face-to-face with Valthar and had a chance to end this, but I didn't do enough. I never do enough to make a difference.

"Maybe we were the ones to fail you," Tivren interjects, his tone laced with regret, and I shake my head, rejecting the notion. "We denied your request. We could have done more to help."

"This is not the end of Aelthar," Soren says, stepping closer and cradling my face in his hands. "We still have time." His words sink in as he holds my gaze, and I let out a shaky breath, allowing him to steady me.

"You two have bonded?" Elarion remarks after a moment, his voice cutting through the tension, and my lips press into a thin line.

"We have," Soren confirms, his tone resolute, and I glance between them, sensing the weight of Elarion's scrutiny.

"Why is everything I do so disappointing to you?" I ask, my frustration bubbling over as I meet Elarion's stare.

"We can afford to lose a prophet," he replies coolly. "We can't afford to lose Soren if you happen to get killed." His words sting, and my eyes narrow with a mix of anger and defiance.

"I swear to the creators, Elarion, I'm going to blast you off an island someday," I retort. How can a fae descended from Sylthara be so intolerable?

"It's bold of you to think you have the skills to do so," he counters, and my fists clench as steam seems to boil from my skin. Before I can act on the impulse, I turn and walk away, needing distance to cool the fire within.

"You of all fae should know it's impossible to keep soul-bounds apart," I hear Sonja tell Elarion, but I don't look back. I need to think, to clear my mind, to find a way through this mess.

When I reach a small treed area near the library, footsteps follow, but I sense they're not a threat I'd like to knock out. Turning, I find Sonja and Zyra approaching steadily.

"Why is he such a prick?" I ask, my voice tinged with exasperation, and Sonja grins faintly.

"He has many reasons," she says simply, and I glance past them to Elarion, then to Soren, who speaks in a low tone with Rennor. Is this why Rennor kept us apart? To prevent our bond from deepening, to ensure Soren's survival if I fell?

"If it makes you feel better, I've wanted to knock Elarion off an island for centuries," Zyra adds, her tone light but her eyes serious. I look down at my feet, guilt creeping in. I pursued Soren, asked for that kiss. Did I drag him into this danger by doing so?

"You're thinking about all this too much," Sonja says, but I shake my head, the thoughts too tangled to unravel.

"He tried to stay away," I mutter, looking up at Soren, who stares back with focused intensity. I slip into our mind-link, finding him waiting there.

Why did Rennor try to keep us apart? I ask silently, feeling an ache bloom in my chest.

I wanted you to be able to move on in case something happens to me, he replies, and tears flood my eyes. I wipe them quickly, turning toward the horizon. I want to ask why he expects that sort of danger, but I'm too terrified to voice it.

"Thalira is here," Zyra says softly, and I look toward the group where Thalira, Soren, and Elarion now stand.

"Something's happening," I say, and we drift back to join them, the air thick with tension.

"I'm glad to see you're still alive," Thalira says, placing a hand on my shoulder and squeezing lightly, her touch a rare comfort.

"What's going on? Don't tell me you were attacked as well," I reply, dreading the thought of more devastation across the dominions that I couldn't prevent.

"We had a few creatures appear, but nothing like what I've heard happening here," she admits, turning to Elarion. "I'm so sorry. If I had known how bad it was, I would have sent assistance."

"You have your own Dominion to look after," Elarion says with a gentle nod, and I wait, sensing there's more to her visit.

"I do have some rather troublesome news," she begins, glancing at the group of fae gathered near the library, assessing them before continuing. "We felt a ripple through the ground—likely shortly after the island fell. We didn't think much of it at first, but then some noticed the sea pulling back into itself."

"No..." I whisper, pressing my hands to my lips as realization dawns, her nod confirming my fear.

"We expect the water to come back in full force and hit the coasts. We are prepared, but we're aware other places..." She glances at me briefly, "may not be as well-suited for a force of water such as this."

"Eldwick..." I breathe, and their eyes turn to me, concern etched into their features.

"We'll go and do what we can," Soren says quickly, grabbing my hand before turning to Rennor and Zyra. "Go back to the palace, gather some of the council, and see how our coasts are faring. The cliff sides should hold, but do what you can." They nod once and drift away, their forms swallowed by shadow as Elarion issues similar commands to his council.

"I'm sorry," Thalira says, and as the words leave her, a gasp and scream erupt. We turn to the group behind us, their eyes fixed on the sky.

A dreadful pit forms in my stomach as I follow their gaze, witnessing more islands plummeting from the heavens, one after another, until only a handful remain alongside the fractured remnants of Celestine. Wind whips fiercely as Elarion bursts with fury, star-drifting away without a word.

I squeeze Soren's hand and lean into him, seeking solace.

Despite my disdain for Elarion and his treatment of me, this is his home, and the sight of its destruction twists my chest with an ache I can't ignore.

Thalira turns to us, tears glistening in her eyes, her grimace a mirror to our despair. "I wish I had better news," she says, and I muster a small, strained grin. "I hope your home fares well."

"Thank you for coming to tell us," I reply, and she nods deeply, offering Soren a nod before she star-drifts, leaving us in the heavy silence.

I let out a deep breath, standing alone with Soren and Sonja, my hands beginning to shake. Not from pain, exhaustion, or adrenaline, but from fear. So much death and destruction has followed me, but it's never touched my home, never threatened Ma or Rory. The thought of losing them now fills me with a guilt I can't shake.

"Take Rhaevor back to our palace," Soren says to Sonja, but my eyes glaze over, my mind spiraling.

"We'll go with you," she offers, but Soren shakes his head.

"It would be better if it's just us two. We won't be long," he insists, and I look at them with blank eyes, my thoughts too scattered to protest.

"We'll be there if you need us," she says, and Soren nods, turning to me as she walks off to find Rhaevor. He cups my face, his thumbs brushing my cheeks as I meet his eyes.

"We'll go to Eldwick and create a shield around the town. We'll take your mom and Rory back to the palace, but I won't risk your life trying to save everyone," he tells me, his voice firm yet gentle. "They will be fine."

"Okay…" I manage, my voice trembling, tears welling up despite my efforts to hold them back.

"This is not your fault," he assures, wiping a tear before it falls fully, and I squeeze my eyes tight. "This is not your fault," he repeats, his words sinking deeper this time. "Are you ready?"

"Yes," I say, and he nods once, then we star-drift into darkness, the weight of our mission pulling us forward.

CHAPTER FORTY-NINE

We land on the pier with a heavy thud, the weathered wood groaning under our weight as if protesting the burden we bring. I turn toward the sea, and my stomach lurches violently. Thalira was right. The water has receded so far it would take hours to walk out to where the waves once lapped, leaving behind a desolate expanse of slick sand and stranded boats tilted awkwardly on their keels. The horizon stretches empty and ominous, a silent prelude to the devastation to come.

Behind me, the town erupts—clamors, shouts, and the rising tide of panic that ripples through Eldwick. This is just one of many coastal towns in the mortal lands, and the realization hits me like a punch: hundreds, perhaps thousands, will be wiped out when that water crashes back in a merciless surge. The thought tightens my chest, a mix of dread and helplessness warring within me.

"I'm going to set some shields around the perimeter. Why don't you go find your mom and Rory?" Soren says, his voice steady but tinged with urgency. He pauses, his hand lingering on my cheek, and leans down to press a soft kiss against my lips, pulling me into a moment of clarity. "We'll do what we can," he adds, his breath warm against my skin.

"I'll be quick," I reply, nodding slowly, the weight of the task ahead pressing down.

"I'm here if you need me," he assures, and I rise to my toes, kissing him harder this time, a desperate affirmation before stepping back.

I turn and walk down the pier toward the town, my boots echoing on the creaking wood. I could star-drift straight to the plaza, grab Ma and Rory, and be back in two seconds. But the townspeople don't need more panic in this fragile moment. Walking feels slower, more natural, a way to ease their fear rather than amplify it.

When I reach Main Street, my stomach lurches again. The scene is chaotic yet methodical. People board up windows and doors with splintered wood, barricading their homes and shops against the unknown. I want to shout for them to flee inland, to run and keep running, but the truth gnaws at me: what chance do they have? These aren't the physically resilient fae; they're mortals, weathered by hardship, unlikely to outpace the deluge. Their best hope lies here, under Soren's shields, and I cling to that fragile comfort.

"Kiera?" a gruff, familiar voice calls from behind, and I glance back to find the entire street lined with people spilling from their shops and homes. Their faces—old, worn, wrinkled beyond their years—stare at me, their tattered clothes fraying at the edges, a stark reminder of how close they teeter to starvation. I never realized how little we all had in Eldwick until now, the simplicity of my past life laid bare.

"She's alive."

"Is that her?"

"She looks different."

"What is she doing here?"

The murmurs follow me as I pass, a constant hum of curiosity and disbelief, but I press on toward the plaza without looking back. There, I spot Ma and Rory frantically packing her herbs and teas, their movements hurried yet precise. My heart aches at the sight— worn hands sorting fragile leaves, a mother and brother I could have protected better, a guilt that gnaws deeper with every step.

"Ma. Rory," I say, stepping up behind them, and they whirl around, wide-eyed with shock.

"Kiera," Ma breathes, throwing herself into my arms. Her entire body trembles, but I hold her steady. "You really are alive."

"I've missed you," I murmur into her, squeezing her tight before pulling back, my voice softening. "But we don't have much time. We have to go."

"Go where? We can't just leave," Rory protests, his words echoing Sonja's defiance when we urged her to abandon Galehaven. "This is our home."

"And we've done everything we can to protect it," I reply, my tone firm but gentle. "But if it doesn't hold, we need to find somewhere safer." Ma steps back, her eyes searching mine.

"What about the rest of the people?" she asks, her voice laced with concern, and I shake my head, holding her gaze with a long, steady stare.

"There's nothing else we can do," I say softly, the admission bitter on my tongue. Ma and Rory exchange a look, and I feel the weight of eyes around the plaza—soft whispers repeating my words, details I wouldn't normally catch but now hear with heightened senses.

"You go," Rory says, his voice resolute. "And I'll stay here and help."

"That's not an option," I counter, shaking my head. "We all go together." My instincts scream to grab them and star-drift out without choice, but I know they'd resent me for it, their autonomy a thread I can't sever.

"Can we grab a few things?" Ma asks, her voice hesitant, and I want to say no and urge them to leave and not look back. But I remember the chance I never had, the sudden uprooting of my own life, and I soften.

"We have to be quick," I concede, and they nod, understanding the urgency.

We make our way back to Main Street where the townspeople have retreated inside, with Rory keeping pace by my side, and Ma close behind. I know as long as I keep them in reach and can star-drift at a moment's notice, I can give them time to gather what they can, a small mercy in the chaos.

"Kiera!" Ma shrieks behind me, and I spin around on my heels, my heart lurching. My eyes widen as I take in the scene—Ma is wrapped in thorny vines, hovering just off the ground, a fae standing beside her with a sinister grin.

"Hello, Kiera," Tormen says, his voice dripping with malice, and Rory rushes past me, fury in his steps.

"You let her go right now!" he yells, but I grab his arm and yank him back behind me.

"Don't," I command, my voice sharp, and Tormen laughs low,

the sound crawling over my skin like a chill.

"How strange it must be for you to realize how weak you truly were when you arrived at my palace," he taunts, and my fists clench. He's right. My early defiance against him, a mortal girl against a fae, now seems foolish given the power I've since wielded.

"What do you want?" I seethe, stepping forward as he raises his arms, surveying the town with a mocking glance.

"I wanted to see the great city of Eldwick before it's washed out to sea," he says, his eyes scanning the gathered townspeople emerging from their dwellings. "To see what you've been so desperately fighting for. And I have to say, I'm not impressed."

"Let her go!" one townsman shouts, stepping closer, joined by others.

"Get out of here!"

"You don't belong here!" Their voices rise in a chorus of defiance, and Tormen chuckles under his breath.

"And now I see where you get your ignorant fight from," he sneers. "How charming." My fists curl tighter, rage simmering beneath my skin.

Black smoke erupts before me, and Soren appears, dripping with shadow. The townspeople gasping and stepping back, murmuring of darkness, fear, and death.

"Kiera…" Rory whispers behind me, grabbing my wrist to pull me away, but I pull my hand back, standing firm.

"Sorry to cut your trip short, Tormen," Soren says, his voice cold and commanding. "But you'll be leaving now."

"You wouldn't want to make a scene in front of all these innocent people, now would you?" Tormen retorts, and I step to Soren's side, knowing he's right. We can't risk a fight here, not with so much collateral damage at stake. "Let's make this easy. Give me the boy, and I'll be on my way."

"You won't be taking anyone," I mutter, my voice low and threatening. "I'll send you straight to the Abyssra if I have to." But he raises his hand, sending vines rushing toward us. I lift my own, sending a sharp blade of air that slices them down before they can reach us.

After days of fighting and honing my powers, it flows like second nature now, responding to my will without effort. And Tormen's narrowed eyes tell me he notices too.

"*Kiera's fae.*"

"*She has powers.*"

"*What happened to her?*"

The townspeople's whispers rise, but Tormen raises his hand, tightening the vines around Ma.

"You'll never learn when to stop fighting, will you?" he says, but I press forward undeterred.

"Take me instead," I offer, and Soren's fists clench, though he remains silent.

"I have no interest in keeping you captive anymore, my dear," Tormen replies, his grin widening. "It would be no fun to watch you rot in a cell. But having your family tied up and tortured, knowing you can't do anything about it. *That* sounds much more appealing."

I unleash a torrent of wind toward him, but he deflects it with a wall of mud and rubble, forcing me to sprint forward. I wrap water up his legs, freezing it into unbreakable ice, and panic floods his eyes. He throws daggers of rock and vine whips, but I cut them down and deflect every blow, my movements precise and instinctive.

He lifts his hand again, and I anticipate another attack, but instead, he reaches for Ma's arm. Realizing he's about to flee, I star-drift to him, landing inches from his face. As he begins to vanish, I grab his arm, and we're swept into a swirl of darkness and green energy I can't control.

I picture Eldwick's beach vividly, hoping to tether us, but when my feet hit the ground, I know that's not where we've landed. I reach for Ma beside me, but she sinks into the ground, vanishing from my grasp. I step back, heart pounding, and hear Tormen's low laugh.

"Of all the places you could have taken me to, you take me to a forest," he sneers, and vines lash out, wrapping around my ankles and wrists, hoisting me high into the trees. I surround myself with air and blast outward, shredding the vines to pieces, my fall cushioned by a soft pulse of wind as I land gently on my feet.

I hadn't meant to bring us here—I'd aimed for water, where I'd have the upper hand—but this must be the limit of my dwindling power.

I summon a waterfall to crash down on Tormen, but he erects a solid dome to deflect it, then sends a ripple through the ground that launches me upward. I swirl a gust of wind around me, suspending myself for a better vantage point, but Tormen raises the ground into a mountain, facing me head-on.

"You'll have nothing, just like I do," he growls, sending slices of the ground toward me. I counter with a gust, splitting them apart through their cracks, shattering them one by one—only to realize the rubble is now falling towards Ma.

I drift to her, erecting an air shield to divert the rubble, then flood the ground with water to soften the dirt around her. Slowly, I lift her out, her trembling form a stark contrast to my racing pulse.

"Are you okay?" I ask, and she nods weakly as she looks up.

"Rory," she whispers, and I glance up at Tormen atop his peak, realizing my mistake. While I freed Ma, he must have returned to town.

"When you love too many things in life, you're more likely to slip up," Tormen taunts, and I see vines tightening around Rory's body and neck, his yell piercing the air.

"Stop!" I scream, darkness erupts, readying to wrap around Tormen, but he vanishes before I can act. "No!" I cry, star-drifting to the platform where he stood, finding it empty. Rage consumes me, and I unleash a blast of air skyward, my body vibrating with fury as I scream into the void.

"I'm sorry…" Soren says softly, and I whip around to face him, my voice breaking.

"What did you do? Why didn't you stop him?" I yell, but his pleading eyes and pale, sunken face tell me the truth—his power must be nearly gone.

"I tried…" he whispers, tears flooding my eyes. "I'm sorry…"

I pace back, glancing at Ma on the ground, her eyes fixed on us. Part of me expects Tormen to return for her, but his absence confirms he got what he wanted. Rory.

"We have to go," Soren urges, reaching for my hand, but I pull away. "The sea is surging; we don't have time."

"I can't leave them here to die," I snap, facing him with anger blazing in my eyes. He looks desperate for retreat, but I can't abandon them. Guilt would haunt me forever.

"I will stand by you," he says, his voice strained, "but I have to ensure I can still get you to safety." I understand. He has just enough power to take us to the Umbral Expanse, his magic drained to the brink.

"That's all I need," I reply, grabbing his arm and star-drifting to Ma to lift her next.

CHAPTER FIFTY

We land back on the pier, the weathered planks groaning under our sudden weight as wind whips in from every direction. The gusts tear at my hair and clothes, carrying the sharp bite of salt and impending doom.

I turn to face the sea, and my stomach drops. The water is still far out in the distance, an unnatural retreat that exposes the muddy seabed, but it's rushing back now, a towering wall of churning foam and debris that won't relent until it claims everything in its path.

I glance back at the town—at Eldwick, my home—and spot the faint glimmer of the shield Soren put up, its ethereal barrier shaking under the assault of the gale. There's no way it's going to hold against this kind of force barreling straight for it, a colossal wave that could swallow the entire village in one merciless gulp.

Which means the only thing standing between Eldwick and this catastrophic surge—is me.

The thought sends a chill through my bones, deeper than the ocean's cold; I've wielded power before, but never against something so vast, so primal. If I fail, their blood will be on my hands, a stain I could never wash away.

"Kiera. We should go. I know you want to save them, but you have to think of yourself too," Ma says, her voice trembling as she clutches my arm, her eyes wide with the same fear that's etched into every line of her weathered face. She's always been the steady one, but now even she looks ready to break.

I shake my head, gently prying her hand away. "I won't have all their blood on my hands," I reply, my voice firmer than I feel inside. "Especially if I don't try."

The words hang between us. I've lost too much already, watched friends and allies fall; I can't add my own people to that list without fighting for them.

"She's strong," Soren says to her, his tone quiet but unwavering, a subtle encouragement that bolsters me as he steps closer.

I suck in a deep breath, closing my eyes to center myself, and dive deep into my mind. There, in the sacred temples of my power, Sylthara soars in graceful loops, her form a whirlwind of ethereal wind, while Lyrisene lurks just at the surface, her serpentine essence coiled like a spring, as if she's been waiting for this very call.

I need to borrow your powers, I plead silently to Lyrisene. *If I don't, people will die—innocents, my family, everyone I've ever known.*

There's a moment's pause, a silent consideration that stretches my nerves taut, as if she's weighing the risk of lending her might to a once mortal vessel like me.

I look out to the water again, and it's closer now. Too close. I know Soren will whisk us away the second he senses my life in true peril, his protective instincts overriding everything, so I plead once more, desperation sharpening my thoughts.

Please. I don't have much time. The words echo in my mind, and in an instant, my body pulses with raw energy, a surge that makes my skin tingle and my veins hum. I raise my hands and see them glowing, just as they did when my powers were first awakened.

I look up again and see a shimmering shield descending around me, around all of us, a dome of protective force manifesting from the power within me. The water is right before us now, a colossal barrier of frothing rage, so I close my eyes and raise my hands higher. I imagine the feel of the sea and focus every ounce of my will on it, commanding it to bend, to yield.

It rushes toward us with a deafening roar, the sound vibrating through my bones, then it slows, rumbling as it curls back into itself before our barrier. I open my eyes to see the water gathering, rising higher instead of retreating, and the pressure building is threatening to burst my bones from within.

I yell out, the strain tearing through my muscles and limbs like fire, shredding me from the inside out. I know I'm wielding too much power, far beyond what my body can handle, but I can't stop, if I let go now, the water would crash in, swallowing Eldwick whole.

"*More*," I grit through clenched teeth, directing the plea toward Lyrisene in my mind, and my arms erupt with intensified power, light bursting through my body as I push the water around us, forcing it to part like a divided river.

"Kiera..." Ma mutters from behind, her voice faint, and tears sweep into my eyes, streaming down my cheeks. A sharp crack echoes, followed by an explosion, and I know Soren's shields around Eldwick have fallen, the sound a death knell that spurs me on.

I scream, raw and primal, as I push all the water away, envisioning a dome encircling the town, the sea bending to my will. The current becomes an extension of me, and I force it outward, away from the pier, away from everything I hold dear.

The surge slows, the relentless rush no longer demanding, the height leveling out as the threat recedes. I squeeze my eyes shut and press my hands down to the ground, channeling the water to seep into the ground, pushing it outward in all directions. I feel the pulse of energy, the life within the waves, and slowly, agonizingly, I let it dissipate, the roar fading to a whisper.

I collapse to my knees, the wood splintering beneath me with a sharp crack, and let the tears fall freely from my face. My entire body shakes uncontrollably, wracked with aftershocks, and I release the powers flooding me, feeling them sink back into my temple as if Lyrisene is gently reeling them in, reclaiming her essence.

Soren kneels at my side, his hand resting warmly on my lower back, a silent comfort, but he doesn't speak, or if he does, I can't hear it over the roar still echoing in my head, the phantom pressure, the lingering light and burn coursing through my veins.

I stare down at my hands pressed into the pier and clench them tightly. Darkness flares out between my fingers, black smoke seeping through the cracks in the wood. For a moment, I think it's a hallucination, a remnant of exhaustion, but when I release my grip, it happens again, tendrils of shadow falling like ink. This time, unlike the borrowed power in the tunnels that felt external, this darkness surges from within me, a part of my core, and the realization sends a chill down my spine. What have I done?

"Will you come with us?" Soren asks gently from behind, his voice cutting through the haze, and I look up to the sea before me, where water still rushes in but with far less fury, the immediate threat averted.

Ma mutters something nearby, her presence a faint pull, and I feel tears well. I have to get her back to safety, away from this nightmare.

I glance back at Eldwick, my vision blurs with fatigue, but I can see the buildings are still standing. Water floods the streets in shallow pools, but the town endures, for now.

"I have to get her back," Soren says, echoing my thoughts, and I stare back to the sea, my vision darkening at the edges, the world tilting.

Eldwick is safe. The people are alive. But Rory is gone, snatched into Tormen's grasp. I know the helplessness of those cells under his palace, the despair that seeps into your bones. I know too much of what he's about to endure, and the guilt threatens to drown me.

I want to pursue Tormen, to keep fighting until Rory's free, but my body betrays me, ready to collapse under the strain. And before I can muster any more strength, my vision blurs completely, and my world fades to black.

SCALE OF ETERNITY
BOOK 2
COMING SOON…

ACKNOWLEDGMENT

Thank you for reading *Withered by Shadows*. Bringing this story to life and finally holding it in my hands has been a dream I scarcely dared to believe would come true. Yet the greatest joy of all has been knowing that you—wonderful readers—are now holding it too.

To my husband: thank you for listening patiently (and enthusiastically) while I rambled endlessly about plots, characters, publishing, and every tiny victory along the way. Your daily love, encouragement, and unwavering belief in me made this book possible.

To my older sister: thank you for pulling me back into the world of books and for every recommendation that followed. Our book talks lit the path that eventually led me here.

To my mom: thank you for never scolding us in high school when the flashlights stayed on long past bedtime, and for being my lifelong cheerleader in every dream I've chased. Your support means the world.

To my younger sister: your love of reading inspired me more than you know. I started writing this story hoping that one day you might want to pick it up and read.

To my two incredible kids: thank you simply for being you—my brightest lights. I hope one day these pages make you proud of your mama.

To my Aunt A and Cousin N: thank you for every book, comic, and graphic novel you slipped into my hands and every nudge to keep reading. You shaped the person—and the writer—I became throughout the years.

To my cats: thank you for curling up on the keyboard, walking across the desk, and purring beside me through countless late-night writing sessions. Your companionship kept loneliness at bay.

With all my heart—thank you.